The O. Henry Prize Stories 2006

The O. Henry Prize Stories 2006

Edited and with an Introduction by
Laura Furman

Jurors
Kevin Brockmeier, Francine Prose,
Colm Tóibín

ANCHOR BOOKS
A Division of Random House, Inc.
New York

The series editor wishes to thank Kris Bronstad, Nell Hanley, Kimberley Jones, and Katie Williams for their help in reading and thinking about short stories that last, and the staff of Anchor Books, whose energy, skill, and enthusiasm make each O. Henry volume a new pleasure.

FOR SOLOMON BARNA

AN ANCHOR BOOKS ORIGINAL, MAY 2006

Copyright © 2006 by Vintage Anchor Publishing, a division of Random House, Inc. Introduction copyright © 2006 by Laura Furman

All rights reserved. Published in the United States by Anchor Books, a division of Random House, Inc., New York, and in Canada by Random House of Canada Limited, Toronto.

Anchor Books and colophon are registered trademarks of Random House, Inc.

Permissions appear at the end of the book.

Cataloging-in-Publication Data for *The O. Henry Prize Stories 2006* is on file at the Library of Congress.

Anchor ISBN-10: 1-4000-9539-5
Anchor ISBN-13: 978-1-4000-9539-1

Book design by Debbie Glasserman

www.anchorbooks.com

Printed in the United States of America
10   9   8   7   6   5   4   3   2   1

Publisher's Note

M ANY READERS have come to love the short story through the simple characters, easy narrative voice and humor, and compelling plotting in the work of William Sydney Porter (1862–1910), best known as O. Henry. His surprise endings entertain readers, even those back for a second, third, or fourth look. One can say "Gift of the Magi" in conversation about a love affair or marriage, and almost any literate person will know what is meant. It's hard to think of many other American writers whose work has been so incorporated into our national shorthand.

O. Henry was a newspaperman, skilled at hiding from his editors at deadline. He wrote to make a living and to make sense of his life. O. Henry spent his childhood in Greensboro, North Carolina, his adolescence and young manhood in Texas, and lived his mature years in New York City. In between Texas and New York, he served out a prison sentence for bank fraud in Columbus, Ohio. Accounts of the origins of his pen name vary; it may have dated from his Austin days, when he was known to call the wandering family cat, "Oh! Henry!" or been inspired by the captain of the guard in the Ohio State Penitentiary, Orrin Henry.

Porter had devoted friends in New York, and it's not hard to see why. He was charming and courteous and had an attractively gallant attitude. He drank too much and neglected his health, which caused his friends concern. He was often short of money; in a letter to a friend asking for a loan of fifteen dollars (his banker was out of town, he wrote), Porter added a post-script: "If it isn't convenient, I'll love you just the same." The banker was unavailable most of Porter's life. His sense of humor was always with him.

Reportedly, Porter's last words were from a popular song, "Turn up the light, for I don't want to go home in the dark."

Eight years after O. Henry's death, in April 1918, the Twilight Club (founded in 1883 and later known as the Society of Arts and Letters) held a dinner in his honor at the Hotel McAlpin in New York City. His friends remembered him so enthusiastically that a group of them met at the Hotel Biltmore in December of that year to establish some kind of memorial to him. They decided to award annual prizes in his name for short-story writers, and formed a Committee of Award to read the short stories published in a year and to pick the winners. In the words of Blanche Colton Williams (1879–1944), the first of the nine series editors, the memorial was intended to "strengthen the art of the short story and to stimulate younger authors."

Doubleday, Page & Company was chosen to publish the first volume, *The O. Henry Memorial Award Prize Stories 1919*. In 1927, the society sold all rights to the annual collection to Doubleday, Doran & Company. Doubleday published *The O. Henry Prize Stories*, as it came to be known, in hardcover, and from 1984 to 1996 its subsidiary, Anchor Books, published it simultaneously in paperback. Since 1997 *The O. Henry Prize Stories* has been published as an original Anchor Books paperback.

Over the years, the rules and methods of selection have varied. As of 2003, the series editor chooses twenty short stories, each one an O. Henry Prize Story. All stories originally written in the English language and published in an American or Canadian periodical are eligible for consideration.

Three jurors are appointed annually. The jurors receive the twenty prize stories in manuscript form, with no identification of author or publication. Each judge, acting independently, chooses a short story of special interest and merit, and comments on that story.

The goal of *The O. Henry Prize Stories* remains to strengthen the art of the short story.

To Katherine Anne Porter (1890–1980)

W HEN SHE WAS seventy, Katherine Anne Porter wrote to a friend that for the rest of her days she would write stories that had been in notes from twenty-five to forty years, as her story "Holiday" had been. "Forty years to write a short story darling! But then you know so well that anything you do is worth a lifetime or nothing." With its brave declarative tone, its suggestion of false starts and stops, and its gallant final declaration, the letter is characteristic of Porter's unwavering artistic integrity.

Hers was a difficult life in which she suffered almost constantly from anxiety, yet she knew how to have a good time. Most important, she did what she set out to do—she wrote stories that will outlast us all. There isn't a false word in them. Each is a wonder of ingenuity in form and language. Because the stories have the feeling of classics—as they might have even when they first appeared—it is easy to overlook Porter's inventiveness and willingness to take chances in her prose.

Katherine Anne Porter was born in Indian Creek, Texas, in 1890 and died in Silver Spring, Maryland, in 1980. A small, beautiful woman, strong but never in good health, Porter fled her complicated family and its past, so steeped in losses and sorrows, to embark at sixteen on her own adventures. All her long wandering life, Porter yearned for a place of her own. She collected furniture and decorations, she bought and sold houses, but she never made herself a home.

Porter spent thirty years in an almighty effort to write her one novel, *Ship of Fools*. Inspired by the journey she took from Vera Cruz, Mexico, to Bremerhaven, Germany, on the S. S. *Werra* in 1931, the book was both a promise and an albatross to a woman who wrote slowly and depended on time to discover the right pattern for her words and images. She finished the book when she was seventy-one, and its huge success provided her with fame and financial security, enabling her to escape "second best and scraps and makeshifts," a phrase she used in one of her most brilliant stories, "Rope."

The story's central characters, He and She, have just moved from the city to the country. He, sent to town to shop, returns without the one thing She wanted—coffee—but with a twenty-four-yard rope. The rope simply took his fancy, but becomes an emblem of their differences. Neither is sure about country life, or their life together. There is no direct dialogue, yet the characters' respective voices are unmistakable. The swiftness of the story and the sureness of technique are marvelous, as is Porter's precise and unvarnished portrait of two people roped in by their own poor idea of love.

Porter's tough-mindedness and technical skill is everywhere in her stories. Read the unsurpassed romance "Pale Horse, Pale Rider," and the time-jumping "The Jilting of Granny Wetherall." Read her heartbreaking "Noon Wine," which could have been written only by someone who knew how hard the land can be, and "Magic," a chilling little tale of enslavement. Read all of Porter, consider how hard it is to carve stories out of a chaotic life, and be grateful for her work.

Contents

Introduction

FOR THE PAST two years, Anchor Books has celebrated the publication of the new O. Henry collection with a panel of the prizewinning authors in a New York City bookstore. On a cold January night in 2005, an audience member posed a good question: Given that the literary forms of story and novel are so different, what are the impulses that lead a writer to pursue one or the other at any given time? What is involved in the choice to write a story or a novel?

Whether or not a particular piece of work becomes a novel or a short story is not only a matter of volition but also one of recognition: the work will be what it will. Some literary works, even in their earliest beginnings, want to be novels, with the form's characteristic layering of possibilities and the forgiving largeness of life itself.

Others want to be stories, with pressure on every small detail and action. To a writer who feels easier with stories, writing a novel can be like working a puzzle that might or might not ever be solved, and which might always be lacking a few crucial pieces. For such a writer, the story is home.

David Means, author of this year's powerful "Sault Ste. Marie," says, "I just love stories, and feel better when I'm able to hold the whole thing in my head and turn it around and around." Anthony Doerr, whose stories appeared in the O. Henry 2002 and 2003 collections, likes being able to focus on an entire story in the course of a day. "For the first few hours, whenever I sit down at the computer, I reread and revise everything I've written in a particular project so far. Only then do I feel ready to push it forward just a bit farther. In a long day of work, I can manage to get from one end of a short story to the other, since I'm perpetually revising, and often only adding a paragraph or two."

Susan Fromberg Schaeffer writes large, lush novels, such as *The Madness of a Seduced Woman*. Her O. Henry 2006 story "Wolves" gives the reader a taste of Schaeffer's courage, her ease with metaphor, and her capacity to take imaginative leaps and make a perfect landing. The story speaks both in a realistic way and also in extended metaphor of a long marriage and the terror of aging.

Terese Svoboda's story, "'80s Lilies," is a marvel of concision. Her images of sheep bones, calla lilies, waves rising like Roy Rogers's Trigger are captivating. In a story of a little more than a thousand words, Svoboda's images drive the drama of a young family seeking refuge in a post-Hiroshima world.

Deborah Eisenberg's characters often try to reconcile past and present, and their struggle to make a whole life from the shards of their experience is the moral core of her work. Her characters can't quite understand either who they are or how they got themselves in the fixes they're in. Kristina of "Window" drifts away from a broken home and into a life with a mysterious man and his beautiful son. She doesn't like the child at first, but she becomes committed to him in ways that ultimately threaten her life.

Alice Munro is a fearless explorer of the story, and it has been her lifework. She appears to relish the challenge of complicating the form as much as possible without breaking it. "Passion" demonstrates a classic Alice Munro dilemma: a young woman, tempted by security in the form of marriage, resists. In "Passion," the conflict is not so much framed as haunted by its beginning: Grace returns to the scene of her crucial decision; revisiting the old place is her way of testing and memorializing a choice that changed her life.

Beneath its realistic surface, William Trevor's "The Dressmaker's Child" has the enchanting power of a fairy tale. It may be seen as the story of a witch who captures a weak and lazy young man through a morally reprehensible act. Equally, it might be the story of a conversion in which a discarded mystery asserts itself over a youth who understands nothing about life but its material tokens: cigarettes, alcohol, cars. Whether readers favor a secular or religious interpretation, they will be drawn into Trevor's world.

In "The Broad Estates of Death" by Paula Fox, Harry and Amelia take a side trip from their honeymoon in New Mexico to visit Harry's estranged and ailing father. Amelia lurches from newly married happiness to understanding the brutality and chaos of her husband's childhood. She comes to see that Harry's past will never be discarded or forgotten, as he wishes, and that she's married a man she doesn't know. The subtle emotional transition revealed through plain, even unremarkable events demonstrates once again why Paula Fox is one of the strongest of American writers.

When Caesar, a convicted murderer, returns to the free world in "Old Boys, Old Girls" by Edward P. Jones, his character is so altered both by the crimes he almost casually committed and by the time he served and lost, that he carries prison inside himself. He is alienated from his ambivalent and clumsy family, from everyone but his old lover, Yvonne, "who believed in unhappiness and who thought happiness was the greatest trick God ever invented." Jones might or might not agree with Yvonne about happiness, but in the story's last moment he opens up new possibilities for Caesar, in a life and a heart that seemed to be all too predictable.

David Means's "Sault Ste. Marie" has the quality of a story told over and over again by the narrator to explain, and expiate, what he has done. The story takes hold of the reader like a kidnapper imprisoning his victim, then asking for understanding. "Sault Ste. Marie" has the haunting power of a confession.

Douglas Trevor's "Girls I Know" is a different sort of confession, the story of a graduate student who wants to slough off the emotional complications of his working-class past. Walt lives in the purgatory of academia, having completed all his work for his doctoral degree except his dissertation on Robert Lowell. Meanwhile, Walt works as a janitor, supplementing his income by selling his sperm. Lowell's aristocratic New England background is of endless interest to Walt, who understands nothing about that class but its privilege, nothing about the poet but his poetry. Enter Ginger, living embodiment of Lowell's class, a person free of Walt's rigid adherence to caste. Trevor's story, alternately funny and moving, brilliantly illustrates the price Walt pays, not for being a snob, but for being a coward.

Laughter may be the rarest reaction a short story can provoke, and it's one O. Henry worked for in his stories. Jackie Kay's "You Go When You Can No Longer Stay" is a delightful surprise of a story, tracing the demise of a too-comfortable relationship. You don't have to be familiar with the ins and outs of contemporary writing to love a story that begins: "It is not so much the fact that we are splitting up that is really worrying me, it is the fact that she keeps quoting Martin Amis."

To understand Melanie Rae Thon's "Letters in the Snow—for kind strangers and unborn children—for the ones lost and most beloved" the reader must enter the heroine's cataclysmic world. We follow Nicole as she swerves between past and present, composing her final messages to the world about the pain she's suffered and caused, recasting the crimes she's committed, and apologizing for her terrible mistakes. The reader becomes adept at working out Nicole's double meanings. As her delusions become clear, Nicole's madness is both original and recognizably moving.

The narrator of the striking "Famine" by Xu Xi calls the past "that country bumpkin's territory" and makes her escape from Hong Kong to New York. From the moment she steps aboard the plane, the act of eating is the narrator's desire. The story posits hunger and greed as equally uncontrollable, and the result is a striking portrait of insatiability.

"Mule Killers" by Lydia Peelle and "The Center of the World" by George Makana Clark take place thousands of miles apart, in Zimbabwe and the rural South, yet both trace the end of one regime and the beginning of another. In Clark's story the characters are in the midst of a political revolution, and in Peelle's an agricultural one, but both stories movingly portray the effect of far-reaching social changes on individual lives.

"Unction" by Karen Brown uses the boredom of office work and of youth as its bass line; the discordant melody is its heroine's capacity for resisting security and even happiness. The story revolves around this sexually awakened girl as a temptress, who is, Eve-like, defined by the unexpected strength of her desire.

Language itself is the secret subject that drives another Eve—a linguist, not a biblical figure—in Neela Vaswani's "The Pelvis Series." In her research, Eve tries to push past the limits of species differences and develops a capacity for generosity and loyalty that's absent in her human relationships. The charming affection Eve feels for her favorite chimp, Lola, is balanced by the cool reality of the primates' life among the scientists.

"Puffed Rice and Meatballs" by Lara Vapnyar begins in "hazy postcoital silence" and journeys back to a frightening passage through puberty. Katya is a Russian teenager who storms a state store, the Soviet version of the Winter Palace, as part of a mob's quest for breakfast cereal. Katya learns that her newly bloomed beauty makes her more vulnerable than strong.

David Lawrence Morse, like Lydia Peelle, appears in the O. Henry 2006 for his first published story. The three characters in Morse's "Conceived"—the passive narrator, his lover, Osa, and her devious sister, Tama—live on top of a fish they call Ceta. The narrator is unquestioningly loyal to the mores and rules of the community, and content with his lot, yet he's drawn to the rebellious, world-changing Osa. Morse does a fine job of working out the details of life atop a great fish, but the imaginative success of the story lies in its convincing portrayal of the narrator's love for Osa.

In "Disquisition on Tears," which is part of a trio of stories called "The Headless Woman," Stephanie Reents portrays the grotesque and frightful dilemma of her narrator with keen intelligence, moving deep into her character's body and pulling back with jokey humor. For anyone who's experienced serious illness, "Disquisition on Tears" is heartachingly familiar country, but it feels like new literary territory.

In the decades since *Love Medicine*, readers have become accustomed to the gracefully complicated characters in Louise Erdrich's novels and stories. Erdrich gives the reader the feeling that there is all the time in the world to contemplate the strangeness and familiarity of human life, always time to tell another tale, to add another twist to what we think is possible, opening our eyes and our imagination.

The narrator of Erdrich's "The Plague of Doves" is a Native American in Minnesota who takes an amble through her family's history of love. Family and tribal history weigh heavily on the story's plot. Only in the last breathtaking moments of "The Plague of Doves" does the narrator become aware of the implications of such an inheritance for her own life, and the responsibilities and dangers of both storytelling and love.

. . .

This year's table of contents shows what a range of magazines are publishing exceptional work, from commercial magazines such as *The New Yorker* and *Harper's*, to the privately owned *One Story* and *Zoetrope*, to little magazines such as *Epoch* and *The Georgia Review* that are supported by universities. Noncommercial magazines give fiction more space than the commercial ones, and represent the best chance writers have to be published, read, and recognized. All readers owe a debt of gratitude to the editors who labor to make their magazines memorable.

Katherine Anne Porter published in small magazines. When she finished "Flowering Judas" she sent it to Lincoln Kirstein of the influential little magazine *Hound and Horn*. In some ways, the literary world is more complicated than it was on that snowy night in 1929 when Katherine Anne Porter mailed off her breakthrough story, but the act is the same: the writer finds the answer to the riddle of the story and sends it, along with her hopes, to an editor. Some things, some good things, don't change.

—*Laura Furman, Austin, Texas*

The O. Henry Prize Stories 2006

Edward P. Jones

Old Boys, Old Girls

T HEY CAUGHT him after he had killed the second man. The law
would never connect him to the first murder. So the victim—a
stocky fellow Caesar Matthews shot in a Northeast alley only two blocks
from the home of the guy's parents, a man who died over a woman who
was actually in love with a third man—was destined to lie in his grave
without anyone officially paying for what had happened to him. It was
almost as if, at least on the books the law kept, Caesar had got away with a
free killing.

Seven months after he stabbed the second man—a twenty-two-year-
old with prematurely gray hair who had ventured out of Southeast for
only the sixth time in his life—Caesar was tried for murder in the second
degree. During much of the trial, he remembered the name only of the
first dead man—Percy, or "Golden Boy," Weymouth—and not the second, Antwoine Stoddard, to whom everyone kept referring during the
proceedings. The world had done things to Caesar since he'd left his
father's house for good at sixteen, nearly fourteen years ago, but he had
done far more to himself.

So at trial, with the weight of all the harm done to him and because he
had hidden for months in one shit hole after another, he was not always
himself and thought many times that he was actually there for killing
Golden Boy, the first dead man. He was not insane, but he was three doors

from it, which was how an old girlfriend, Yvonne Miller, would now and again playfully refer to his behavior. Who the fuck is this Antwoine bitch? Caesar sometimes thought during the trial. And where is Percy? It was only when the judge sentenced him to seven years in Lorton, D.C.'s prison in Virginia, that matters became somewhat clear again, and in those last moments before they took him away he saw Antwoine spread out on the ground outside the Prime Property nightclub, blood spurting out of his chest like oil from a bountiful well. Caesar remembered it all: sitting on the sidewalk, the liquor spinning his brain, his friends begging him to run, the club's music flooding out of the open door and going thumpety-thump-thump against his head. He sat a few feet from Antwoine, and would have killed again for a cigarette. "That's you, baby, so very near insanity it can touch you," said Yvonne, who believed in unhappiness and who thought happiness was the greatest trick God had invented. Yvonne Miller would be waiting for Caesar at the end of the line.

He came to Lorton with a ready-made reputation, since Multrey Wilson and Tony Cathedral—first-degree murderers both, and destined to die there—knew him from his Northwest and Northeast days. They were about as big as you could get in Lorton at that time (the guards called Lorton the House of Multrey and Cathedral), and they let everyone know that Caesar was good people, "a protected body," with no danger of having his biscuits or his butt taken.

A little less than a week after Caesar arrived, Cathedral asked him how he liked his cellmate. Caesar had never been to prison but had spent five days in the D.C. jail, not counting the time there before and during the trial. They were side by side at dinner, and neither man looked at the other. Multrey sat across from them. Cathedral was done eating in three minutes, but Caesar always took a long time to eat. His mother had raised him to chew his food thoroughly. "You wanna be a old man livin on oatmeal?" "I love oatmeal, Mama." "Tell me that when you have to eat it every day till you die."

"He all right, I guess," Caesar said of his cellmate, with whom he had shared fewer than a thousand words. Caesar's mother had died before she saw what her son became.

"You got the bunk you want, the right bed?" Multrey said. He was sitting beside one of his two "women," the one he had turned out most recently. "She" was picking at her food, something Multrey had already warned her about. The woman had a family—a wife and three children—but they would not visit. Caesar would never have visitors, either.

"It's all right." Caesar had taken the top bunk, as the cellmate had already made the bottom his home. A miniature plastic panda from his youngest child dangled on a string hung from one of the metal bedposts. "Bottom, top, it's all the same ship."

Cathedral leaned into him, picking chicken out of his teeth with an inch-long fingernail sharpened to a point. "Listen, man, even if you like the top bunk, you fuck him up for the bottom just cause you gotta let him know who rules. You let him know that you will stab him through his motherfuckin heart and then turn around and eat your supper, cludin the dessert." Cathedral straightened up. "Caes, you gon be here a few days, so you can't let nobody fuck with your humanity."

He went back to the cell and told Pancho Morrison that he wanted the bottom bunk, couldn't sleep well at the top.

"Too bad," Pancho said. He was lying down, reading a book published by the Jehovah's Witnesses. He wasn't a Witness, but he was curious.

Caesar grabbed the book and flung it at the bars, and the bulk of it slid through an inch or so and dropped to the floor. He kicked Pancho in the side, and before he could pull his leg back for a second kick Pancho took the foot in both hands, twisted it, and threw him against the wall. Then Pancho was up, and they fought for nearly an hour before two guards, who had been watching the whole time, came in and beat them about the head. "Show's over! Show's over!" one kept saying.

They attended to themselves in silence in the cell, and with the same silence they flung themselves at each other the next day after dinner. They were virtually the same size, and though Caesar came to battle with more muscle, Pancho had more heart. Cathedral had told Caesar that morning that Pancho had lived on practically nothing but heroin for the three years before Lorton, so whatever fighting dog was in him could be pounded out in little or no time. It took three days. Pancho was the father of five children, and each time he swung he did so with the memory of all five and what he had done to them over those three addicted years. He wanted to return to them and try to make amends, and he realized on the morning of the third day that he would not be able to do that if Caesar killed him. So fourteen minutes into the fight he sank to the floor after Caesar hammered him in the gut. And though he could have got up he stayed there, silent and still. The two guards laughed. The daughter who had given Pancho the panda was nine years old and had been raised by her mother as a Catholic.

That night, before the place went dark, Caesar lay on the bottom bunk and looked over at pictures of Pancho's children, which Pancho had taped on the opposite wall. He knew he would have to decide if he wanted Pancho just to move the photographs or to put them away altogether. All the children had toothy smiles. The two youngest stood, in separate pictures, outdoors in their First Communion clothes. Caesar himself had been a father for two years. A girl he had met at an F Street club in Northwest had told him he was the father of her son, and for a time he had believed her. Then the boy started growing big ears that Caesar thought didn't belong to anyone in his family, and so after he had slapped the girl a few times a week before the child's second birthday she confessed that the child belonged to "my first love." "Your first love is always with you," she said, sounding forever like a television addict who had never read a book. As Caesar prepared to leave, she asked him, "You want back all the toys and things you gave him?" The child, as if used to their fighting, had slept through this last encounter on the couch, part of a living-room suite that they were paying for on time. Caesar said nothing more and didn't think about his 18k.-gold cigarette lighter until he was eight blocks away. The girl pawned the thing and got enough to pay off the furniture bill.

Caesar and Pancho worked in the laundry, and Caesar could look across the noisy room with all the lint swirling about and see Pancho sorting dirty pieces into bins. Then he would push uniform bins to the left and everything else to the right. Pancho had been doing that for three years. The job he got after he left Lorton was as a gofer at construction sites. No laundry in the outside world wanted him. Over the next two weeks, as Caesar watched Pancho at his job, his back always to him, he considered what he should do next. He wasn't into fucking men, so that was out. He still had not decided what he wanted done about the photographs on the cell wall. One day at the end of those two weeks, Caesar saw the light above Pancho's head flickering and Pancho raised his head and looked for a long time at it, as if thinking that the answer to all his problems lay in fixing that one light. Caesar decided then to let the pictures remain on the wall.

Three years later, they let Pancho go. The two men had mostly stayed at a distance from each other, but toward the end they had been talking, sharing plans about a life beyond Lorton. The relationship had reached the point where Caesar was saddened to see the children's photographs come off the wall. Pancho pulled off the last taped picture and the wall was suddenly empty in a most forlorn way. Caesar knew the names of all the children. Pancho gave him a rabbit's foot that one of his children had given him. It was the way among all those men that when a good-luck piece had run out of juice it was given away with the hope that new ownership would renew its strength. The rabbit's foot had lost its electricity months before Pancho's release. Caesar's only good-fortune piece was a key chain made in Peru; it had been sweet for a bank robber in the next cell for nearly two years until that man's daughter, walking home from third grade, was abducted and killed.

One day after Pancho left, they brought in a thief and three-time rapist of elderly women. He nodded to Caesar and told him that he was Watson Rainey and went about making a home for himself in the cell, finally plugging in a tiny lamp with a green shade which he placed on the metal shelf jutting from the wall. Then he climbed onto the top bunk he had made up and lay down. His name was all the wordplay he had given Caesar, who had been smoking on the bottom bunk throughout Rainey's efforts to make a nest. Caesar waited ten minutes and then stood and pulled the lamp's cord out of the wall socket and grabbed Rainey with one hand and threw him to the floor. He crushed the lamp into Rainey's face. He choked him with the cord. "You come into my house and show me no respect!" Caesar shouted. The only sound Rainey could manage was a gurgling that bubbled up from his mangled mouth. There were no witnesses except for an old man across the way, who would occasionally glance over at the two when he wasn't reading his Bible. It was over and done with in four minutes. When Rainey came to, he found everything he owned piled in the corner, soggy with piss. And Caesar was again on the top bunk.

They would live in that cell together until Caesar was released, four years later. Rainey tried never to be in the house during waking hours; if he was there when Caesar came in, he would leave. Rainey's name spoken by him that first day were all the words that would ever pass between the two men.

A week or so after Rainey got there, Caesar bought from Multrey a calendar that was three years old. It was large and had no markings of any sort, as pristine as the day it was made. "You know this one ain't the year we in right now," Multrey said as one of his women took a quarter from Caesar and dropped it in her purse. Caesar said, "It'll do." Multrey prized the calendar for one thing: its top half had a photograph of a naked woman of indeterminate race sitting on a stool, her legs wide open, her pussy aimed dead at whoever was standing right in front of her. It had been Multrey's good-luck piece, but the luck was dead. Multrey remembered what the calendar had done for him and he told his woman to give Caesar his money back, lest any new good-fortune piece turn sour on him.

The calendar's bottom half had the days of the year. That day, the first Monday in June, Caesar drew in the box that was January 1st a line that went from the upper left-hand corner down to the bottom right-hand corner. The next day, a June Tuesday, he made a line in the January 2nd box that also ran in the same direction. And so it went. When the calendar had all such lines in all the boxes, it was the next June. Then Caesar, in that January 1st box, made a line that formed an X with the first line. And so it was for another year. The third year saw horizontal marks that sliced the boxes in half. The fourth year had vertical lines down the centers of the boxes.

This was the only calendar Caesar had in Lorton. That very first Monday, he taped the calendar over the area where the pictures of Pancho's children had been. There was still a good deal of empty space left, but he didn't do anything about it, and Rainey knew he couldn't do anything, either.

The calendar did right by Caesar until near the end of his fifth year in Lorton, when he began to feel that its juice was drying up. But he kept it there to mark off the days and, too, the naked woman never closed her legs to him.

In that fifth year, someone murdered Multrey as he showered. The killers—it had to be more than one for a man like Multrey—were never found. The Multrey woman who picked at her food had felt herself caring for a recent arrival who was five years younger than her, a part-time deacon who had killed a Southwest bartender for calling the deacon's wife "a woman without one fuckin brain cell." The story of that killing—the bartender was dropped headfirst from the roof of a ten-story building—became legend, and in Lorton men referred to the dead bartender as "the Flat-Head Insulter" and the killer became known as "the Righteous Desulter." The Desulter, wanting Multrey's lady, had hired people to butcher him. It had always been the duty of the lady who hated food to watch out for Multrey as he showered, but she had stepped away that day, just as she had been instructed to by the Desulter.

In another time, Cathedral and Caesar would have had enough of everything—from muscle to influence—to demand that someone give up the killers, but the prison was filling up with younger men who did not care what those two had been once upon a time. Also, Cathedral had already had two visits from the man he had killed in Northwest. Each time, the man had first stood before the bars of Cathedral's cell. Then he held one of the bars and opened the door inward, like some wooden door on a person's house. The dead man standing there would have been sufficient to unwrap anyone, but matters were compounded when Cathedral saw a door that for years had slid sideways now open in an impossible fashion. The man stood silent before Cathedral, and when he left he shut the door gently, as if there were sleeping children in the cell. So Cathedral didn't have a full mind, and Multrey was never avenged.

There was an armed-robbery man in the place, a tattooer with homemade inks and needles. He made a good living painting on both muscled and frail bodies the names of children; the Devil in full regalia with a pitchfork dripping with blood; the words "Mother" or "Mother Forever" surrounded by red roses and angels who looked sad, because when it came to drawing happy angels the tattoo man had no skills. One pickpocket had had a picture of his father tattooed in the middle of his chest; above the father's head, in medieval lettering, were the words "Rotting in Hell," with the letter "H" done in fiery yellow and red. The tattoo guy had told Caesar that he had skin worthy of "a painter's best canvas," that he could give Caesar a tattoo "God would envy." Caesar had always told him no, but then he awoke one snowy night in March of his sixth year and realized that it was his mother's birthday. He did not know what day of the week it was, but the voice that talked to him had the authority of a million loving mothers. He had long ago forgotten his own birthday, had not even bothered to ask someone in prison records to look it up.

There had never been anyone or anything he wanted commemorated on his body. Maybe it would have been Carol, his first girlfriend twenty years ago, before the retarded girl entered their lives. He had played with the notion of having the name of the boy he thought was his put over his heart, but the lie had come to light before that could happen. And before the boy there had been Yvonne, with whom he had lived for an extraordinary time in Northeast. He would have put Yvonne's name over his heart, but she went off to work one day and never came back. He looked for her for three months, and then just assumed that she had been killed somewhere and dumped in a place only animals knew about. Yvonne was indeed dead, and she would be waiting for him at the end of the line, though she did not know that was what she was doing. "You can always trust unhappiness," Yvonne had once said, sitting in the dark on the couch, her cigarette burned down to the filter. "His face never changes. But happiness is slick, can't be trusted. It has a thousand faces, Caes, all of them just ready to reform into unhappiness once it has you in its clutches."

So Caesar had the words "Mother Forever" tattooed on his left bicep. Knowing that more letters meant a higher payment of cigarettes or money or candy, the tattoo fellow had dissuaded him from having just plain "Mother." "How many hours you think she spent in labor?" he asked Caesar. "Just to give you life." The job took five hours over two days, during a snowstorm. Caesar said no to angels, knowing the man's ability with happy ones, and had the words done in blue letters encased in red roses. The man worked from the words printed on a piece of paper that Caesar had given him, because he was also a bad speller.

The snow stopped on the third day and, strangely, it took only another three days for the two feet of mess to melt, for with the end of the storm came a heat wave. The tattoo man, a good friend of the Righteous Desulter, would tell Caesar in late April that what happened to him was his own fault, that he had not taken care of himself as he had been instructed to do. "And the heat ain't helped you neither." On the night of March 31st, five days after the tattoo had been put on, Caesar woke in the night with a pounding in his left arm. He couldn't return to sleep so he sat on the edge of his bunk until morning, when he saw that the "e"s in "Mother Forever" had blistered, as if someone had taken a match to them.

He went to the tattoo man, who first told him not to worry, then patted the "e"s with peroxide that he warmed in a spoon with a match. Within two days, the "e"s seemed to just melt away, each dissolving into an ugly pile at the base of the tattoo. After a week, the diseased "e"s began spreading their work to the other letters and Caesar couldn't move his arm without pain. He went to the infirmary. They gave him aspirin and Band-Aided the tattoo. He was back the next day, the day the doctor was there.

He spent four days in D.C. General Hospital, his first trip back to Washington since a court appearance more than three years before. His entire body was paralyzed for two days, and one nurse confided to him the day he left that he had been near death. In the end, after the infection had done its work, there was not much left of the tattoo except an "o" and an "r," which were so deformed they could never pass for English, and a few roses that looked more like red mud. When he returned to prison, the tattoo man offered to give back the cigarettes and the money, but Caesar never gave him an answer, leading the man to think that he should watch his back. What happened to Caesar's tattoo and to Caesar was bad advertising, and soon the fellow had no customers at all.

Something had died in the arm and the shoulder, and Caesar was never again able to raise the arm more than thirty-five degrees. He had no enemies, but still he told no one about his debilitation. For the next few months he tried to stay out of everyone's way, knowing that he was far more vulnerable than he had been before the tattoo. Alone in the cell, with no one watching across the way, he exercised the arm, but by November he knew at last he would not be the same again. He tried to bully Rainey Watson as much as he could to continue the façade that he was still who he had been. And he tried to spend more time with Cathedral.

But the man Cathedral had killed had become a far more constant visitor. The dead man, a young bachelor who had been Cathedral's next-door neighbor, never spoke. He just opened Cathedral's cell door inward and went about doing things as if the cell were a family home—straightening wall pictures that only Cathedral could see, turning down the gas on the stove, testing the shower water to make sure that it was not too hot, tucking children into bed. Cathedral watched silently.

Caesar went to Cathedral's cell one day in mid-December, six months before they freed him. He found his friend sitting on the bottom bunk, his hands clamped over his knees. He was still outside the cell when Cathedral said, "Caes, you tell me why God would be so stupid to create mosquitoes. I mean, what good are the damn things? What's their function?" Caesar laughed, thinking it was a joke, and he had started to offer something when Cathedral looked over at him with a devastatingly serious gaze and said, "What we need is a new God. Somebody who knows what the fuck he's doing." Cathedral was not smiling. He returned to staring at the wall across from him. "What's with creatin bats? I mean, yes, they eat insects, but why create those insects to begin with? You see what I mean? Creatin a problem and then havin to create somethin to take care of the problem. And then comin up with somethin for that second problem. Man oh man!" Caesar slowly began moving away from Cathedral's cell. He had seen this many times before. It could not be cured even by great love. It sometimes pulled down a loved one. "And roaches. Every human bein in the world would have the sense not to create roaches. What's their function, Caes? I tell you, we need a new God, and I'm ready to cast my vote right now. Roaches and rats and chinches. God was out of his fuckin mind that week. Six wasted days, cept for the human part and some of the animals. And then partyin on the seventh day like he done us a big favor. The nerve of that motherfucker. And all your pigeons and squirrels. Don't forget them. I mean really."

In late January, they took Cathedral somewhere and then brought him back after a week. He returned to his campaign for a new God in February. A ritual began that would continue until Caesar left: determine that Cathedral was a menace to himself, take him away, bring him back, then take him away when he started campaigning again for another God.

There was now nothing for Caesar to do except try to coast to the end on a reputation that was far less than it had been in his first years at Lorton. He could only hope that he had built up enough goodwill among men who had better reputations and arms that worked a hundred percent.

In early April, he received a large manila envelope from his attorney. The lawyer's letter was brief. "I did not tell them where you are," he wrote. "They may have learned from someone that I was your attorney. Take care." There were two separate letters in sealed envelopes from his brother and sister, each addressed to "My Brother Caesar." Dead people come back alive, Caesar thought many times before he finally read the letters, after almost a week. He expected an announcement about the death of his father, but he was hardly mentioned. Caesar's younger brother went on for five pages with a history of what had happened to the family since Caesar had left their lives. He ended by saying, "Maybe I should have been a better brother." There were three pictures as well, one of his brother and his bride on their wedding day, and one showing Caesar's sister, her husband, and their two children, a girl of four or so and a boy of about two. The third picture had the girl sitting on a couch beside the boy, who was in Caesar's father's lap, looking with interest off to the left, as if whatever was there were more important than having his picture taken. Caesar looked at the image of his father—a man on the verge of becoming old. His sister's letter had even less in it than the lawyer's: "Write to me, or call me collect, whatever is best for you, dear one. Call even if you are on the other side of the world. For every step you take to get to me, I will walk a mile toward you."

He had an enormous yearning at first, but after two weeks he tore everything up and threw it all away. He would be glad he had done this as he stumbled, hurt and confused, out of his sister's car less than half a year later. The girl and the boy would be in the backseat, the girl wearing a red dress and black shoes, and the boy in blue pants and a T-shirt with a cartoon figure on the front. The boy would have fallen asleep, but the girl would say, "Nighty-night, Uncle," which she had been calling him all that evening.

An ex-offenders' group, the Light at the End of the Tunnel, helped him to get a room and a job washing dishes and busing tables at a restaurant on F Street. The room was in a three-story building in the middle of the 900 block of N Street, Northwest, a building that, in the days when white people lived there, had had two apartments of eight rooms or so on each floor. Now the first-floor apartments were uninhabitable and had been padlocked for years. On the two other floors, each large apartment had been divided into five rented rooms, which went for twenty to thirty dollars a week, depending on the size and the view. Caesar's was small, twenty dollars, and had half the space of his cell at Lorton. The word that came to him for the butchered, once luxurious apartments was "warren." The roomers in each of the cut-up apartments shared two bathrooms and one nice-sized kitchen, which was a pathetic place because of its dinginess and its fifty-watt bulb, and because many of the appliances were old or undependable or both. Caesar's narrow room was at the front, facing N Street. On his side of the hall were two other rooms, the one next to his housing a mother and her two children. He would not know until his third week there that along the other hall was Yvonne Miller.

There was one main entry door for each of the complexes. In the big room to the left of the door into Caesar's complex lived a man of sixty or so, a pajama-clad man who was never out of bed in all the time Caesar lived there. He could walk, but Caesar never saw him do it. A woman, who told Caesar one day that she was "a home health-care aide," was always in the man's room, cooking, cleaning, or watching television with him. His was the only room with its own kitchen setup in a small alcove— a stove, icebox, and sink. His door was always open, and he never seemed to sleep. A green safe, three feet high, squatted beside the bed. "I am a moneylender," the man said the second day Caesar was there. He had come in and walked past the room, and the man had told the aide to have "that young lion" come back. "I am Simon and I lend money," the man said as Caesar stood in the doorway. "I will be your best friend, but not for free. Tell your friends."

He worked as many hours as they would allow him at the restaurant, Chowing Down. The remainder of the time, he went to movies until the shows closed and then sat in Franklin Park, at Fourteenth and K, in good weather and bad. He was there until sleep beckoned, sometimes as late as two in the morning. No one bothered him. He had killed two men, and the world, especially the bad part of it, sensed that and left him alone. He knew no one, and he wanted no one to know him. The friends he had had before Lorton seemed to have been swept off the face of the earth. On the penultimate day of his time at Lorton, he had awoken terrified and thought that if they gave him a choice he might well stay. He might find a life and a career at Lorton.

He had sex only with his right hand, and that was not very often. He began to believe, in his first days out of prison, that men and women were now speaking a new language, and that he would never learn it. His lack of confidence extended even to whores, and this was a man who had been with more women than he had fingers and toes. He began to think that a whore had the power to crush a man's soul. "What kinda language you speakin, honey? Talk English if you want some." He was thirty-seven when he got free.

He came in from the park at two forty-five one morning and went quickly by Simon's door, but the moneylender called him back. Caesar stood in the doorway. He had been in the warren for less than two months. The aide was cooking, standing with her back to Caesar in a crisp green uniform and sensible black shoes. She was stirring first one pot on the stove and then another. People on the color television were laughing.

"Been out on the town, I see," Simon began. "Hope you got enough poontang to last you till next time." "I gotta be goin," Caesar said. He had begun to think that he might be able to kill the man and find a way to get into the safe. The question was whether he should kill the aide as well. "Don't blow off your friends that way," Simon said. Then, for some reason, he started telling Caesar about their neighbors in that complex. That was how Caesar first learned about an "Yvonny," whom he had yet to see. He would not know that she was the Yvonne he had known long ago until the second time he passed her in the hall. "Now, our sweet Yvonny, she ain't nothin but an old girl." Old girls were whores, young or old, who had been battered so much by the world that they had only the faintest wisp of life left; not many of them had hearts of gold. "But you could probably have her for free," Simon said, and he pointed to Caesar's right, where Yvonne's room was. There was always a small lump under the covers beside Simon in the bed, and Caesar suspected that it was a gun. That was a problem, but he might be able to leap to the bed and kill the man with one blow of a club before he could pull it out. What would the aide do? "I've had her myself," Simon said, "so I can only recommend it in a pinch." "Later, man," Caesar said, and he stepped away. The usual way to his room was to the right as soon as he entered the main door, but that morning he walked straight ahead and within a few feet was passing Yvonne's door. It was slightly ajar, and he heard music from a radio. The aide might even be willing to help him rob the moneylender if he could talk to her alone beforehand. He might not know the language men and women were speaking now, but the language of money had not changed.

. . .

It was a cousin who told his brother where to find him. That cousin, Nora Maywell, was the manager of a nearby bank, at Twelfth and F Streets, and she first saw Caesar as he bused tables at Chowing Down, where she had gone with colleagues for lunch. She came in day after day to make certain that he was indeed Caesar, for she had not seen him in more than twenty years. But there was no mistaking the man, who looked like her uncle. Caesar was five years older than Nora. She had gone through much of her childhood hoping that she would grow up to marry him. Had he paid much attention to her in all those years before he disappeared, he still would not have recognized her—she was older, to be sure, but life had been extraordinarily kind to Nora and she was now a queen compared with the dirt-poor peasant she had once been.

Caesar's brother came in three weeks after Nora first saw him. The brother, Alonzo, ate alone, paid his bill, then went over to Caesar and smiled. "It's good to see you," he said. Caesar simply nodded and walked away with the tub of dirty dishes. The brother stood shaking for a few moments, then turned and made his unsteady way out the door. He was a corporate attorney, making nine times what his father, at fifty-seven, was making, and he came back for many days. On the eighth day, he went to Caesar, who was busing in a far corner of the restaurant. It was now early September and Caesar had been out of prison for three months and five days. "I will keep coming until you speak to me," the brother said. Caesar looked at him for a long time. The lunch hours were ending, so the manager would have no reason to shout at him. Only two days before, he had seen Yvonne in the hall for the second time. It had been afternoon and the dead lightbulb in the hall had been replaced since the first time he had passed her. He recognized her, but everything in her eyes and body told him that she did not know him. That would never change. And, because he knew who she was, he nodded to his brother and within minutes they were out the door and around the corner to the alley. Caesar lit a cigarette right away. The brother's gray suit had cost $1,865.98. Caesar's apron was filthy. It was his seventh cigarette of the afternoon. When it wasn't in his mouth, the cigarette was at his side, and as he raised it up and down to his mouth, inhaled, and flicked ashes, his hand never shook.

"Do you know how much I want to put my arms around you?" Alonzo said.

"I think we should put an end to all this shit right now so we can get on with our lives," Caesar said. "I don't wanna see you or anyone else in your family from now until the day I die. You should understand that, Mister, so you can do somethin else with your time. You a customer, so I won't do what I would do to somebody who ain't a customer."

The brother said, "I'll admit to whatever I may have done to you. I will, Caesar. I will." In fact, his brother had never done anything to him, and neither had his sister. The war had always been between Caesar and their father, but Caesar, over time, had come to see his siblings as the father's allies. "But come to see me and Joanie, one time only, and if you don't want to see us again then we'll accept that. I'll never come into your restaurant again."

There was still more of the cigarette, but Caesar looked at it and then dropped it to the ground and stepped on it. He looked at his cheap watch. Men in prison would have killed for what was left of that smoke. "I gotta be goin, Mister."

"We are family, Caesar. If you don't want to see Joanie and me for your sake, for our sakes, then do it for Mama."

"My mama's dead, and she been dead for a lotta years." He walked toward the street.

"I know she's dead! I know she's dead! I just put flowers on her grave on Sunday. And on three Sundays before that. And five weeks before that. I know my mother's dead."

Caesar stopped. It was one thing for him to throw out a quick statement about a dead mother, as he had done many times over the years. A man could say the words so often that they became just another meaningless part of his makeup. The pain was no longer there as it had been those first times he had spoken them, when his mother was still new to her grave. The words were one thing, but a grave was a different matter, a different fact. The grave was out there, to be seen and touched, and a man, a son, could go to that spot of earth and remember all over again how much she had loved him, how she had stood in her apron in the doorway of a clean and beautiful home and welcomed him back from school. He could go to the grave and read her name and die a bit, because it would feel as if she had left him only last week.

Caesar turned around. "You and your people must leave me alone, Mister."

"Then we will," the brother said. "We will leave you alone. Come to one dinner. A Sunday dinner. Fried chicken. The works. Then we'll never bother you again. No one but Joanie and our families. No one else." Those last words were to assure Caesar that he would not have to see their father.

Caesar wanted another cigarette, but the meeting had already gone on long enough.

Yvonne had not said anything that second time, when he said "Hello." She had simply nodded and walked around him in the hall. The third time they were also passing in the hall, and he spoke again, and she stepped to the side to pass and then turned and asked if he had any smokes she could borrow.

He said he had some in his room, and she told him to go get them and pointed to her room.

Her room was a third larger than his. It had an icebox, a bed, a dresser with a mirror over it, a small table next to the bed, a chair just beside the door, and not much else. The bed made a T with the one window, which faced the windowless wall of the apartment building next door. The beautiful blue-and-yellow curtains at the window should have been somewhere else, in a place that could appreciate them.

He had no expectations. He wanted nothing. It was just good to see a person from a special time in his life, and it was even better that he had loved her once and she had loved him. He stood in the doorway with the cigarettes.

Dressed in a faded purple robe, she was looking in the icebox when he returned. She closed the icebox door and looked at him. He walked over, and she took the unopened pack of cigarettes from his outstretched hand. He stood there.

"Well, sit the fuck down before you make the place look poor." He sat in the chair by the door, and she sat on the bed and lit the first cigarette. She was sideways to him. It was only after the fifth drag on the cigarette that she spoke. "If you think you gonna get some pussy, you are sorely mistaken. I ain't givin out shit. Free can kill you."

"I don't want nothin."

"'I don't want nothin. I don't want nothin.'" She dropped ashes into an empty tomato-soup can on the table by the bed. "Mister, we all want somethin, and the sooner people like you stand up and stop the bullshit, then the world can start bein a better place. It's the bullshitters who keep the world from bein a better place." Together, they had rented a little house in Northeast and had been planning to have a child once they had been there two years. The night he came home and found her sitting in the dark and talking about never trusting happiness, they had been there a year and a half. Two months later, she was gone. For the next three months, as he looked for her, he stayed there and continued to make it the kind of place that a woman would want to come home to. "My own mother was the first bullshitter I knew," she continued. "That's how I know it don't work. People should stand up and say, 'I wish you were dead,' or 'I want your pussy,' or 'I want all the money in your pocket.' When we stop lyin, the world will start bein heaven." He had been a thief and a robber and a drug pusher before he met her, and he went back to all that after the three months, not because he was heartbroken, though he was, but because it was such an easy thing to do. He was smart enough to know that he could not blame Yvonne, and he never did. The murders of Percy "Golden Boy" Weymouth and Antwoine Stoddard were still years away.

He stayed that day for more than an hour, until she told him that she had now paid for the cigarettes. Over the next two weeks, as he got closer to the dinner with his brother and sister, he would take her cigarettes and food and tell her from the start that they were free. He was never to know how she paid the rent. By the fourth day of bringing her things, she began to believe that he wanted nothing. He always sat in the chair by the door. Her words never changed, and it never mattered to him. The only thanks he got was the advice that the world should stop being a bullshitter.

On the day of the dinner, he found that the days of sitting with Yvonne had given him a strength he had not had when he had said yes to his brother. He had Alonzo pick him up in front of Chowing Down, because he felt that if they knew where he lived they would find a way to stay in his life.

At his sister's house, just off Sixteenth Street, Northwest, in an area of well-to-do black people some called the Gold Coast, they welcomed him, Joanie keeping her arms around him for more than a minute, crying. Then they offered him a glass of wine. He had not touched alcohol since before prison. They sat him on a dark-green couch in the living room, which was the size of ten prison cells. Before he had taken three sips of the wine, he felt good enough not to care that the girl and the boy, his sister's children, wanted to be in his lap. They were the first children he had been around in more than ten years. The girl had been calling him Uncle since he entered the house.

Throughout dinner, which was served by his sister's maid, and during the rest of the evening, he said as little as possible to the adults—his sister and brother and their spouses—but concentrated on the kids, because he thought he knew their hearts. The grownups did not pepper him with questions and were just grateful that he was there. Toward the end of the meal, he had a fourth glass of wine, and that was when he told his niece that she looked like his mother and the girl blushed, because she knew how beautiful her grandmother had been.

At the end, as Caesar stood in the doorway preparing to leave, his brother said that he had made this a wonderful year. His brother's eyes teared up and he wanted to hug Caesar, but Caesar, without smiling, simply extended his hand. The last thing his brother said to him was "Even if you go away not wanting to see us again, know that Daddy loves you. It is the one giant truth in the world. He's a different man, Caesar. I think he loves you more than us because he never knew what happened to you. That may be why he never remarried." The issue of what Caesar had been doing for twenty-one years never came up.

His sister, with her children in the backseat, drove him home. In front of his building, he and Joanie said goodbye and she kissed his cheek and, as an afterthought, he, a new uncle and with the wine saying, Now, that wasn't so bad, reached back to give a playful tug on the children's feet, but the sleeping boy was too far away and the girl, laughing, wiggled out of his reach. He said to his niece, "Good night, young lady," and she said no, that she was not a lady but a little girl. Again, he reached unsuccessfully for her feet. When he turned back, his sister had a look of such horror and disgust that he felt he had been stabbed. He knew right away what she was thinking, that he was out to cop a feel on a child. He managed a goodbye and got out of the car. "Call me," she said before he closed the car door, but the words lacked the feeling of all the previous ones of the evening. He said nothing. Had he spoken the wrong language, as well as done the wrong thing? Did child molesters call little girls "ladies"? He knew he would never call his sister. Yes, he had been right to tear up the pictures and letters when he was in Lorton.

He shut his eyes until the car was no more. He felt a pained rumbling throughout his system and, without thinking, he staggered away from his building toward Tenth Street. He could hear music coming from an apartment on his side of N Street. He had taught his sister how to ride a bike, how to get over her fear of falling and hurting herself. Now, in her eyes, he was no more than an animal capable of hurting a child. They killed men in prison for being that kind of monster. Whatever avuncular love for the children had begun growing in just those few hours now seeped away. He leaned over into the grass at the side of the apartment building and vomited. He wiped his mouth with the back of his hand. "I'll fall, Caesar," his sister had said in her first weeks of learning how to ride a bicycle. "Why would I let that happen?"

He ignored the aide when she told him that the moneylender wanted to talk to him. He went straight ahead, toward Yvonne's room, though he had no intention of seeing her. Her door was open enough for him to see a good part of the room, but he simply turned toward his own room. His shadow, cast by her light behind him, was thin and went along the floor and up the wall, and it was seeing the shadow that made him turn around. After noting that the bathroom next to her room was empty, he called softly to her from the doorway and then called three times more before he gave the door a gentle push with his finger. The door had not opened all the way when he saw her half on the bed and half off. Drunk, he thought. He went to her, intending to put her full on the bed. But death can twist the body in a way life never does, and that was what it had done to hers. He knew death. Her face was pressed into the bed, at a crooked angle that would have been uncomfortable for any living person. One leg was bunched under her, and the other was extended behind her, but both seemed not part of her body, awkwardly on their own, as if someone could just pick them up and walk away.

He whispered her name. He sat down beside her, ignoring the vomit that spilled out of her mouth and over the side of the bed. He moved her head so that it rested on one side. He thought at first that someone had done this to her, but he saw money on the dresser and felt the quiet throughout the room that signaled the end of it all, and he knew that the victim and the perpetrator were one and the same. He screwed the top on the empty whiskey bottle near her extended leg.

He placed her body on the bed and covered her with a sheet and a blanket. Someone would find her in the morning. He stood at the door, preparing to turn out the light and leave, thinking this was how the world would find her. He had once known her as a clean woman who would not steal so much as a needle. A woman with a well-kept house. She had been loved. But that was not what they would see in the morning.

He set about putting a few things back in place, hanging up clothes that were lying over the chair and on the bed, straightening the lampshade, picking up newspapers and everything else on the floor. But, when he was done, it did not seem enough.

He went to his room and tore up two shirts to make dust rags. He started in a corner at the foot of her bed, at a table where she kept her brush and comb and makeup and other lady things. When he had dusted the table and everything on it, he put an order to what was there, just as if she would be using them in the morning.

Then he began dusting and cleaning clockwise around the room, and by midnight he was not even half done and the shirts were dirty with all the work, and he went back to his room for two more. By three, he was cutting up his pants for rags. After he had cleaned and dusted the room, he put an order to it all, as he had done with the things on the table—the dishes and food in mouseproof canisters on the table beside the icebox, the two framed posters of mountains on the wall that were tilting to the left, the five photographs of unknown children on the bureau. When that work was done, he took a pail and a mop from her closet. Mice had made a bed in the mop, and he had to brush them off and away. He filled the pail with water from the bathroom and soap powder from under the table beside the icebox. After the floor had been mopped, he stood in the doorway as it dried and listened to the mice in the walls, listened to them scurrying in the closet.

At about four, the room was done and Yvonne lay covered in her unmade bed. He went to the door, ready to leave, and was once more unable to move. The whole world was silent except the mice in the walls.

He knelt at the bed and touched Yvonne's shoulder. On a Tuesday morning, a school day, he had come upon his father kneeling at his bed,

Caesar's mother growing cold in that bed. His father was crying, and when Caesar went to him his father crushed Caesar to him and took the boy's breath away. It was Caesar's brother who had said they should call someone, but their father said, "No, no, just one minute more, just one more minute," as if in that next minute God would reconsider and send his wife back. And Caesar had said, "Yes, just one minute more." The one giant truth. . . , his brother had said.

Caesar changed the bed clothing and undressed Yvonne. He got one of her large pots and filled it with warm water from the bathroom and poured into the water cologne of his own that he never used and bath-oil beads he found in a battered container in a corner beside her dresser. The beads refused to dissolve, and he had to crush them in his hands. He bathed her, cleaned out her mouth. He got a green dress from the closet, and underwear and stockings from the dresser, put them on her, and pinned a rusty cameo on the dress over her heart. He combed and brushed her hair, put barrettes in it after he sweetened it with the rest of the cologne, and laid her head in the center of the pillow now covered with one of his clean cases. He gave her no shoes and he did not cover her up, just left her on top of the made-up bed. The room with the dead woman was as clean and as beautiful as Caesar could manage at that time in his life. It was after six in the morning, and the world was lighting up and the birds had begun to chirp. Caesar shut off the ceiling light and turned out the lamp, held on to the chain switch as he listened to the beginnings of a new day.

He opened the window that he had cleaned hours before, and right away a breeze came through. He put a hand to the wind, enjoying the coolness, and one thing came to him: he was not a young man anymore.

He sat on his bed smoking one cigarette after another. Before finding Yvonne dead, he had thought he would go and live in Baltimore and hook up with a vicious crew he had known a long time ago. Wasn't that what child molesters did? Now, the only thing he knew about the rest of his life was that he did not want to wash dishes and bus tables anymore. At about nine thirty, he put just about all he owned and the two bags of trash from Yvonne's room in the bin in the kitchen. He knocked at the door of the woman in the room next to his. Her son opened the door, and Caesar asked for his mother. He gave her the hundred and forty-seven dollars he had found in Yvonne's room, along with his radio and tiny black-and-white television. He told her to look in on Yvonne before long and then said he would see her later, which was perhaps the softest lie of his adult life.

On his way out of the warren of rooms, Simon called to him. "You comin back soon, young lion?" he asked. Caesar nodded. "Well, why don't you bring me back a bottle of rum? Woke up with a taste for it this mornin." Caesar nodded. "Was that you in there with Yvonny last night?" Simon said as he got the money from atop the safe beside his bed. "Quite a party, huh?" Caesar said nothing. Simon gave the money to the aide, and she handed Caesar ten dollars and a quarter. "Right down to the penny," Simon said. "Give you a tip when you get back." "I won't be long," Caesar said. Simon must have realized that was a lie, because before Caesar went out the door he said, in as sweet a voice as he was capable of, "I'll be waitin."

He came out into the day. He did not know what he was going to do, aside from finding some legit way to pay for Yvonne's funeral. The D.C. government people would take her away, but he knew where he could find and claim her before they put her in potter's field. He put the bills in his pocket and looked down at the quarter in the palm of his hand. It was a rather old one, 1967, but shiny enough. Life had been kind to it. He went carefully down the steps in front of the building and stood on the sidewalk. The world was going about its business, and it came to him, as it might to a man who had been momentarily knocked senseless after a punch to the face, that he was of that world. To the left was Ninth Street and all the rest of N Street, Immaculate Conception Catholic Church at Eighth, the bank at the corner of Seventh. He flipped the coin. To his right was Tenth Street, and down Tenth were stores and the house where Abraham Lincoln had died and all the white people's precious monuments. Up Tenth and a block to Eleventh and Q streets was once a High's store where, when Caesar was a boy, a pint of cherry-vanilla ice cream cost twenty-five cents, and farther down Tenth was French Street, with a two-story house with his mother's doilies and a foot-long porcelain black puppy just inside the front door. A puppy his mother had bought for his father in the third year of their marriage. A puppy that for thirty-five years had been patiently waiting each working day for Caesar's father to return from work. The one giant truth . . . Just one minute more. He caught the quarter and slapped it on the back of his hand. He had already decided that George Washington's profile would mean going toward Tenth Street, and that was what he did once he uncovered the coin.

At the corner of Tenth and N, he stopped and considered the quarter again. Down Tenth was Lincoln's death house. Up Tenth was the house where he had been a boy, and where the puppy was waiting for his father. A girl at the corner was messing with her bicycle, putting playing cards in the spokes, checking the tires. She watched Caesar as he flipped the quarter. He missed it and the coin fell to the ground, and he decided that that one would not count. The girl had once seen her aunt juggle six coins, first warming up with the flip of a single one and advancing to the juggling of three before finishing with six. It had been quite a show. The aunt had shown the six pieces to the girl—they had all been old and heavy one-dollar silver coins, huge monster things, which nobody made anymore. The girl thought she might now see a reprise of that event. Caesar flipped the quarter. The girl's heart paused. The man's heart paused. The coin reached its apex and then it fell.

Jackie Kay

You Go When You Can No Longer Stay

I T IS NOT so much that we are splitting up that is really worrying me, it is the fact that she keeps quoting Martin Amis. The other day we were in our bedroom having a silly argument about where things hang in the wardrobe when she said to me, "Like Martin Amis says, you go when you can no longer stay." It seemed odd to me. I looked outside the window into our street and saw Mr. Davies post a letter. I saw three-down's white cat walk daintily along our wall, and then jump off. I often say nothing at all when she says something that is perturbing. It seemed odd to me, because here we are two very long-term lesbians, who have been in it so long we look as if we could have knitted each other up, been in it so long we have grown to look the same, wear similar clothes and have almost identical expressions on our plain faces, that Martin Amis should be coming into our lives in this way.

I hadn't even realized she was so keen on him until she made that remark; the one thing we don't share is books. It is the only area of our lives where we are both truly different. I read thrillers and human interest books, about somebody who has done something that I am not likely to do, or somebody who is interested in something that I know nothing about. She reads novels and then she rereads the novels she has read. And sometimes she reads slim volumes of poetry which always look a little sinister and have very peculiar titles. We are not the kind of couple that share a book, one after the other, which is maybe a shame, and maybe if we had been that kind of couple we wouldn't be splitting up now. It seems to me from the amount that she has started quoting Martin Amis that she's had a secret passion for him all along.

We were in the kitchen the other day arguing again about sex. It is a sore point between us. A kind of Achilles' heel. "All marriage turns into a sibling relationship," she said terrifically confidently.

"Who said that?" I asked with a sickening, sinking heart. She paused, stirring her coffee.

"Do you want a coffee?" she said.

"No thank you," I said. "Don't tell me it was Martin Amis."

"Yes," she said defensively. "He's quite right. You just don't fancy each other after a while."

"I fancy you," I said, then instantly regretted it.

"No you don't, you think you do," she said, adding a big splash of milk into the coffee mug. "Sure you don't want a cup?" she said.

"All right then," I said. And she quite gleefully got another mug out of the kitchen cupboard. I think I bought the mug but I can't be sure. She smiled at me. When she smiles at me, I remember who she is.

Then she said, "You become far too similar, especially two women. It's like looking in the mirror. You need a bit of difference to feel real passion."

"Oh," I said, and sipped at my coffee anxiously.

"Life is too short not to feel passion," she said. I knew where it was all going, but I didn't want her to tell me. I wanted to hide. I wanted to run up the stairs and hide in the airing cupboard. I couldn't stop thinking about my eighty-two-year-old mother who was even fonder of Hilary than she was of me, who had taken years to accept our relationship and then had finally totally embraced it. My old mother would be devastated. I felt edgy just thinking about it.

"Do you want a Jaffa with your coffee?" she asked me, as if a Jaffa could be the answer to all my troubles, as if a Jaffa could truly console.

"Yes please," I said. I'd got into the habit of saying yes to as many things as possible, thinking that if I said yes enough she might stop saying no. She put three Jaffas on my plate but I noticed she took none for herself.

"Aren't you having any?" I asked her, a bit alarmed.

"No," she said.

"Why not?" I said.

"Oh for goodness' sake, Ruth, stop trying to control me. After a while all relationships turn into power struggles," she said. "Would you ask that same question of a friend?"

"I'm just wondering why you put three on a plate for me if you're not having any yourself," I said suspiciously. I was becoming very suspicious of her because she had started to change all of her habits and it was very worrying to me.

"Do you know something?" she said, very nastily. "I think you are going mad."

"Does Martin Amis say that?" I said furiously. "Does he say one person in a couple during a breakup will always accuse the other of going mad?"

She sighed and shook her head. She was actually looking quite beautiful these days. The person I didn't want to hear about was clearly making her feel good about herself. "I'm just trying to have a cup of coffee with you, that's all. If I can't have a cup of coffee with you without fighting, we will have to put the house on the market even sooner than we said. As Martin Amis says, you go when you can no longer stay," she said, standing up in the kitchen and drinking her coffee. She wouldn't sit down these days. There it was again, that bloody awful quote. It was deliberate then. She knew it was agitating me; she'd started to repeat it at random in whatever corner of our house we found ourselves in. I could even hear it in my sleep.

She left the room, coffee in hand, and I heard her playing music up the stairs. She'd taken to playing music a lot recently, another big change for her. This was a thin voice I didn't much like, one of those new English jazz singers with a very insipid style. I preferred the Dinah Washingtons of this world. I got up from the table and put two of the Jaffa Cakes in the bin. I gave the third to our dog. I saw what she was up to. She was trying to fatten me up as she lost weight. Well, we were both a little on the generous side. I was about three stone overweight and Hilary was at least two. Whenever we went out to a big lesbian do, I noticed that we weren't the only long-term couple that was overweight. I used to think that was happiness, being fat together, rolling about from one side of the big double bed to the other. Most of our old relationship revolved around food. Our idea of a super day used to be a day when we were both off work. (Now I notice her days off don't coincide with mine anymore.) Hilary didn't have to go into the Council which was depressing her and I didn't have to go into the Tax Office which was depressing me. We'd get into our big bed with lots of treats—a couple of Chow Mein Pot Noodles, a big plate of chocolate biscuits, a big tub of cookies and cream Häagen-Dazs. Bliss. And we'd watch *The Maltese Falcon* for the umpteenth time or *Now Voyager* or *All About Eve*. Heaven. A day like that was even nicer if it was raining outside. At the end of *Now Voyager*, we'd both say that line together, "Oh Jerry, don't let's ask for the moon. We have the stars," and clutch at each other as if we were frightened of losing everything.

A lot of the people who know us often get us mixed up as though we were identical twins. Some people call me Hilary and Hilary Ruth. It's a bit silly because we don't really look all that alike. Admittedly we do both buy similar-looking clothes in Marks & Spencer. Our casual clothes days and smart clothes days are always the same. But recently Hilary has started to shop in Harvey Nichols. I went in there one day on my own and took a look at some of the prices. They actually made me feel quite ill and I felt terribly worried. That night I said to Hilary, "I don't think shopping at Harvey Nichols on your salary is very sensible."

She was reading the new Martin Amis at the time, *Yellow Dog*. "This is about a man who suddenly becomes very violent," she said quite menacingly.

I said, "I feel as if I'm living with a gambler. You have run up massive bills on our joint Visa."

"I told you we should never have had a joint account," Hilary said, and got up and opened a bottle of red wine, which was another curious thing, because we only usually have a nice bottle of white, a Chardonnay, at the weekend. Now Hilary has taken to red wines, big heavy reds like Cabernet Sauvignons and Riojas, and she's taken to drinking them during the week. She slurped her wine. I suddenly noticed that she'd lost quite a bit of weight.

"Anyway, I think you should be a bit more careful," I said, trying to sound calm.

"I think you should stop being a control freak," she said. Then she got up and left the room again, taking her glass and the bottle with her. I heard the music go on up the stairs. She was playing it really quite loud. This time it was Otis Redding. We haven't played Otis Redding for years.

She came running back down the stairs. I thought she was going to apologize, but she just picked up *Yellow Dog* without a word and went back upstairs. I could hear Otis singing "Sitting on the Dock of the Bay."

I was annoyed at myself. I started clearing away the remains of our meal. I noticed that Hilary had left all of her rice. She'd eaten her salad though. I didn't know quite what to do with myself because we usually watched *Frost* on the TV together or *Miss Marple* or *Midsomer Murders*. But lately Hilary had said, "That isn't me, watching *Frost*. That's you." She'd started saying this a lot recently. "I'm not the kind of person who does such and such or who says such and such or who watches such and such." I wondered furiously if Martin Amis had put her up to that too. Perhaps there was something in one of his books that advised people in long-term relationships to stop doing everything that they used to enjoy doing. Perhaps he, being so resolutely heterosexual, so smug with his roll-ups, was trying to destroy the lesbian relationship. I suddenly had a brain-wave. If she was reading him, the only thing I could do to read her was read him too. I rushed into Waterstone's in town and bought everything they had by him. I hid the books under the spare room bed, the spare room which I have now been consigned to. Hilary needs space to think about what we should do, she has said. She needs space and calm. For my part I have stopped reading my murder mysteries for the moment. Hilary always looked down upon them. Of course she thinks she is much cleverer than me. "It's always the woman that gets it," she'd say whenever I picked up another thriller.

I've started to feel very odd within my own life. It's most peculiar to feel lonely inside your own life. It's a secret, of course, because nobody would know and all of our friends still think everything is fine between us, though I must say they have all taken to admiring Hilary recently and saying things like, "You're looking great." This morning we had breakfast together which was a nice change. Sunday breakfast. Hilary had bacon and egg but no toast and no newspapers. She has even given up the Sunday papers; I'm not sure why. When I asked her about it, she said, "Do I have to explain everything to you?" Then when she saw my slightly hurt face, she said, "I'm engrossed in *Yellow Dog* and newspapers are a huge waste of time."

I suggested we go out for a Sunday walk or a run in the car in the afternoon. Hilary said yes, good idea. I felt very pleased about this because it seemed to me that if we could go out for a walk in some beautiful country-side normal life might return, encouraged by the light on the hills or a gushing waterfall. "Shall we go to Coniston Water or Derwent Water and then go for Sunday lunch in a pub somewhere?" I said excitedly.

"No, I don't want to make a big production out of it," Hilary said. "Let's just go to the park with Orlando. I've got other things I want to do today." The dog was wagging her tail as Hilary fetched the lead, wagging her tail frantically.

It was a freezing cold day. I had my scarf tied firmly around my neck. Hilary looked a bit bare but I daren't suggest she put a scarf on. I rather like the winter cold if I am well wrapped up. We were walking side by side, with our golden retriever Orlando running on happily in front of us, when Hilary suddenly said to me, "I thought it best that we talk about this outside of the house rather than in. You know I have not been happy for some time."

"I didn't know that," I said, hurt.

"Oh come on. You did, darling," Hilary said, quite gently. I shook my head and put my hands in my pockets. Our dog ran back towards us. I picked up her stick and threw it again really quite far. It was truly an astonishingly beautiful winter day; even the clouds were lit up from behind as if they had highlights in their hair. "Isn't it lovely light today?" I said. "Isn't it absolutely gorgeous?"

"Why won't you let me talk about this?" Hilary said.

"Don't spoil our walk, darling," I said, picking up the stick again and throwing it. It was the coldest it has been yet. Freezing bitter cold, but still very beautiful, beautiful in an icy, frosty way. The ducks and the geese were sitting on top of the ice on the pond as if they were on holiday. Hilary sighed beside me. I could tell she was about to try again.

"I know that you are finding this hard, that's only natural. I know that we thought we'd be together forever. But stuff happens; life changes. We have to move on."

I walked beside her. At least she hadn't quoted again from Martin Amis, nor had she told me her name. I presumed it was a she anyway. I didn't want to know her name; I didn't want to know what she looked like; I didn't want to know anything about her. "Could you at least do me one favor?" I asked Hilary. "Could you tell me nothing about her, nothing at all?"

"That's silly," Hilary said. "I'm not buying into that. I've done nothing to be ashamed of."

"You've stopped loving me," I said, quietly.

"We weren't good for each other anymore," she said. I looked at her and suddenly noticed that she'd lost at least three stone. "How have you lost all this weight?" I asked her. "I don't want to tell you," she said. "I don't want you copying that too. You copy everything. If you hadn't copied everything, we might still have been lovers."

"What do I copy?" I said, feeling extremely alarmed.

"Nothing," she said. "Never mind." We walked round the pond in silence. I noted a few things, I think, about the geese but I can't remember what they were.

I noticed that Hilary was sweating quite profusely even though the temperature was subzero. I sneaked a look at her. She had that mad look on her face, eyebrows knitted together, quite unappealing if I am honest. It occurred to me that she might be having her menopause and that all of these changes of behavior were actually the change of life. She had after all been behaving very erratically recently, flying off the handle at the slightest thing. "Are you having a hot flush?" I asked her.

"No I certainly am not!" she said.

But it was out and now I knew. Hilary was having her menopause and keeping it secret from me. That explained everything: it explained why she no longer wanted to share the double bed. The sheets were probably soaking in the middle of the night! It explained the temper tantrums and the outbursts. "Why didn't you just tell me? For goodness' sake, we are both lesbians," I said.

"You might describe yourself like that. You know I don't," she said.

"Well, whatever, why didn't you tell me you were having hot flushes?" Hilary is three years younger than I am and I could tell she was fuming, absolutely fuming about getting her change of life first.

"It can happen at any age," I said. "I've just been lucky I haven't had mine yet. I was a late starter with my periods. When you start late, you apparently have your menopause later. Did you start yours early?"

"Don't do this," Hilary said, beside herself now. "I am not having my menopause. I don't know how many times I have to say this," she said, tired. "This is typical of you. You are in denial. I am in love. This is a love story of all the strange things happening to me so late in the goddamned day."

She wasn't going to get me this time with that Martin Amis. I said, "When I come in the door I go tee hee hee. The place kills me."

She said, "Have you been reading him?"

"Yes," I said, quite pleased.

"See, I told you you always had to copy me," she said, apoplectic with rage now. "And now you've gone out and got him. Nothing's sacred."

I smiled. I shouted *Or-lan-do,* my voice going up and down merrily. "Who is going to have the dog?" I said.

"I am," Hilary said. "I'm much fonder of Orlando than you are. Orlando is my dog."

"She is not," I said indignantly.

"I don't think I want to do this," Hilary said.

"Do what?" I said, still like a fool feeling a little hopeful.

"Have these silly fights. We are two grown-ups. We have to be able to sort this out amicably. It's not like we have kids."

"Having a dog is like having a kid," I said.

"It is not. Don't be stupid."

We walked in silence then round the pond for the third time. I couldn't count the amount of times we have walked round and round and round that pond. I thought of all the walks over our twenty-five years together. Our walking books are the only books we truly share, tiny leaflet-sized books that tell us of lengths and grades of difficulty in Strathglass and surrounding glens. I thought of our favorite walk from just below Beinn Mhor, and the lovely waterfall in the woods up the hill from the old sheep fanks. And the odd little cemetery you come across as you reach the end of the walk. Rumor has it that once a burial party arrived there from Tomich village minus the coffin. I thought of all the walks over all the years—off the beaten track and out of breath. Parts of the country, we used to believe, truly belonged to us: the Lakes, the Highlands, the Peak District. I couldn't bear to think of Hilary anywhere, in any of these places with some other love, her dark fleece zipped up, her walking boots thick with mud, and a map in her hand. I looked at Hilary. I couldn't imagine her even wearing a fleece in the future. She looked so slim now; she looked like somebody else, oddly focused and deliberate-looking, as if the resolve to do this had made her quite certain of herself. I couldn't quite believe it. Hilary had slimmed her way out of my hands. If only I'd followed her example I could have squeezed myself through to where she had gone. When we got inside our cream kitchen, I thought she might have a cup of tea and a scone and jam for old times' sake. "Scones are a thing of the past," Hilary said and I had the impression that she wasn't quoting from Martin Amis this time.

It seemed to me that Hilary wanted to consign our whole life to the past. The other day I arrived home, very excited, with a classic copy of the *Dandy*—December 30, 1972. Hilary and I have collected comics for over ten years and have spent many a happy hour laughing over the antics of Dennis the Menace or Desperate Dan or Beryl the Peril. I said triumphantly, "Look what I've just found!" thinking that Hilary would remember our love through Beryl the Peril's impersonation of an Abominable Snowman. But Hilary just stared at it a little disdainfully and said, "You can have the comic collection, that was always more your thing. I'll have the CDs."

I put the kettle on and got out a fresh jar of rhubarb-and-ginger jam. I pulled the little bit of tracing paper off the top. I opened our cake tin and took out one of yesterday's homemade scones, a nice batch that had risen properly. I buttered my scone quite thickly and spread the nippy jam over it. I made a fresh pot of tea and put the cozy on. I sat down alone at the table. I poured us both a mug of tea. Hilary watched me eat my scone with some satisfaction, sipping at her mug of tea, standing, leaning against the fridge. She said nothing. She eyed me eating my scone. I wasn't the least bit bothered. I thought ahead to nighttime in the spare room. I said to myself secretly another Martin Amis line: "Jesus Christ if I could make it into bed and get my eyes shut without seeing a mirror." She smiled at me and I smiled back at her and both of our faces looked the same. We both had his tight, cool grin.

Lydia Peelle

Mule Killers

M Y FATHER was eighteen when the mule killers finally made it to his father's farm. He tells me that all across the state that year, big trucks loaded up with mules rumbled steadily to the slaughterhouses. They drove over the roads that mules themselves had cut, the gravel and macadam that mules themselves had laid. Once or twice a day, he says, you would hear a high-pitched bray come from one of the trucks, a rattling as it went by, then silence, and you would look up from your work for a moment to listen to that silence. The mules when they were trucked away were sleek and fat on oats, work-shod and in their prime. *The best color is fat,* my grandfather used to say, when asked. But that year, my father tells me, that one heartbreaking year, the best color was dead. Pride and Jake and Willy Boy, Champ and Pete were dead, Kate and Sue and Orphan Lad; Orphan Lad was dead.

In the spring of that year, in the afternoon of one rain-brightened day, my father's father goes to Nashville and buys two International Harvester tractors for eighteen hundred dollars, cash. "We've got no choice nowadays," he tells the IHC man, counting out the bills and shaking his head. He has made every excuse not to buy what everyone has come to call a mule killer, but finally the farm's financial situation has made the decision for him. Big trucks deliver the tractors and unload them in the muddy yard in front of the barn, where for a day they hunch and sulk like children. My grandfather's tobacco fields stretch out behind them, shimmering in the spring heat. Beyond the slope of green, the Cumberland River is just visible through a fringe of trees, swollen and dark with rain.

The next morning after chores my grandfather calls in the hands to explain the basics of the new machines, just the way the man in Nashville has done for him. He stands next to one of the tractors for a long time, talking about the mechanics of it, one hand resting on its flank. Then with all the confidence he can muster he climbs up to start it. He tries three times before the tractor shivers violently, bucks forward, and busts the top rail of a fence. "This one ain't entirely broke yet," my grandfather jokes, struggling to back it up.

"Reckon you'll break it before it breaks you?" someone calls out, and only half of the men laugh. Most of them are used to sleeping all down the length of a tobacco row until the mules stop, waking just long enough to swing the team and start on back up the next. They all know when it's lunchtime because the mules bray, in unison, every day at five to twelve.

My father stands with the men who are laughing, laughing with them and scuffing up dust with his boot, though he is nervous about these tractors. His light eyes are squinted in the sun, and he slouches—he has his father's height, and he carries it apologetically. He is trying hard to keep certain things stuffed deep inside his chest: things like fear, sadness, and uncertainty. He expects to outgrow all of these things very soon, and in the meantime, he works hard to keep them hidden. Lately, he has become secretive about the things he loves. His love is fierce and full, but edged in guilt. He loves Orphan Lad: Orphan's sharp shoulders and soft ears, the mealy tuck of his lower lip. Music. Books and the smell of books, sun-warm stones, and Eula Parker, who has hair thick and dark as soil. He has loved her since he was ten and once sat next to her at church; during the sermon she pinched him so hard his arm was red until Tuesday, and he had secretly kissed that red butterfly bruise. But Orphan will soon be gone, and none of the hands read books, and he laughs at the tractors just as he would laugh if one of these men made a rude comment about Eula Parker; because the most important thing, he believes, is not to let on that he loves anything at all.

Late that night, some of the hands sit on the porch to dip snuff and drink bitter cups of coffee. My father sits with them, silent on the steps. When he is with people he often finds pockets in the noise that he can crawl into and fill with his own thoughts, soft familiar thoughts with worn rounded corners. At this particular moment he is turning an old thought of Eula Parker over and over in his mind: he is going to marry her. If he goes so far as to conjure dark-haired children for them, I don't know, but he does build a house where they sit together on a porch, a vast and fertile farm on the other side of the river, and on this night, a shed full of bright chrome tractors, twice as big as the ones that rest still warm and ticking in his father's mule barn. He plants a flower garden for her at the foot of the porch, he buys a big Victrola for the dining room and a smaller, portable one for picnics. Guiltily he touches just the edges of one of these picnics: Eula's hair loose and wild, a warm blanket by a creek, cold chicken and hard boiled eggs, drowsiness, possibility.

In a moment his pocket of quiet is turned inside out: the hands roar with laughter at the punch line of a joke and the screen door clatters as my grandfather comes out to the porch. "You all ever gonna sleep?" he asks them and smiles. He is an old man, nearing sixty, and the thin length of his body has rounded to a stoop, like a sapling loaded with snow. But his eyes are still the eyes of a young man, even after years and years in the sun, and they are bright as he smiles and jokes. My father stands up and leans against a post, crossing his arms. His father winks at him, then waves his hand at the men and steps back into the house, shaking his head and chuckling.

My grandfather understood mule power. He celebrated it. He reveled in it. He always said that what makes a mule a better worker than the horse or the donkey is that he inherited the best from both of them: strong hindquarters from his dam and strong shoulders from his sire. He said *the gospel according to mule is push and pull.* When his wife died young of a fever, it was not a horse but Orphan Lad who pulled her coffin slowly to the burying grounds, a thing the prouder men of the county later felt moved to comment on in the back room of the feed store. My grandfather was a man who never wore a hat, even to town. *Uncover thy head before the Lord,* he said, and the Lord he believed to be everywhere: in the trees, the chimneys of houses, the water of the creek, under Calumet cans rusting in the dirt.

. . .

Eula Parker is a slippery and mysterious girl, and my father's poor heart is constantly bewildered by her fickle ways. Like the day he walked her home from church and she allowed him to hold her cool hand, but would not let him see her all the way to the front door. Or the times when she catches him looking at her, and drops her eyes and laughs—at what, he cannot guess. With a kit he burns her name into a scrap of pine board and works up the courage to leave it at the door of her parents' house in town: when he walks by the next day and it is still there, he steals it back and takes it home to hide it shamefully beneath his bed. At church she always sits with the same girl, fifth pew back on the left, and he positions himself where he can see her: her hair swept up off her neck, thick purple-black and shining, the other girl's hanging limply down, onion paper pale. Afterward, when people gather in the yard, the other girl always smiles at him, but he never notices: he is watching to see if Eula smiles, because sometimes she does and sometimes she doesn't. His love fattens on this until it is round and full, bursting from every seam.

At night, when he is sure his father is sleeping, he sticks the phonograph needle in a rubber eraser and holds the eraser in his front teeth. Carefully, with his nose inches from the record, he sets the needle down. With a hiss and crackle, the music reverberates through the hollows of his mouth and throat without making a sound in the room. Ignoring the cramp in his neck, this is how he listens to his favorite records night after night. Wild with thoughts of Eula with her hair like oil. Her snakecharming eyes. Her long fine hands. How she teases him. He dreams he finds pieces of his heart in the boot scraper at her door.

On a warm and steamy afternoon my father makes a trip to town to buy new needles for the Victrola. He walks along the side of the road and passing cars do not give him any room. Several times he has to jump into the tick-heavy weeds that grow at the road's edge. At the river a truck heavy with mules from a farm to the north passes him and bottoms out on the bridge: he keeps his head to the side until it is out of sight. Soon the truck will come for the last of his father's herd. *Oh, Orphan.* On the coldest mornings of his boyhood, his father had let him ride Orphan to school, bareback with two leads clipped to the halter. When they got to the schoolhouse he'd jump down and slap the mule's wide wonderful haunch, and the big animal would turn without hesitation and walk directly home to be harnessed and hitched for the day's work.

When my father gets to town it is still and hot. The street is empty, buildings quiet, second-story shutters closed like eyes. He buys a tin of needles at the furniture store and lingers to look at the portable record players, nestled neat and tidy in their black cases. When finally he steps out of the store, head bowed in thought, he nearly runs into two girls who stand bent close in serious conversation.

When they look up and see that it is him, they both politely say hello. Eula looks up at the store awning behind him. The other girl, the girl with the onion pale hair, she looks down at the toe of her boot. He hears himself ask, "Want to go for a soda?" His voice is like a round stone that drops right there on the sidewalk. Eula's face closes like a door. But the other girl. The other girl, she guesses so.

He takes her to the only drugstore in town and they sit at the counter and order two sodas. She doesn't speak. They watch the clerk stocking packages on the high shelves along the wall, sliding his wooden ladder along the track in the ceiling with a satisfying, heavy sound. She seals her straw with her finger and swizzles it around the glass. She crosses her right ankle over her left, then her left ankle over her right, then hooks her heels onto the bottom of the stool. My father compliments her on her dress. The clerk drops a bag of flour and curses, then apologizes to the girl. There are hollow fly carcasses wedged into the dusty seam of the counter and the warped wood floor. Even with two ceiling fans running, the air is hot and close.

This must have been the middle of August: though my father doesn't tell me this, it is easy enough to count backwards and figure for myself. The walls of the store are painted a deep green and the paint has bubbled in some places. My father's mind fails him as he searches for something to say. He watches her twist a strand of hair around her finger, but she feels his eyes on her and abruptly stops, folding her hands in her lap.

"So, you and Eula, y'all sit together at church," he says, forgetting to make it a question.

Puzzled, the girl nods her head. She has not yet said a word. Perhaps she is having trouble believing that she is sitting here at this counter, having a soda with a boy. Or she is worrying that her hair is too pale and limp, or her wrists too big, or her dress too common. She has never believed she would find herself in this situation, and so has never rehearsed.

"I've always thought this time of year is the saddest," she finally says, looking up at my father. He lays his hand on the counter and spreads out his fingers. His chin tilts forward as if he is about to speak. Then the sleigh bells on the door jingle, shiver when it slams shut. It is Eula. She doesn't look at them. She brushes her sweat-damp hair back with two fingers and asks the clerk for something—what?—my father's ears are suddenly filled—she is asking the clerk for a tin of aspirin, peering up at the shelves behind him and blinking her snakecharming eyes. The clerk stares too long before turning to his ladder. My father considers socking him one in that plug ugly face. Eula raps her fingers along the edge of the counter and hums tunelessly and still she won't look their way.

At this moment, my father feels his heart dissolve into a sticky bright liquid. Jealousy has seized her, she has followed them here—he is certain. Finally, a staggering proclamation of her love. His heart has begun to trickle down into the soles of his feet when the girl somehow catches Eula's eye and ripples her fingers at her.

Hello.

Then Eula unfolds her long body towards them, and smiles. An enormous, beautiful, open-faced smile: a smile with no jealousy hidden behind it at all. She takes her change and paper sack from the clerk and turns, one hand stretched out towards the door. She is simply going to leave. She is going to walk out the door and leave them here to their sodas and silence. At this point my father, frantic, takes hold of the girl on the stool next to him, leans her in Eula's direction, and kisses her recklessly, right on the mouth.

My father tells me this story in the garden, bent over and searching through the knee-high weeds for long thick stalks of asparagus, clipping them with his pocketknife and handing them to me. Here he stops and straightens and squints east, and I know his back is starting to bother him. Why he never told me the story when I was a boy, I don't know: I am twice as old now as he was, the year of the mule killers. But still he skips the part of the story where I come in.

It doesn't matter; I can imagine it. Before the door has even closed after Eula, something has changed in my father, and as he slides from his stool he firmly takes the girl's hand. He leads her out of the drugstore, glancing back once more at the pock-faced clerk, who is carefully smoothing Eula's bill into the cash register drawer. Slowly they make their way somewhere: back to the farm, most likely, where his father is sitting with the hands at supper. He takes her to the hayloft, a back field, the mule barn, the spring-house: any place that was dark and quiet for long enough that my father could desperately try to summon Eula's face, or else hope to forever blot it from his mind. Long enough that I, like a flashbulb, could snap into existence.

Mercy, mercy, mercy, my grandfather said, that day they finally took Orphan. *He'll be all right.* He pinched the bridge of his nose and looked away when they tried to load him onto the truck. The mule's big ears swung forward, his narrow withers locked, and he would not budge when he got to the loading ramp. It took four men to finally get him up, and they saw his white eye swiveling madly when they looked in through the slats. *Not stubborn, just smart,* my grandfather said to the ground, then again pinched his nose and leaned against the truck as two more mules were loaded up. His herd was so big that this was the last of three trips. He had intended to send Orphan with the first load, but had put it off and put it off.

Ain't it some kind of thanks, my grandfather said as he latched up the back of the truck, the mules inside jostling to get their footing, and Orphan's long ear had swiveled back at the sound of his voice. The best of them brought three or four cents a pound as dog meat; some of them would merely be heaved six deep into a trench that would be filled over with dirt by men on tractors. The hollow report of hooves on the truck bed echoed even after the truck had pulled onto the road and turned out of sight. The exact same sound could be heard all through the county, all across the hills of Tennessee and up through Kentucky, across Missouri and Kansas and all the way out west, even, you could hear it. The mules' job, it was finished.

When the back of the truck is finally shut, my father is high above, hiding in the hayloft. At church the pale haired girl had pulled him into the center aisle just before the service and told him her news, the news of me. All through the sermon his mind had flipped like a fish, and he had stared hard at the back of Eula's neck, trying to still that fish. In the hayloft he thinks of this moment as he listens to the shouts of the truck driver and the engine backfiring once before the mules are pulled away, but he doesn't come to the edge, he doesn't look down for one last glimpse of Orphan Lad.

Late that night my father creeps to the Victrola in the living room and carefully opens the top of the cabinet. He slides a record onto the turntable and turns the crank, then sets his eraser and needle between his teeth and presses it to the first groove. A fiddle plays, is joined by a guitar, and then a high lonesome voice starts in about heartbreak. Every time he listens to his records like this, the first notes take him by surprise. When the music starts to fill his head, he can't believe it is coming from the record on the turntable and not from a place within himself. He closes his eyes and imagines Eula Parker is in the room, dancing behind him in a dark red dress. He moves his face across the record, following the groove with the needle, and spit collects in the pockets of his cheeks. *Eula, Eula, Eula.* He lets her name roll around in his head until it is unclear, too, whether this sound is coming from the record on the turntable, or from the deepest hollows of his heart.

Three weeks after the last load of mules is taken, one of the tractors overturns on a hill down by the river and nearly kills one of the hands. It is not an unexpected tragedy. My grandfather is the only one with the man, and he pulls him out from underneath the seat and searches through the grass for three scattered fingers while the machine's engine continues to choke and whir. He drives the man to the hospital in Nashville and doesn't return until late that night. His trip home is held up by a wreck at the bridge that takes nearly an hour to be cleared away. When he finally arrives back, his son is waiting up on the porch to tell him about the pale haired girl.

My father has rehearsed what he will say dozens of times to the fence posts and icebox, but when he sees his father's brown blood-caked forearms and hands, he is startled enough to forget what it was. Weary and white in the face, my grandfather sits down next to him on the top step and touches his shoulder.

"Son," he says, "you're gonna see a future I can't even stretch my mind around. Not any of it. I can't even begin to imagine."

If my father had understood what his father was trying to tell him, maybe he would have waited until the morning to say what he now says. Maybe he would never have said anything, packed up a small bag and a portable Victrola and left town for good. Abandoned love and any expectation of it. Instead he confesses to my grandfather, all in a rush, the same way he might have admitted that he had broken the new mower, or left the front gate open all night.

My grandfather stares hard at my father's knee and is quiet a long time.

"This is wrong," he says. Repeats it. "You got no choice but to take care of it. This is wrong."

In those days this was my grandfather's interpretation of the world, a thing was either right or it was wrong. Or so it seemed to my father, and he was getting tired of it.

"No, sir," he says, lips tight. "That's not what I intend. I'm in love with someone else." He takes a breath. "I'm gonna marry Eula Parker." Even as he speaks her name he is startled by this statement, like it is a giant carp he has yanked from the depths of the river. It lies on the step before both of them, gasping in the open air.

My grandfather looks at him with sadness rimming his eyes and says quietly, "You should've thought of that before."

"But you see," my father says, as if explaining to a child, "I love her."

My grandfather grips his knees with his big hands and sighs. He reaches out for his son's arm, but my father brushes him away, stands up, and walks heavily across the porch. When he goes into the house, he lets the screen door slam behind him, and it bangs twice in the casement before clicking shut.

Late that night, after washing the dishes of a silent dinner, my father sits on the porch sharpening his pocketknife. He taps his bare feet against the hollow stairs and even whistles through his teeth. His father's words have still not completely closed in around him. Though an uneasiness is slowly creeping up, he is still certain that the future is bright chrome and glorious, full of possibility. Behind him, the strings of the banjo gently twang as they go flat in the cooling air. It is the first night of the year that smells of autumn and my father takes a few deep breaths as he leans against the porch railing and looks out into the yard. This is when he sees something out under the old elm, a long twisted shape leaning unsteadily against the thick trunk of the tree.

He steps off the porch onto the cool grass of the yard, thinking first he sees a ghost. As he gets closer to the shape, he believes it next to be a fallen limb, or one of the hands, drunk on moonshine, then, nothing but a forgotten ladder, then—with rising heart—Eula come to call for him in her darkest dress. But when he is just a few yards away from the tree, he sees it is just his father, leaning with his back to the house, arms at his sides. He is speaking quietly, and my father knows by the quality of his voice that he is praying. He has found him like this before, in the hayfield at dusk or by the creek in the morning, eyes closed, mumbling simple private incantations. My father is about to step quietly back to the porch when his father reaches a trembling hand to the tree to steady himself, then lets his shoulders collapse. He blows his nose in his hand and my father hears him swallow back thick jumbled sobs. When he hears this, when he realizes his father is crying, he turns and rushes blindly back to the house, waves of heat rising from beneath his ribs like startled birds from a tree.

Once behind the closed door of his room, my father makes himself small as possible on the edge of his unmade bed. Staring hard at the baseboard, he tries to slow his tumbling heart. He has never, ever seen his father cry, not even when his mother died. Now, having witnessed it, he feels like he has pulled the rug of manhood out from under the old man's feet. He convinces himself that it must be the lost mules his father was praying for, or the mangled man who lies unconscious in the hospital bed in Nashville, and that this is what drove him to tears. It is only much later, picking asparagus in the ghost of a garden, that he will admit who his father had really been crying for: for his son, and for his son.

These days, my father remembers little from the time before the tractors. The growl of their engines in his mind has long since drowned out the quieter noises: the constant stamping and shifting of mule weight in the barn, the smooth sound of oats being poured into a steel bucket. He remembers the steam that rose from the animals after work. Pooled heaps of soft leather harness waiting to be mended on the breakfast table. At the threshold of the barn door, a velvet-eared dog that was always snapping its teeth at flies. Orphan standing dark and noble in the snow, a sled hooked to his harness. Eula Parker in a dark blue hat laughing and saying his name, hurrying after him and calling out *Wait, Wait,* one warm Sunday as he left church for home.

He remembers too his mother's cooking spices lined up in the cupboard where they had been since her death, faded inside their tins without scent or taste. When he knew he was alone in the house, it gave him some comfortable sadness to take them out one by one and open them, the contents of each as dusty and gray as the next. He has just one memory of her, just an image: the curve of her spine and the fall of her hair when she had once leaned over to sniff the sheets on his bed, the morning after he'd wet it. This is all he has of her: one moment, just one, tangled in those little threads of shame.

In the same way I only have one memory of my grandfather, one watery picture from when I was very young. When my mother and father would rock me on the porch at night, my grandfather sat with them in a straight backed chair, playing the banjo. He would tie a little tissue paper doll to his right wrist, and it danced and jumped like a tiny white ghost. I remember sitting on my mother's lap one night, and in the darkness the only things I could see were the tissue doll, the white moon of the banjo face, my mother's pale hair. I remember watching that doll bobbing along with my grandfather's strumming, and from time to time, the white flash of his teeth when he smiled. And I can hear him sing just a piece of one of the old songs: *I know'd it, indeed I know'd it, yes, I know'd it, my bones are gonna rise again.*

This is the story that my father tells me as he bends like a wire wicket in the garden, or, I should say, what once was my mother's garden. He parts the tangle of weeds to find the asparagus, then snaps off the tough spears with his knife, straightening slowly from time to time to stretch his stiff and rounded back. The garden is like a straight-edged wilderness in the middle of the closely mowed lawn, a blasted plot of weeds and thorns and thistle. Nothing has grown here since my mother died and there was no one who wanted to tend it. Nothing except the asparagus, which comes up year after year.

Paula Fox

The Broad Estates of Death

A T NOON they began their descent from the Organ Mountains to the valley below. The road swung from side to side, now hidden by an escarp, then flung into sight as it followed the declining slope. After a sharp turn, Harry Tilson drove the car onto a fenced shoulder and turned off the ignition. Amelia, his wife, yawned and stretched. Harry removed his jacket and folded it across the backseat. Above and behind them, the mountains baked in the midday sun.

"What's in the valley?" she asked.

"Nothing."

She picked up the map lying on the seat between them.

"When will we be there?" she asked.

"An hour or less," he answered.

"Are you scared yet? To see him?"

"I don't know. I don't think so."

He hadn't seen his father, Ben, in twenty-three years. Amelia dropped the map. "How can anyone fold these things?" she asked. The United States lay across her knees covered with the penciled record of their journey from New York City to New Mexico.

"What a long way," she murmured.

Harry stared through the open window at the pale and heat-drained land below. The visit to his father, old and sick, probably dying, had been planned as a side trip during their vacation in Taos. All morning the mountains had obscured their destination.

Until Harry glimpsed the valley, he had not expected to feel much of anything. But now, along with mounting unease, the past began to own him. It was incomprehensible, all of it. Yet he had constructed from what he recalled of his early life a comic patter for himself and his listeners. It nearly convinced him he had a place to come from, early years, all that.

The stories he told were not so comic. He didn't know why he told them. Perhaps there was something satisfying in the responses he evoked when, in the guise of regional lore, he spoke of nomadic wanderings in search of work, skeletal Fords containing all that he and his father owned, whippings administered with baling wire after his mother died giving birth to his brother, who died a few months later of some childhood disease. Sometimes in midsentence, as he remembered the traveling fairs that passed seasonally through the valley towns, recalling in the wake of their gaudy, vacuous gaiety his hope that life would be different when he was older and smarter, Harry would fall silent. But he discovered that silence had its uses too.

Now, as he gazed down at it, he was astonished to perceive the valley actually existed, and he was confronted with an almost shameful truth that he was unable to find words for. The smell of wild sage assaulted his nostrils. He closed his eyes briefly and found he was straining to catch the sound of something stirring in the silence of the mountains, just as he had when he was a child. All of it had happened. He turned on the ignition and gripped the wheel.

"Did you always live around here when you were little?" Amelia asked.

Harry put the car into second gear; the grade was steep. "Yes," he said, then, "What? I'm sorry . . ."

"I asked—"

"I know what you asked." A truck gained on them, passed, and left behind a sound of grinding gears.

"Yes, what?" she asked.

"About living here? Yes. I said yes before. When he—"

"Your father?"

"We stayed near the river. That's where the work was."

Amelia made another try at refolding the map. The ineffectual rustle of the paper irritated him.

"I had a gift for finding the cheapest cars," he said.

"When you were little?" she asked.

"I was ten. That's not little."

"Oh," she said. He sensed her disbelief. Why did she bother to question him? If he turned to look at her now he knew there would be a certain plaintive sweetness in her face.

"And then?" she asked.

"Then," he began, accelerating as the road gradually leveled off, "we packed the car and set off until we found work. He drank up the take. Saturdays, he'd end up in a saloon with a hustler and no money. I'd load them both into the car, drive them to wherever we were camped. Sometimes the lady made me breakfast—"

"—when you were ten?"

"When I was a few years older. They cried all over me," he said. His tone made her feel vaguely implicated, and she moved closer to the passenger door.

"It doesn't look as if you could get anything to grow around here," she observed somewhat stiffly.

Harry sighed and loosened his grip on the wheel. They had reached the valley floor. A few cattle stood here and there staring at the daylight, as they might have stared at darkness.

"You always think you can," Harry said. "This is a bad month. But when they irrigate—you could plant a telephone pole and it would take root."

She offered him a cigarette, and as he took it from her fingers he glanced at her and smiled briefly. Their marriage was recent, their experience of each other still fresh. Everything in the car was about them, of them—their maps and cigarettes, the suitcases in which their clothes were intermingled, a half-empty bottle of whiskey that rolled around the car floor.

He was recalling other cars, heaps of clanging, rusty parts, his father's clothes and his bundled into blankets.

She was looking at him. He was such a solitary being that she imagined him self-conceived—no parents, no past. For all his stories, she did not associate him with the complex accumulation of experience she sensed in other people.

. . . .

"Look! There's a house," she said, startled, expecting only horizon and sky.

"We're almost there," he said. "Mrs. Coyle wrote the place was north of Las Cruces."

"How can people live like that?" she asked, turning her head to keep the house in view for a minute longer. It looked to her like a lump of yellow earth that had been scooped up roughly from the ground. What seemed like a doorway gave on to darkness. An inner tube rested against the dirt wall, and near it a chicken stood in a pose of expectancy. There was no other sign of life.

"It's a sod shack," he said. "You'd be surprised what you can live like."

Amelia, with their destination only minutes away, asked him a question that had bothered her since letters from Mrs. Coyle, the district nurse, and a Doctor Treviot, had arrived, telling Harry of Ben Tilson's stroke. "Will your father be crippled?" Her voice held a tremor that belied her air of detachment.

"It'll be all right," Harry said. "It's not catching. Only his right arm was affected." He had casually put his arm around her shoulder as he spoke. But he felt a sudden pain in his gut and withdrew the arm abruptly.

"What's the matter?"

"It's just that I'm getting tired of driving," he replied. He wondered why he had bothered to try and reassure her. His father could have no meaning for her, and for him Ben Tilson was a monthly check and a tax deduction. Ben was a wreck, the doctor had written. No one knew what held him together.

He knew, he thought, watching the road without seeing it, instead seeing his father, asleep in an irrigation ditch after eighteen hours of work, spring up as the water reached his bare feet, a nightmare figure blackened with mud. It was a contemptible life for a man. What was the use of such endurance? He despised the memory—that vision of Ben, a furious scarecrow, drunk with fatigue, digging the irrigation ditch still deeper to receive the flow of water.

"There it is," Harry said. They had rounded a curve, and just beyond it, oasislike, was a clump of cottonwood trees and, nailed to the trunk of one of them, a sign that read COYLE. Harry parked a few feet from the house. The siding and window frames were nearly bare of paint; the window shades were drawn, and a sheet-iron roof reflected the sunlight with brutal intensity.

For a brief moment, the two of them sat unmoving. Amelia sensed in Harry a vast exercise of will as he reached across her and opened the door, then got out on his side. As she stepped to the ground, she saw a gray stoop and several scrawny chickens roosting on its steps. A dog the color of charred wood gazed at her blankly before resting its head back on its paws. Harry waved his hand at the stoop, and the chickens flew lumpishly into the scrub grass. The dog rose and wagged its skinny tail just as Mrs. Verbena Coyle opened the screen door. She regarded them silently until a smile widened her lips to reveal small discolored teeth. Not a hair escaped from the thick braids wound round her head. Her pale eyes were unblinking. The heavy contours of her face were smooth; mass upon mass, moon-like and placid.

"I knew it was you as soon as I heard the car," she said. "Ben's been waiting all morning—wouldn't eat his lunch. Think you might make him eat it?"

Harry went up the steps quickly, and Amelia followed. Mrs. Coyle continued. "I tell him he's got to eat meat if he's going to get better"—she paused to extend a hand to Harry. "'I'll be on my feet soon, Verbena,' he says."

Mrs. Coyle advanced a step and held out her other hand to Amelia. "Is he any better?" Harry asked.

"He's not," Mrs. Coyle answered firmly. "There comes a time in an illness where it don't matter if you have a good day." She looked up at the sky and smacked her lips. "He's a sick man, Mr. Tilson." She released both their hands and folded her own across her stomach. "When I found him laying out in the shack, holding on to his old flatiron—he'd dug a hole right in the dirt floor with it, you know—I thought he was gone for sure. But the doctor did a lot for him. He even gets around a bit, but he's weak. That real weakness," the last words said emphatically. She nodded to Amelia. "I'm a trained nurse, you know, the only one for miles around."

"Could we see him now?" Harry asked.

"That's what you come for, isn't it?" Mrs. Coyle said. "You go round the house and I'll meet you in the back. Ben's in a little shed my husband fixed up." She entered the house.

Harry backed down the two steps and stood irresolutely, frowning down at his shoes.

"Isn't she something!" Amelia spoke in a low voice.

"Did you leave the cigarettes in the car?"

"I've got them right here," she replied quickly, holding the pack out to him. But he turned from her and set off for the back of the house. Only natural, she said to herself, inevitable.

A few cottonwood trees stood between them and the dusty lonesome-looking two-lane road. The heat sang in the silence. The air had the texture of warmed glue.

Mrs. Coyle met them at the back door. She was accompanied by a little pale man who, as she walked, slipped in and out of sight behind her as though he were in league with her shadow.

"In there," she said and waved toward an oversize chicken coop. At her words the small man took a giant step and Mrs. Coyle looked at him with rapt amusement, then turned to them, smiling archly. "This is my husband, Gulliver Coyle," she said. Mr. Coyle grinned eerily at them and nodded. Amelia noticed how knobby his fingers were, and she recalled the dry flaked furrows they had driven past.

"Come on," Harry urged her, as though she'd held back. She felt the sting of resentment. How ridiculous he looked in his finely tailored jacket, his costly slacks, as he stood in front of the shed. The dog had slunk around the house to make a part of their group.

Mrs. Coyle, as though seized by impulse, strode up to the shed door and opened it. "They're here, Ben! Your boy's here with his wife," she cried as she stood aside to let Harry and Amelia precede her. Amelia stood back to wait for Mr. Coyle, but he shook his head no, moving his abused hands in clumsy amiability. Amelia stepped across the threshold. The room contained a bed, a rocking chair, and a tall dresser from which two middle drawers were missing. The rungs of the iron headrest were patched with white paint. An old man lay on the edge of the bed. He lifted his left hand in greeting as Amelia walked toward him. But he was looking past her, at Harry. His eyes were large, faded blue, and veined. The control apparent in the way he held his long-lipped mouth so stiffly gave way to the faintest of smiles. He barely parted his lips to speak.

"Well . . . it's been a long time," he said in a thin, grainy voice. Harry held out a hand, which the old man touched with his fingers. "I see your hair's thinning," Ben Tilson said. He looked at Amelia then. "I lost mine young, too. Seems to run in the family." There was a moment of silence, which ended when Mrs. Coyle said with arch severity, "Will you eat your lunch now, Ben? I'll bring it in." He didn't look at her or answer, and she left the shed.

Harry sat in the rocking chair. Amelia knew he was under a strain, but still, there was no other place to sit, and she stood awkwardly in the middle of the small room until Ben pointed down at his bed with a semblance of the authority of a man who knows how to deal with women. In the space he made for her by moving a few inches very slowly, she sat down on sheets thin and gray from years of washing.

"Don't worry," Ben said. "I can move if you crowd me." She looked from father to son; a resemblance echoed back and forth between them.

"Everything going good for you?" Ben asked.

"Fairly well," Harry answered. Couldn't he give his father the satisfaction of knowing how far he had traveled away from this awful place? Harry had a fundamental frugality, she thought, a reluctance to admit obligation to anyone or anything.

"Remember your aunt Thyra?" Ben asked.

"Sure . . . of course," Harry said.

"Well, she got into trouble up in Albuquerque," Ben went on. "She kept on borrowing money, signing papers she couldn't understand."

"What did she want money for?" asked Harry irritably. "I thought you wrote last year that Winslow was doing pretty well?"

"Women get queer around a certain age, I guess. She decided she'd missed out on the grander things, bought herself one of them hairless Mexican dogs, took up smoking, bought a truckload of clothes and fifteen silk ties for Winslow. Not to leave out expensive liquor."

Harry began to laugh. Broken, sibilant, it sounded like weeping. He bent over and covered his face with his hands. When he took them away a moment later, only a faint smile remained.

They all heard Mrs. Coyle nearing the shed as she crooned to the chickens. She entered the room carrying a small tray on which a plate crowded a jelly glass of milk. "Here you are, Ben. Show your boy how you can eat!"

She put the tray on the dresser, walked between Harry and Amelia, and began to plump up the thin pillows behind Ben's head, arranging his shoulders against them with demonstrative efficiency. Ben's eyes were half-shut, but his left hand moved convulsively. His right arm was immobile on the cotton coverlet. Once the tray was on his lap, he stared up at Mrs. Coyle. With ferocity, as though the sentiment had been hoarded until this moment, he said, "I don't want this stuff!"

Mrs. Coyle, her authority questioned, was at a loss. She sighed heavily. "Well—then I'll attend to my other charges," she said, crossing to a door on the other side of the room Amelia hadn't noticed. It led to another room, into which Mrs. Coyle disappeared.

Harry asked Amelia for matches. As she began searching her bag, Mrs. Coyle reappeared, her plump hands each placed on the heads of two children who clung to her skirt.

Framed by folds of cotton were the pale protuberant foreheads and silken-skinned faces of two little girls, thick pleats of skin around their slanted eyes.

"Alice and Pearly are going to have a little walk, then their lunch, then their naps," Mrs. Coyle said in a singsong voice.

"Get this tray off'n me," Ben demanded. Harry carried the tray to the dresser as Mrs. Coyle left with the children.

"Amelia . . . you've forgotten to give me the matches," Harry said. Amelia held out a book of them as Ben's voice trembled in the close air of the room. "Verbena takes care of lots of folks around here," he said.

"I thought I'd drop in on Dr. Treviot, Dad," Harry said.

"He can't tell you nothing I don't know," Ben said. "When you're old and sick, doctors get this secret organization all rigged up. It's all about you, but you can't join it."

"No secrets," Harry said briskly. "I'll stick to the facts."

"The facts!" exclaimed Ben scornfully, just as Mrs. Coyle knocked on the door and stuck her head into the room. "Mr. Coyle is playing with the children," she announced. "Perhaps you'd come over to the kitchen, Mr. Tilson, now that I've got some time."

Amelia smiled at Ben, who didn't smile back, and followed Harry and Mrs. Coyle into the yard. Mr. Coyle was just rounding the house holding the hands of the girls. They moved torpidly beside him, their faded smocks flattened against their legs. Amelia turned from them into Mrs. Coyle's huge smile. "Perhaps you'd keep old Ben company while your husband and I talk business," she said.

Amelia cast a pleading glance at Harry; he ignored her.

She went back to the shed. The old man looked at her without much interest as she resumed her seat on the bed. "Well. . . ," he sighed.

"I've never been to this part of the country before," Amelia said. Perplexed when Ben didn't answer her right away, she fell silent.

"Harry's mother died young," he said suddenly.

"Yes. He told me."

"You were saying?"

"I've never been out here," she repeated.

"Oh?" He spoke with faint interest. Could he be falling asleep or was it that she'd lost his attention? It was as if she'd never appeared in the room. Then his voice came out of the absence in his face. His lips parted and revealed a few brown teeth.

". . . like his mother," Ben said, continuing an inner story. He went on. "When he was little, he had fat little legs, short like this—" He placed his index finger in the dead hollow of his right arm. "No longer than my forearm. I used to run him down paths, and those fat little legs of his . . . My! He could run!" They looked at each other for a long moment. Amelia thought, it's not going to be so hard. But she felt some betrayal of Harry. Had he ever thought his father knew him in such a way?

"He always did have friends," the old man went on. "Wherever we went and stopped a bit." He looked warily at Amelia. "Maybe you didn't know that?"

"No, I didn't," she said.

"I'll be getting dressed now," he said gruffly. With his good left arm, he lifted his right onto his lap.

"Shall I go get Mrs. Coyle to help you?"

"I'll manage," he said.

She left the shed. The chickens were gathered around a pile of potato peelings. Amelia avoided them, repulsed by their scrawniness.

Harry was sitting at the kitchen table with the Coyles. Mr. Coyle was staring at his wife with doggy admiration. No one looked up as Amelia came into the kitchen.

"Your father is getting dressed," she said sharply.

Mrs. Coyle nodded. "Sure he is. He expects you to take him around the valley to visit old friends. He doesn't hardly get anywhere these days."

Harry got to his feet. "Is there anything else?" he asked.

"I've tried to tell you all of it," Mrs. Coyle replied. "There'll be no point in your seeing the doctor."

"I'd like to use your bathroom," Harry said with a touch of plaintiveness.

"Mr. Coyle will show you the facilities," Mrs. Coyle said. Her husband rose obediently, and Harry followed him out of the kitchen. The clump of their footsteps sounded very loud, as though the house were hollow. Mrs. Coyle made no effort to detain Amelia, and after a minute she walked out of the kitchen. Ben, wearing khaki pants and a faded blue work shirt, leaned against the shed door. She ran to him, but he waved her away.

"Where's the car?" he wanted to know.

Slowly, they made their way to the front of the house. He wouldn't let her take his good arm. Once they were inside the car, he seemed to ignore her. After several minutes, he reached across her and pressed the horn.

"He'll be along soon," she said.

"What's he doing in there?" Ben asked irritably. Harry emerged from the house to the sagging porch, wiping his mouth fastidiously with a handkerchief. Ben moved one foot back and forth, and Amelia felt on her cheek a drop of sweat like a tear.

"Where to?" Harry said as he got into the car.

"Toward town," Ben said.

Here and there houses like shacks rose into the yellow light of the still afternoon. Once, Amelia saw a truck without wheels, abandoned in a field. A dog ran by the side of the road, its pink tongue hanging out. They went past a porch upon which an old person sat in a rocking chair, unmoving, mouth open to the heat. As they drove by a store, Ben poked Amelia with unexpected familiarity. "You can buy a pork chop or a hoe in our store . . ." Next to it stood a gas station with a large tin bucket in front of a solitary gas tank.

"Stop here," Ben directed. Harry pulled off the road in front of what Amelia guessed was a boardinghouse. After the motor died, the two men got out of the car without a backward glance. Amelia scrambled out and followed them as they approached the steps leading up to a narrow swayed porch. In the shade of its overhang stood a cluster of old men. Their work clothes were shapeless with use and age. It crossed Amelia's mind that if touched, they'd turn to dust.

Ben neared the steps cautiously, his head down. Harry walked beside him. Amelia sensed a struggle between them as Ben edged away from his son, holding the dead arm with his other. As he placed his foot on the first of three steps, the old men began to shout his name again and again. One did a short buck-and-wing. Amelia imagined she heard the click-clack of ghostly bones.

When Ben reached the porch, he looked back triumphantly at Harry. Look what I've done, his look seemed to say; I'm somebody here in my own country.

He introduced her: "Amelia, my daughter-in-law." His voice loud. Amelia smiled, and it seemed to suffice, because the old men, Ben along with them, drifted to the other end of the porch. Amelia looked around for Harry and found him a few steps behind her. He pointed at Ben, shook his head, and sighed exaggeratedly. They listened to the loud guffaws, the moments of silence broken sharply by the rise of someone's cracked old voice, a faint mumble.

"I'll wait in the car," Amelia said. She was nearly asleep when Harry and Ben rejoined her.

That afternoon they paid another visit. All the way to the Sherman ranch, Ben was loquacious. He told stories about his friends, the ones they had just seen on the boardinghouse porch. Their stories all bore the same stamp of misfortune—long droughts, disastrous storms, grudging harvests. They had outlived it all, Ben said, they had the last laugh.

No one has the last laugh, Amelia thought.

They parked in a driveway of sorts and entered a darkened room that held a stale coolness. A rancher's huge, callused hand swept a black tomcat from a chair.

"Get off there, cat," Mr. Sherman said. "You sit right down here, Ben. It's fine to see you. So your boy come home and brought his new wife? Well now, Mrs. Tilson, why don't you go visit with Mrs. Sherman?" He pointed toward the kitchen.

Mrs. Sherman, the middle-aged woman in a housedress who had greeted them at the front door, was making coffee. She wiped her hands on her dress and pulled out a chair at a round table for Amelia.

"You must find it different here from back East."

"Yes, it is." From the other room, she could hear the men's voices rising and falling. What could wake her up fully? Her eyes nearly closed, she looked up to see Mrs. Sherman pouring coffee into thick white mugs. She was speaking about children.

"No. We don't have any," Amelia replied listlessly to the question.

"Whatever would that be like?" exclaimed Mrs. Sherman. "My children are all grown up and they've moved away. I don't know why I bother with that cat. It spends its nights getting into fights and coming home limping with its ears unstitched. I suppose you got to have something around that's alive and don't fight with you."

"Those two children Mrs. Coyle takes care of—" Amelia began impulsively.

"Pearly's my niece's little girl. Alice comes from somewhere down the valley. Bless Verbena. It isn't everybody who would bother."

"But there are special places for children like that," Amelia insisted, remotely outraged that anyone would bless Mrs. Coyle.

"I suppose so," replied Mrs. Sherman. She put the mugs of coffee on a tray and started off to the parlor. Amelia followed, carrying a sugar bowl and a pitcher of milk. Mrs. Sherman served Ben first, placing the mug on a stool where he could reach it.

"I'm not supposed to drink coffee," Ben said. "But I will, thank you. If Verbena was here she'd knock it out of my hand." He drank the coffee slowly, only his eyes closing to show his pleasure. Amelia sat down beside Harry. He seemed unaware of her. No one spoke or moved until Ben put his emptied mug down.

"You've got to take care of yourself, Ben," Mrs. Sherman said in a kindly voice.

"Yeah. . . ," the old man sighed, opening his eyes, his mouth slack. Mr. Sherman, who had been watching him, turned his attention to Harry.

"You going back East soon?" he asked.

"This afternoon," replied Harry, shooting a warning glance at Amelia.

"It's a short visit," Mrs. Sherman remarked. Nothing more was said. And what if they were leaving? Amelia asked herself. What could be solved if they stayed longer? People went off and returned, again and again until they died. Generations of tomcats left and came back, staying home until their wounds healed. The heat was immutable.

Harry stood up and handed his mug to Mrs. Sherman. "Dad," he said. Ben looked blankly about the room. "We're going?" he asked. He too got to his feet, but this time he took Harry's arm.

"It's been grand to see you," Mrs. Sherman said. Ben nodded as though he didn't know the Shermans.

"Come again, soon," Mr. Sherman said.

Outside, the intensity of the light had diminished. As they drove back to the Coyles' house, Amelia saw far ahead the Organ Mountains, shadowed, mysterious in the twilight.

Mrs. Coyle was waiting for them on the porch. "I'm glad you brought my boy home safe," she called out amiably. Ben grunted, but whether it was from disgust or the effort of moving, Amelia couldn't guess. They walked with him to the shed, Mrs. Coyle following like fate. The sky grew plum-colored.

As soon as they went inside, Ben lay down on his bed. Mrs. Coyle covered him with a blanket and left.

"We'll be on our way," Harry said.

Ben stared up at them, his eyes empty.

"I'll keep in touch," Harry promised.

"Goodbye," Amelia said and held out her hand. He touched it with one finger. At the door, Amelia turned back. Ben hadn't moved. There was such desolation in the whole look of him, though there was no expression on his face she could name.

While Harry spoke to Mrs. Coyle, Amelia went to the car. It's over, she realized.

Harry reached into the car for his jacket, still folded across the back seat, and got in. He felt in his pockets for cigarettes and turned on the ignition at the same time. Mrs. Coyle lifted a fat white arm, the broad hand dipped, and she turned slowly and entered her house. Just as the Tilsons drove onto the road, Amelia looked back once more and saw Mr. Coyle with something between a leap and a run suddenly appear on the driveway. He too waved, then stood still, staring after them.

They drove for a while in silence.

Neela Vaswani

The Pelvis Series

1

Eve's father swung her onto his shoulders and gave her a ride to the indoor forest. She pinched his ears. She was farseeing: a giraffe.

"Duck," her father said as they passed through a door hanging with vines.

A white, plastic sky arched above. She heard a trickle of water, distant screeches of birds. She grabbed a hunk of her father's hair and gently kicked him; he lowered her to the ground.

At a fork in the path, they peered through the simulated fog seeping rhythmically from vents. Set back against the plastic horizon, between the trees, a small door framed a patch of real sky. Moisture dripped from the ceiling.

Her father raised a hand, cupped his ear. She heard crickets chirping; she nodded. To the left, watching them through a glass wall, was a chimpanzee.

Eve and her father walked down the Ape Path. The chimp kept pace, his brackish eyes inscrutable, his thick lashes feminine and curious. Eve watched the chimp, close enough to touch, to understand. She squeaked her fingers along the glass. In the dense foggy air, she knew the chimp by his steps, his eyes; she knew her father by his neck, the wedge of his back. Her tongue was flat in her mouth: blank, unnecessary.

When the path veered away from the glass enclosure, the chimp disappeared from her view. She yanked on her father's hand, and he lifted her to his shoulders.

2

On a dig in South Africa (fieldwork for her linguistics doctorate), Eve unearthed a chimpanzee. It was 3.5 million years dead. She gazed into the empty eye sockets and beige muzzle of the intact skull. An hour later, she found shards of spine.

She worked on the computer, reconstructing the placement of the chimpanzee's larynx. The partially reassembled skeleton lay on a table covered with black velvet, a cushion and contrasting background for the bones. With the help of the resident biologist—a timorous man with clumps of red back hair welling above his collar—Eve deduced the larynx to be high in the throat, restricting the range of sound.

She massaged her own larynx, low, like all *Homo sapiens*. She hummed a high note and made a cage of her fingers around the vibration.

That night, Eve got drunk. Three beers for each member of the American team and four each for the Africans because they haggled better, with charm. The hairy biologist produced a bottle of tequila and the Africans clapped and shouted for Eve as she tossed back five shots in five minutes. "You look like Ghana woman," one man said, and touched her helixed hair. "Where are your people from?"

"Could be Ghana. Could be anywhere," she said.

A game of charades was organized by the paleontologists who insisted on dividing: one team named Leakey, one, Johanssen. Eve sat next to the biologist and his tequila. When the Leakey group said that sound in charades was as legitimate as Piltdown Man, the game turned into a fight.

Eve leaned into the biologist: "So, Red, do you feed that animal on your back, or what? We all want to know."

He laughed and pulled a comb from his pocket. "Want to give it a whirl?" he asked, and rapped the comb sharply against her forehead.

"Not here," she said and staggered from the lab.

In the dark, on a mound of mistakenly excavated twentieth century rabbit, lion, and hyena bones, Eve sat with her legs sprawled in front of her. The titanic sky rolled down to the earth in every direction, so that Eve stared straight ahead and still looked into the black star-crowded night, a piece of velvet studded with white bones. The biologist tapped her shoulder, and she leaned her head back.

"Gimme that comb," she said, "and take off that dirty shirt." A primitive fear, of decay, of the unknown, taunted her from the tar-pit sky. She knew it was eternal and complete. She was fragile, an inevitable fossil. The biologist removed his shirt.

Eve looked at him, at his red fringed pelt and triangular head. Against the night, his silhouette rose pointed and stout, blotting stars. She felt safe; his shape, like a tent, spoke of community. Reaching up, she pulled him onto the pile of bones. "They're sharp," he complained, and shrank from the triumph in her voice when she said, "I don't feel anything," and closed her eyes against the sky and the words and the unknown.

The biologist sat meekly, allowing her to tug at his red back hair, wincing when she untangled a snarl. "It's nice," she whispered to him, her legs clamped around his pale fleecy waist, her fingers wielding the comb like a crude weapon.

3

For her dissertation research, Eve took a job in Texas working with language-impaired children. One of her cases could not speak; eight-year-old Jamie vocalized and gestured, but was usually unable to make herself understood. During her frequent tantrums, she wrapped her hands with her blond, waist-length hair and punched her mother mechanically.

No matter how her mother tied Jamie's hair, the child shook it loose. When she began yanking it out in fits of frustration, her mother cut it into a bob that curved around Jamie's face in shaggy points. With her short hair, Jamie was unwilling to punch, so she created a new expression of anger. By pointing at the fridge she demanded a juice box and then emptied it in one crushing squeeze, one livid slurp. She tossed the flattened juice box to the floor, then pounced on it and tore it to shreds with her hands and teeth, saving the mutilated plastic straws as trophies. If seriously confounded, she pulled out her own eyebrows and eyelashes and would not allow her mother to attach fake ones. Both speech therapy and sign language failed to help Jamie.

Eve investigated alternate methods. She read about a pygmy chimpanzee, or bonobo, named Kanzi, who learned to communicate through a system of lexigrams, a language called Yerkish.

The system pleased Eve: a computerized board covered with arbitrary symbols, each symbol representing a word: noun, adjective, or verb in the shape of a spiral, square, semicircle, rod. She saw possibilities: *I want pasta, I miss you, I'm tired.* A total of seven hundred potential words lined the lexigram board. The center performing the chimpanzee research also sponsored a program for speech-impaired children.

Eve wrote letters, e-mailed, telephoned the center, bombarding anyone who would listen with her credentials and interests. She said she would move to Georgia and agreed to learn the lexigram process first with chimpanzees, then humans, as the center requested.

She was granted a three-year internship (with no pay). She promised Jamie and her mother that she would send for them as soon as she began work with children.

4

When they met, Lola grabbed Eve's hand and brought her to the TV. They spent the afternoon watching a Discovery program on the migration patterns of monarch butterflies. Lola was a bonobo, with immense gaps between her teeth and hands textured like olive meat. She was fond of placing towels on her head; when she pulled the ends around her face, she looked uncommonly like Mother Teresa, benevolent and wise. In sunlight, red highlights streaked her long, black fur. Her ears wiggled when it thundered. She laughed easily, explosive, sounding like seagulls cavorting around a Dumpster. Because of a mild case of arthritis, she was not very dexterous, even clumsy when climbing. The red of her lips bled almost up to her nostrils, and a deep cove of wrinkled forehead interrupted her soft hair. If embarrassed, she covered her face with her hands.

"Lola, Lo-lo-lo-lo, Lola," Eve sang to her.

What amazed Eve most was the level of comprehension she read in Lola's eyes. She showed her pictures of Jamie, her own parents, her cat. She learned that Lola was pregnant and that her mother had died when she was eight. When Eve was twenty-four, her parents died in an airplane crash. As soon as she told Lola, she found herself clasped in a vigorous embrace.

The pregnancy was Lola's third; all her babies had been stillborn. Lola told Eve this using the lexigrams to say, "My babies quiet." She also told Eve she liked bananas and oranges and disliked the woman with white hair who mopped the floors ("Dirty White Head"), and she hid Eve's car keys at the end of each day—always in a different spot. Arriving home, Eve worked on her dissertation and wrote letters to Jamie and her mother. She sent them pictures of Lola playing dress-up and drinking vodka and cranberry juice with the American Sign Language chimps: Fouts, Jane, and Darwin. From the ASL chimps Lola learned the hand-signs for "GIMME," "MORE," and "HURRY," which she eventually combined into a sentence, "HURRY, GIMME MORE." In turn, she taught her friends the lexigrams for "Lola pretty" and "Please hug."

Hats and scarves and accessories of any kind thrilled Lola. She loved to try on clothes and look in the mirror; sometimes her hands flew to her face in embarrassment, sometimes her smile stretched happy and gapped. She had a collection of postcards, reproduced prints by Frida Kahlo (her favorite: *Diego on My Mind*) and Georgia O'Keeffe (she ignored the flower paintings but was fascinated by the bone and sky pieces). She adored UPS deliverers; ripping open packages was one of her assigned chores. She danced to polka music, LL Cool J. She played darts—the bull's-eye a photograph of Noam Chomsky. But only one activity, car rides, evoked cheers of delight. When Eve told her they were going for a drive, Lola wrapped an orange silk scarf around her head, Grace Kelly style. She took her backpack and stuffed it full of bananas, audio tapes, magazines (she demanded *Playgirl* whenever she was in estrus or if she had just encountered her favorite man, a grad student with green eyes who was studying bisexuality and face-to-face copulation in bonobos). Beethoven remained her favorite composer, from childhood through adulthood, particularly the Seventh Symphony conducted by Herbert von Karajan. Once she and Eve turned onto the open road, Lola put Beethoven in the deck, rolled down her window, and stuck out her hand, tapping against the side of the car and causing many near accidents. She had a hatred for policemen on motorcycles, especially if they wore sunglasses, and Eve always had to speed in case Lola tried to unseat a cop with her long arms.

In winter, Lola pouted. Forced to stay indoors, she used the lexigram board to sign "Bad oranges," and "Dirty Eve take Good Lola outside."

The year Eve came to the language center, the winter was unusually long. Mid-April, the first warm day, Lola followed Eve around, sensing a treat. "Yes, Lola," Eve told her. "We're going for a car ride."

Lola donned her maternity tank top, her gravid stomach bulging, her baby due in two months. She waddled around, fanning herself with the portable lexigram sheet as Eve packed a picnic basket with grapes, cheese sandwiches, a jar of pickles, and napkins. She stowed the basket in the trunk of the car.

With all the windows rolled down, orange scarf wrapped around her head, and wind rippling her sleek, conditioned fur, Lola waved at houses and children looking out the back of a school bus. She whipped her face into a frenzy of terrifying expressions, the children laughing encouragement and forcing their arms joyfully out the side-windows to give her the finger. She gave it back. The wind inflated the orange scarf and she broke the sideview mirror trying to look inside her mouth.

When they stopped at a gas station, the attendant ran from Lola, who got out of the car and stood on one leg, stretching the other above her head. He locked himself in the booth and stared at Lola's pendulous breasts, full stomach, and red engorged sex. Since Lola was always allowed to pay for gas, Eve handed her a ten-dollar bill and told her to slide it gently under the slot. The attendant whimpered and cried as Lola gave him the money, grunting her friendly grunt.

As they neared the park, Lola became pensive and quiet. Usually when Eve asked her what she was thinking about, Lola ignored her. Eve reached out and touched Lola's head. She asked her, "What are you thinking about?" Lola poked at the lexigram "Mommy."

"Are you thinking of your Mommy?" asked Eve. "Wuhh, wuh, wuh," Lola replied in her guttural voice, and twisted her toes. Eve patted Lola's stomach, sagging under the bottom of the tank top. Tilting the lexigram board, she tapped "Mommy," then patted Lola's stomach again and wondered if she herself would ever be a mother. At thirty-eight, three years younger than Lola, she did not feel ready for children.

"Tell me, Lola, what's in your stomach?" Eve asked, and Lola pointed triumphantly to the symbol "Baby." They turned into the park.

Black fur gleaming red, Lola led the way to a path they had used once in the fall, peeled off her tank top, and unwound the orange scarf from her head. She hardly walked bipedally now, preferring the protective four-hand stance, her back shielding the life inside her. The woods smelled faintly of scallions. Lola gathered sorrel for Eve and daffodils for herself, some of which she ate. Nostrils flared, she loped ahead, scouting. When the sun drifted behind clouds, the air turned cool. Eve mimicked thrush and sparrow calls, trying to engage the birds in conversation. Lola swatted at mosquitoes and ate the ones she caught. "Good protein," Eve told her.

On the bank of a small creek, they spread out a blanket and unpacked the picnic basket. A crow circled above them and called out, the sound echoing. The crow chased its own voice, spinning in wide, flirtatious circles. "Too bad humans understand echoes," Eve said to Lola. "We could have been spared some loneliness." She folded the paper napkins into triangles.

Once Lola gave birth, the center would concentrate on teaching her baby and monitoring how much he learned from his mother (they already knew it was a boy, but did not tell Lola). When the baby turned three, Lola would stop working altogether—money at the center had to be re-served for learning chimps and postretirement upkeep was expensive. The center tried to accrue money to study old age in chimpanzees, but no donors were interested, and Lola would be sent to a conservancy with other retired chimps and bonobos, a better fate than the last set of aged ASL chimps who had been shipped to a research institute and injected with hepatitis.

Eve wondered if she would be friends with Lola's son as she watched her trying to open the jar of pickles, grunting in frustration. Holding the jar out to Eve, Lola mimed a twisting motion with her right hand and fur-rowed her brow pleadingly.

They ate the entire jar of pickles, Lola teaching Eve how to eat with her toes. When they finished eating, they lay on their sides and flipped through magazines. It began to rain. Plashes of water fell onto the magazines, sticking the pages together. Out of the blanket, they made a roof and huddled together.

5

Lola retired at forty-five, Jamie's second year in the children's program, and the year Eve finished her dissertation and was hired as a permanent member of the center. It was Eve who arranged for Lola's send-off picnic at her favorite park. Numerous guest speakers signed up for the event: a specialist on hominid teeth Eve knew from her days on the dig, an ethnologist, a cultural anthropologist. Eve had ordered round tables, white tablecloths, and peach napkins folded into swans (in honor of chimpanzee Washoe and her creation of WATER BIRD) for the wealthy sponsors' table and Lola's center table where Pan—Lola's three year-old son—Eve, Fouts, Jane, and Darwin also sat. Green and white balloons tossed above the back of each chair. Eve was wearing a new spring dress, white and sheer, flecked with little pink roses. She had twisted her hair and forced earrings through her long-closed piercings.

Lola jabbered to Pan and fed him carrots. She tried to rub up against a handsome paleontologist from Kenya. A few children chased stray programs skipping across the lawn. Eve's group of speech-impaired children sat at the next table, Jamie happily among them. The child's hair was long again, almost to her waist. She sat on her mother's lap and used a lexigram board to demand more coleslaw. After only three months in the program, Jamie had begun to communicate. Lately, she combined sign language with lexigrams. Sometimes she said "Mommy" or "Eve" in a whisper. She and Lola wore the same pink party hat.

The paleontologist from Kenya gave Lola a plastic model of a human pelvis. She sniffed it lovingly and toyed with herself. One speaker remained: Eve. After her introduction, she walked up to the podium and stood under an oversized green umbrella stamped with white chimpanzees. She tapped the microphone, unexpectedly nervous. She saw Lola lying on her back with Pan balanced on her hands and feet, playing airplane. Pan giggled, sounding like a small seagull. His fur glowed with a red hue.

Eve talked about Lola and her accomplishments as a student and mother, her generosity, her love of paintings, dogs, Mississippi John Hurt, her long sentences. She told the story of Roger Fouts and Washoe, the ASL chimp, and the day a deaf girl came to the house to visit. Sitting in the kitchen, the child saw Washoe through the window, and at the same time that she signed "MONKEY" to Washoe, Washoe signed "BABY" to the child. Human-raised and cross-fostered, Washoe thought of herself as a *Homo sapiens*. The first time she met other chimpanzees she disdainfully referred to them as "BLACK BUGS," but after a few days she called them "MAN" or "WOMAN," deciding they were all one people, all primates.

<h1 style="text-align:center">6</h1>

The picnic was over. Stars crammed the sky; the moon was a tilted crescent. Lola had consumed three pounds of grapes and seven chili dogs. Pan was frisky from too much iced tea. Eve supervised the removal of the tables and chairs, and made sure the microphone was returned to the soundman. She took out her earrings and put them in her backpack. She was tired.

At ten, the lights in the park went out. Eve, Lola, and Pan ambled to the van together. The crickets buzzed like power tools: screw guns, circ saws, drills. Lola carried the plastic pelvis and led the way through the woods. She knew where the van was parked. Eve always forgot.

When they came out of the trees and onto the blacktop, they stopped and looked at the sky. The stars pulsed and blazed, the Milky Way cloudy, like the wax on a plum.

"Orion," Eve said to the chimps. "And look! There are the Pleiades."

Lola waved the pelvis. She stood bipedally, and so did Pan. Silently, they gazed up. The crickets buzzed and clicked. A thin cloud sidled in front of the moon. Eve stared at the stars, searching for a pattern.

She asked Lola for the pelvis. She looked at the sky through the hip sockets so the stars were framed in white circles of bone. On the back of Lola's "Pelvis with Moon" postcard she had read that Georgia O'Keeffe held flowers and bones against the sky to see the objects clearly, to get a sense of foreground and distance.

She pulled her eye farther away from the hip socket: the curve of white bone, the black sky pitted with light.

"Pelvis with Stars," she said to Lola, and gave the bone back to her. "Like your painting. You know the one?"

Lola held the bone up to her own eyes and hooted. She signed "SKY" to Pan, who copied the gesture, sweeping the air with his hand. He begged for the pelvis in high, pleading grunts.

"Good. Yes. Sky," Eve said to Pan, making the motion herself.

Lola watched Pan's hand, then grabbed his thumb and moved it away from his fingers.

"It was a bit slurred," Eve agreed.

Pan tried again, his hand in front of his face, the arc smooth, expansive. He kept his eyes on his mother: "SKY."

Lola chuffed and gave him the pelvis.

"That's right," Eve said, looking up. "Sky."

David Lawrence Morse

Conceived

O UR VILLAGE is built on a great fish—Ceta—so sizeable we have room for nineteen huts, built with the bones we find floating on the sea. Osa always thought it more precarious than it is—we have the huts lashed down with great belts of kelp, for those rare moments when the seas get aggressive. Our huts are grouped in two rows, facing each other across the bony length of Ceta's spine, extending from her dorsal fin to her blowhole. My hut is closest to the blowhole, so I can monitor it, keep it free of debris—fish lice like to force their way into those warm, wet recesses. And even a small child, crawling loose and free, is liable to fall in, become wedged in the delicate tracheal membranes, suffocating our gentle Ceta. Who knows what she would do in such a situation? Thrash and flail the sea, flinging our meager posts and provisions miles across the deep? Perhaps, but Ceta is the gentlest of beasts, and also the wisest—she would see the futility in such aggression, knowing with a beast's instinctual wisdom that there's no cure for calamity once it has lodged itself inside. No, I imagine her simply sinking calmly into the sea, giving her flukes one last flip as if in apology, or farewell. Either way that would be the end of us.

It is my duty to see that Ceta has everything she needs. I swim into her mouth daily, clutching the great bony beak of a swordfish, with which to pick her baleen clean—the bigger fish sometimes get stuck between those hard, horny plates, causing her some discomfort. Of course it's not easy work, finding my way in that great black chasm, swimming through the whirling swirl of krill, but Ceta is patient and tries to keep her gullet shut so I won't get swallowed up inside. Sometimes these days I think of giving in to the temptation, of releasing my grip on the baleen, letting my body be taken up in that violent stream, swallowed along with millions of krill for the sake of a larger life. But that would mean abandoning my duty, and I assume Ceta's stomach would have no room for the likes of me—I'm a stubborn man and probably not easily digested.

Other villagers take care of the remaining matters—harvesting the fish lice, our primary source of food, also a danger to Ceta if too many accumulate too quickly. Lice attach themselves to her skin, trying to suck the very life out of her. But if you know how to grip them—just above the gut—they pluck right off, and make for easy eating—succulent, nothing but muscle, tasty raw or pickled in vats of brine. And our drinking water must be collected—every few minutes Ceta spouts forth a mighty mist, the water always remarkably warm no matter the temperature of the sea, and free of all trace of salt.

Osa loved Ceta almost as much as I did, but was afraid she might suddenly make a dive for the deep, giving up her commitment to a surface existence. But Osa had many such fears. I never knew anyone who regarded the simple things of life with such simultaneous passion and suspicion. She was afraid of drowning, though she loved to swim. Afraid of swallowing her own teeth (they might make a meal of her from the inside out), though she loved to eat. Her greatest fear was of being misunderstood, though the life she lived was a mystery. But not a mystery to me, or at least I thought as much at the time. Understood? What is there to understand? We live on a fish on the sea. We eat fish lice and occasionally a lungfish, a tench, or a snook. We play with our children and make love with our wives. Life is good, life is not so good. We are glad, we are not so glad. What is there, I would ask my Osa, to understand?

I call her my Osa, though she was never properly mine—not my wife, anyway—only my companion. Companions are not allowed to marry unless and until they have produced a child—human life is too precarious to allow a couple to pass through life without propagation. If after a few seasons the companions have not succeeded, then they are separated and a new pair is arranged. I was Osa's second companion. Her first was set adrift on a raft of bones after he was discovered to be impotent, which is

not punishable in and of itself (we are not, after all, pitiless) except combined with his deceit—the couple, it was judged, had flaunted our cus-
toms regarding fertility in order to attend to their own notions of
togetherness. Osa herself never confessed—it was her younger sister Tama
who overheard them discussing it and told the elders. Osa was only spared
the same sentence because as a probable childbearer she was entitled to
another chance.

As for me, I was surprised to find Osa was interested at all. Her first
companion, Conger, was one of the men who rode bareback on the dolphins, hunting with spears the larger game—swordfish, mako sharks—as
much to protect our Ceta from attack as for fresh meat and hides. Osa
would often ride the dolphins with them—not on the hunts but at other
times, just for fun—and I would sit in envy, not of their prowess but of the
wonderfully free way in which they rode. But some months after Conger
had been exiled, Osa began to join me in the sea when I would inspect
Ceta's sides for signs of illness or evidence of attacks. We would swim
underneath her, admiring her massive dimensions, her jaws yawning open
and her throat swelling to twice its size, swallowing the sea. Once we
found a fresh wound on her belly—a gash of jagged flesh as long as my
arm, the tooth of a mako shark lodged in the fat—which fascinated Osa so
much I couldn't bring her to leave, even with another shark attack surely
imminent. Wounds, scars, scabs, blisters, sores—the evidence of injuries
and how they healed—these captivated her. The body and its processes
was her passion, and the reason she became obsessed with me, too—caretaker of the largest body in the sea.

Though ours was not her first companionship, I was surprised to find
she approached it with the passion and even ingenuousness as if it were. In
our first weeks together, we were en route on our fish from the seas of summer to those of fall, the cool darkness of the deep, by degrees, seeping
closer to the sea's surface. We moved together into one of the huts set aside
for companions, and she brought with her many additions—variously
colored sea stars to surround our pallet and a briny ball of orange, with
brilliant, serpentine tendrils, to hang like the sun from our ceiling. The
waters were still moderately warm at that time and we spent our days
splashing and laughing and swimming with the others, the quicker swim-
mers among us catching tench for all to eat, the smaller children taking
turns on the blowhole to be shot wriggling into the air, a few of us lying

flat on Ceta's flukes to be flipped high into the sky, and my own Osa climbing onto the backs of the dolphins and holding on for the ride. At her goading the two of us dove down into the cold sea-deep, and there, unseen, lost in darkness, suspended together in the giant writhing silence, I first knew the reach and rush of lust.

And yet she didn't conceive, and soon our fish had brought us to winter seas, stretching before us calm and cold, Osa said, as a corpse. The sun far-flung, for months unmoving above, and I found my Osa gradually given to fits of ill-humor. She hated the cold and monotony of those winter seas, where nothing much exists but ourselves and the occasional shadow of something silent in the deep, and her body began to show it. Her brown hair, a surge of curls and tresses, began to wilt, become long and sodden as seaweed. Her eyelids thickened; the soft corners of her mouth hardened with suspicion. In winter we rely almost entirely on the fish louse for food, but Osa lost her taste for these, needing variety. And while others enjoyed the weather of these winters—the crisp, brisk touch of the sun—Osa was always chilled.

Her younger sister Tama—who had told the elders of Conger's impotency—didn't help matters—there were no boys her age to flirt with, and she was having to wait for male attention until she grew a few years older. Tama frequently frustrated my efforts to care for Ceta, hiding the sword-fish beak I used to clean the baleen, or worse, using the beak to dig holes into Ceta's skin, which I would then rub down for hours with vats of shark fat. But when I mentioned this to Osa she refused to scold her sister and insisted that I leave her alone as well. "She's harmless," Osa said, "just a girl really. And can you blame her if she's bored?"

"Bored?" I asked. "How could one be bored? We're surrounded by the sea, the sky, the stars. Every day Ceta swims us somewhere different—the colors of the waters—see how they're changing!" But Osa's sympathies seemed to be more with her sister than with me, and the two of us grew increasingly hostile. She was suspicious in her misery, sure that I disapproved, which was true, except I would not admit it, instead offering limp, bitter sympathies. I could be caretaker, but only of something I thought deserved being taken care of—what reason did Osa have for her petty ways? "What reason?" she asked. "What reason does Ceta have for bringing us here?" I told her Ceta didn't need a reason—any more than did the sun for sinking into the sea. "Then I don't need a reason, either," she said.

"Maybe one day I'll be riding a dolphin and decide to keep holding on, and never let go. Dolphins know where the warm waters are, and never leave them." In such moments Osa would become perfectly still, riveted by her own resentments, her cheeks reddening—in her anger she would forget to breathe. I was infatuated with her passions but angered when the passions ran her the other way—from love of our life to hatred of it. She began to grant me little intimacy, though even at our most estranged I was fervent for it, from sheer lust, but also from the growing realization that our time together would soon be ended by the elders unless our love proved fruitful.

The days were long in those winter waters and the nights nonexistent. Osa spent much of the time on our pallet, preoccupied with picking the calluses from her feet, or from mine, when I would let her. Or she would lie on the pallet resting on her elbows, studying the pallid gray patterns of Ceta's skin. When she did leave the hut, she would wander about looking for the sunburned boys—bribing them until they agreed to sit still while she peeled off their skin.

Our village spent much of these white nights in revelry, amid music of the drum and fife, spinning and slipping and dancing across Ceta's mottled skin, free from the haunts and sluggishness of sleep. I often observed these revelries—finding it enjoyable to watch others enjoying themselves—but Osa remained much in our hut, determined to sleep— even with no night to necessitate it—so she would not miss her dreams.

Sometimes she would describe these dreams to me, full of things none of us had ever seen: beings like fish that swam through the air rather than the sea; an expanse of surface, like our Ceta's back except more vast, more firm, and fixed; and from that surface, things growing upwards, like seaweed but without need of water for support, fixed instead of floating, whispering in the breeze. She told me these were things she had dreamed into existence. She said that life inflicted wounds and that dreams were the mind's means of healing. She asked me if I ever dreamed and I—taken aback and even offended by her visions—lied for the first time in my life and told her I didn't. I told her dreams were the things of fools and prophets. She assumed I meant her to be a fool and left me alone on the pallet; I might have stopped her but found I couldn't. In truth I didn't know which she was—fool or prophet—and didn't know if she knew, either.

Yet we maintained a fascination with each other—there were still flashes of passion. As once when we crawled onto our hut's roof, a shelf of kelp, to watch the winter lights—great green glowing bands dancing in the sky. Swoot swoot BOOM went the blowhole, and the spout shot high into those green sky lights, and we were awash in the heated mist, the seaweed soft and supple under our backs, and Osa asked me what did it all mean. I didn't know any more than she did, but I did know that wasn't what she wanted to hear, and for once I obliged her, and gave her meanings—fool that I was—as I understood them right then: that there was no such thing as time, only the glow of the moment; that there was no such thing as truth, only the blur of feeling and belief. She gasped and her eyes regained their wide, wild delight. "We shouldn't be up here," she said. "We could fall through." And then we fell to each other with such force that that is exactly what we did—fell through—the kelp suddenly letting us go so quickly and completely that it seemed impossible it had ever held us, and as we fell we remained embraced, suspended for a moment, blind in the green misty light, before we landed on the pallet, on Ceta's forgiving back, with an unforgiving thud.

"Where have you been?" she asked afterwards. She was resting on my chest, her head rising and falling with my breaths.

"Where else? I've been right here."

"You mean with me?"

"Well, yes."

"You only love the idea of me. And I love the idea of you. But that's not enough. Our love needs a body."

"That's what a child is," I said, "or could be."

She was quiet for a while. Every few minutes the blowhole boomed. "No," she said. "No, it's not. A child would just be floating right along with us. We wouldn't love our child, just the idea of our child."

"What's wrong with floating?" I asked. "That's the way the world works."

"But what if we weren't living on Ceta anymore? What if Ceta were free to swim and dive and leap out of the water like other fish, and we were free, too, without clinging to her back like lice. What if we found a place where what was under us wasn't always moving? Then I could settle down with you."

"What do you mean 'then'?" I said. "There's no such thing as 'then.' There's only now. Now is the same as it's always been. And always will be."

Again she was silent, and said bitterly, "I see." And I could feel the bones in her back stiffening, feel them constricting, until she rolled off my chest and away from me, and we lay there silently, separately, rising and falling with Ceta's tremendous breaths.

I can't remember which arrived first that spring—the rumors or the bird. The rumors said that the elders were already thinking of separating Osa and me; it was no secret, though I'd tried to keep it so, that we were having difficulties. She now refused intimacy except on rare occasions, though at the same time, she refused to be finished with me. She thought she could somehow win me over to her dreams of things, and didn't believe me when I said I never dreamed. "You talk in your sleep," she said. "Sometimes you cry out—that's how I know you're lying." And it was true I was having dreams—but not like Osa's—her views had gotten under my skin, and I had secretly begun to fear what would happen to us if Ceta ever died. We had lived on her back for generations, so that we could no more imagine her dying than the sun itself, but then again, wasn't she a fish, just like the other fish of the sea? I began having nightmares, dreaming of an ocean of bones and foam and blood. I dreamed of Ceta sinking, and of the villagers lashed to her back, sinking through an abyss of krill. And yet my role as Ceta's caretaker was a sacred responsibility I could not easily disavow—as long as I continued to administer to her needs, then surely she would continue serving us dutifully as she had always done. And besides, I asked Osa, where were we to go? She was determined that I admit the possibility of her nightly visions, and I was determined that she admit the actuality of our situation.

I tried to seduce her while she slept, but she would wake, angry, and leave. She would go back to her father's hut. Sometimes when this happened Tama would make her way down Ceta's long bony spine, balancing, her arms outstretched like fins. She would sing to herself, "Osa's home, Osa's home," loud enough that the villagers in their huts on either side might hear. When she arrived at my hut she would stop in the doorway, a hand on the frame, looking at me, and announce, "Osa's home."

"Yes, I know."

"Do you know why?"

"Because she loves her little sister."

"Don't be a fool," she would say—reproving me, but reproving Osa, too, whose love could not be had or held so simply. And then she would make up a preposterous list of reasons why her sister had gone home: Osa lost her eyes again—Papa is gluing on new ones. Osa forgot to kiss the great fish in the sky goodbye before she was born—she has to go back and be born again. Osa likes to sleep with Papa. Osa peeled off all her skin.

One day she didn't stop at the doorway but slipped inside, keeping her hands behind her. She started again in her list: Osa swallowed a fish louse whole. Osa exploded. Osa came home to find her sister but her sister turned into a bird.

"What's a bird?" I asked.

"Here," she said, and held out her cupped hands. Inside them was the strangest thing I'd ever seen, like something out of Osa's dreams. A snout like that of a swordfish, long and beaked, which opened and shut and emitted strange squeaks. A plump body, shaped more like a large fish egg than a fish itself, with a thin, wrinkled membrane of skin, and strange, soft fins that alternately extended and were tucked away.

"What is it?" I asked.

"A bird, silly," Tama said. "Osa created it, in one of her dreams. But she's never seen a real one. I'm the only one who has. Me, and now you, too."

"Where did you get it?"

"It got me. It landed on my head. Here, you can hold it," she said, and reached toward me, but the bird sprang out of her hand and began swimming through the air, beating what I only knew then to call its fins. "That's okay," she said. "In Osa's dreams that's called flying." The bird flew out my cabin door but Tama remained unconcerned. "It'll come back," she said. "I'm its new home."

Only the bird didn't come back, but was seen by various villagers swimming—flying—in and out of huts, over heads and under arms, until it landed in the hands of Tope, one of the elders, a timid man with enormous eyes, who clutched at it and almost broke its neck before his wife got it into a makeshift cage. There was a commotion in the village such as had not been seen since years before, when an old woman named Daee declared our great fish pregnant, and it was only after many speeches from me that I convinced the village Ceta wasn't pregnant but was only suffering from indigestion. "How could she possibly conceive?" I told them at the time. "She's twice as big as any fish out there."

Everyone took the bird's arrival as a sign—the question was, of what? Some thought it meant the end of times, which brought leaping and laughter from some, crying from others. Some quarreled, hitting each other in the knees with bones. Others played the fife and drum, marching up and down Ceta's spine. Others feasted, opening up the reserves of pickled plaice, or plucking off fresh fish lice and biting them in half. Games of gobo, shinny, and battledore, wrestling and fencing, spouting contests among the boys. Only in the uproar, the villagers lost track of the bird itself, and when a line formed around Tope's hut, waiting to give him his ceremonial, congratulatory whacks on the back for a notable deed done, it was discovered that Tope himself no longer had the bird—he said it was at Turbot's. Turbot said it was at Tautog's. Tautog said it was at Sprat's. Sprat didn't know where it was, or even that it existed, Sprat having died the previous week. His widow beat the villagers out of her hut with a dead lungfish.

Late that night, Osa returned to the hut, as I knew she would. There was no moon and the night was black and the sea winds unusually strong for the season, and I felt as if I were lost and swirling inside the sea-filled jaws of a beast even greater than Ceta, without even her bony baleen to hold on to, to keep me from giving myself to the rush of darkness swallowing us all. Osa paused in the doorway; I couldn't see her but could feel her presence, her eyes wide and fixed on where she knew my body would be lying. She feared doorways—that feeling of being caught in between—but she lingered there, as her sister had done so many times before.

"Would you believe me if I told you I conceived the bird in a dream?" she asked, her voice trembling, her words tumbling down onto me as if from a great height. I was staring into the night through the tattered hole in the roof, which she'd insisted I never repair, so that the mist from Ceta's breaths was continually drizzling down upon us.

"No," I said.

"Would you believe me if I said the bird flew to us from a great expanse of something called land, and that we could live there, you and I?"

"No," I said.

"Would you believe me if I said I have conceived a child? Our child?"

My heart kicked at my breast, but though I wanted to believe her, again I said no. To believe one of her conceits was to believe them all, and to believe them all was to risk the ruination of the precarious life it was my responsibility to preserve.

"I see," she said and was silent. Ceta's spouts boomed and the warm mist fell upon us, and I could feel Osa sinking away from me, sinking back into the night.

By noon the next day the entire village had been given to understand that Osa was with child—it was Tama who triumphantly spread the word. The village decided the mysterious bird must have been a messenger bringing the news, and there were whispers that Osa was to bear a child of great strength and courage. Most were pleased that the end of times was to be put off after all, though a few dissenters said the child might be the one who would one day wreak the ruin. All of the men—including Osa's father—lined up to whack me on the back (some of the shark hunters hit harder than they should), and in the afternoon three elder women arrived with pillows and fragrances and a tiara of pike teeth for the blessed mother-to-be. Only Osa had not yet returned to our hut from the night before, and I had not gone to find her—from preoccupation and obstinacy. The women stumbled about in the hut, embarrassed and concerned and titillated, adjusting and readjusting the pillows on the pallet and chattering.

"It's a hardness on a woman, who's with child."

"A man's no help anyways."

"Could be a demon-child."

"No telling what a woman might do."

"Come to her good sense eventually."

The villagers were befuddled. Marriage festivities were in order and yet couldn't proceed if the couple didn't seem inclined to be together. As for me, in the following days I busied myself in the sea with Ceta. Now that she'd returned us to warmer waters I had many duties: cleaning the yellow algae from beneath her flippers, rubbing down her flippers and dorsal fin with vats of shark fat, filing the barnacles off her flukes. Routine duties, but pleasurable all the same, keeping me busy in the sea and out of my vacant, newly fragranced hut. As for Osa, I missed her terribly, and strove to know if what she said was true—that she had conceived a child. And yet I remained tormented by my own suspicions. What of what she'd said did she herself believe? We were suffering, as we had all along, from two different kinds of obstinacy—Osa's driven by the fervency of dream and belief; mine more like a disease, trapped within the accumulated fat of habit, insulation against a fear of the mysterious, that would not let me yield, and would not let me go.

A week passed. One of the elders—Tope himself, who had found and lost the messenger bird—came to me, his enormous eyes drifting in his cavernous sockets, and questioned me tepidly about the nature of our disagreements, suggesting I do what I could to solve them. Tama could be heard about the village, singing out "Osa's home" to whomever looked as if they might want to hear. But she did not come again to my doorway, instead solving everyone's problems by coming to the elder women late one afternoon, crying and saying with a mixture of shame, anger, and dismay that Osa was not pregnant after all. Osa had neglected to throw away the strips of kelp she'd used to clean herself, and Tama had found these and was here bringing them to the elders. The elders made their decision swiftly, this being Osa's second offense against fertility, that she was to be put on a raft of bones and set adrift at sea.

The entire village seemed in agreement, except her father, who tarried in the doorway when the shark hunters arrived to carry her away. But even he put up little fight—just a gatherer of fish lice his entire life. It was said Osa seemed willing to go, that she seemed to have salvaged from her suffering if not dignity then at least a degree of defiance. It was said she forgot to kiss our Ceta, the great fish, goodbye. It was said she took nothing with her. It was said that her raft didn't drift at all, but seemed moved by unseen currents, and that a bird flew overhead, leading, circling, following.

It was Tama who said these things, lingering, swinging in my doorway. It was Tama who told me proudly that it was her own blood that had bloodied the kelp, her first time, and just in time, for Osa really had conceived a child, but had placed her sister under oath not to tell.

"Why?" I asked, cringing, my airways constricting. "Because she wanted to die?"

"Oh, don't be such a fool," she said.

Only now I have little choice but to be the fool, love-lost, fearful of what may become of us, lying on my back by night, showered by Ceta's mists, admiring and scrutinizing the nature of her spouts. Are they coming less frequently? Are they blowing at not quite their former height? Is our Ceta slowing down? I do not know, and cannot, nor can I know what became of my Osa alone out there on a raft of bones, but every day I keep watch on the horizon for that mysterious expanse of something called land, and imagine my Osa running and spinning and dancing across it, our child clinging to her back, laughing, holding on for the ride.

William Trevor

The Dressmaker's Child

C AHAL SPRAYED WD-40 onto the only bolt his spanner wouldn't shift. All the others had come out easily enough but this one was rusted in, the exhaust unit trailing from it. He had tried to hammer it out, he had tried wrenching the exhaust unit this way and that in the hope that something would give, but nothing had. Half five, he'd told Heslin, and the bloody car wouldn't be ready.

The lights of the garage were always on, because shelves had been put up in front of the windows that stretched across the length of the wall at the back. Abandoned cars, kept for their parts, and cars and motorcycles waiting for spares, and jacks that could be wheeled about took up what space there was on either side of the small wooden office, which was at the back also. There were racks of tools, and workbenches with vises along the back wall, and rows of new and reconditioned tires, and drums of grease and oil. In the middle of the garage there were two pits, in one of which Cahal's father was at the moment, putting in a clutch. There was a radio, on which advice was being given about looking after fish in an aquarium. "Will you turn that stuff off?" Cahal's father shouted from under the car he was working on, and Cahal searched the wave bands until he found music of his father's time.

He was an only son in a family of girls, all of them older, all of them gone from the town—three to England, another in Dunnes in Galway, another married in Nebraska. The garage was what Cahal knew, having kept his father company there since childhood, given odd jobs to do as he grew up. His father had had help then, an old man who was related to the family, whose place Cahal eventually took.

He tried the bolt again but the WD-40 hadn't begun to work yet. He was a lean, almost scrawny youth, dark-haired, his long face usually unsmiling. His garage overalls, over a yellow T-shirt, were oil-stained, gone pale where their green dye had been washed out of them. He was nineteen years old.

"Hullo," a voice said. A man and a woman, strangers, stood in the wide-open doorway of the garage.

"Howya," Cahal said.

"It's the possibility, sir," the man inquired, "you drive us to the sacred Virgin?"

"Sorry?" And Cahal's father shouted up from the pit, wanting to know who was there. "Which Virgin's that?" Cahal asked.

The two looked at one another, not attempting to answer, and then it occurred to Cahal that they were foreign people, who had not understood. A year ago a German had driven his Volkswagen into the garage, with a noise in the engine, so he'd said. "I had hopes it'd be the big end," Cahal's father admitted afterward, but it was only the catch of the bonnet gone a bit loose. A couple from America had had a tire put on their hired car a few weeks after that, but there'd been nothing since.

"Of Pouldearg," the woman said. "Is it how to say it?"

"The statue you're after?"

They nodded uncertainly and then with more confidence, both of them at the same time.

"Aren't you driving, yourselves, though?" Cahal asked them.

"We have no car," the man said.

"We are traveled from Ávila." The woman's black hair was silky, drawn back and tied with a red-and-blue ribbon. Her eyes were brown, her teeth very white, her skin olive. She wore the untidy clothes of a traveler: denim trousers, a woolen jacket over a striped red blouse. The man's trousers were the same, his shirt a nondescript shade of grayish blue, a white kerchief at his neck. A few years older than himself, Cahal estimated they'd be.

"Ávila?" he said.

"Spain," the man said.

Again Cahal's father called out, and Cahal said two Spanish people had come into the garage.

"In the store," the man explained. "They say you drive us to the Virgin."

"Are they broken down?" Cahal's father shouted.

He could charge them fifty euros, Pouldearg there and back, Cahal considered. He'd miss Germany versus Holland on the television, maybe the best match of the Cup, but never mind that for fifty euros.

"The only thing," he said, "I have an exhaust to put in."

He pointed at the pipe and silencer hanging out of Heslin's old Vauxhall, and they understood. He gestured with his hands that they should stay where they were for a minute, and with his palms held flat made a pushing motion in the air, indicating that they should ignore the agitation that was coming from the pit. Both of them were amused. When Cahal tried the bolt again it began to turn.

He made the thumbs-up sign when exhaust and silencer clattered to the ground. "I could take you at around seven," he said, going close to where the Spaniards stood, keeping his voice low so that his father would not hear. He led them to the forecourt and made the arrangement while he filled the tank of a Murphy's Stout lorry.

When Cahal's father had driven a mile out on the Bantry Road, he turned at the entrance to the stud farm and drove back to the garage, satisfied that the clutch he'd put in for Father Shea was correctly adjusted. He left the car in the forecourt, ready for Father Shea to collect, and hung the keys up in the office. Heslin from the courthouse was writing a check for the exhaust Cahal had fitted. Cahal was getting out of his overalls, and when Heslin had gone he said the people who had come wanted him to drive them to Pouldearg. They were Spanish people, Cahal said again, in case his father hadn't heard when he'd supplied that information before.

"What they want with Pouldearg?"

"Nothing only the statue."

"There's no one goes to the statue these times."

"It's where they're headed."

"Did you tell them, though, how the thing was?"

"I did of course."

"Why they'd be going out there?"

"There's people takes photographs of it."

Thirteen years ago, the then bishop and two parish priests had put an end to the cult of the wayside statue at Pouldearg. None of those three men, and no priest or nun who had ever visited the crossroads at Pouldearg, had sensed anything special about the statue; none had witnessed the tears that were said to slip out of the downcast eyes when pardon for sins was beseeched by penitents. The statue became the subject of attention in pulpits and in religious publications, the claims made for it fulminated against as a foolishness. And then a curate of that time demonstrated that what had been noticed by two or three local people who regularly passed by the statue—a certain dampness beneath the eyes—was no more than raindrops trapped in two overdefined hollows. There the matter ended. Those who had so certainly believed in what they had never actually seen, those who had not noticed the drenched leaves of overhanging boughs high above the statue, felt as foolish as their spiritual masters had predicted they one day would. Almost overnight the Weeping Virgin of Pouldearg became again the painted image it had always been. Our Lady of the Wayside, it had been called for a while.

"I never heard people were taking photographs of it." Cahal's father shook his head as if he doubted his son, which he often did and usually with reason.

"A fellow was writing a book a while back. Going around all Ireland, tracking down the weeping statues."

"It was no more than the rain at Pouldearg."

"He'd have put that in the book. That man would have put the whole thing down, how you'd find the statues all over the place and some of them would be O.K. and some of them wouldn't."

"And you set the Spaniards right about Pouldearg?"

"I did of course."

"Drain the juice out of young Leahy's bike and we'll weld his leak for him."

The suspicions of Cahal's father were justified: the truth had no more than slightly played a part in what Cahal had told the Spanish couple about Pouldearg. With fifty euros at the back of his mind, he would have considered it a failure of his intelligence had he allowed himself to reveal that the miracle once claimed for the statue at Pouldearg was without foundation.

They had heard the statue called Our Lady of Tears as well as Our Lady of the Wayside and the Sacred Virgin of Pouldearg by a man in a Dublin public house with whom they had drifted into conversation.

They'd had to repeat this a couple of times before Cahal grasped what they were saying, but he thought he got it right in the end. It wouldn't be hard to stretch the journey by four or five miles, and if they were misled by the names they'd heard the statue given in Dublin it was no concern of his. At five past seven, when he'd had his tea and had had a look at the television, he drove into the yard of Macey's Hotel. He waited there as he'd said he would. They appeared almost at once.

They sat close together in the back. Before he started the engine again Cahal told them what the cost would be and they said that was all right. He drove through the town, gone quiet as it invariably did at this time. Some of the shops were still open and would remain so for a few more hours—the newsagents' and tobacconists', the sweetshops and small groceries, Quinlan's supermarket, all the public houses—but there was a lull on the streets.

"Are you on holiday?" Cahal asked.

He couldn't make much of their reply. Both of them spoke, correcting one another. After a lot of repetition they seemed to be telling him that they were getting married.

"Well, that's grand," he said.

He turned out onto the Loye Road. Spanish was spoken in the back of the car. The radio wasn't working or he'd have put it on for company. The car was a black Ford Cortina, a hundred and eighty thousand miles on the clock, that his father had taken in part exchange. They'd use it until the tax sticker expired and then put it aside for spares. Cahal thought of telling the passengers that in case they'd think he hadn't much to say for himself, but he knew it would be too difficult. The Christian Brothers had had him labeled as not having much to say for himself, and it had stuck in his memory, worrying him sometimes in case it caused people to believe he was slow. Whenever he could, Cahal tried to give the lie to that by making a comment.

"Are you here long?" he inquired, and the girl said they'd been two days in Dublin. He said he'd been in Dublin himself a few times. He said it was mountainy from now on, until they reached Pouldearg. The scenery was beautiful, the girl said.

He took the fork at the two dead trees, although going straight would have got them there, too, longer still but potholes all over the place. It was a good car for the hills, the man said, and Cahal said it was a Ford, pleased that he'd understood. You'd get used to it, he considered, with a bit more practicing you'd pick up the trick of understanding them.

"How'd you say it in Spanish?" he called back over his shoulder. "A statue?"

"Estatua," they both said, together. *"Estatua,"* they said.

"Estatua," Cahal repeated, changing gears for the hill at Loye.

The girl clapped her hands, and he could see her smiling in the rearview mirror. God, a woman like that, he thought. Give me a woman like that, he said to himself, and he imagined he was in the car alone with her, that the man wasn't there, that he hadn't come to Ireland with her, that he didn't exist.

"Do you hear about St. Teresa of Ávila? Do you hear about her in Ireland?" Her lips opened and closed in the rearview mirror, her teeth flashing, the tip of her tongue there for a moment. What she'd asked him was as clear as anyone would say it.

"We do of course," he said, confusing St. Teresa of Ávila with the St. Teresa who'd been famous for her humility and her attention to little things. "Grand," Cahal said of her also. "Grand altogether."

To his disappointment, Spanish was spoken again. He was going with Minnie Fennelly, but, no doubt about it, this woman had the better of her. The two faces appeared side by side in his mind's eye and there wasn't a competition.

He drove past the cottages beyond the bridge, the road twisting and turning all over the place after that. It said earlier on the radio there'd be showers but there wasn't a trace of one, the October evening without a breeze, dusk beginning.

"Not more than a mile," he said, not turning his head, but the Spanish was still going on. If they were planning to take photographs they mightn't be lucky by the time they got there. With the trees, Pouldearg was a dark place at the best of times. He wondered if the Germans had scored yet. He'd have put money on the Germans if he'd had any to spare.

Before they reached their destination, Cahal drew the car onto the verge where it was wide and looked dry. He could tell from the steering that there was trouble and found it in the left front wheel, the tire leaking at the valve. Five or six pounds it would have lost, he estimated.

"It won't take me a minute," he reassured his passengers, rummaging behind where they sat, among old newspapers and tools and empty paint tins, for the pump. He thought for a moment it mightn't be there and wondered what he'd do if the spare tire was flat, which sometimes it was if a car was a trade-in. But the pump was there and he gave the partially deflated tire a couple of extra pounds to keep it going. He'd see how things were when they reached Pouldearg crossroads.

When they did, there wasn't enough light for a photograph, but the man and woman went up close to the Wayside Virgin, which was more lopsided than Cahal remembered from the last time he'd driven by it, hardly longer than a year ago. The tire had lost the extra pressure he'd pumped in, and while they were occupied he began to change the wheel, having discovered that the spare tire wasn't flat. All the time he could hear them talking in Spanish, although their voices weren't raised. When they returned to the car it was still jacked up and they had to wait for a while, standing on the road beside him, but they didn't appear to mind.

He'd still catch most of the second half, Cahal said to himself when eventually he turned the car around and began the journey back. You never knew how you were placed as regards how long you'd be, how long you'd have to wait for people while they poked about.

"Was she all right for you?" he asked them, turning on the headlights so that the potholes would show up.

They answered in Spanish, as if they had forgotten that it wouldn't be any good. She'd fallen over a bit more, he said, but they didn't understand. They brought up the man they'd met in the public house in Dublin. They kept repeating something, a gabble of English words that still appeared to be about getting married. In the end, it seemed to Cahal that this man had told them people received a marriage blessing when they came to Pouldearg as penitents.

"Did you buy him drinks?" he asked, but that wasn't understood, either.

They didn't meet another car, nor even a bicycle, until they were farther down. He'd been lucky over the tire: they could easily have said they wouldn't pay if he'd had them stranded all night in the hills. They weren't talking anymore; when he looked in the mirror they were kissing, no more than shadows in the gloom, arms around one another.

It was then, just after they'd passed the dead trees, that the child ran out. She came out of the blue cottage and ran at the car. He'd heard of it before, the child on this road who ran out at cars. It had never happened to himself, he'd never even seen a child there any time he'd passed, but often it was mentioned. He felt the thud no more than a second after the headlights picked out the white dress by the wall and then the sudden movement of the child running out.

Cahal didn't stop. In his mirror the road had gone dark. He saw something white lying there but said to himself he had imagined it. In the back of the Cortina the embrace continued.

Sweat had broken out on the palms of Cahal's hands, on his back and his forehead. She'd thrown herself at the side of the car and his own door was what she'd made contact with. Her mother was the unmarried woman of that cottage, many the time he'd heard that said in the garage. Fitzie Gill had shown him damage to his wing and said the child must have had a stone in her hand. But usually there wasn't any damage, and no one had ever mentioned damage to the child herself.

Bungalows announced the town, all of them lit up now. The Spanish began again, and he was asked if he could tell them what time the bus went to Galway. There was confusion because he thought they meant tonight, but then he understood it was the morning. He told them, and when they paid him in Macey's yard the man handed him a pencil and a notebook. He didn't know what that was for, but they showed him, making gestures, and he wrote down the time of the bus. They shook hands with him before they went into the hotel.

In the very early morning, just after half past one, Cahal woke up and couldn't sleep again. He tried to recall what he'd seen of the football, the moves there'd been, the saves, the yellow card shown twice. But nothing seemed quite right, as if the television pictures and snatches of the commentary had come from a dream, which he knew they hadn't. He had examined the side of the car in the garage and there'd been nothing. He had switched out the lights of the garage and locked up. He'd watched the football in Shannon's and hadn't seen the end because he lost interest when nothing much was happening. He should have stopped; he didn't know why he hadn't. He couldn't remember braking. He didn't know if he'd tried to; he didn't know if there hadn't been time.

The Ford Cortina had been seen setting out on the Loye Road and then returning. His father knew the way he'd gone, past the unmarried woman's cottage. The Spaniards would have said in the hotel they'd seen the Virgin. They'd have said in the hotel they were going on to Galway. They could be found in Galway for questioning.

In the dark Cahal tried to work it out. They would have heard the bump. They wouldn't have known what it was, but they'd have heard it while they were kissing. They would remember how much longer it was before they got out of the car in Macey's yard. It hadn't been a white dress, Cahal realized suddenly; it trailed on the ground, too long for a dress, more like a nightdress.

He'd seen the woman who lived there a few times when she came in to the shops, a dressmaker they said she was, small and wiry with dark inquisitive eyes and a twist in her features that made them less appealing than they might have been. When her child had been born to her, the father had not been known—not even to herself, so it was said, though possibly without justification. People said she didn't speak about the birth of her child.

As Cahal lay in the darkness, he resisted the compulsion to get up in order to go back and see for himself; to walk out to the blue cottage, since to drive would be foolish; to look on the road for whatever might be there, he didn't know what. Often he and Minnie Fennelly got up in the middle of the night in order to meet in the back shed at her house. They lay on a stack of netting there, whispering and petting one another, the way they couldn't anywhere in the daytime. The best they could manage in the daytime was half an hour in the Ford Cortina out in the country somewhere. They could spend half the night in the shed.

He calculated how long it would take him to walk out to where the incident had occurred. He wanted to; he wanted to get there and see nothing on the road and to close his eyes in relief. Sometimes dawn had come by the time he parted from Minnie Fennelly, and he imagined that, too, the light beginning as he walked in from the country feeling all right again. But more likely he wouldn't be.

"One day that kid'll be killed," he heard Fitzie Gill saying, and someone else said the woman wasn't up to looking after the kid. The child was left alone in the house, people said, even for a night while the woman drank by herself in Leahy's, looking around for a man to keep her company.

That night, Cahal didn't get back to sleep. And all the next day he waited for someone to walk into the garage and say what had been found. But no one did, and no one did the next day, either, or the day after that. The Spaniards would have gone on from Galway by now, the memories of people who had maybe noticed the Ford Cortina would be getting shaky. And Cahal counted the drivers who he knew for a fact had experienced similar incidents with the child and said to himself that maybe, after all, he'd been fortunate. Even so, it would be a long time before he drove past that cottage again, if ever he did.

Then something happened that changed all that. Sitting with Minnie Fennelly in the Cyber Café one evening, Minnie Fennelly said, "Don't look, only someone's staring at you."

"Who is it?"

"D'you know that dressmaker woman?"

They'd ordered chips and they came just then. Cahal didn't say anything, but knew that sooner or later he wasn't going to be able to prevent himself from looking around. He wanted to ask if the woman had her child with her, but in the town he had only ever seen her on her own and he knew that the child wouldn't be there. If she was, it would be a chance in a thousand, he thought, the apprehension that had haunted him on the night of the incident flooding his consciousness, stifling everything else.

"God, that one gives me the creeps!" Minnie Fennelly muttered, splashing vinegar onto her chips.

Cahal looked round them. He caught a glimpse of the dressmaker, alone, before he quickly looked back. He could still feel her eyes on his back. She would have been in Leahy's; the way she was sitting suggested drunkenness. When they'd finished their chips and the coffee they'd been brought while they were waiting, he asked if she was still there.

"She is, all right. D'you know her? Does she come into the garage?"

"Ah no, she hasn't a car. She doesn't come in."

"I'd best be getting back, Cahal."

He didn't want to go yet, while the woman was there. But if they waited they could be here for hours. He didn't want to pass near her, but as soon as he'd paid and stood up he saw they'd have to. When they did she spoke to Minnie Fennelly, not him.

"Will I make your wedding dress for you?" the dressmaker offered. "Would you think of me at all when it'll be the time you'd want it?"

And Minnie Fennelly laughed and said no way they were ready for wedding dresses yet.

"Cahal knows where he'll find me," the dressmaker said. "Amn't I right, Cahal?"

"I thought you didn't know her," Minnie Fennelly said when they were outside.

Three days after that, Mr. Durcan left his prewar Riley in because the hand brake was slipping. He'd come back for it at four, he arranged, and said before he left, "Did you hear that about the dressmaker's child?"

He wasn't the kind to get things wrong. Fussy, with a thin black mustache, his Riley Sports the pride of his bachelor life, he was as tidy in what he said as he was in how he dressed.

"Gone missing," he said now. "The Gardai are in on it."

It was Cahal's father who was being told this. Cahal, with the cooling system from Gibney's bread van in pieces on a workbench, had just found where the tube had perished.

"She's backward, the child," his father said.

"She is."

"You hear tales."

"She's gone off for herself, anyway. They have a block on a couple of roads, asking was she seen."

The unease that hadn't left him since the dressmaker had been in the Cyber Café began to nag again when Cahal heard that. He wondered what questions the Gardai were asking; he wondered when it was that the child had taken herself off; although he tried, he couldn't piece anything together.

"Isn't she a backward woman herself, though?" his father remarked when Mr. Durcan had gone. "Sure, did she ever lift a finger to tend that child?"

Cahal didn't say anything. He tried to think about marrying Minnie Fennelly, although still nothing was fixed, not even an agreement between themselves. Her plump, honest features became vivid for a moment in his consciousness, the same plumpness in her arms and her hands. He found it attractive, he always had, since first he'd noticed her when she was still going to the nuns. He shouldn't have had thoughts about the Spanish girl, he shouldn't have let himself. He should have told them the statue was nothing, that the man they'd met had been pulling a fast one for the sake of the drinks they'd buy him.

"Your mother had that one run up curtains for the back room," his father said. "Would you remember that, boy?"

Cahal shook his head.

"Ah, you wouldn't have been five at the time, maybe younger yet. She was just after setting up with the dressmaking, her father still there in the cottage with her. The priests said give her work on account she was a charity. Bedad, they wouldn't say it now!"

Cahal turned the radio on and turned the volume up. Madonna was singing, and he imagined her in the getup she'd fancied for herself a few years ago, suspenders and items of underclothes. He'd thought she was great.

"I'm taking the Toyota out," his father said, and the bell from the forecourt rang, someone waiting there for petrol. It didn't concern him, Cahal told himself as he went to answer it. What had occurred on the evening of Germany and Holland was a different thing altogether from the news Mr. Durcan had brought, no way could it be related.

"Howya," he greeted the school-bus driver at the pumps.

The dressmaker's child was found where she'd lain for several days, at the bottom of a fissure, half covered with shale, in the exhausted quarry half a mile from where she'd lived. Years ago the last of the stone had been carted away and a barbed-wire fence put up, with two warning notices about danger. She would have crawled in under the bottom strand of wire, the Gardai said, and a chain-link fence replaced the barbed wire within a day.

In the town the dressmaker was condemned, blamed behind her back for the tragedy that had occurred. That her own father, who had raised her on his own since her mother's early death, had himself been the father of the child was an ugly calumny, not voiced before, but seeming now to have a natural place in the paltry existence of a child who had lived and died wretchedly.

"How are you, Cahal?" Cahal heard the voice of the dressmaker behind him when, early one November morning, he made his way to the shed where he and Minnie Fennelly indulged their affection for one another. It was not yet one o'clock, the town lights long ago extinguished except for a few on Main Street. "Would you come home with me, Cahal? Would we walk out to where I am?"

All this was spoken to his back while Cahal walked on. He knew who was there. He knew who it was; he didn't have to look.

"Leave me alone," he said.

"Many's the night I rest myself on the river seat and many's the night I see you. You'd always be in a hurry, Cahal."

"I'm in a hurry now."

"One o'clock in the morning! Arrah, go on with you, Cahal!"

"I don't know you. I don't want to be talking to you."

"She was gone for five days before I went to the Guards. It wouldn't be the first time she was gone off. A minute wouldn't go by without she was out on the road."

Cahal didn't say anything. Even though he still didn't turn round he could smell the drink on her, stale and acrid.

"I didn't go to them any quicker for fear they'd track down the way it was when the lead would be fresh for them. D'you understand me, Cahal?"

Cahal stopped. He turned round and she almost walked into him. He told her to go away.

"The road was the thing with her. First thing of a morning she'd be running at the cars without a pick of food inside her. The next thing is she'd be off up the road to the statue. She'd kneel to the statue the whole day until she was found by some old fellow who'd bring her back to me. Some old fellow'd have her by the hand and they'd walk in the door. Oh, many's the time, Cahal. Wasn't it the first place the Guards looked when I said that to the sergeant? Any woman'd do her best for her own, Cahal."

"Will you leave me alone!"

"Gone seven it was, maybe twenty past. I had the door open to go in to Leahy's and I seen the black car going by and yourself inside it. You always notice a car in the evening time, only the next thing was I was late back from Leahy's and she was gone. D'you understand me, Cahal?"

"It's nothing to do with me."

"He'd have gone back the same way he went out, I said to myself, but I didn't mention it to the Guards, Cahal. Was she in the way of wandering in her nightdress? was what they asked me and I told them she'd be out the door before you'd see her. Will we go home, Cahal?"

"I'm not going anywhere with you."

"There'd never be a word of blame on yourself, Cahal."

"There's nothing to blame me for. I had people in the car that evening."

"I swear before God, what's happened is done with. Come back with me now, Cahal."

"Nothing happened, nothing's done with. There was Spanish people in the car the entire time. I drove them out to Pouldearg and back again to Macey's Hotel."

"Minnie Fennelly's no use to you, Cahal."

He had never seen the dressmaker up close before. She was younger than he'd thought, but still looked what she was—a fair bit older than himself, maybe twelve or thirteen years. The twist in her face wasn't ugly, but it spoilt what might have been beauty of a kind, and he remembered the flawless beauty of the Spanish girl and the silkiness of her hair. The dressmaker's hair was black, too, but wild and matted, limply straggling, falling to her shoulders. The eyes that had stared so intensely at him in the Cyber Café were bleary. Her full lips were drawn back in a smile, one of her teeth slightly chipped. Cahal walked away and she did not follow him.

That was the beginning; there was no end. In the town, though never again at night, she was always there: Cahal knew that was an illusion, that she wasn't always there but seemed so because her presence on each occasion meant so much. She tidied herself up; she wore dark clothes, which people said were in mourning for her child; and people said she had ceased to frequent Leahy's public house. She was seen painting the front of her cottage, the same blue shade, and tending its bedraggled front garden. She walked from the shops of the town, and never now stood, hand raised, in search of a lift.

Continuing his familiar daily routine of repairs and servicing and answering the petrol bell, Cahal found himself unable to dismiss the connection between them that the dressmaker had made him aware of when she'd walked behind him in the night, and knew that the roots it came from spread and gathered strength and were nurtured, in himself, by fear. Cahal was afraid without knowing what he was afraid of, and when he tried to work this out he was bewildered. He began to go to Mass and to confession more often than he ever had before. It was noticed by his father that he had even less to say these days to the customers at the pumps or when they left their cars in. His mother wondered about his being anemic and put him on iron pills. Returning for a couple of days at a weekend, his sister who was still in Ireland said the trouble must surely be to do with Minnie Fennelly.

During all this time—passing in other ways quite normally—the child was lifted again and again from the cleft in the rocks, still in her nightdress as Cahal had seen her, laid out and wrapped as the dead are wrapped. If he hadn't had to change the wheel he would have passed the cottage at a different time and the chances were she wouldn't have been ready to run out, wouldn't just then have felt inclined to. If he'd explained to the Spaniards about the Virgin's tears being no more than rain he wouldn't have been on the road at all.

The dressmaker did not speak to him again or seek to, but he knew that the fresh blue paint, and the mourning clothes that were not, with time, abandoned, and the flowers that came to fill the small front garden were all for him. When a little more than a year had passed since the evening he'd driven the Spanish couple out to Pouldearg, he attended Minnie Fennelly's wedding to Des Downey, a vet from Athenry.

The dressmaker had not said it, but it was what there had been between them in the darkened streets: that he had gone back, walking out as he had wanted to that night when he'd lain awake, that her child had been there where she had fallen on the road, that he had carried her to the quarry. And Cahal knew it was the dressmaker, not he, who had done that.

He visited the Virgin, always expecting that she might be there. He knelt, and asked for nothing. He spoke only in his thoughts, offering reparation and promising to accept whatever might be visited upon him for associating himself with the mockery of the man the Spaniards had met by chance in Dublin, for mocking the lopsided image on the road, taking fifty euros for a lie. He had looked at them kissing. He had thought about Madonna with her clothes off, not minding that she called herself that.

Once when he was at Pouldearg Cahal noticed the glisten of what had once been taken for tears on the Virgin's cheek. He touched the hollow where this moisture had accumulated and raised his dampened finger to his lips. It did not taste of salt, but that made no difference. Driving back, when he went by the dressmaker's blue cottage she was there in the front garden, weeding her flower beds. Even though she didn't look up, he wanted to go to her and knew that one day he would.

Stephanie Reents

Disquisition on Tears

A NEW NOISE captured my attention: the sound of someone driving a nail into sheet metal. I couldn't stop listening to it, and I couldn't stop shaking. Each time the nail was struck, vibrations moved from my head, down through my arms and legs, out the tips of my toes and fingers and into the air. I glanced around the living room, expecting to see ordinary objects like the coffee table and the bookshelves and the fringed lamp shade reflecting the way I felt, but everything seemed normal, except for the woman in the African batik whose beaded headdress began to streak like tears down her head and neck. I closed my eyes, and the pounding continued for what seemed like hours until gradually the sound became gentler, and I realized that it was noon, and someone was knocking.

Very few people came to my door because my house was hidden. It was off the street, across a gravel lot, and through a gate that swelled in the heat and rain and would not budge unless you threw your weight against it. The path from the gate to the house was blocked by an overgrown pomegranate bush covered with rotting fruit that had been recently infested with small black bugs. When I left the fruit unpicked, I imagined flocks of dark birds covering the small bush and pecking at the dry husks. The person at my door had most likely walked underneath the pomegranate bush, oblivious to the threat of the bugs raining down, not that this had happened, but I imagined it happening. I had grown accustomed to always expecting the worst, except for the flock of birds, which would have been beautiful, like a handful of confetti suspended in the sky.

I eased myself up from the couch. My pants felt damp, and I realized that I had wet myself while I was captivated by the noise. This was not unusual; the pain that pinned me to the couch was so intense that I often lost control of different things. It was as though my body still wept, even though I no longer cried.

Through the front window, I saw a woman without a head. I pressed my knuckles into my eyes, hoping that when the static cleared she would be gone, though I didn't count on it. In my experience, the universe was more apt to bring things than to take them away, and just as I expected, the woman remained. Her shoulders were like an empty table, an unexpected horizontal line. Her T-shirt wasn't crooked even though she had no neck to anchor it. I squinted. In one hand, she cradled her head as if it were a baby while with the other, she rapped steadily on the door. Suddenly, she stopped knocking and lifted her head up to the screen and swiveled it back and forth, taking everything in.

"Hello," she said. "Anyone home?"

I screamed.

"Am I catching you at a bad time?" she asked, as if by screaming, I'd told her nothing more than that she was inconveniencing me. "I can come back. . . ."

I tiptoed back to the couch, but behind me I heard the door opening. I screamed again.

"I can come back," the woman repeated, now standing in my living room in front of a poster of impressionistic, pastel-colored sunbathers that my nurse had brought to cheer things up.

I turned and faced her. She was holding her head in both hands and nodding it up and down. There was a chance I could escape; though I moved as if the ground shifted beneath me like choppy water, she would surely be slowed by having to navigate without her head in its normal place.

"If there's a better time . . ." She trailed off.

She was so polite that I started to feel inhospitable. And also curious. The truth was, I wanted her to go away. But I also wanted to know how she got by. She reminded me of a blind man I'd met in Boise, Idaho, who took photographs. He didn't even pretend he could see; he usually held his camera right under his chin or above his head. When the film was developed, he asked people to describe the pictures to him. "I had a sense," he'd say about every image. He photographed me eating lunch. I was having a bad year, but that day was especially bad because I couldn't stop thinking about the MRI the following week, when I'd find out whether any new tumors had germinated in my skull. I was wearing a silk scarf, instead of the long, red wig that everyone admired, because it was very hot in Boise, the hottest week on record since the summer of 1927. The next day, the blind man appeared at my table where I was trying to stay cool by sipping tea, and handed me a white envelope. "I have a sense that you're sad," he said. "But melancholia is exquisite." We talked for a while, and later, we went to bed. Often, before I had an MRI, I'd wind up in bed with someone—sometimes a stranger, sometimes a friend around whom I'd been too shy—aroused by my fear that it could be my last intimate act. It was like breakup sex, my friends teased, except that it wasn't like that at all. The blind man played the flute beautifully, but as far as the sex went, he was clumsy and rough.

When I woke up after our lovemaking, he handed me a photograph: "Tell me what you see here," he said. The picture was bright and blank, as if he had pointed his camera at the sun or the surface of a lake. I had a terrible feeling that this was what the blind man saw, but that he couldn't put it into words since it was the only thing he'd ever seen. "Why are you leaving?" he inquired when he heard me snapping my shirt. "Not disturbing, is it?" It scared me to tell him that it was both dark and bright at the same time, nothing and something. I had enough problems of my own.

Meanwhile, of course, the woman was waiting.

"Hey," she called, impatience edging into her voice. "I can come back. Tell me when would be good for you, and I'll come back." She shook her head in an exasperated way. Her brow scrunched together, and she moved the head both up and down and sideways. I thought of how long it must have taken to master that gesture with her hands, instead of her neck.

"Why are you here?" I finally asked. "Was I expecting you?"

"We had an appointment," she answered. She kept the head very still, but I could tell from the way her shoulders jumped that she was upset. "I'll check my calendar to confirm the time and date. . . ." She trailed off.

"I believe you," I said, even though I didn't. I had a terrible premonition that she was peddling something, like knives, and that her head was a prop that she would use in her sales routine. I imagined her pitch: "I'll cut off my head before your very eyes. Slides through gristle, clean as a whistle."

"Can I bring my cooler in?" she asked. "I'll need it."

"Sure."

She was silent, concentrating, I guess, on getting herself back into the house. I should have offered to help her, but I didn't think it was my responsibility. Finally, when she was seated, with the cooler at her feet and her head in her lap, she said, "That's much better. But it's a bit dark in here."

It was strange to see the head lodged in the V of her legs and tilted back, looking both up and forward, as if it belonged to a body lying in a dentist's chair.

"It's because you've been outside in the sun," I answered. "Your eyes will adjust."

"They won't actually. My pupils don't dilate. It's a rare condition. Not that it's terribly severe, but it can be a nuisance. The worst part is that I can't see in the dark. In fact, I prefer light of the kind that today has brought us. Bright, glaring light. Then everything appears crystal clear."

"Can you see me?" I asked.

The woman tilted the head forward. "No, can you say something again, please?"

"I'm without hair," I said, because I had forgotten the word to describe myself.

"Bald?" She turned the head slightly so that it was more or less looking in my direction. "I can see the outline of you. But your features are blurry. Is there a reason you can't turn on a light or two? It would help me immensely."

My hands twisted into a knot in my lap. Before this woman's arrival, I'd been trying to remember something about the type of car that I'd rented in Spain ten years ago. My friend Lilly and I had driven around Spain for over a month in the kind of car that didn't have a top. It was frustrating. I could remember the feeling of the wind in my hair, as if a giant hand were collecting my hair in a ponytail, and I could recall the smells, the hot brittleness of southern Spain, and the heaviness of Barcelona, and I could see the straw colored fields that ran to the edges of the walled towns. One of them boasted a Roman aqueduct built without a speck of mortar. I couldn't fathom how I could remember such an odd and unnecessary word like aqueduct, but it was lodged in my head along with ambivalent, catatonic, deracinate, contumacious, petard, noctilucent, leman, fillip, and countless other words that I once memorized for standardized tests, but never used in conversation. These words were like packing peanuts in my brain, burying the real goods (like the word for a car without a top) so deep that I'd never be able to pull them out. Each day, I seemed to spend more time up to my elbows in the box, senselessly grasping at anything I could touch.

I had thought about calling Lilly before my headache came and asking her about the car, but I had bothered her last week, phoning her up to find out the word to describe her and her sister, people who are born at the same time to the same mother: twins, she blurted out. Then she said she had to run, but she would call back soon. You could say I was a twin: me before the tumors, and me after. If you looked closely at pictures of her (minus the hair), the resemblance was there, especially in the eyes. Our personalities had diverged, though. She wore high, strappy heels and danced all night, made decisions in a blink, laughed until she cried, and enjoyed noisy arguments. I had turned into an introvert. I padded around in ballet slippers that my mother gave me and worried that it was obvious when I wore diapers. My life had slowed down.

I reluctantly turned on a light.

"Is that better?"

"Yes, now I can see."

"What business do we have?" I asked.

"You told me you wanted a disquisition on tears."

Here was another word I knew, disquisition. A perfectly useless word that was an obstacle to remembering the term for a car without a top. "Why did I want that?"

"You didn't say. You called and made an appointment. I've spent over three days doing the research. But if you're not feeling well, I understand, and we can make an appointment for another day."

I could tell that the woman was lying. Her shoulders were bunched together again, and the head in her lap was biting its lips.

"You're feeling uncomfortable?" she said. "If you're feeling the slightest bit uncomfortable, I can put on my head pack. Would that be easier for you?"

It was true. I didn't know where to look when she was speaking. My natural inclination was to focus on her shoulders, but her head wasn't there.

"Would it be inconvenient?"

"Not at all. Notatall," she said in a slightly more jaunty voice. "Usually I do put it on, but for some reason, I didn't this morning."

I suddenly wondered how she drove. Maybe mounted on the steering wheel was a giant head-sized cup. "When did I call?" I had no recollection of calling her, but it was possible that I had called and forgotten. This happened with increasing frequency—conversations were being misfiled in my short-term memory, or disappearing completely, just as the birds would have vanished after lighting on the pomegranate tree and picking it clean.

She giggled, placing her hand over her mouth. The gesture was so strange and small. The whole point of giggling into your hand was bringing your hand all the way from your lap to your mouth. This gesture was abbreviated.

"What's so funny?" I asked.

"The way you're dressed. That heavy coat on a hot day like this. Now that I can see, I couldn't help but notice."

It was true I was wearing my winter parka. The hood was trimmed with fur, though I was not so cold that I had pulled it up. The inside of my house felt cool, but outside, where it was so hot that Popsicles melted before you could take a bite, it was blindingly, head-achingly bright.

"And your socks." I was wearing socks with toes like the fingers of mittens. The woman pointed at them with one hand and with the other she jiggled her head as if she were convulsing with laughter. The head turned bright red and coughed, sputtering saliva. "Oh dear me," she said, pounding her chest. "Oh dear me. I think I may be choking." She spluttered on. "Would. You. Be. Kind. Enough. To. Get. Me." While her torso shook, her head froze. Her eyes opened as wide as a mannequin's, and her mouth twisted, as if someone playing a practical joke had put her lips on sideways. I had a terrible premonition that if she didn't stop choking she might die in my living room.

I went to the kitchen for a glass of water. Moving made me realize that I had a rash like fine sandpaper on my butt from sitting in my wet underpants. I considered going into the bathroom to shed my damp clothes and apply talcum powder or a soothing cream, but I was afraid it would take too long. The bathroom was dizzying with all of its similarly shaped containers. I might accidentally slather toothpaste on my butt, in which case I'd have to scrub it off, thus aggravating the rash. Such mishaps had happened before. Once I had brushed my teeth with A and D ointment; another time, I had squirted nasal decongestant into my eyes. In another context, these mix-ups might have made amusing anecdotes, but in the context of my cancer they weren't—at least not to others. I might laugh to death about them privately, but that was no fun.

I almost forgot about the woman, but then I saw the glass of water in my hand and I remembered and returned to the living room.

The woman brought it to her mouth, like a blind person using memory rather than sight. Cupping her head right beneath the chin, she tilted the glass, dribbling tiny sips into her open lips. I glanced away; it was as if I was watching something very private, like a mother nursing a baby or a bald woman being fitted with a wig.

"Thank you," she said. "I haven't laughed that much in years. My lung capacity isn't what it used to be."

I looked at her in disbelief. "Leave," I said.

Her face was still red, but her mouth was working just fine. Circling her lips into an O, she brought her hands to her temples and gripped her head like she was putting it in a vise. Again, it was a gesture that didn't work and was so wrong I wanted to laugh aloud.

"You're a headless freak," I said, hoping to offend her as much as she had offended me and drive her away.

"Tell me something I don't know." She giggled.

"You're a fright," I said. "There should be a law requiring you to wear a prosthetic device."

"And you're a fright, too," she answered. "Sitting alone in your house day after day."

"I have my reasons," I said. "I'm very sick, and it's difficult for me to leave."

"Why don't people take you out?"

"They do when they have time. But people are busy."

"Don't you have friends?"

I stopped to consider her question. It was true that I did have friends, but when I got sick and the tumors persisted against the doctors' aggressive attacks upon them, the friendships became difficult. I suspected that many of my friends thought I was going to die, and pretending that I was not going to die was a burden too heavy for them to carry. It was true that for a long time, I thought I was going to live. So shoot me. I was alive, and I thought I'd keep living. Also, I stopped calling them; it was so tiring trying to comfort them.

The phone rang.

"Aren't you going to get it?" the woman asked.

"No," I said.

"It's probably one of your friends," she said.

I didn't answer.

The phone continued to ring. I had gotten rid of my machine because the little red eye, staring at me without blinking, reminded me that I was always home. I didn't wish to abandon the idea that I might have been out doing fabulously fun things, if I had only gotten the calls. Which was why I didn't answer the phone, especially when I was focused on plucking my eyebrows into extinction, hair by hair.

I was missing half of one eyebrow, but I was lucky to have any eyebrows at all. "Your body's holding on to its vanity," a doctor had chuckled, and I had laughed too, not because I understood the joke, but because it was good to share laughter with someone.

"I can't stand to hear it ring," she said. "How can you bear it?"

"Look," I said, "when I finally came to terms with the fact that I was going to die, many of my friends, who thought I was going to die much earlier, had stopped being my friends. It sounds cruel, and at first I thought it was, but they were living, moving on, and I interfered with this."

"What about your other friends?" the woman asked.

"They're still my friends because they've always believed that I'll live," I said. "And when I was still optimistic, this suited me, but now their hopefulness fits me like old clothes."

The woman stood up and was heading toward the phone when it stopped. She sat back down. "No wonder you're by yourself."

"It was probably my father," I answered.

Her eyes lit up. For emphasis, she grabbed her head and moved it in my direction, as if scrutinizing me. "Your father? Does he live in town?"

"Indonesia. He has a coconut grove." This was obviously a lie. My father had been dead for ten years. My mother lived several states away, and after lengthy negotiations, she had agreed to leave me alone until I absolutely needed her. It was easier on both of us.

"Right," she said, clearly indicating that she didn't believe me. "Does he use a long bamboo pole to knock coconuts from the trees?"

She laughed. She was cradling her head in her hands again, rolling it back and forth like a basketball. Suddenly, I had a sick feeling that she was going to toss her head and expect me to catch it. Because my eye-hand coordination had been damaged with my third surgery, I knew I would miss it, and when I missed it, I didn't know whether her head would bounce like a basketball, explode like a ripe tomato, dent like a cheap aluminum pot, or get scrambled like the brain of a carelessly shaken baby.

And what would happen to her body if her head were lying on the floor? How would she find it?

I started to sniffle.

"Ah ha," the woman said in a way that suggested she had caught me doing something naughty, "over the phone you said that you no longer cried. But I knew you were lying."

My own head began to hurt again. I could feel the pain pulsing like a sound wave from a small node buried in my front temporal lobe.

"Did you know," she said, "that crying is like urinating, defecating, or exhaling, that it rids the body of its waste and pain? Did you know that there is a difference in the chemical composition of tears that you shed when you're peeling an onion and those that fall when you're feeling sad or distressed? In a study of normal men and women, researchers found that women cry five times as often as men, that the typical teary episode lasts six minutes, that people are most likely to cry in the evening when they let down their guards, that there is no correlation between crying and age, except that babies younger than two months old do not shed tears because their tear ducts are not fully formed. Were you aware of this? Were you aware of any of this?"

She lifted her head from her lap, her thumbs pressed into her ears, and offered it to me like a gift. But then I realized the gesture was a rhetorical flourish, an exclamation point at the end of her speech.

"Now," she continued, "I want to show you something."

She carefully placed her head back into the valley of her legs and opened the cooler. I wondered whether she was going to feed me. Offering food—casseroles, cold cuts, homemade cookies—was one of the few ways that people were comfortable expressing their care. I hoped she would.

She removed a small plastic container. Dip? I wondered. Perhaps she'd prepare crudités? I liked everything, except for celery, whose strings got tangled in my teeth.

"This is onion dip," she said.

I eagerly peeled back the lid, but was surprised to find nothing but an inch of colorless liquid.

"Onion tears," she said, and then I realized I had misheard her. "Smell them, and tell me what they remind you of."

"Nothing," I said, "except perhaps an old, plastic margarine container."

She laughed. "And now smell this: brimming tears, most typical of the crying behavior of the human male."

I stuck my nose into the container. "These are familiar," I said, thinking for a moment. "They remind me of something from my childhood, the mixture of hot water and salt that my mother made when I'd hurt myself."

"Epsom salts," she said. "Exactly. And now this: cascading tears, a normal sign of women's pain and suffering."

The scent of the liquid was cloying, like the breath of a woman who kept her lips pressed together and rarely spoke. My visitor handed me another container: sobbing tears that smelled like a pot boiling over and bursting into flames. It was difficult for me to believe that all the containers fit into the small cooler, and that they held so many different types of tears: of willful toddlers, of irritation caused by small bugs and grains of sand, of yawns and sneezes, of fear, of silent weeping, of rage and disappointment, of crocodiles and other forms of fakery. She handed me container after container, and each one smelled like something that came to me in words that I found in my head and brought to the tip of my tongue without a thought. It was the first time in months I hadn't gotten terribly stuck in the middle of trying to remember something.

"I've saved the best for last," she said.

"We're at the end?" I asked, feeling a bit sad and disappointed.

Her head deflated slightly, like a balloon with a slow leak, or the way faces look early in the morning before they've regained their shape.

"I'm afraid so," she answered. "Lacrimae mortis."

The container was the size of a baby food jar, and there was barely a teaspoon of liquid in the bottom.

"This is rare, very difficult to collect."

I sniffed it gingerly. The liquid smelled of hospital, like brightly lit ammonia and anonymous starched sheets and uniforms, like the humiliation of the bedpan and the toilet bowl, like sapped blood, like an electric razor when it overheats, like bouquets with too much baby's breath and the distance between the sky and the window when you're not allowed outside, like greasy telephone receivers and plastic IV veins, like the staleness of the television playing for too long. The smell was so simple, so familiar, so disappointing. The pain got louder, and the container tipped, the drops of tears spilling across my lap as if I had wet myself again. I closed my eyes and concentrated. Someone was knocking somewhere, and I listened.

David Means

Sault Ste. Marie

E RNIE DUG in with the tip of his penknife, scratching a line into the plastic top of the display case, following the miniature lock system as it stepped down between Lake Superior and Lake Huron. At the window, Marsha ignored us both and stood blowing clouds of smoke at the vista . . . a supertanker rising slowly in the lock, hefted by water . . . as if it mattered that the system was fully functioning and freight was moving up and down the great seaway. As if it mattered that ore was being transported from the hinterlands of Duluth (a nullifyingly boring place) to the eastern seaboard and points beyond. As if it mattered that the visitor's center stood bathed in sunlight, while behind the gift counter an old lady sat reading a paperback and doing her best to ignore the dry scratch of Ernie's knife, raising her rheumy eyes on occasion, reaching up to adjust her magnificent hair with the flat of her hand.—I'm gonna go see that guy I know, Tull, about the boat I was telling you about, Ernie announced, handing me the knife. He tossed his long black hair to the side, reached into his pants, yanked out his ridiculously long-barreled .44 Remington Magnum, pointed it at the lady, and said,—But first I'm going to rob this old bag.— Stick 'em up, he said, moving toward the lady, who stared over the top of her paperback. Her face was ancient; the skin drooped from her jaw, and on her chin bits of hair collected faintly into something that looked like a Vandyke. A barmaid beauty remained in her face, along with a stony resilience. Her saving feature was a great big poof of silvery hair that rose like a nest and stood secured by an arrangement of bobby pins and a very fine hairnet.—Take whatever you want, she said in a husky voice, lifting her hands out in a gesture of offering.—As a matter of fact, shoot me if you feel inclined. It's not going to matter to me. I'm pushing eighty. I've lived the life I'm going to live and I've seen plenty of things and had my heart broken and I've got rheumatoid arthritis in these knuckles so bad I can hardly hold a pencil to paper. (She lifted her hand and turned it over so we could see the claw formation of her fingers.)—And putting numbers into the cash register is painful.—Jesus Christ, Ernie said, shooting you would just be doing the world a favor, and too much fun, and he tucked the gun back in his pants, adjusted the hem of his shirt, and went to find this guy with the boat. Marsha maintained her place at the window, lit another cigarette, and stared at the boat while I took Ernie's knife from the top of the display case and began scratching where he left off. Finished with the matter, the old lady behind the gift counter raised the paperback up to her face and began reading. Outside, the superfreighter rose with leisure; it was one of those long ore boats, a football field in length, with guys on bicycles making the journey from bow to stern. There was probably great beauty in its immensity, in the way it emerged from the lower parts of the seaway, lifted by the water. But I didn't see it. At that time in my life, it was just one more industrial relic in my face.

A few minutes later, when Ernie shot the guy named Tull in the parking lot, the gun produced a tight little report that bounced off the side of the freighter that was sitting up in the lock, waiting for the go-ahead. The weight line along the ship's hull was far above the visitor's station; below the white stripe, the skin of the hull was shoddy with flakes of rust and barnacle scars. The ship looked ashamed of itself exposed for the whole world to see, like a lady with her skirt blown up. The name on the bow, in bright white letters, was HENRY JACKMAN. Looking down at us, a crew member raised his hand against the glare. What he saw was a sad scene: a ring of blue gunsmoke lingering around the guy Ernie shot, who was muttering the word fuck and bowing down while blood pooled around his crotch. By the time we scrambled to the truck and got out of there, he was trembling softly on the pavement, as if he were trying to limbo-dance under an impossibly low bar. I can assure you now, the guy didn't die that morning. A year later we came face-to-face at an amusement park near

Bay City, and he looked perfectly fine, strapped into a contraption that would—a few seconds after our eyes met—roll him into a triple corkscrew at eighty miles an hour. I like to imagine that the roller-coaster ride shook his vision of me into an aberration that stuck in his mind for the rest of his earthly life.

For what it's worth, the back streets of Sault Ste. Marie, Michigan, were made of concrete with nubs of stone mixed in, crisscrossed with crevices, passing grand old homes fallen into disrepair—homes breathing the smell of mildew and dry rot from their broken windows. Ernie drove with his hand up at the noon position while the police sirens wove through the afternoon heat behind us. The sound was frail, distant, and meaningless. We'd heard the same thing at least a dozen times in the past three weeks, from town to town, always respectfully distant, unraveling, twisting around like a smoke in a breeze until it disappeared. Ernie had a knack for guiding us out of bad situations. We stuck up a convenience store, taking off with fifty bucks and five green-and-white cartons of menthol cigarettes. Then a few days later we hog-tied a liquor-store clerk and made off with a box of Cutty Sark and five rolls of Michigan Scratch-Off Lotto tickets. Under Ernie's leadership, we tied up our victims with bravado, in front of the fish-eyed video monitors, our heads in balaclavas. We put up the V sign and shouted: Liberation for all! For good measure, we turned to the camera and yelled: Patty Hearst lives! The next morning the *Detroit Free Press* Sunday edition carried a photo, dramatically smudgy, of the three of us bent and rounded off by the lens, with our guns in the air. The accompanying article speculated on our significance. According to the article, we were a highly disciplined group with strong connections to California, our gusto and verve reflecting a nationwide resurgence of Weathermen-type radicals.—A place to launch the boat will provide itself, Ernie said, sealing his lips around his dangling cigarette and pulling in smoke. Marsha rooted in the glove box and found a flaying knife, serrated and brutal-looking, with a smear of dried blood on the oak handle. She handed it to me, dug around some more, and found a Baggie with pills, little blue numbers; a couple of bright reds, all mystery and portent. She spun it around a few times and then gave out a long yodel that left our ears tingling. Marsha was a champion yodeler. Of course we popped the pills and swallowed them dry while Ernie raged through the center of town, running two red lights, yanking the boat behind us like an afterthought. Marsha had her feet on the dash, and her hair tangled beautifully around her eyes and against her lips. It was the best feeling in the world to be running from the law with a boat in tow, fishtailing around corners, tossing our back wheels into the remnants of the turn, rattling wildly over the potholes, roaring through a shithole town that was desperately trying to stay afloat in the modern world and finding itself sinking deeper into squalor beneath a sky that unfurled blue and deep. All this along with drugs that were, thank Christ, swiftly going about their perplexing work, turning the whole show inside out and making us acutely aware of the fact that above all we were nothing much more than a collection of raw sensations. Marsha's legs emerging beautiful from her fringed cutoff shorts—the shorts are another story—and her bare toes, with her nails painted cherry red, wiggling in the breeze from the window. The seaway at the bottom of the street, spread out in front of a few lonely houses, driftwood gray, rickety and grand, baking in the summer heat. They crackled with dryness. They looked ready to explode into flames. They looked bereft of all hope. In front of a Victorian, a single dog, held taut by a long length of rope, barked and tried to break free, turning and twisting and looping the full circumference of his plight. We parked across the street, got out of the truck, and looked at him while he, in turn, looked back. He was barking SOS. Over and over again. Bark bark bark. Bark bark bark. Bark bark bark. Bark bark bark. Bark bark bark. Until finally Ernie yanked his gun from his belt, pointed quickly, with both hands extended for stability, and released a shot that materialized as a burst of blooming dust near the dog; then another shot that went over his head and splintered a porch rail. The dog stopped barking and the startled air glimmered, got brighter, shiny around the edges, and then fell back into the kind of dull haze you find only in small towns in summer, with no one around but a dog who has finally lost the desire to bark. The dog sat staring at us. He was perfectly fine but stone-still. Out in the water a container ship stood with solemnity, as if dumbfounded by its own passage, covered in bright green tarps.—We're gonna drop her right here, Ernie said, unleashing the boat, throwing back restraining straps, trying to look like he knew what he was doing. The water was a five-foot fall from the corrugated steel and poured cement buttress of the wall. The Army Corps of Engineers had constructed a breakwall of ridiculous proportions. We lifted the hitch, removed it from the ball, and wiggled the trailer over so that the bow of the boat hung over the edge. Then without consultation—working off the mutual energies of our highs—we lifted the trailer and spilled the boat over the edge. It landed in the water with a plop, worked hard to right itself, coming to terms with its new place in the world, settling back as Ernie manipulated the rope and urged it along to some ladder rungs. To claim this was anything but a love story would be to put Sault Ste. Marie in a poor light. The depleted look in the sky and the sensation of the pills working in our bloodstream, enlivening the water, the slap and pop of the metal hull over the waves. The superfreighter (the one with green tarps) looming at our approach. To go into those details too much would be to bypass the essential fact of the matter. I was deeply in love with Marsha. Nothing else in the universe mattered. I would have killed for her, I would have swallowed the earth like an egg-eating snake. I would have turned inside out in my own skin. I was certain that I might have stepped from the boat and walked on the water, making little shuffling movements, conserving my energy, doing what Jesus did but only better. Jesus walked on water to prove a point. I would have done it for the hell of it. Just for fun. To prove my love. Up at the bow Ernie stood with his heel on the gunwale, one elbow resting on a knee, looking like the figurehead on a Viking ship. I sat in the back with Marsha, watching as she held the rubber grip and guided the motor with her suspiciously well-groomed fingers. I could see in the jitteriness of her fingers that she was about to swing the boat violently to the side. Maybe not as some deeply mean-spirited act but just as a joke on Ernie, who was staring straight ahead, making little hoots, patting his gun, and saying,—We're coming to get you. We're gonna high-jack us a motherfucking superfreighter, boys. I put my hand over Marsha's and held it there. Her legs, caught in the fringed grip of her tight cutoff jeans, were gleaming with spray. (She'd amputated the pants back in a hotel in Manistee, laying them over her naked thighs while we watched, tweaking the loose threads out to make them just right.) Tiny beads of water clung to the downy hairs along the top of her thighs, fringed with her cutoff jeans, nipping and tucking up into her crotch. Who knows? Maybe she was looking at my legs, too, stretched against her own, the white half-moon of my knees poking through the holes in my jeans. When I put my hand over hers I felt our forces conjoin into a desire to toss Ernie overboard.

. . . .

Two nights later we were alone in an old motel, far up in the nether regions of the Upper Peninsula, near the town of Houghton, where her friend Charlene had OD'ed a few years back. Same hotel, exactly. Same room, too. She'd persuaded me that she had to go and hold a wake for her dead friend. (—I gotta go to the same hotel, she said.—The same room.) The hotel was frequented mainly by sailors, merchant-marine types, a defiled place with soggy rank carpet padding and dirty towels. In bed we finished off a few of Tull's pills. Marsha was naked, resting on her side as she talked to me in a solemn voice about Charlene and how much they had meant to each other one summer, and how, when her own father was on a rage, they would go hide out near the airport, along the fence out there, hanging out and watching the occasional plane arrive, spinning its propellers wildly and making tipping wing gestures as if in a struggle to conjure the elements of flight. Smoking joints and talking softly, they poured out secrets the way only stoner girls can—topping each other's admissions, one after the other, matter-of-factly saying yeah, I did this guy who lived in Detroit and was a dealer and he, like, he like was married and we took his car out to the beach and spent two days doing it. Listening to her talk, it was easy to imagine the two of them sitting out there in the hackweed and elderberry on cooler summer nights, watching the silent airstrips, cracked and neglected, waiting for the flight from Chicago. I'd spent my own time out in that spot. It was where Marsha and I figured out that we were bound by coincidence: our fathers had both worked to their deaths in the paint booth at Fisher Body, making sure the enamel was spread evenly, suffering from the gaps in their masks, from inhaled solvents, and from producing quality automobiles.

I was naked on the bed with Marsha, slightly buzzed, but not stoned out of my sense of awareness. I ran my hand along her hip and down into the concave smoothness of her waist while she, in turn, reached around and pawed and cupped my ass, pulling me forward against her as she cried softly in my ear, just wisps of breath, about nothing in particular except that we were about to have sex. I was going to roll her over softly, expose her ass, find myself against her, and then press my lips to her shoulder blades as I sank in. When I got to that point, I became aware of the ashen cinder-block smell of the hotel room, the rubber of the damp carpet padding, the walls smeared with mildew, and the large russet stains that marked the dripping zone inside the tub and along the upper rim of the toilet. Outside, the hotel—peeling pink stucco, with a pale blue slide curling into an empty pool—stood along an old road, a logging route, still littered with the relics of a long-past tourist boom. The woods across from the place were thick with undergrowth, and the gaps between trees seemed filled with the dark matter of interstellar space. When we checked in it was just past sunset, but the light was already drawn away by the forest. It went on for miles and miles. Just looking at it too long would be to get lost, to wander in circles. You could feel the fact that we were far up along the top edge of the United States; the north pole began its pull around there, and the aurora borealis spread across the sky. I like to think that we both came out of our skin, together, in one of those orgasmic unifications. I like to think that two extremely lonely souls—both fearing that they had just killed another human being—united themselves carnally for some wider, greater sense of the universe; I like to think that maybe for one moment in my life, I reached up and ran my hand through God's hair. But who knows? Who really knows? The truth remains lodged back in that moment, and that moment is gone, and all I can honestly attest to is that we did feel a deep affection for our lost comrade Ernie at the very moment we were both engaged in fornication. (That's the word Ernie used: I'd like to fornicate with that one over there, or I'm going to find me some fornication.) We lay on the bed and let the breeze come through the hotel window—cool and full of yellow pine dust—across our damp bellies. The air of northern Michigan never quite matches the freshness of Canada. There's usually a dull iron-ore residue in it, or the smell of dead flies accumulating between the stones on shore. Staring up at the ceiling, Marsha felt compelled to talk about her dead friend. She lit a smoke and took a deep inhalation and let it sift from between her teeth. (I was endlessly attracted to the big unfixed gap-tooth space between her two front ones.) Here's the story she told me in as much detail as I can muster:

Charlene was a hard-core drifter, born in Sarnia, Ontario, across the lake from Port Huron. Her grandmother on her mother's side raised her, except for a few summers—the ones in our town—with her deranged autoworker father. She was passed on to her grandfather on her father's side for some reason, up in Nova Scotia. Her grandfather was an edgy, hard drinker who abused her viciously. Along her ass were little four-leaf-clover scar formations. She ran away from her grandfather, back to her grandmother in Sarnia, and then ran away from her and crossed the International Bridge to Detroit, where she hooked up with a guy named Stan, a maintenance worker at a nursing home, who fixed air conditioners and cleared dementia-plugged toilets. Stan was into cooking crank in his spare time. They set up a lab in a house near Dearborn, in a pretty nice neighborhood, actually. Then one day there was an explosion and Stan got a face full of battery acid. She left him behind and hooked up with another cooker, named King, who had a large operation in a house near Saginaw. She worked with him and helped out, but she never touched the stuff and was angelic and pious about it. Even King saw a kind of beauty in Charlene's abstinence, Marsha said. For all the abuse she had suffered she had a spiritual kind of calm. Her eyes were, like, this amazingly deep blue color. Aside from her scars and all, she still had the whitest, purest skin, Snow White skin, the kind that you just want to touch, like a cool smooth stone. She just got more and more beautiful until eventually the guy named King couldn't stand the gentleness in her eyes and, maybe to try to change things around, he started to beat her face like a punching bag. One afternoon, under the influence of his own product, he had a couple of friends hold her down while he struck her face with a meat pounder, just hammered it, until she was close to death—maybe actually dead. Maybe she left her body and floated above herself and looked down and saw a guy with long shaggy hair and a silver meat hammer bashing her face in and decided it just wasn't worth dying in that kind of situation and so went back into her body. (Marsha was pretty firm in her belief about this part.) Charlene's cheekbones were broken, her teeth shattered. It took about twenty operations on her jaw and teeth just to chew again. Even then, chewing never felt right; her fake teeth slipped from the roof of her mouth, she talked funny, and a ringing sounded in her ears when she tried to smile. When she laughed too hard, her mouth would clamp up and she'd hear a chiming sound, high in pitch, like bells, and then the sound of windswept rain, or wind in a shell, or wind through guy wires, or a dry, dusty windswept street, or the rustling of tissue paper, or a sizzling like a single slice of bacon in a pan, or a dial tone endlessly unwinding in her eardrum. Forever she was up over herself looking down, watching King go at her, the two guys holding onto her shoulders, her legs scissor-kicking, the flash of the hammer until it was impossible to know what was going on beneath the blood. When Marsha met her again—a year or so later, in the break room at Wal-Mart, she had this weirdly deranged face; the out-of-place features demanded some thought to put straight. I mean it was a mess, Marsha said. Her nose was folded over. The Detroit team of plastic and oral surgeons just couldn't put poor Charlene back together again. A total Humpty Dumpty. No one was going to spend large amounts of money on a face of a drifter, anyway. Marsha forced herself to look. Then Charlene told her the story of King, the reasons for the damage, and the whole time Marsha didn't remove her eyes from the nose, the warped cheeks, the fishlike mouth. She tried as hard as she could to see where the beauty had gone and what Charlene must've been like before King mashed her face, the angelic part, because she kind of doubted her on that part of the story. As far as she could remember, from their nights together getting stoned outside the airport fence, Charlene had been, well, just a normal-looking kid. But listening to her talk, she put the pieces together and saw that, yeah, yeah, yeah, maybe this mishmash of features had once been beautiful. Her eyes were certainly bright blue, and wide, and she had pale milky skin. That night after work they decided to go out together, not to a bar where she'd get hassled but just to buy some beer and go to Charlene's apartment and drink. She had some little pills she called goners, good God goners, something like that. So they went to her apartment, took the pills, drank some beer, and decided to watch *Blue Velvet*. Whatever transpired next, according to Marsha, was amazing and incredibly sensual; they were stoned together, watching the movie, and suddenly between them there grew a hugely powerful sense of closeness; when Marsha looked down at her on the couch, Charlene appeared to her too gorgeous not to kiss (that's how she put it, exactly). Her mouth was funny because her teeth were out, so it was just softness and nothing else, and then, somehow, they undressed—I mean it wasn't like a first for either of us, Marsha said—and she fell down between Charlene's knees, and made her come, and then they spent the night together. A few days later, Charlene quit her job and split for Canada, back over the bridge, and then the next thing Marsha heard she was up north at this hotel with some guys and then she OD'ed.

The story—and the way she told it to me, early in the morning, just before dawn—as both of us slid down from our highs, our bodies tingling and half asleep, turned me on in a grotesque way. To get a hard-on based on a story of abuse seemed wrong, but it happened, and we made love to each other again, for the second time, and we both came wildly and lay there for a while until she made her confession.—I made that up, completely. I never knew a drifter named Charlene from Canada, and I certainly wouldn't sleep with a fuckface reject like that. No way. I just felt like telling a story. I felt like making one up for you. I thought it would be interesting and maybe shed some light on the world. The idea—the angelic girl, the perfect girl, the one with perfect beauty getting all mashed up like that. That's something I think about a lot. She sat up, smoking a cigarette, stretching her legs out. Dawn was breaking outside. I imagined the light plunging through the trees, and the log trucks roaring past. For a minute I felt like knocking her on the head. I imagined pinning her down and giving her face a go with a meat hammer. But I found it easy to forgive her because the story she made up had sparked wild and fanciful sex. I kissed her and looked into her eyes and noticed that they were sad and didn't move away from mine (but that's not what I noticed). What did I notice? I can't put words to it except to say she had an elegiac sadness there, and an unearned calm, and that something had been stolen from her pupils.—You weren't making that up, I said.—You couldn't make that shit up, she responded, holding her voice flat and cold.—So it was all true.—I didn't say that. I just said you couldn't make that shit up.

We're gonna get nailed for what we did, she said, later, as we ate breakfast. Around us truckers in their long-billed caps leaned into plates of food, clinking the heavy silverware, devouring eggs in communal silence. A waitress was dropping dirty dishes into the slop sink, lifting each of them up and letting them fall, as if to test the durability of high-grade, restaurant-quality plates.—We're gonna get nailed, I agreed. I wasn't up for an argument about it. The fact was, our stream of luck would go on flowing for a while longer. Then I'd lose Marsha and start searching for a Charlene. For his part, the world could devour plenty of Ernies; each day they vaporized into the country's huge horizon.—He's probably dead. He knew how to swim, but he didn't look too confident in his stroke.—Yeah, I agreed. Ernie had bobbed up to the surface shouting profanities and striking out in our direction with a weird sidestroke. His lashing hands sustained just his upper body. The rest was sunken out of sight and opened us up to speculation as to whether his boots were on or off. After he was tossed from the boat, he stayed under a long, long time. When he bobbed up, his face had a wrinkled, babyish look of betrayal. He blew water at us, cleared his lips, and in a firm voice said,—You're dead, man, both of you. Then he cursed my mother and father and the day they were born, Marsha's cunt and her ass and her mother and father and God and the elements and the ice-cold water of the seaway and the ship, which was about four hundred yards away (—come on, motherfuckers, save my ass). He kept shouting like this until a mouthful of water gagged him. We were swinging around, opening it up full-throttle, looping around, sending a wake in his direction and heading in. When we got to the breakwall we turned and saw that he was still out there, splashing, barely visible. The ship loomed stupidly in the background, oblivious to his situation. A single gull spiraled overhead, providing us with an omen to talk about later. (Gulls are God's death searchers, Marsha told me. Don't be fooled by their white feathers or any of that shit. Gulls are best at finding the dead.) Then we got back in Tull's truck and headed through town and out, just following roads north toward Houghton, leaving Ernie to whatever destiny he had as one more aberration adrift in the St. Lawrence Seaway system. For a long time we didn't say a word. We just drove. The radio was playing an old Neil Young song. We turned it up, and then up some more, and left it loud like that, until it was just so much rattling noise.

Karen Brown

Unction

T HEY GATHERED each morning at seven o'clock in the bookbinding machine shop, in the back where the parts were stored in long, narrow metal bins and stacked on metal shelving to the ceiling. Fans spun the dusty heat. They drank cups of dark coffee. They moved, their teenaged bodies dull and inarticulate, to the plywood counter where thick sheaves of computer printouts listed the parts they needed to count. It was a summer job, this inventory. Lily was pregnant, seventeen, and no one knew, not Orlando, the young draftsman, who taught her to drive his Renault, or Tish, the owner's niece, who brought in bags of the watermelon candy Lily secretly craved, not even Matthew, with his soft hair in his eyes, with his bashful glances that made her feel a part of herself had come undone, a blouse button, the clasp to her shorts, the silent, swift unraveling of her heart.

She could not tell you, now, who the father was. There had been a succession of boys at the time. She would leave her parents' house and walk the three blocks to the center of the small town, to the outdoor mall and its fountain, onto the town green's damp evening grass, and meet her friends, and wait for the boys. They would appear like gliding birds in their cars, paint jobs shining from a new waxing, the tires thick and ready to grab the parking lot's black asphalt. They stuck their heads out of car windows, their hair wet from the shower, from a quick swim in oval-shaped pools, from the lake in Suffield where some of them skied and a few would die in a boat accident the following summer. They lived without any fear of death. They stuck their heads out into the wind and grinned and promised a fearlessness that she would desire more than the inexpert movements of their hands on her body, their mouths' wet urgency, their rising heat beneath her sliding palms.

They would never force themselves on her. She was practiced at how to make them want her. It became a simple game. Each boy was a new beginning. Each had an eventual parting, signaled by a new girl in the passenger seat of his car, or a general disregard that she learned to intuit, never an angry rebuff, never with any malice, just a folding away of himself from her, a closing off that made her sad at first. She would remember the smell of his upholstery, the salty taste of the skin on his throat, the way his mouth parted, or how he used his tongue. She would pine for the places they parked: the meadow beyond the reservoir, the smell of the grass dampened by rain. She would miss his groans, his efforts moving inside her, the way he fell panting afterward. She held their faces the same in her hands. She gazed into their eyes. They all had a way of not looking back, of shielding themselves, as if from the force of her love.

The father of her child might have been any of them from that spring, or early summer. She did not know for sure about herself until the end, in August, when the heat in the machine shop was the worst, and the black grit settled grimly on the handrails of the tall rolling ladders they moved up and down the aisles of shelving, seeking out the parts. Her breasts hurt. She drank her coffee in the morning, and promptly threw it up. Only Matthew noticed waiting outside the ladies' room for her, the worry in his eyes something they pretended wasn't there. He would brush her hair from her face. He would grin wildly, to make her smile. In the afternoons, he would sit on one of the high ladders and draw caricatures of all of them, or the comic book superheroes he created. His body, large and ungainly, would curl in on itself, double over. His arm bent along the wide white paper moved lithe and supple, like the appendage of someone else. He would present the drawings to her, rolled up into long tubes, paper clipped at the ends. She sensed her happiness was, to him, of the utmost importance.

There were six of them that summer, hired to work the seven to five o'clock inventory. At first, she did not spend much time getting to know any of them. She took her list and went off into the aisles of shelving, working on deciphering the language of screws and pins and bolts and clamps. She found time went faster this way. At lunch, she bought a sandwich from the truck that came and parked in the lot. The machine shop used to manufacture the bookbinding machine parts, but it had been closed for two years. Only a husband and wife ran the shipping department. There was Matthew, hired to build the wooden crates, to operate the forklift, and to pack things up to ship. A few machines remained operable. Two men ran those. Most parts were made in another of the owner's factories down by the Connecticut River, a bigger, more efficient place. The sense of the small bookbinding machine shop was of desolation and decline. Its dirt and grease, ground into the brick floor, were ancient, from another time. The sun lit the high row of narrow windows filmed by dust, a pinkish orange. There was no other source of light beyond the hanging fluorescent lamps. Each morning she came into the heat of the shop and felt a new raw wave of despair.

They worked without any supervision. After a week they grew bored. There was no one to please with their progress through the stacks of computer printouts. Lily knew that up in the front offices women in accounts receivable gossiped and split blueberry crumb cake, purchasing agents lounged in each other's offices, sipping from cans of soft drinks, tipping cigarette ashes into cupped palms. The office manager carried on an affair with a file clerk, the blinds to his office drawn, and a receptionist sat at a switchboard facing the double glass doors, by the American flag in its stand, waiting to greet the mailman. There were foreign engineers, three of them, spread out in cubicles, their suit jackets draped over the backs of their chairs, their drawings clipped to slanted tables, their ashtrays spilling over with the ends of hand-rolled cigarettes.

That summer, none of the office workers ever came to the back, except for Celie, one of the purchasing agents, who checked on things occasionally. She wore bright floral skirts and high heels and dangling earrings. She seemed uncomfortable in the dark shop, as if she might become soiled. She would stop in at shipping with her stack of paperwork, and then head to the other end of the shop, where the parts were kept, where by the second week the six of them sprawled on the metal steps of the rolling ladders, sat in folding chairs around the computer printouts, pretending to look busy. Orlando had the best performance. He would hold the print-out like a book in his arms, and thumb through it. He kept a pencil behind his ear, and always seemed to appear from around a shelf, at the appropriate moment to report in to her.

"We've got all the Rounder Backer parts accounted for," he'd say.

Celie would smile at him, making a special effort. Her earrings shook and made a sound like small bells. "Wow!" she'd say, shaking her head. "Good."

Orlando had applied as a draftsman just out of trade school. The summer inventory was the only job open, but they had emphasized there was potential to learn, and the possibility of a later position. In the beginning, Orlando worked to entrench himself. He brought the engineers samples from his family's bakery. He made a round of the front offices daily, presenting himself, an affable employee. Lily begged the driving lessons from him. She knew he would have to steal time from the company he was trying so desperately to join, that he did not want to do it. But she saw, too, that summer there was something about her that no one could refuse. After lunch, they drove in circles around the empty back lot where the machinists used to park. Orlando gripped the door handle when the car jerked and stalled. Sometimes, he cried out in Portuguese, and put his hand over his heart when her foot confused the clutch and the brake, and she came too close to the shop's brick wall. Lily liked the smell of his car, the afternoon sun warming up a mixture of talcum powder and the baked crust of the bread he'd brought in that morning. She liked the way she could confuse him, how in the little car with her he stammered, no longer the expert.

During work hours Orlando was the only one who could describe the parts they sought, their size and shape, what to actually look for in the narrow bins. But by the third week of inventory they grew weary of consulting him, and they counted anything, their hands oily from the screws' threads, gray with dust from the castings piled up on the floor, their part numbers raised metal that no one, in the dim lighting, could truly read. If it looked like a lever arm, Jamie said, then it was the lever arm on the list.

Lily suspected that Jamie was working the job, like she was, as some form of penance. Lily had been hired to work in the shop's front office that winter. She got the job from her school disciplinary counselor, who met with her one afternoon after she had been discovered inebriated in French class. It had been French V, Advanced, and the other students, with their straight A averages and bowl-shaped haircuts and polyester button-downs, had been shocked. Madame Dorn had led her by the hand out of the room. She had chastised her in French. You disappoint me, she'd said. They stood in the beige brick hallway, on the pale and shining waxed floor tiles. Lily remembered the bright blue of her eye shadow, the way her small hands had clung to her wrists, the sound of the verb, *décevoir*, like an unending and upturned sadness. The disciplinary counselor was gruff and stocky with a broad face. He was missing half of one of his thumbs. He set up the interview with the bookbinding shop's office manager.

"You need this," he said. "Keep you out of trouble."

She worked every day after school making blueprints on the large machine. All the drawings of parts were stored flat in long metal file drawers. She kept them in order, filed by their part numbers, some of them very old on tobacco colored paper worn at the edges. She found that making the blueprints, the mindless feeding of drawings into the big machine, its emanating heat and hum and ammonia smell, kept her content, and she was grateful, in a way, for the job. When they'd assigned her to the summer inventory, she found she'd become good at accepting whatever she was given.

Jamie had been hired under similar circumstances through a friend of his father. A safe occupation for the summer. He wasn't resentful. With his paychecks, he claimed, he would put a down payment on the Trans-Am his father had already refused him. Jamie kept his blond hair cropped short. His eyes perused her when he looked, lingered, needy and intent on her face, her mouth, on the slope of her shoulders down to her breasts. Tish came in each morning, primly, in a different colored sleeveless blouse, carrying her canvas tote bag. Her father wanted her to learn the value of hard work, she told them, crossing her brown eyes. She would leave each afternoon, her face shining, her blouse ringed with sweat under her arms. The other girl working with them, Geri, was tall and had a long, bushy mane of hair that she spent time twisting and piling and clipping back. She wore her boyfriend's UCONN T-shirts. Even these, Jamie announced, could not hide the bouncing effect of her large breasts. Geri was good-natured about Jamie's observations. She stuck her tongue out at him, and disappeared down an aisle of shelving.

"Do you think she wants me to follow her?" he would ask Lily. "We could fuck in D row, under the Smyth sewer bolts." Lily and Jamie did the least amount of work. They sat at the plywood counter amid the print-outs, rifling through them, organizing them, pretending to mark things off. They separated the work into piles for everyone. Jamie smoked Camels, dropping his butts on the floor and grinding them with the toe of his boot. He looked over at her.

"This is unendurable," he said, his eyes fastening on her bare legs spread out under the counter. She looked back at him, and shook her head, refusing him, her body taken over by an inexpressible lethargy, an emptying of desire. She felt drawn into a current of deep and swirling water. No one seemed angry that she did less work. Matthew wheeled the big ladders around for her. Tish brought her the watermelon candy. Matthew and Orlando, finally, unbolted the green vinyl couch from the break room's linoleum floor. They carried it to the back wall of the shop, beneath the high row of windows, hidden away behind the last aisle of shelving. They said it was for everyone to take turns. Jamie offered to double up with Geri. But they relinquished it to Lily, who fell asleep every afternoon, her eyelids heavy, her limbs lifeless, her body drawn under invisible tidewater.

Once in a while, the Russian engineer would saunter through the shop. He would make a point of walking over, and stop, and ask for Lily. He needed a blueprint made. He couldn't find a drawing. He wore his dark suit pants and polished shoes. His shoe leather creaked, making his foot-falls menacing. Matthew's face reddened when he saw him approaching. They made up excuses so Lily would not have to speak to him. That spring, the engineer had asked Lily to model, to pose wearing a nautical shirt and white shorts and a sailor's hat, with a bow thruster he had devel-oped and patented for the owner as a side job. She had agreed, flattered at first. Celie in purchasing had done her makeup in the ladies' room. The engineer had taken the photos himself with a Nikon. He stood, stiff and unfriendly, issuing orders. He had her straddle the design, something that looked like a heavy, riveted pipe. Then, she stood up beside it with one hand on her hip. Frustrated, he gripped the fleshy part of her arm above her elbow to position her, and his thumb and forefinger left a darkening print.

They took the photos in the machine shop. The late afternoon shone serene and unconcerned through the high row of windows, and the dust swirled about. She was not ready to reveal to the adult world her own knowledge of sex, and so she pretended she did not read anything in his eyes' movements over her body, his positioning of her, roughly, in the poses of his liking. She could endure his gaze under this pretense, her hips and mouth prodded to assume falsely, awkwardly, the expression of seduction. Later, the engineer tried to persuade her to attend a trade show with them in Boston and hand out brochures, offering to pay her hotel room, her traveling expenses. But the office manager intervened, pointing out that she was a minor, and Celie had taken her aside. "Don't go," she'd said, grimacing. "I wouldn't if I were you," fully convinced of Lily's ignorance concerning the engineers in their suits, their thick waists and formality, their other uses for her they were not telling. The engineer improvised with a photo made into a life-sized cutout to stand alongside their display—Lily in her sailor's hat, a hand placed on her outthrust hip, her look conveying a disarming innocence.

Matthew had been in the shop during the shoot. They took the photos once everyone left for the day, and he stayed under the pretense of working late, suspicious of the engineer's intentions from the first. Later, he drew a scathing caricature of the Russian holding his camera, his oversized head stern, his one exposed eye sly and lascivious. During the summer inventory, Matthew would draw a whole series of his characters. They were heroes from fantasy stories, men and women who had survived the last battle on earth, who lived to fight a latex-suited foe from space, or mutant animals, lion mouthed, vulture winged, left to inhabit earth's dark recesses. The human survivors wore only remnants of their old clothing. Their near naked bodies swirled in motion, spun on muscled calves, swung weapons that looked cumbersome and medieval. Their faces tightened in anger or horror or pain. Their eyes glared or softened or filled with tears. Matthew would bring the drawings to her, shyly, when the others weren't around. Lily had never seen anything so beautiful emerge from a pencil on paper before. She held the drawings in her hands and her hands shook. The characters looked back at her from the tumult of their movements, frozen in the midst of their unfolding stories.

She wouldn't say much. She would hand them back and look at him and smile, and she could see he knew what she felt, that she believed his ability was a gift, something that resided in some self other than the one maneuvering a forklift, stacking castings on wooden pallets, searching out one hundred and five Casing-In bolts. His caricatures of all of them brought out their beauty, the small defect in each of their personalities—Orlando's simpering, his debonair nose; Tish's crossed eyes and self-deprecating smile; Geri's horsy face, its lack of imagination; Jamie's rakishness, a Camel hanging from his bottom lip. Of herself, Lily could only sense a kind of tragic weakness, her eyes too wide, too seemingly childlike, and she believed he had gotten her wrong. He would not draw any others of her, only real sketches he would not show her until later, near the end of the summer.

The notes came first. They were Lily's idea, grown out of the impossible state of her body, its languidness, its inconceivable separate heartbeat. It had been late afternoon. She had been asleep, and it began to rain. The rain on the shop roof was like something rising and building to a heightened pitch, the sound of it hollow and metallic. It woke her, and its thrumming made her lonely. She felt slighted by the condition of her body, as if it no longer had any other use than the one that now occupied it without her permission. She came around from the back of the rows of shelving and found Jamie with his cigarette at the counter. He gave her a look and then glanced over at Geri, moping on one of the ladders, her fingers flaying her hair.

"I like that big head of hair," he said. "I want to put my hands in it."

Lily tore a piece of the computer printout. She wrote this down with one of the pencils, in cursive script. "Put it in a bin on her list," she said.

"Add something else," he told her, grinning.

Lily wrote what she believed Jamie would want from Geri, what he wanted to do to her. *I can't keep this a secret,* she wrote. *I am overcome with lust.*

Jamie stubbed out his cigarette. He looked over Geri's abandoned list, and took off down the aisles. She didn't find the note at first. They watched her, waiting. They went off with their own lists, keeping an eye on her. Lily climbed to the top of a ladder and found the heat had collected there. She took the bin down to the floor and spent the afternoon counting and losing track and recounting three hundred and twenty feeder nuts, finally placing them in piles of twenty-five on the brick floor. At the end of the day lining up to punch out, they noticed Geri's face, flushed, distracted. Tendrils of her hair stuck to her forehead. She said nothing about a note. But Lily saw her eyes take in the fine sheen on Orlando's dark skin, the way Matthew's pants had slid down on his hips. She saw them sweep across the broad space between Jamie's shoulder blades. Lily saw her wonder what his back looked like without his shirt. In her eyes was lit a kind of startled heat.

The notes, unsigned, unmentioned, would become the mystery that kept them searching in the bins of parts. Lily wrote confessions of desire and Jamie placed the notes in bins on everyone's list. *Yesterday, I couldn't breathe, watching you,* and, *I want, more than anything right now, to taste your mouth.* There was a certain stealth required, a cruel urge to unsettle and disconcert. Tish came to work in lip-gloss, which she reapplied every hour or so, her thin lips glimmering and suddenly soft. Orlando grew a small, slim mustache and wore sleeveless tank tops. Geri arrived one morning in a halter, her breasts pressing the V of the front, spilling out over the edge of the fabric. Jamie leaned back in his chair, ecstatic. Lily ate the watermelon candies, placing them one after another into her mouth, letting them dissolve on her tongue, and wrote about what hands would feel like on someone's chest, sliding up a smooth stomach, riding down below the curve of a waist, the rise of hips, the warm, damp place between legs. She felt her body surge and slip into some region of wakefulness, a kind of knowing that mixed with the smell of the oiled parts, the paper and ink of the computer printouts, the artificial watermelon, the plywood counter where she piled the candy's cellophane wrappers.

Only Matthew seemed unchanged. He still gave her his quiet, thoughtful glances. He still waited for her in the mornings outside the ladies' room, his back pressing the brick wall, his arms folded patiently across his chest. He drew her when she least expected it. He would need only one or two quick looks, and those he would take while she was busy, unaware. Once in a while, she would catch him, and they would meet each other's expression without knowing what their own reflected, hers sorrowful and lost, his fueled with love. Tish believed that Matthew had penned her notes. She came to Lily with them all smoothed out and pressed together, in a kind of order.

"Look at these," she said.

Lily looked. She already knew what messages they held. She had, she realized, intended her to believe that Matthew had written them. She had mentioned his large Catholic family, the three sisters, the four brothers, the nieces and nephews, the value he placed on their closeness, the uncreased and simple sacrifice. Lily had thought they would make a nice couple. She had wanted Tish to pursue and capture him, to spare him from herself. In Matthew's notes she had written things she believed Tish might reveal. Her respect for her father's stringent rules, her mother's alcoholism, her loss, at fifteen, of a boyfriend to leukemia. Some of these were things Lily had learned. Others, she had made up. She held the scraps of paper in her hands, and saw, through the disguised handwriting, the thoughtlessness with which she allowed the notes to lead lives of their own, assume their own history, their stories stretching out to contain moments that had not even happened yet.

"What should I do?" Tish asked. Her small lips trembled.

Lily shrugged, wordless with regret. Already, Jamie had tried to approach Geri and been rebuffed. Now, sitting at the top of her tall ladder, twirling her hair, Geri looked down at Orlando's head bent counting over a bin, with a wistful longing. Orlando thought his notes came from Tish. He confided in Jamie and raised an eyebrow, and ran his tongue over his lips. "I can taste that gloss," he said.

Jamie became surly. "I'm done with this," he said. They stopped writing and hiding the notes. He sulked for three days, refusing to count anything, smoking his cigarettes, and dropping his fist down on the counter top. The spell of the notes faded and was replaced with Jamie's irritableness. No one had the nerve to approach anyone else. No one knew how to feed all their wanting. Lily felt responsible, her own body, she believed, immune. But then she fell asleep late one afternoon on the green couch, and when she woke she could tell, from the slant of light, the way it colored the grimy brick, the gray metal shelves, that it was later than she'd ever slept. Matthew was there, near the top of one of the rolling ladders.

"I didn't want to wake you," he said. His voice floated from above her, resonant and strange. She knew the shop was empty, that everyone had gone.

"What time is it?" she asked. She imagined her mother waiting outside in the parking lot to pick her up, her exasperation, her refusal to go inside and inquire, the easy assumption that Lily had left with someone else. Now, she imagined her parents sat at the dining table, silent and still assuming that Lily was with a friend, or at the mall, or any number of places that Lily had invented in the past to appease them. Their cutlery clanked against the china. Her father glanced up occasionally as if to speak. In the flickering crystals of the chandelier, in the polished handles of the silver, the colors of the room bled, the magenta of her mother's blouse, her father's Kelly green golf shirt, the still brilliant but wilting centerpiece of flowers, all of it tinged with presentiment.

"I can give you a ride home," Matthew said. He descended the ladder. She slid over on the couch, and motioned for him to sit beside her. He hesitated, then dropped onto the vinyl cushion, casually, looking away. He let his hands rest on his thighs. She stared at the curve of his neck, his cheek. He would not turn to face her.

"Don't do that," he said, barely a whisper.

Lily could see the twilight slipping through the narrow windows, its sifted particles converging. She felt the air in the shop like a presence on her skin. She rose up onto her knees. She turned his face toward her with her hands. He was caught there, and resigned, he allowed her to look at him. His face stayed impassive. His eyes confounded her, like those of his characters. She slid her hands down his shoulders. She felt the tops of his arms, their hardened muscles. Her hands came to rest on his.

"Why didn't you write to me as you?" he asked.

She felt a conflagration of loss. She felt consumed.

He did not know, exactly, what to do with her. But he had a restless sense of what he needed, and how to get it. His mouth was soft and clumsy. His hands, large knuckled, tentative, touched her face, her eyes and mouth, her nose and ears. They smelled of the oil from the bins. They settled on her body like a blessing. She felt the ache in her rise to the surface of his fingers. She had, she admitted, allowed herself to imagine this. She had even created the story of what might come after, his large family ready to take her in, to tend to her, to accept her body and its child as his. She saw bureau drawers layered with tiny, pastel-colored clothes, lamplight in an attic room, a window looking out into the ruffling dusk of waving leaves. She saw herself relent to this unfolding, her loneliness purged in soft breath and fine hair and the lulling scent of milk. But lying with him on the vinyl cushion, their hip bones pressed together, his need released, his love at her disposal, she felt only the betrayal, keen edged, merciless, and knew nothing in her grasp would ever ward against loss.

She did not finish out the summer. He would never know how her body swelled, or didn't. Her breasts filled, or not. She kept only one of his drawings, that of herself just awakened on the couch. He drew it that day from above, on the ladder. In it, the twilight is a color on the brick. The vinyl couch casts its own darker shadow. Her legs are folded, one on top of the other. She looks up. In her eyes he has placed a perfect, earnest love. She leans on one arm and the other curves in a motion of possession over her abdomen. Everything, then, still part of the story.

Terese Svoboda

'80s Lilies

T HE CALLA LILIES in New Zealand say we are dead, just step off the jade-strewn, rimed high-tide line here and a wave will rise up like Trigger, like some silent-movie stallion, and suck us under, suck us beneath a continental shelf stuck out so far the waves whiten before they break. So too the calla lilies, all white and wild like that, all about to break in the greeny drizzle that the wind whips, all these wild calla lilies that will bear us away.

I see the lilies and I say, Let's get off the bus. Then the bus's burring keeps on without us as we stand at the upper ridge of lilies, before they spill off the grave mounds corraled by wooden fences and multiply right onto the waves. Lilies from old settlers' tombs, I say into the silencing wind with you tucking the baby onto my back, and as far as we can see, green drizzle, jade beaches, white cups in clumps flattened by wind.

Mind the waves, she says. They will jump the beach and pull you in.

She comes abreast of us, nearly green-skinned in the green mist with a small-sized boy, just as green, tugging at the end of her arm. Does she mean for us to mind those waves—or for him, the green monkey among the lilies?

I hold up a rock. Jade? Really jade? I ask.

Tourists, she says in a tone that can't be confused. Tourists don't come here, she says.

Really? They skip this bit? I thumb toward all that various beauty. Those terrible tourists.

She laughs and my husband and I say all the little things against the wind that makes her lean toward us down the length of the beach until we are at her car that she unlocks and leaves in, waving. We wave back, a few more little things on our lips.

The baby takes away our wonder at the place and its people, the baby has his wants. At the end of the road the woman has driven away from sits a pub, curiously free of all the lilies, as if bulldozed free. We order pints there, then we ask after rooms since the green mist can only give way to dark.

They have rooms.

We remark on the sheep smell of these rooms, and the drizzle-colored pub interior, its darts bent and broken, the dark growlings and the stares from the pub fiends, two steamy goldminers, silent and filthy in their mining gear, flakes of dirt, green not gold, falling from them onto their table, and we order another pint.

Going to the ladies', with the baby asleep, milk lip aquiver, I trip over huge bones in the corridor, vastly gnarled, prehistoric big gray bones that must be the source of the sheep stink. The dog that gnaws at such bones, as terrible an animal as he must be, thumps and growls from inside some further door when I shut mine, but he's quiet when I emerge, as if he has plans.

I haven't. I haven't said yes yet to the room or to another pint. I just want to talk about those bones but at our seat there's no one to note my near miss with the bone-guarding dog, no man or child.

One of the two miners nods to the window. Out there, he says. She has them in her car.

Where else would you be putting up but here? she shouts over new pell-mell rain. I have tea, she says.

We rode the ferry that sinks, the ferry with a crèche where the children are roped to rockers through the big waves that slap the island apart, the ferry that, however, did not sink when we crossed, but allowed us, vomitous, to board that bus.

That ferry's no problem, she says. Look in the phone book.

I open the phone book and the first page lists all the calamities: tidal wave, earthquake, floods, volcanic eruptions, and numbers to call. Such a safe place, I say they say. So safe for children.

We are fleeing, we explain, to some safe place. We're sure this time they'll drop it. We thought, Here's a place we'll be safe, and gave the airlines our gold card.

They don't laugh, she and her husband. Just the way she doesn't laugh at the green rock I pull out of my bag, the rock that must be worth money. Their house is full of toys my baby knows and toys my husband can feel the remote of, and books I have read and admired. Her husband has my husband's charm, and why not? They do nothing similar for work but charm makes the men match.

The baby inspects all the toys their boy brings so I can talk while she cooks, because cooking is the point of visiting, isn't it, she says, a place where everyone meets. Then you can go back, if you like. After tea.

I look out into the pell-mell greeny rain and, even in the looking, smell sheep, hear that growl. When real night falls about two drinks after tea—what is surely dinner—when the rain isn't seen but felt, they won't let us go, they make up beds.

Their boy bounces a ball off the baby's head and the baby smiles.

We all visit a gold mine in the morning, their idea.

Maybe they wanted to have sex, I whisper to my husband as he settles a hard hat onto his head.

A little late, he says.

We walk deep into the mines posted Do Not Enter and they say, Don't mind the signs, the baby is fine.

This is where we're going when it happens, says her husband. And he explains what he heard on TV yesterday, how it will blow ash all over the globe in ways nobody knew. Everywhere will be caught in the grip of its terrible winter.

Winter—you are obsessed with having seasons that don't match ours, I say. I look at my husband. So here is not safe either is our glance exchanged.

We walk along in the dark.

I expect a room of gold all aglitter at the end, jutting ore burnished to a sun's strength. What we get to is a small cave lit with mirrors that leave little flashes of faraway light on the dull rock.

Our faces facing the mirrors are just one gray ball, then another.

Their boy drops a rock down a shaft and it doesn't hit bottom. While we wait, the baby wakes as if the rock hits hard, and his wails echo all down the tunnel. We walk back through his wails, it's that physical.

We stay one more night. We stay up late and my husband says, Maybe the threat will blow over.

Blow over. We all laugh, drinking the wine from the grapes that grow among the lilies. Then we talk movies, all the same ones we have seen as if together.

We really came to see you, I say. Does it matter if we flee if you are here?

In the morning they tell us they do not write, they will not. No letters.

Consider them written, says my husband.

We take the next bus, a dark cave filled with more miners abandoning mines. The settlers we leave behind, such settlers as they are, wearing our clothes nearly exactly, franchise for franchise, who wave as our bus burrs off past the lilies, the big waves behind them lapping and reaching.

Alice Munro

Passion

WHEN GRACE goes looking for the Traverses' summer house, in the
Ottawa Valley, it has been many years since she was in that part
of the country. And, of course, things have changed. Highway 7 now
avoids towns that it used to go right through, and it goes straight in places
where, as she remembers, there used to be curves. This part of the Canadian Shield has many small lakes, which most maps have no room to identify. Even when she locates Sabot Lake, or thinks she has, there seem to be
too many roads leading into it from the county road, and then, when she
chooses one, too many paved roads crossing it, all with names that she
does not recall. In fact, there were no street names when she was here,
more than forty years ago. There was no pavement, either—just one dirt
road running toward the lake, then another running rather haphazardly
along the lake's edge.

Now there is a village. Or perhaps it's a suburb, because she does not
see a post office or even the most unpromising convenience store. The
settlement lies four or five streets deep along the lake, with houses strung
close together on small lots. Some of them are undoubtedly summer
places—the windows already boarded up, as they always were for the
winter. But many others show all the signs of year-round habitation—
habitation, in many cases, by people who have filled the yards with plastic
gym sets and outdoor grills and training bikes and motorcycles and picnic

tables, where some of them sit now having lunch or beer on this warm September day. There are other people, not so visible—students, maybe, or old hippies living alone—who have put up flags or sheets of tinfoil for curtains. Small, mostly decent, cheap houses, some fixed to withstand the winter and some not.

Grace would have turned back if she hadn't caught sight of the octagonal house with the fretwork along the roof and doors in every other wall. The Woods house. She has always remembered it as having eight doors, but it seems there are only four. She was never inside, to see how, or if, the space is divided into rooms. Mr. and Mrs. Woods were old—as Grace is now—and did not seem to be visited by any children or friends. Their quaint, original house now has a forlorn, mistaken look. Neighbors with their ghetto blasters and their half-dismembered vehicles, their toys and washing, are pushed up against either side of it.

It is the same with the Travers house, when she finds it, a quarter of a mile farther on. The road goes past it now, instead of ending there, and the houses next door are only a few feet away from its deep, wraparound veranda.

It was the first house of its kind that Grace had ever seen—one story high, the roof continuing without a break out over that veranda, on all sides—a style that makes you think of hot summers. She has since seen many like it, in Australia.

It used to be possible to run from the veranda across the dusty end of the driveway, through a sandy, trampled patch of weeds and wild strawberries, and then jump—no, actually, wade—into the lake. Now Grace can hardly even see the lake, because a substantial house—one of the few regular suburban houses here, with a two-car garage—has been built across that very route.

What was Grace really looking for when she undertook this expedition? Perhaps the worst thing would have been to find exactly what she thought she was after—the sheltering roof, the screened windows, the lake in front, the stand of maple and cedar and balm-of-Gilead trees behind. Perfect preservation, the past intact, when nothing of the kind could be said of herself. To find something so diminished, still existing but made irrelevant—as the Travers house now seems to be, with its added dormer windows, its startling blue paint—might be less hurtful in the long run.

And what if it had been gone altogether? She might have made a fuss, if anybody had come along to listen to her; she might have bewailed the loss. But mightn't a feeling of relief have passed over her, too, of old confusions and obligations wiped away?

Mr. Travers had built the house—that is, he'd had it built—as a surprise wedding present for Mrs. Travers. When Grace first saw it, it was perhaps thirty years old. Mrs. Travers's children were widely spaced: Gretchen, twenty-eight or twenty-nine, already married and a mother herself; Maury, twenty-one, going into his last year of college; and then there was Neil, in his mid-thirties. But Neil was not a Travers. He was Neil Borrow. Mrs. Travers had been married before, to a man who had died. For a few years, she had earned her living, and supported her child, as a teacher of business English at a secretarial school. Mr. Travers, when he referred to this period in her life before he'd met her, spoke of it as a time of hardship almost like penal servitude, something that would barely be made up for by a whole lifetime of comfort, which he would happily provide.

Mrs. Travers herself didn't speak of it that way at all. She had lived with Neil in a big old house broken up into apartments, not far from the railway tracks in the town of Pembroke, and many of the stories she told at the dinner table were about events there, about her fellow-tenants, and the French-Canadian landlord, whose harsh French and tangled English she imitated. The stories could have had titles, like the stories by James Thurber that Grace had read in *The Anthology of American Humor,* found unaccountably on the library shelf at the back of her grade-ten classroom. "The Night Old Mrs. Cromarty Got Out on the Roof." "How the Postman Courted Miss Flowers." "The Dog Who Ate Sardines."

Mr. Travers never told stories and had little to say at dinner, but if he came upon you looking, for instance, at the fieldstone fireplace he might say, "Are you interested in rocks?" and tell you how he had searched and searched for that particular pink granite, because Mrs. Travers had once exclaimed over a rock like that, glimpsed in a road cut. Or he might show you the not really unusual features that he personally had added to the house—the corner cupboard shelves swinging outward in the kitchen, the storage space under the window seats. He was a tall, stooped man with a soft voice and thin hair slicked over his scalp. He wore bathing shoes when he went into the water and, though he did not look fat in his clothes, a pancake fold of white flesh slopped over the top of his bathing trunks.

. . .

Grace was working that summer at the hotel at Bailey's Falls, just north of Sabot Lake. Early in the season, the Travers family had come to dinner there. She had not noticed them—it was a busy night, and they were not at one of her tables. She was setting up a table for a new party when she realized that someone was waiting to speak to her.

It was Maury. He said, "I was wondering if you would like to go out with me sometime."

Grace barely looked up from shooting out the silverware. She said, "Is this a dare?" Because his voice was high and nervous, and he stood there stiffly, as if forcing himself. And it was known that sometimes a party of young men from the cottages would dare one another to ask a waitress out. It wasn't entirely a joke—they really would show up, if accepted, though sometimes they only meant to park, without taking you to a movie or even for coffee. So it was considered rather shameful, rather hard up, of a girl to agree.

"What?" he said painfully, and then Grace did stop and look at him. It seemed to her that she saw the whole of him in that moment, the true Maury. Scared, fierce, innocent, determined.

"O.K.," she said quickly. She might have meant, O.K., calm down, I can see it's not a dare. Or, O.K., I'll go out with you. She herself hardly knew which. But he took it as agreement, and at once arranged—without lowering his voice, or noticing the looks that he was getting from the diners around them—to pick her up after work the following night.

He did take her to the movies. They saw *Father of the Bride*. Grace hated it. She hated girls like Elizabeth Taylor's character—spoiled rich girls of whom nothing was ever asked but that they wheedle and demand. Maury said that it was just a comedy, but she told him that that was not the point. She could not quite make clear what her point was. Anybody would have assumed that it was because she worked as a waitress and was too poor to go to college, and because, if she wanted that kind of wedding, she would have to save up for years to pay for it herself. (Maury did think this, and was stricken with respect for her, almost with reverence.)

She could not explain or even quite understand that it wasn't jealousy she felt, it was rage. And not because she couldn't shop like that or dress like that but because that was what girls were supposed to be like. That was what men—people, everybody—thought they *should* be like: beautiful, treasured, spoiled, selfish, pea-brained. That was what a girl had to be, to be fallen in love with. Then she'd become a mother and be all mushily devoted to her babies. Not selfish anymore, but just as pea-brained. Forever.

Grace was fuming about this while sitting beside a boy who had fallen in love with her because he had believed—instantly—in the integrity and uniqueness of her mind and soul, had seen her poverty as a romantic gloss on that. (He would have known she was poor not just because of her job but because of her strong Ottawa Valley accent.)

He honored her feelings about the movie. Indeed, now that he had listened to her angry struggles to explain, he struggled to tell her something in turn. He said he saw now that it was not anything so simple, so *feminine*, as jealousy. He saw that. It was that she would not stand for frivolity, was not content to be like most girls. She was special.

Grace was wearing a dark-blue ballerina skirt, a white blouse, through whose eyelet frills the upper curve of her breasts was visible, and a wide rose-colored elasticized belt. There was a discrepancy, no doubt, between the way she presented herself and the way she wanted to be judged. But nothing about her was dainty or pert or polished, in the style of the time. A bit ragged around the edges, in fact. Giving herself Gypsy airs, with the very cheapest silver-painted bangles, and the long, wild-looking, curly dark hair that she had to put into a snood when she waited on tables.

Special.

He told his mother about her, and his mother said, "You must bring this Grace of yours to dinner."

It was all new to her, all immediately delightful. In fact, she fell in love with Mrs. Travers, almost exactly as Maury had fallen in love with her, though it was not in her nature, of course, to be as openly dumbfounded, as worshipful, as he was.

Grace had been brought up by her aunt and uncle, really her great-aunt and great-uncle. Her mother had died when she was three years old, and her father had moved to Saskatchewan, where he now had another family. Her stand-in parents were kind, even proud of her. But they were not given to conversation. The uncle made his living caning chairs, and he had taught Grace how to cane so that she could help him and eventually take over the business when his eyesight failed. But then she had got the job at

Bailey's Falls for the summer, and though it was hard for him—and for her aunt as well—to let her go, they believed that she needed a taste of life before she settled down.

She was twenty years old and had just finished high school. She should have finished a year earlier, but she had made an odd choice. In the very small town where she lived—it was not far from Mrs. Travers's Pembroke—there was nevertheless a high school that offered five grades, to prepare students for the government exams and what was then called senior matriculation. It was never necessary to study all the subjects offered, and at the end of her first year in grade thirteen—what should have been her final year—Grace took examinations in history and botany and zoology and English and Latin and French, receiving unnecessarily high marks. But there she was in September, back again, proposing to study physics and chemistry, trigonometry, geometry, and algebra, though these subjects were considered particularly hard for girls. She did creditably well in all three branches of mathematics and in the sciences, though her results were not as spectacular as they had been the year before. She thought, then, of teaching herself Greek and Spanish and Italian and German, so that she could try those exams the following year—those subjects were not taught by any teacher at her school—but the principal took her aside and told her that this was getting her nowhere, since she was not going to be able to go to college, and, anyway, no college required such a full plate. Why was she doing it? Did she have any plans?

No, Grace said, she just wanted to learn everything you could learn for free. Before she started her career of caning.

It was the principal who knew the manager of the inn at Bailey's Falls and said that he would put in a word for her if she wanted to try for a summer waitressing job. He, too, mentioned getting "a taste of life."

So even the man in charge of learning in that place did not believe that learning had to do with life. He thought that what she had done was crazy, as everyone else did.

Except Mrs. Travers, who had been sent to business college, instead of a real college, in order to make herself useful, and who now wished like anything, she said, that she had crammed her mind first with what was useless.

. . .

By trading shifts with another girl, Grace managed to get Sundays off, from breakfast on. This meant that she always worked late on Saturdays. In effect, it meant that she had traded time with Maury for time with Maury's family. She and Maury could never see a movie now, never have a real date. Instead, he would pick her up when she got off work, around eleven at night, and they would go for a drive, stop for ice cream or a hamburger—Maury was scrupulous about not taking her into a bar, because she was not yet twenty-one—then end up parking somewhere.

Grace's memories of these parking sessions—which might last till one or two in the morning—proved to be much hazier than her memories of sitting at the Traverses' round dining table or, after everybody had finally got up and moved, with coffee or fresh drinks, on the tawny leather sofa or the cushioned wicker chairs at the other end of the room. (There was never any fuss about doing the dishes; a woman Mrs. Travers called "the able Mrs. Abel" would come in the morning.)

Maury always dragged cushions onto the rug and sat there. Gretchen, who never dressed for dinner in anything but jeans or Army pants, usually sat cross-legged in a wide chair. Both she and Maury were big and broad-shouldered, with something of their mother's good looks—her wavy caramel-colored hair, warm hazel eyes, easily sun-browned skin. Even, in Maury's case, her dimple. (The other waitresses called Maury "cute" and "hunky," and respected Grace somewhat more since she had got him.) Mrs. Travers, however, was barely five feet tall, and under her bright muumuus seemed not fat but sturdily plump, like a child who hasn't stretched up yet. And the shine, the intentness, of her eyes, the gaiety that was always ready to break out in them, had not been inherited. Nor had the rough red, almost a rash, on her cheeks, which was probably a result of going out in any weather without thinking about her complexion, and which, like her figure, like her muumuus, showed her independence.

There were sometimes guests, in addition to Grace, on these Sunday evenings. A couple, maybe a single person as well, usually close to Mr. and Mrs. Travers's age, and not unlike them. The women would be eager and witty, and the men quieter, slower, more tolerant. These people told amusing stories in which the joke was often on themselves. (Grace has been an engaging talker for so long now that she sometimes gets sick of herself, and it's hard for her to remember how novel these dinner conversations once seemed to her. On the rare occasions when her aunt and uncle had had company, there had been only praise of and apology for the food, discussion of the weather, and a fervent wish for the meal to be finished as soon as possible.)

After dinner at the Travers house, if the evening was cool enough, Mr. Travers lit a fire, and they played what Mrs. Travers called "idiotic word games," for which, in fact, people had to be fairly clever to win. Here was where somebody who had been rather quiet at dinner might begin to shine. Mock arguments could be built up in defense of preposterous definitions. Gretchen's husband, Wat, did this, and so, after a bit, did Grace, to Mrs. Travers's and Maury's delight (with Maury calling out, to everyone's amusement but Grace's, "See? I told you. She's smart"). Mrs. Travers herself led the way in this making up of ridiculous words, insuring that the play did not become too serious or any player too anxious.

The only time there was a problem was one evening when Mavis, who was married to Mrs. Travers's son Neil, came to dinner. Mavis and Neil and their two children were staying nearby, at her parents' place down the lake. But that night she came by herself—Neil was a doctor, and he was busy in Ottawa that weekend. Mrs. Travers was disappointed, but she rallied, calling out in cheerful dismay, "But the children aren't in Ottawa, surely?"

"Unfortunately not," Mavis said. "But they're thoroughly awful. They'd shriek all through dinner. The baby's got prickly heat, and God knows what's the matter with Mikey."

She was a slim, suntanned woman in a purple dress, with a matching wide purple band holding back her dark hair. Handsome, but with little pouches of boredom or disapproval hiding the corners of her mouth. She left most of her dinner untouched on her plate, explaining that she had an allergy to curry.

"Oh, Mavis. What a shame," Mrs. Travers said. "Is this new?"

"Oh, no. I've had it for ages, but I used to be polite about it. Then I got sick of throwing up half the night."

"If you'd only told me . . . What can we get you?"

"Don't worry about it. I'm fine. I don't have any appetite anyway, what with the heat and the joys of motherhood."

She lit a cigarette.

Afterward, in the game, she got into an argument with Wat over a definition he'd used, and when the dictionary proved it acceptable she said, "Oh, I'm sorry. I guess I'm just outclassed by you people." And when it came time for everybody to hand in their own word on a slip of paper for the next round she smiled and shook her head. "I don't have one."

"Oh, Mavis," Mrs. Travers said.

And Mr. Travers said, "Come on, Mavis. Any old word will do."

"But I don't have any old word. I'm sorry. I just feel stupid tonight. The rest of you just play around me."

Which they did, everybody pretending that nothing was wrong, while she smoked and continued to smile her determined, unhappy smile. In a little while she got up and said that she couldn't leave her children on their grandparents' hands any longer. She'd had a lovely and instructive visit, and now she had to go home.

"I must give you an Oxford dictionary next Christmas," she said to nobody in particular before she left, with a merry, bitter little laugh. The Traverses' dictionary, which Wat had used, was an American one.

When she was gone, none of them looked at one another. Mrs. Travers said, "Gretchen, do you have the strength to make us all a pot of coffee?" And Gretchen went off to the kitchen, muttering, "What fun. Jesus wept."

"Well. Her life is trying," Mrs. Travers said. "With the two little ones."

On Wednesdays, Grace got a break between clearing breakfast and setting up dinner, and when Mrs. Travers found out about this she started driving up to Bailey's Falls to bring her down to the lake for those free hours. Maury would be at work then—he was spending the summer with the road gang repairing Highway 7—and Wat would be in his office in Ottawa and Gretchen would be off with the children, swimming or rowing on the lake. Usually Mrs. Travers herself would announce that she had shopping to do or letters to write, and she would leave Grace alone in the big, cool, shaded living-dining room, with its permanently dented leather sofa and crowded bookshelves.

"Read anything that takes your fancy," Mrs. Travers said. "Or curl up and go to sleep, if that's what you'd like. It's a hard job—you must be tired. I'll make sure you're back on time."

Grace never slept. She read. She barely moved, and her bare legs below her shorts became sweaty and stuck to the leather. Quite often she saw nothing of Mrs. Travers until it was time for her to be driven back to work.

In the car, Mrs. Travers would not start any sort of conversation until enough time had passed for Grace's thoughts to have shaken loose from whatever book she had been in. Then she might mention having read it herself, and say what she had thought of it—but always in a way that was both thoughtful and lighthearted. For instance, she said, of *Anna Karenina*, "I don't know how many times I've read it, but I know that first I identified with Kitty, and then it was Anna—oh, it was awful with Anna—and now, you know, the last time, I found myself sympathizing with Dolly. When she goes to the country, you know, with all those children, and she has to figure out how to do the washing, there's the problem about the washtubs—I suppose that's just how your sympathies change as you get older. Passion gets pushed behind the washtubs. Don't pay any attention to me, anyway. You don't, do you?"

"I don't know if I pay much attention to anybody." Grace was surprised at herself, wondered if she sounded conceited. "But I like listening to you talk."

Mrs. Travers laughed. "I like listening to myself, too."

Somehow, by the middle of the summer Maury had begun to talk about their being married. This would not happen for quite a while, he said— not until after he was qualified and working as an engineer—but he spoke of it as something that she, as well as he, must be taking for granted. "When we are married," he'd say, and, instead of questioning or contradicting him, Grace would listen curiously.

When they were married, they would have a place on Sabot Lake. Not too close to his parents, not too far away. It would be just a summer place, of course. The rest of the time they would live wherever his work might take them. It could be anywhere—Peru, Iraq, the Northwest Territories. Grace was delighted by the idea of such travels—rather more than she was by the idea of what he spoke of, with a severe pride, as "our own home." None of this seemed at all real to her, but then the idea of helping her uncle, of taking on the life of a chair-caner in the town and in the very house where she had grown up, had never seemed real either.

Maury kept asking her what she had told her aunt and uncle about him, when she was going to take him home to meet them. In fact, she had said nothing in her brief weekly letters, except to mention that she was "going out with a boy who works around here for the summer." She might have given the impression that he worked at the hotel.

It wasn't as if she had never thought of getting married. That possibility had been in her mind, along with the life of caning chairs. In spite of the fact that nobody had ever courted her, she had felt sure that it *would* happen someday, and in exactly this way—with the man making up his mind immediately. He would see her and, having seen her, he would fall in love. In her imagination, he was handsome, like Maury. Passionate, like Maury. Pleasurable physical intimacies followed.

But this was the thing that had not happened. In Maury's car, or out on the grass under the stars, she was willing. And Maury was ready, but not willing. He felt that it was his responsibility to protect her. And the ease with which she offered herself threw him off balance. He sensed, perhaps, that it was cold—a deliberate offering that he could not understand and that did not fit in at all with his notions of her. She herself did not realize how cold she was—she believed that her show of eagerness would lead to the pleasures she knew about, in solitude and in her imagination, and she felt that it was up to Maury to take over. Which he would not do.

These sieges left them both disturbed and slightly angry or ashamed, so that they could not stop kissing, clinging, and using fond words to make it up to each other as they said good night. It was a relief to Grace to be alone, to get into bed in the hotel dormitory and blot the last couple of hours out of her mind. And she thought it must be a relief to Maury, too, to be driving down the highway by himself, rearranging his impressions of his Grace so that he could stay wholeheartedly in love with her.

Most of the waitresses left after Labor Day, to go back to school or college. But the hotel was going to stay open till October, for Thanksgiving, with a reduced staff—Grace among them. There was talk, this year, of opening again in early December for a winter season, or at least a Christmas season, but nobody on the kitchen or dining-room staff seemed to know if this would really happen. Grace wrote to her aunt and uncle as if the Christmas season were a certainty and they should not expect her back anytime soon.

Why did she do this? It was not as if she had other plans. Maury was in his final year at college. She had even promised to take him home at

Christmas to meet her family. And he had said that Christmas would be a good time to make their engagement formal. He was saving up his summer wages to buy her a diamond ring.

She, too, had been saving her wages, so that she would be able to take the bus to Kingston, to visit him during his school term.

She spoke of this, promised it, so easily. But did she believe, or even wish, that it would happen?

"Maury is a sterling character," Mrs. Travers said. "Well, you can see that for yourself. He will be a dear, uncomplicated man, like his father. Not like his brother. Neil is very bright. I don't mean that Maury isn't— you certainly don't get to be an engineer without a brain or two in your head—but Neil is . . . He's deep." She laughed at herself. "*Deep unfathomable caves of ocean bear*—What am I talking about? For a long time, Neil and I didn't have anybody but each other. So I think he's special. I don't mean he can't be fun. But sometimes people who are the most fun can be melancholy, can't they? You wonder about them. But what's the use of worrying about your grown-up children? With Neil I worry a lot, with Maury only a tiny little bit. And Gretchen I don't worry about at all. Because women have always got something, haven't they, to keep them going?"

The house on the lake was never closed up till Thanksgiving. Gretchen and the children had to go back to Ottawa, of course, for school. And Maury had to go to Kingston. Mr. Travers could come out only on weekends. But Mrs. Travers had told Grace that she usually stayed on, sometimes with guests, sometimes by herself.

Then her plans changed. She went back to Ottawa with Mr. Travers in September. This happened unexpectedly—the Sunday dinner that week was canceled.

Maury explained that his mother got into trouble, now and then, with her nerves. "She has to have a rest," he said. "She has to go into the hospital for a couple of weeks or so, and they get her stabilized. She always comes out fine."

Grace said that Mrs. Travers was the last person she would have expected to have such troubles. "What brings it on?"

"I don't think they know," Maury said. But after a moment he added,

"Well. It could be her husband. I mean, her first husband. Neil's father. What happened with him, et cetera."

What had happened was that Neil's father had killed himself.

"He was unstable, I guess. But I don't know if it even is that. It could be her age, and female problems and all that sort of thing. But it's O.K.—they can get her straightened out easy now, with drugs. They've got terrific drugs. Don't worry about it."

By Thanksgiving, as Maury had predicted, Mrs. Travers was out of the hospital and feeling well. Thanksgiving dinner would take place at the lake, as usual. And it was being held on Sunday, instead of Monday—that was also customary, to allow for the packing up and closing of the house. And it was fortunate for Grace, because Sunday was still her day off.

The whole family would be there, even Neil and Mavis and their children, who were staying at Mavis's parents' place. No guests—unless you counted Grace.

By the time Maury brought her down to the lake on Sunday morning, the turkey was already in the oven. The pies were on the kitchen counter—pumpkin, apple, wild blueberry. Gretchen was in charge of the kitchen, as coordinated a cook as she was an athlete. Mrs. Travers sat at the kitchen table, drinking coffee and working on a jigsaw puzzle with Gretchen's younger daughter, Dana.

"Ah, Grace," she said, jumping up for an embrace—the first time she had ever done this—and with a clumsy motion of her hand scattering the jigsaw pieces.

Dana wailed, "*Grand*-ma," and her older sister, Janey, who had been watching critically, scooped up the pieces.

"We can easy put them back together," she said. "Grandma didn't mean to."

"Where do you keep the cranberry sauce?" Gretchen asked.

"In the cupboard," Mrs. Travers said, still squeezing Grace's arms and ignoring the destroyed puzzle.

"*Where* in the cupboard?"

"Oh. Cranberry sauce," Mrs. Travers said. "Well, I make it. First I put the cranberries in a little water. Then I keep it on low heat—no, I think I soak them first—"

"Well, I haven't got time for all that," Gretchen said. "You mean you don't have any canned?"

"I guess not. I must not have, because I make it."

"I'll have to send somebody to get some."

"Dear, it's Thanksgiving," Mrs. Travers said gently. "Nowhere will be open."

"That place down the highway, it's always open." Gretchen raised her voice. "Where's Wat?"

"He's out in the rowboat," Mavis called from the back bedroom. She made it sound like a warning, because she was trying to get her baby to sleep. "He took Mikey out in the boat."

Mavis had driven over in her own car, with Mikey and the baby. Neil was coming later—he had some phone calls to make.

And Mr. Travers had gone golfing.

"It's just that I need somebody to go to the store," Gretchen said. She waited, but no offer came from the bedroom. She raised her eyebrows at Grace. "You can't drive, can you?"

Grace said no.

Mrs. Travers sat down, with a gracious sigh.

"Well," Gretchen said. "Maury can drive. Where's Maury?"

Maury was in the front bedroom looking for his swimming trunks, though everybody had told him that the water was too cold for swimming. He said that the store would not be open.

"It will be," Gretchen said. "They sell gas. And if it isn't there's that one just coming into Perth—you know, with the ice-cream cones."

Maury wanted Grace to come with him, but the two little girls, Janey and Dana, were begging her to come see the swing that their grandfather had put up under the Norway maple at the side of the house.

As Grace was going down the steps, she felt the strap of one of her sandals break. She took both shoes off and walked without difficulty on the sandy soil, across the flat-pressed plantain and the many curled leaves that had already fallen.

First she pushed the children in the swing, then they pushed her. It was when she jumped off, barefoot, that one leg crumpled and she let out a yelp of pain, not knowing what had happened.

It was her foot, not her leg. The pain had shot up from the sole of her left foot, which had been cut by the sharp edge of a clamshell.

"Dana brought those shells," Janey said. "She was going to make a house for her snail."

"He got away," Dana said.

Gretchen and Mrs. Travers and even Mavis had come running out of the house, thinking that the cry had come from one of the children.

"She's got a bloody foot," Dana said. "There's blood all over the ground."

Janey said, "She cut it on a shell. Dana left those shells here—she was going to build a house for Ivan. Ivan her snail."

A basin was brought out, with water to wash the cut and a towel, and everyone asked how much it hurt.

"Not too bad," Grace said, limping to the steps, with both girls competing to hold her up and generally getting in her way.

"Oh, that's nasty," Gretchen said. "But why weren't you wearing your shoes?"

"Broke her strap," Dana and Janey said together, as a wine-colored convertible swerved neatly into the parking space by the house.

"Now, that is what I call opportune," Mrs. Travers said. "Here's the very man we need. The doctor."

This was Neil—the first time that Grace had ever seen him. He was tall, thin, impatient.

"Your bag," Mrs. Travers cried gaily. "We've already got a case for you."

"Nice piece of junk you've got there," Gretchen said. "New?"

Neil said, "Piece of folly."

"Now the baby's awake," Mavis said, with a sigh of unspecific accusation. She went back into the house.

"Don't tell me you haven't got it with you," Mrs. Travers said. But Neil swung a doctor's bag out of the backseat, and she said, "Oh, yes, you have. That's good. You never know."

"You the patient?" Neil said to Dana. "What's the matter? Swallow a toad?"

"It's her," Dana said with dignity. "It's *Grace*."

"I see. *She* swallowed the toad."

"She *cut her foot*."

"On a clamshell," Janey said.

Neil said, "Move over," to his nieces, and sat on the step below Grace. He carefully lifted the foot and said, "Give me that cloth or whatever," then blotted away the blood to get a look at the cut. Now that he was so close to her, Grace noticed a smell that she had learned to identify over the summer, working at the inn—the smell of liquor edged with mint.

"Hurts?" he asked.

Grace said, "Some."

He looked briefly, though searchingly, into her face. Perhaps wondering if she had caught the smell and what she had thought about it.

"I bet. See that flap? We have to get under there and make sure it's clean, then I'll put a stitch or two in it. I've got some stuff I can rub on it, so that won't hurt as much as you might think." He looked up at Gretchen. "Hey. Let's get the audience out of the way here."

He had not spoken a word, as yet, to his mother, who now said again what a good thing it was that he had come along just when he did.

"Boy Scout," he said. "Always prepared."

His hands didn't feel drunk, and his eyes didn't look it. Nor did he look like the jolly uncle he had impersonated when he talked to the children, or the purveyor of reassuring patter he had chosen to be with Grace. He had a high pale forehead, a crest of tight curly gray-black hair, bright gray but slightly sunken eyes, high cheekbones, and rather hollowed cheeks. If his face relaxed, he would look somber and hungry.

When the cut had been dealt with, Neil said that he thought it would be a good idea to run Grace into town, to the hospital. "For an antitetanus shot."

"It doesn't feel too bad," Grace said.

Neil said, "That's not the point."

"I agree," Mrs. Travers said. "Tetanus—that's terrible."

"We shouldn't be long," he said. "Here. Grace? Grace, I'll get you to the car." He held her under one arm. She had strapped on the good sandal, and managed to get her toes into the other, so that she could drag it along. The bandage was very neat and tight.

"I'll just run in," he said, when she was sitting in the car. "Make my apologies."

Mrs. Travers came down from the veranda and put her hand on the car door.

"This is good," she said. "This is very good. Grace, you are a godsend. You'll try to keep him away from drinking today, won't you? You'll know how to do it."

Grace heard these words, but didn't give them much thought. She was too dismayed by the change in Mrs. Travers, by what looked like an increase in bulk, a stiffness in her movements, a random and rather frantic air of benevolence. And a faint crust showing at the corners of her mouth, like sugar.

The hospital was three miles away. There was a highway overpass above the railway tracks, and they took this at such speed that Grace had the impression, at its crest, that the car had lifted off the pavement and they were flying. There was hardly any traffic, so she wasn't frightened, and anyway there was nothing she could do.

Neil knew the nurse who was on duty in Emergency, and after he had filled out a form and let her take a passing look at Grace's foot ("Nice job," she said without interest) he was able to go ahead and give the tetanus shot himself. ("It won't hurt now, but it could later.") Just as he finished, the nurse came back into the cubicle and said, "There's a guy in the waiting room who wants to take her home."

She said to Grace, "He says he's your fiancé."

"Tell him she's not ready yet," Neil said. "No. Tell him we've already gone."

"I said you were in here."

"But when you came back," Neil said, "we were gone."

"He said he was your brother. Won't he see your car in the lot?"

"But I parked out back in the doctor's lot."

"*Pret*-ty *trick*-y," the nurse said, over her shoulder.

And Neil said to Grace, "You didn't want to go home yet, did you?"

"No," Grace said, as if she'd seen the word written in front of her, on the wall. As if she were having her eyes tested.

Once more she was helped to the car, sandal flopping from the toe strap, and settled on the creamy upholstery. They took a back street out of the lot, an unfamiliar way out of town.

She knew that they wouldn't see Maury. She did not think of him. Still less of Mavis.

Describing this passage, this change in her life, later on, Grace might say—she did say—that it was as if a gate had clanged shut behind her. But at the time there was no clang—acquiescence simply rippled through her, and the rights of those left behind were smoothly canceled out.

Her memory of this day remained clear and detailed for a long time, though there was a variation in the parts of it she dwelled on.

And even in some of those details she must have been wrong.

First they drove west, on Highway 7. In Grace's recollection, there was not another car on the highway, and their speed approached the flight on the highway overpass. This cannot have been true—there must have been people on the road, people on their way home from church that Sunday morning, or on their way to spend Thanksgiving with their families. Neil must have slowed down when driving through villages, and around the many curves on the old highway. She was not used to driving in a convertible with the top down, wind in her eyes, taking charge of her hair. It gave her the illusion of constant perfect speed—not frantic but miraculous, serene.

And though Maury and Mavis and the rest of the family had been wiped from her mind, some scrap of Mrs. Travers did remain, hovering, delivering in a whisper and with a strange, shamed giggle, her last message.

You'll know how to do it.

Grace and Neil did not talk, of course. As she remembers it, you would have had to scream to be heard. And what she remembers is, to tell the truth, hardy distinguishable from her idea, her fantasies at that time, of what sex should be like. The fortuitous meeting, the muted but powerful signals, the nearly silent flight in which she herself figured more or less as a captive. An airy surrender, her flesh nothing now but a stream of desire.

They stopped, finally, in Kaladar, and went into the hotel—the old hotel that is still there. Taking her hand, kneading his fingers between hers, slowing his pace to match her uneven steps, Neil led her into the bar. She recognized it as a bar, though she had never been in one before. (Bailey's Falls Inn did not yet have a license, so drinking was done in people's rooms, or in a rather ramshackle nightclub across the road.) This bar was just as she would have expected—a big, dark, airless room, with the chairs and tables rearranged in a careless way after a hasty cleanup, the smell of Lysol not erasing the smell of beer, whiskey, cigars, pipes, men.

A man came in from another room and spoke to Neil. He said, "Hello there, Doc," and went behind the bar.

It occurred to Grace that it would be like this everywhere they went—people would know Neil.

"You know it's Sunday," the man said in a stern, almost shouting voice, as if he wanted to be heard out in the parking lot. "I can't sell you anything in here on a Sunday. And I can't sell anything to her, ever. She shouldn't even be in here. You understand that?"

"Oh, yes, sir. Yes, indeed, sir," Neil said. "I heartily agree, sir."

While both men were talking, the man behind the bar had taken a bottle of whiskey from a hidden shelf and poured some into a glass and shoved it across the counter to Neil.

"You thirsty?" he asked Grace. He was already opening a Coke. He gave it to her without a glass.

Neil put a bill on the counter, and the man shoved it away.

"I told you," he said. "Can't sell."

"What about the Coke?" Neil said.

"Can't sell."

The man put the bottle away. Neil drank what was in the glass very quickly. "You're a good man," he said. "Spirit of the law."

"Take the Coke along with you. Sooner she's out of here the happier I'll be."

"You bet," Neil said. "She's a good girl. My sister-in-law. Future sister-in-law. So I understand."

"Is that the truth?"

They didn't go back to Highway 7. Instead, they took the road north, which was not paved but was wide enough and decently graded. The drink seemed to have affected Neil's driving in the opposite way than it was supposed to. He had slowed down to the seemly, even cautious rate that this road required.

"You don't mind?" he said.

Grace said, "Mind what?"

"Being dragged into any old place."

"No."

"I need your company. How's your foot?"

"It's fine."

"It must hurt some."

"Not really. It's O.K."

He picked up the hand that was not holding the Coke bottle, pressed the palm of it to his mouth, gave it a lick, and let it drop.

"Did you think I was abducting you for fell purposes?"

"No," Grace lied, thinking how like his mother that word was. *Fell.*

"There was a time when you would have been right," he said, just as if she had answered yes. "But not today. I don't think so. You're safe as a church today."

The changed tone of his voice, which had become intimate, frank, and quiet, and the memory of his lips pressed, his tongue flicked, across her skin, affected Grace to such an extent that she was hearing the words but not the sense of what he was telling her. She could feel a hundred flicks of his tongue, a dance of supplication, all over her skin. But she thought to say, "Churches aren't always safe."

"True. True."

"And I'm not your sister-in-law."

"Future. Didn't I say future?"

"I'm not that, either."

"Oh. Well. I guess I'm not surprised. No. Not surprised."

Then his voice changed again, became businesslike.

"I'm looking for a turnoff up here, to the right. There's a road I ought to recognize. Do you know this country at all?"

"Not around here, no."

"Don't know Flower Station? Ompah? Poland? Snow Road?"

She had not heard of them.

"There's somebody I want to see."

A turn was made, to the right, with some dubious mutterings on his part. There were no signs. This road was narrower and rougher, with a one-lane plank-floored bridge. The trees of the hardwood forest laced their branches overhead. The weather had been strangely warm this year, and the leaves were still green, except for the odd one here and there that flashed out like a banner. There was a feeling of sanctuary. For miles, Neil and Grace were quiet, and there was still no break in the trees, no end to the forest. But then Neil broke the peace.

He said, "Can you drive?" And when Grace said no he said, "I think you should learn."

He meant right then. He stopped the car, got out, and came around to her side, gesturing to her to move behind the wheel.

"No better place than this."

"What if something comes?"

"Nothing will. And we can manage if it does. That's why I picked a straight stretch."

He did not bother explaining anything about how cars ran—he simply showed her where to put her feet, and made her practice shifting the gears, then said, "Now go, and do what I tell you."

The first leap of the car terrified her. She ground the gears, and she thought he would put an end to the lesson immediately, but he just laughed. He said, "Whoa, easy. Easy. Keep going," and she did. He did not comment on her steering, except to say, "Keep going, keep going, keep on the road, don't let the engine die."

"When can I stop?" she said.

"Not till I tell you how."

He made her keep driving until they came out of the tunnel of trees, and then he instructed her about the brake. As soon as she had stopped, she opened the door so that they could trade sides, but he said, "No. This is just a breather. Soon you'll be getting to like it." And when they started again she began to see that he might be right. Her momentary surge of confidence almost took them into a ditch. Still, he laughed when he had to grab the wheel, and the lesson continued.

She drove for what seemed like miles, and even went—slowly—around several curves. Then he said that they had better switch back, because he could not get a feeling of direction unless he was driving.

He asked how she felt now, and though she was shaking all over she said, "O.K."

He rubbed her arm from shoulder to elbow and said, "What a liar." But did not touch her, beyond that, did not let any part of her feel his mouth again.

He must have got his feeling of direction back when they came to a crossroads some miles on, for he turned left, and the trees thinned out and they climbed a rough road up to a village, or at least a roadside collection of buildings. A church and a store, neither of them open to serve their original purposes but probably lived in, to judge by the vehicles around them and the sorry-looking curtains in the windows. There were a couple of houses in the same state, and, behind one of them, a barn that had fallen in on itself, with old dark hay bulging out between its cracked beams like swollen innards.

Neil exclaimed in celebration at the sight of this place, but did not stop there.

"What a relief," he said. "What—a—relief. Now I know. Thank you."

"Me?"

"For letting me teach you to drive. It calmed me down."

"Calmed you down?" Grace said. "Really?"

"True as I live." Neil was smiling, but he did not look at her. He was busy looking from side to side, across the fields that lay along the road after it had passed through the village. He was talking as if to himself. "This is it. Got to be it. Now we know."

And so on, till he turned onto a lane that didn't go straight but wound around through a field, avoiding rocks and patches of juniper. At the end of the lane was a house, in no better shape than the houses in the village.

"Now, this place," he said, "this place I am not going to take you into. I won't be five minutes."

He was longer than that.

She sat in the car, in the shade. The door to the house was open—just the screen door closed. The screen had mended patches in it, newer wire woven in with the old. Nobody came to look at her, not even a dog. And now that the car had stopped, the day filled up with an unnatural silence. Unnatural because on such a hot afternoon you would expect the buzzing and chirping of insects in the grass and in the juniper bushes. Even if you couldn't see them, their noise would seem to rise out of everything growing on the earth, as far as the horizon. But it was too late in the year, maybe too late even to hear geese honking as they flew south. At any rate, she didn't hear any.

It seemed that they were up on top of the world here. The field fell away on all sides; only the tips of the trees were visible, because they grew on lower ground.

Whom did Neil know, who lived in this house? A woman? It didn't seem possible that the sort of woman he would want could live in a place like this, but then there was no end to the strangeness that Grace could encounter today. No end to it.

Once, this had been a brick house, but someone had begun to take the brick walls down. Plain wooden walls had been bared underneath, and the bricks that had covered them were roughly piled in the yard, maybe waiting to be sold. The bricks left on the wall in front of her formed a diagonal line, a set of steps, and Grace, with nothing else to do, leaned back to count them. She did this both foolishly and seriously, the way you would pull petals off a flower, but not with any words so blatant as *He loves me, he loves me not.*

Lucky. Not. Lucky. Not. That was all she dared.

She found that it was hard to keep track of the bricks arranged in this zigzag fashion, especially since the line flattened out above the door.

Then she knew. What else could it be? A bootlegger's place. She thought of the bootlegger in the town where her aunt and uncle lived—a raddled, skinny old man, morose and suspicious. He sat on his front step with a shotgun on Halloween night. And he painted numbers on the sticks of firewood stacked by his door so he'd know if any were stolen. She thought of him—or this one—dozing in the heat, in his dirty but tidy room (she knew that it would be that way by the mended patches in the screen), getting up from his creaky cot or couch, covered with a stained quilt that some woman related to him, some woman now dead, had made long ago.

Not that she had ever been inside the bootlegger's house, but the partitions were thin, back home, between the threadbare ways of living that were respectable and those that were not. She knew how things were.

How strange that she'd thought of becoming one of them—a Travers. Marrying Maury. A kind of treachery, it would be. But not a treachery to be riding with Neil, because he wasn't fortunate—he knew some of the things that she did.

And then in the doorway it seemed that she could see her uncle, stooped and baffled, looking out at her, as if she had been away for years and years. As if she had promised to come home and then had forgotten about it, and in all this time he should have died but he hadn't.

She struggled to speak to him, but he was lost. She was waking up, moving. She was in the car with Neil, on the road again. She had been asleep with her mouth open and she was thirsty. He turned to her for a moment, and she noticed, even with the wind blowing around them, a fresh smell of whiskey.

"You awake? You were fast asleep when I came out of there," he said. "Sorry—I had to be sociable for a while. How's your bladder?"

That was a problem she had been thinking about, in fact, while she was waiting. She had seen a toilet behind the house, but had felt shy about getting out and walking to it.

He said, "This looks like a possible place," and stopped the car. She got out and walked in among some blooming goldenrod and Queen Anne's lace and wild asters, to squat down. He stood in the flowers on the other side, with his back to her. When she got into the car, she saw the bottle, on the floor beside her feet. More than a third of its contents seemed already to be gone.

He saw her looking.

"Oh, don't worry," he said. "I just poured some in here." He held up a flask. "Easier when I'm driving."

On the floor there was also another Coca-Cola. He told her to look in the glove compartment for a bottle opener.

"It's cold!" she said in surprise.

"Icebox. They cut ice off the lakes in the winter and store it in sawdust. He keeps it under the house."

"I thought I saw my uncle in the doorway of that house," she said. "But I was dreaming."

"You could tell me about your uncle. Tell me about where you live. Your job. Anything. I just like to hear you talk."

There was a new strength in his voice, and a change in his face, but it wasn't the manic glow of drunkenness. It was as if he'd been sick—not terribly sick, just down, under the weather—and was now wanting to assure her that he was better. He capped the flask and laid it down and reached for her hand. He held it lightly, a comrade's clasp.

"He's quite old," Grace said. "He's really my great-uncle. He's a caner—that means he canes chairs. I can't explain that to you, but I could show you how, if we had a chair to cane—"

"I don't see one."

She laughed, and said, "It's boring, really."

"Tell me about what interests you, then. What interests you?"

She said, "You do."

"Oh. What about me interests you?" His hand slid away.

"What you're doing now," Grace said determinedly. "Why."

"You mean drinking? Why I'm drinking?" The cap came off the flask again. "Why don't you ask me?"

"Because I know what you'd say."

"What's that? What would I say?"

"You'd say, 'What else is there to do?' Or something like that."

"That's true," he said. "That's about what I'd say. Well, then you'd try to tell me why I was wrong."

"No," Grace said. "No. I wouldn't."

When she'd said that, she felt cold. She had thought that she was serious, but now she saw that she'd been trying to impress him, to show that she was as worldly as he was, and in the middle of that she had come on a rock-bottom truth, a lack of hope that was genuine, reasonable, everlasting. There was no comfort in what she saw, now that she could see it.

Neil said, "You wouldn't? No. You wouldn't. That's a relief. You are a relief, Grace."

In a while he said, "You know, I'm sleepy. Soon as we find a good spot I'm going to pull over and go to sleep. Just for a little while. Would you mind that?"

"No. I think you should."

"You'll watch over me?"

"Yes."

"Good."

The spot he found was in a little town called Fortune. There was a park on the outskirts, beside a river, and a graveled space for cars. He settled the seat back, and at once fell asleep. Evening had come on as it did now, around suppertime, proving that this wasn't a summer day after all. A short while ago, people had been having a Thanksgiving picnic here—there was still some smoke rising from the outdoor fireplace, and the smell of hamburgers in the air. The smell did not make Grace hungry, exactly—it made her remember being hungry, in other circumstances.

Some dust had settled on her, with all the stopping and starting of her driving lesson. She got out and washed her hands and her face as well as she could, at an outdoor tap. Then, favoring her cut foot, she walked slowly to the edge of the river, saw how shallow it was, with reeds breaking the surface. A sign there warned that profanity, obscenity, or vulgar language was forbidden in this place and would be punished.

She tried the swings, which faced west. Pumping herself high, she looked into the clear sky—faint green, fading gold, a fierce pink rim at the horizon. Already the air was getting cold.

She had thought that it was touch. Mouths, tongues, skin, bodies, banging bone on bone. Inflammation. Passion. But that wasn't what she'd been working toward at all. She had seen deeper, deeper into him than she could ever have managed if they'd gone that way.

What she saw was final. As if she were at the edge of a flat dark body of water that stretched on and on. Cold, level water. Looking out at such dark, cold, level water, and knowing that it was all there was.

It wasn't the drinking that was responsible. Drinking, needing to drink—that was just some sort of distraction, like everything else, from the thing that was waiting, no matter what, all the time.

She went back to the car and tried to rouse him. He stirred but wouldn't waken. So she walked around again to keep warm, and to practice the easiest way with her foot—she understood now that she would be working again, serving breakfast in the morning.

She tried once more, talking to him urgently. He answered with various promises and mutters, and once more he fell asleep. By the time it was really dark she had given up. Now, with the cold of night settled in, some other facts became clear to her: that they could not remain here, that they were still in the world, after all, that she had to get back to Bailey's Falls.

With some difficulty, she got him over into the passenger seat. If that did not wake him, it was clear that nothing could. It took her a while to figure out how the headlights went on, and then she began to move the car, jerkily, slowly, back onto the road.

She had no idea of directions, and there was not a soul on the street to ask. She just kept driving, to the other side of the town, and there, most blessedly, was a sign pointing the way to Bailey's Falls, among other places. Only nine miles.

She drove along the two-lane highway, never at more than thirty miles an hour. There was little traffic. Once or twice a car passed her, honking, and the few she met honked also. In one case, it was probably because she was going so slowly, and, in the other, because she did not know how to dim the lights. Never mind. She couldn't stop to get her courage up again. She had to just keep going, as he had said. Keep going.

At first she did not recognize Bailey's Falls, coming upon it in this unfamiliar way. When she did, she became more frightened than she had been in all the nine miles. It was one thing to drive in unknown territory, another to turn in at the inn gates.

He was awake when she stopped in the parking lot. He didn't show any surprise at where they were, or at what she had done. In fact, he told her, the honking had woken him, miles back, but he had pretended to be still asleep, because the important thing was not to startle her. He hadn't been worried, though. He'd known that she would make it.

She asked if he was awake enough to drive now.

"Wide awake. Bright as a dollar."

He told her to slip her foot out of its sandal, and he pressed it here and there, before saying, "Nice. No heat. No swelling. Your arm hurt from the shot? Maybe it won't." He walked her to the door, and thanked her for her company. She was still amazed to be safely back. She hardly realized that it was time to say goodbye.

As a matter of fact, she does not know, to this day, if those words were spoken or if he only caught her, wound his arms around her, held her so tightly, with such continuous, changing pressure that it seemed as if more than two arms were needed, as if she were surrounded by him, his body strong and light, demanding and renouncing all at once, telling her that she was wrong to give up on him, everything was possible, but then again that she was not wrong, he meant to stamp himself on her and go.

Early in the morning, the manager knocked on the dormitory door, calling for Grace.

"Somebody on the phone," he said. "Don't bother getting up—they just wanted to know if you were here. I said I'd go and check. O.K. now."

It would be Maury, she thought. One of them, anyway. But probably Maury. Now she'd have to deal with Maury.

When she went down to serve breakfast—wearing running shoes, one loosely laced—she heard about the accident. A car had gone into a bridge abutment halfway down the road to Sabot Lake. It had been rammed right in—it was totally smashed and burned up. There were no other cars involved, and apparently no passengers. The driver would have to be identified by dental records. Or probably had been, by this time.

"One hell of a way," the manager said. "Better to go and cut your throat."

"It could've been an accident," said the cook, who had an optimistic nature. "Could've just fell asleep."

"Yeah. Sure."

Her arm hurt now, as if it had taken a wicked blow. She couldn't balance her tray, and had to carry it in front of her, using both hands instead.

She did not have to deal with Maury face-to-face. He wrote her a letter.

Just say he made you do it. Just say you didn't want to go.

She wrote back five words. *I did want to go.*

She was going to add, *I'm sorry,* but stopped herself.

Mr. Travers came to the inn to see her a few days later. He was polite and businesslike, firm, cool, not unkind. She saw him now in circumstances that let him come into his own. A man who could take charge, who could tidy things up. He said that it was very sad, they were all very sad, but alcoholism was a terrible thing. When Mrs. Travers was a little better, he was going to take her on a trip, a vacation, somewhere warm.

Then he said that he had to be going. He had many things to do. As he shook her hand to say goodbye, he put an envelope into it.

"We both hope you'll make good use of this," he said.

The check was for a thousand dollars. Immediately she thought of sending it back or tearing it up, and sometimes even now she thinks that that would have been a grand thing to do. But in the end, of course, she was not able to do it. In those days, it was enough money to insure her a start in life.

George Makana Clark

The Center of the World

For dinner, I warmed an opened tin of meat paste in the convection oven, a massive appliance that in times past accommodated a prison loaf large enough to feed thirty-nine boys. The cooking smells rose with the heat into the rafters of the empty dining facility.

Days come to an abrupt end in the eastern highlands, and by the time I rose from the table, the view of the glen had already been replaced by my reflection on the windowpanes. I switched off the transistor radio, silencing the Christmas carols and war bulletins. Insurgents had crossed the Zambezi to fire up the faraway north country in these, the closing weeks of 1972.

As the last and sole ward of the Outreach Mission for Troubled Boys, it fell upon me to put out the lights and lock up. A framed map hung above the exit, paper continents arranged against a sea of blue felt. Africa rode too high on the equator, Rhodesia slightly left of middle, locating the mission dead center of the world.

Outside a man was unhitching a dented horse trailer from the Very Reverend's Range Rover. Mrs. Philips stood on the veranda of the rectory, arms folded, making certain the man left the blankets and tackle, which were not part of the purchase agreement. The Very Reverend had already retired for the night. Since the Prisons Department canceled its contract with the mission, he slept more than he was awake, leaving his wife to supervise the dissolution of his life's work.

"Where are you off to?" she asked me.

I shrugged. The stables no longer needed mucking. Earlier in the week a representative from the Rhodesian Security Forces had collected all the mission horses, excepting the mare that drowned in the river.

Mrs. Philips turned back to the rectory wherein her husband lay, the windows shuttered against his failure. "Go on then," she muttered.

I watched the man drive away with the battered trailer. Once, when the trailer was filled with horses, a green mamba had crawled inside and gotten itself stamped to a pulp. This was how the dents had been made. The mission cook told me this in the days before he ran away to join the war of liberation. He used to say that I collected stories like other boys collect dead bugs.

In my pocket was the typed notice I'd retrieved from the morning garbage:

NOTICE OF CREMATION AND DISPOSITION
H. Takafakare Crematory
"Pay your last respects, not your lifetime earnings"
This is to respectfully inform concerned persons that the burning and disposal of all remains correlative to the deceased will be conducted by end of removal day.

I started along the dirt track that cut across the compound. Each morning women from the trust land raised their yokes and tramped down the mountain path through the mission to fetch water from the river. In their stories they referred to the track as Three Man Road.

Before their relocation to the trust land, the water drawers had inhabited a village on the river near a sacred kopje where heaven joined with earth. Always they beat the ground with their walking sticks as they followed the track that took them back to the river of their youth. Their descent into the glen took less than an hour; the laden climb back to the trust land consumed the balance of their lives.

As they walked, the women took turns reciting a communal narrative that began in a time when God and animals still spoke to people. On the occasions when I accompanied them, the women spoke English, happy to have an audience. Always the cadence of their voices rose and fell with the beat of the walking sticks. And when the final words were uttered, *"That is all,"* and the women found themselves stranded in the present day, someone would cry out, *"A story!"* evoking a chorus from the others: *"Bring it!"* and the water drawers would begin again, reaching back into the days of creation.

I followed the track past the quiet stables, the abandoned outbuildings, the darkened dormitory that had once housed the criminal youth of our nation. These days Rhodesia needed her troubled boys for the war, and any interest in their redemption had evaporated. A soft tremor ran through the ground, making the soles of my feet itch. The glen lay on the southernmost boundary of a tectonic plate that stretched the length of Africa. It was a shifting, unsettled place and such quakes had become increasingly common, though nothing ever came of them.

The track crooked around the mission chapel, then traced the riverbank half a mile to the foot of a kopje that rose up from the bottom of the glen. Some ancient cataclysm had sheared away the summit, giving it the appearance of a colossal altar. A pillar of smoke spiraled up from the kopje into the gloaming.

I began my climb, stepping along one of the twin ruts that angled across the steep face, my footprints superimposed over the imprint of a balding tire. Snow fell against my face as I neared the top, the flakes warm on my cheeks. I brushed at them and my fingers came away gray and greasy.

The ground grew level beneath my feet as I reached the broad, flattened crest. In the darkness I could make out a brick oven that bulged and billowed amid a field of ash. A concrete-block house stood at the oven's mouth, illuminated by its flames. Chimes hung from the eaves, hollow bones that twisted and came together in dull, yet musical, clacks.

The owner of the field was named Mr. Takafakare, a failed sweet potato farmer given to great fits of coughing. He stood over a charred husk that had once been the neck and shoulder of the drowned mare. A lorry had been backed up to the oven, a chain saw in its empty bed.

"Come to see the horse-burning," Mr. Takafakare said.

I blinked through the pong of charred hair and fat. Mr. Takafakare gave a short bark of laughter that trailed into a phlegmy burr. "You almost missed it, young sir." He produced a perfectly white handkerchief, cleared his throat, and spat. The wind lifted flakes of burnt bone and tissue into a swirl of carbon waste that rose and fell from the field.

Mr. Takafakare had bought the field to grow sweet potatoes, and later added the kiln as a side business. He came on the idea after listening to an African Service radio broadcast in which an agriculturalist from the Ministry of Lands touted carbon as an excellent source for fertilizer. Mr. Takafakare quickly discovered there was no market for sweet potatoes grown in human ash, and the path of his life turned away from farming and toward burning. For twenty years the oven exhaled the marrow of blackened bones into his face, forcing him to retreat each night into his house where he buried his nose and mouth in freshly laundered linen handkerchiefs. Therein he spat and blew the corporeal residue of landless Shona, low-caste Indians, vagrants of mixed race, and diseased livestock.

Mr. Takafakare broke the mare's cremains in half with the edge of the spade, and they reared up in a flurry of sparks and ash that made me step back and cover my nose and mouth with my sleeve. My gaze fell upon a girl who stood atop a ladder against the roof of the house. She held a laundry basket on her hip, the tip of her nose barely visible beyond the line of her cheek. Moses-in-the-boat grew in a window box next to her, pointed tongues of purple and green wagging in the blasted air. The girl's skin and hair were a uniform gray, save for the brown of her forearms which looked as though they had been recently immersed in water. I watched her spread her father's handkerchiefs to wind-dry on the asbestos roof.

The cremator followed my gaze to his daughter. He might have told me to go home, but he knew I'd come from the mission and he didn't want any trouble. Ash rose in devils that swirled through the lower rungs as the girl descended the ladder with her empty basket.

Mr. Takafakare buried his face in his handkerchief, blew noisily, then presented her to me. "This is my child, Madota." It is a custom to give children names that reflect a family problem at the time of the birth, and so Mr. Takafakare called his daughter *Madota*, which in the Shona language means ashes. She stood before me in the light of the oven, enveloped in an aura of silence.

"A demon lives inside her," Mr. Takafakare told me. "She cannot speak." He shifted uneasily. "Come inside and eat something," he said finally.

Madota guided me into the house, her fingers exerting subtle pressures against my elbow. The furnishings inside were spare: a cooking pot and three metal bowls; a cardboard box containing groceries for the week; the typewriter and thesaurus which had produced the notice in my pocket; a sprung mattress, dark and shiny in the place where Mr. Takafakare lay alone each night in his own sweat; a bucket of river water; a neatly made doss where his daughter slept; and four gray volumes, Winston Churchill's *The History of the English-Speaking Peoples*, each with a facsimile signature of the former British prime minister scrawled across its cover in cramped, golden script, the handwriting of a megalomaniac. Their former owner was a teacher at the trust land school who died intestate. Mr. Takafakare had taken the books with the corpse as payment for the latter's removal, and now kept the volumes stacked on the floor for use as a stool.

An unframed picture of Mr. Takafakare's dead wife was affixed to the wall, her wedding ring suspended from a tack. Mrs. Takafakare's constitution had been defeated by the fine layer of human ash that covered every surface and utensil of that unclean house. It was said she left behind a corpse so diminished that when her husband folded and fed it into his oven the flames only licked at the shroud before subsiding. In desperation Mr. Takafakare doused his wife with petrol and she went up in a bituminous cloud that filled the sky until a cleansing rain erased it two days later.

Madota wiped the ash from the kitchen table before seating me in front of a large bowl of peanut butter soup. It tasted faintly of carbon, and I realized she had heated it atop the brick kiln. Her almond eyes followed each spoonful of soup to my mouth. I stared back, suddenly aware that I was eating her dinner.

I poured the unfinished soup into the sink and sat atop *The History of the English-Speaking Peoples*. Madota squatted on her haunches beside me and the earth trembled lightly as we looked out the window into a galaxy of stars that wavered in the heat of the brick oven. Her fingers were corded with muscle and tendon from a lifetime of wringing handkerchiefs. They squeezed my hand with a silent request. *Talk to me.*

I'd never spoken at length to a girl before and, as the warmth of her hand seeped into mine, I began to recite the stories I'd collected from the water drawers, braiding one into the next. "This happened in a time," I began, "when people still listened to God and animals."

As I spoke, Mr. Takafakare looked up at me from his mattress across the room, distressed with the way things were turning in these, the last months of his life. I had seen blood mixed with ash and mucus in his handkerchiefs and knew that soon Mr. Takafakare would be fed into his own oven.

The night wind rolled off the mountains, carrying away the heat from the oven, and the mare's remains cooled and fell to join the rest of the forgotten animals and ancestors that blanketed the flat summit of the kopje. Outside, hyenas, lured by the smell of charred meat, ploughed the field with their noses, breaking bones with their jaws and filling their bellies with ashes.

Four streams flowed down from the mountains that walled the glen. They came together to form the river, a topographical feature that, coupled with the abundance and variety of fruit trees, convinced the Very Reverend that he had found the location of Eden. He lobbied the Ministry of Lands and National Resources to bulldoze a Shona village and shift its inhabitants to the trust land on the mountainous periphery of the glen, so that he might establish the mission upon the geographical origins of his faith.

The Very Reverend no longer rose for breakfast. Mrs. Philips and I ate fried eggs at opposite ends of the dining facility, the tink of our flatware sounding unnaturally loud against the china plate in that cavernous place. When the mission's funding got the ax, the older boys were offered commuted sentences to join the Rhodesian Security Forces, while the younger ones were sent to industrial schools to serve out the remainder of their time. The boys had come to the mission with no place in the world, and many cried as they were taken away. With only a month left in my sentence, I'd been allowed to stay while Mrs. Philips disposed of its assets.

I could hear the voices of the water drawers outside as they went down to the river with clay urns suspended from their yokes, always following the dirt track across the mission grounds. Half crippled by age, they refused the convenience of the communal faucet in the trust land, preferring instead to fetch their water and gossip from the river.

In the early days of the mission the Very Reverend had ordered an end to this trespass but his servants refused to interfere with the women. I sometimes followed them as far as the banks where shards of sunlight floated on the dark currents, forcing me to avert my eyes as I listened to the words that streamed from their mouths.

Mrs. Philips surprised me by speaking. "I need you to help me dress the Very Reverend and bring him out onto the veranda."

"I've got things to do," I said. The Very Reverend's passion for discipline had faded with his spirits, and I no longer tried to invent excuses.

Mrs. Philips pushed her eggs around on the plate for a few moments. "When I was your age," she said finally, "I also believed the world revolved around me." I rose and quit the table, vaguely disappointed that she didn't ask where I was going.

Outside, two men struggled to push a pump organ through the double doors of the chapel, an uphill battle. The chapel had been built too close to the river and the altar end was sunk deep into the vlei.

The kopje was a short ride from the mission, but all the horses were gone, and so I began the interminable walk to Madota's house. Red locusts crunched beneath my feet, spilling their eggs into the dirt, a sign, according to the water drawers, that the rains were coming. The women had warned me away from the kopje. They believed cremation was the worst form of desecration, that without the body, the spirits of the burned would become homeless and unpredictable.

I arrived to find Mr. Takafakare forcing a corpse into a crouching position. The brick kiln was only four feet square.

"Back again, young sir. I'm afraid my daughter must go into the mountain to collect camphor basil to help with my coughing." He shook his head regretfully. "Perhaps you can come back next week."

Madota's fingers settled lightly on the ball of my shoulder. *Come.*

And so I accompanied Madota down the kopje, her father staring after us. We walked along the riverbank. My feet sank in the black vlei and I felt as if I were moving in a dream. "Here is where the mare drowned," I said. "The one your father was burning when I first came to your house." Already it had faded into a brief anecdote to associate with the moment of our meeting.

The track turned up at the chapel, and Mrs. Philips watched in silence as we crossed the mission compound. A panel van was parked by the dining facility entrance, a sandwich board affixed to its roof: "Convert your used appliances to cash. We Buy It All!!"

The track climbed out of the glen and into the mountains that rose above the curve of the earth. Far above the mission, we passed by the foundations of a coriander plantation abandoned by Franciscan monks—Manicaland is littered with the ruins of forgotten missions—and I told Madota how, in olden times, the friars would move naked through the groves at night, fertilizing the rows of coriander with their semen. Her bare feet registered no sound as she stepped over the dead branches and leaves that littered our path.

The ground shuddered softly beneath us and we held hands for balance. Three Man Road crossed the mountain highway where market vendors choked on the dust and diesel that filled the mouth of the trust land.

My calves ached as I struggled to match Madota's pace, her form seeming always to hover ahead of and above me, ringed in light, a sign that the air was thinning and my mind was starved for oxygen. My words became lost in the roar that filled my ears.

Three Man Road came to an end in a profane place where God molded Past, Present, and Future into a single creature that chased itself in circles. All this I had learned from the women as they drew their water from the river. Deadfall blew across the clearing. "South-blown leaves," I said, parroting the water drawers, "rain to follow."

Madota turned back to me, and her fingers found the base of my skull. *Kiss me.* I leaned toward her face, and her mouth swallowed my words before I could give them voice. Above, the sun moved unnoticed in its sky, the mountain air collected the moisture it had dispensed at dawn, and clouds erased the glen below us.

The river, straightened by age, bisected the glen into perfect halves. Each morning I walked its banks toward Madota's house, past the place where the drowned mare had lain for two days undiscovered, its stomach bloating with combustible gases until it produced a corpse that burnt with such intense heat that the oven bricks began to melt. In order to prevent further damage to his livelihood, Mr. Takafakare took to crouching by the mouth of the warped oven, its door open wide, as he tried to gauge the heat by the intensity of the blast that struck him full face. He endured this awful proximity for almost a month before finally resolving to travel across the mountains to Umtali where he could purchase a pyrometer.

Mr. Takafakare had never left the glen, and so he asked me to come with him. The low clouds hung motionless in the surrounding air as the lorry struggled up the mountain face. Mr. Takafakare stuffed camphor basil into his mouth while he drove, grinding it into a leafy bolus that filled all the gaps in his teeth. I spread a Survey Unit Reserve map across my lap, ready to call out directions once we reached unfamiliar territory. Rhodesia had been featureless before the English-speaking peoples came to chart and name it, one of Churchill's "empty places of the globe."

"Why do the water drawers think the kopje is sacred?" I asked.

The lorry whirred and lurched up the steep grade in low gear, while Mr. Takafakare chewed on the camphor basil and my question. "In the beginning of the world," he said, finally, "God tore apart the mountains, and the village was buried in ash. Some ran away. When they returned, the kopje had been cut in half." Three Man Road floated before us on the clouds. "Our ancestors took this as a sign that it was a sacred place and they began to bury their dead here, in a crouching position, shoulder to shoulder, generations upon generations, until the ground was filled. This is why I was allowed to buy the field. Even the Europeans refuse to live in this place." He wanted to say more, but he fell into a coughing fit that peppered the windscreen with festive flecks of green and red.

We followed Three Man Road to a highway that ran through the mountains, but the lorry rolled to a stop before we could crest the first peak. Mr. Takafakare turned in his seat and looked down on the glen. Perhaps he was afraid if we continued, we would drive off the face of the earth. He remained that way for several minutes, twisted in his seat, staring back on the road he had taken, the unmuffled engine idling and backfiring.

"You all right?" I asked.

He straightened in his seat and executed a three-point turn on the horizon of the world, and we returned to the kopje without the pyrometer.

That night at the mission, I dreamed Mr. Takafakare was pushing me into his oven. I awoke crouching beneath my blanket, flames lapping at the wallpaper. The Very Reverend had splashed diesel fuel over the dormitory floorboards and lighted it.

I wrapped myself in my bedclothes and crawled through the smoke toward a gauzy rectangle of starlight framed by flaming curtains. Once outside, I threw off the burning blankets and rolled in the dirt, my lungs heaving.

The building was a lost cause by the time I reached the water hose, so I soaked the ground to keep the fire from spreading to the rectory. The Very Reverend quoted scripture as Mrs. Philips led him away from the collapsing structure, the sparks catching and dying in her hair. "Take heed to thyself," he shouted at me, "that thou offer not thy burnt offerings in every place that thou seeist."

Mr. Takafakare was an outcast among the people who engaged his services, and he did not object when I offered to ride with him as he conducted his final removals. On these occasions he recited accounts, punctuated by coughs and throat clearings, of the first ancestors who founded the bulldozed village. Mr. Takafakare brought along the power saw when the removal was something large, a bull for instance that had succumbed to foot and mouth, its four stomachs heaving with gases. A dolly was required for medium-size removals such as a fighting dog, usually a ridgeback or a wild cape dog, its teeth sharpened with metal files, blood spattered waist high on the walls of the pit, wounds daubed with leopard's bane in a last-ditch effort to prevent blood loss and rouse the animal from shock. In the case of something small, say an infant dead of tuberculosis, Mr. Takafakare would conduct the removal in a dignified manner with gloved hand.

Once we removed one of the water drawers who had died in the trust land. We took her from a single-room house, its concrete-block walls cracked and seamed from seismic stress. A communal patch of stunted mealie struggled to survive in the granite and rime soil.

Madota traveled in the back with the corpse while I rode in the cab next to Mr. Takafakare, his head tilted back to keep blood from streaming out of his nose. He downshifted the lorry as we passed through the mission, slowing almost to a stop. "Here is the place where the dead woman was born. She was my cousin." Mr. Takafakare chuckled, then fell to coughing. "Don't look so surprised," he said, "It was my village as well." As he laughed, a thin trickle of blood stretched from his nostril to his lip. He nodded toward his daughter. "She also knows all the stories of our village, stupid girl." I looked over my shoulder to the lorry bed where Madota lay across the blanket to keep it from blowing off the corpse. She was mouthing words to the bundle, stories, perhaps, of a village she never knew. Mr. Takafakare stared at his surd daughter in the rearview mirror.

"Small matter, young sir," he said. "We have lost our place in the world, and our stories mean nothing anymore."

The rains, summoned by the spawning locusts, came to the eastern highlands, filling the glen. The river burst its banks and swollen currents swept away the mission chapel, leaving only naked pillars that canted in the vlei, indistinguishable from the handful of concrete headstones that marked the graves of boys and servants who'd died at the mission since its founding. There was rain enough to overfill the urns, but still the women came down to the river for their water. They shrugged when I told them that Mr. Takafakare could recite a story for everything within the horizons of the glen. "How would you know if he was lying?" one of them asked.

In the gray days that followed, the field atop the kopje became a lake of char. While Mr. Takafakare struggled through the sheeting rain to fire his oven, I remained indoors with Madota, reading to her the stories of the English-speaking peoples which Churchill had taken and bound in volumes, his masterwork organized into chapters, books, and volumes—divisions, regiments, and battalions of words that advanced inexorably until they overwhelmed his audience.

My court sentence expired amid a series of unsubtle omens. The earth quaked and shook the glass panes from the window over the cot I'd set up in the stables, and I woke beneath a blanket of broken glass. Crows flew in through the empty frame and nested in the rafters, from which they would spatter my pillow and bedclothes with their white feces.

The same day, Mrs. Philips put her luggage and husband out on the veranda and locked the rectory. Disnested, the Very Reverend peered out at the compound through the gray lens of rain. His boys, horses, and servants had been taken away to fight on different sides of the war, and the mission had the look of a razed military barracks.

I held an umbrella over Mrs. Philips's head while she loaded the detritus of her life into the back of the Range Rover. The Very Reverend had located his faith in the center of a map, but as he looked back through the rear window, he seemed not to know where he was. They drove away, leaving the buildings to collapse upon themselves and the land to become as it was in the beginning, a profane, uncreated place without form and void.

The absence of the Very Reverend and Mrs. Philips left my routine unaltered. I rose from the spattered cot each morning to help Madota pick camphor basil for her dying father and search the ash for hollow ear and finger bones suitable for chimes. At sunset, I lay beside her on the roof with the drying handkerchiefs, making shapes out of the clouds in the red sky, while below us Mr. Takafakare fed his oven with scrub mahogany and fighting dogs. The oven flames continued to burn ungoverned without the pyrometer, and he kept the door agape, judging the heat by the force with which it struck his face and blistered his lungs. The sweat evaporated before it left his pores, and his skin became indistinguishable from the oven's brick. I reckoned he would die before the rains came again, leaving all his stories sealed within his voiceless daughter.

I sat up on the roof and pointed to a cloud. "There. A horse," I said to Madota, but already the wind had pulled the image apart, and it looked as though flames were coming from its back.

We descended from the roof with the gloaming to take our places amid the volumes of *The History of the English-Speaking Peoples*. Madota listened, as she had done all her life, while I spun out a filament of lore to drape across our sliver of world, my words clacking together over our heads like the dull music of her bone-chimes. Whereas Churchill was driven to account for all the English-speaking peoples across the globe, I recounted the meager lore that fell within my circumscribed horizon. We differed, he and I, only in the scope of our compulsions.

I talked myself to sleep, my head cradled in Madota's lap, and dreamed of us alone in the valley as it had been in the beginning. *An unbroken canopy of ancient forest flanks a winding river. Granite mountains spill out fire and magma, the ground undulant and volatile beneath our feet. Madota leads me into a grove of young fruit trees, her fingers speaking with pressures against my arm.* I woke to the sound of phlegmy throat clearing, my hand on Madota's breast, Mr. Takafakare standing over us.

"Perhaps you should go now, young sir."

The sun burned away the mist and sparked against quartz deposits that shot through the jet granite mountains, forcing me to squint out over the glen as I stood in the splintered threshold of the dining facility. Winds rippled through the forest canopy, turning each leaf in light and shadow. The previous night someone had prized open the door, ransacked the pantry, and stolen the flatware, dishes, food, tables, and chairs, as well as the frame

and the blue-felt backing for the Very Reverend's map. The paper continents swirled like leaves at my feet.

The water drawers stumped hopelessly along the track that ran through
the mission compound. They numbered fewer than when I had arrived at
the mission a year earlier. As young brides, their husbands had been press-
ganged to improve the glen with grass buffers, dip tanks, drain strips, gal-
ley dams, and a highway to bring the bulldozers that would push over
their village. Now the women lived as widows amid concrete-block houses
and dusty fields pegged out in grids, and their granddaughters drew water
from a faucet.

Above, I could see the brightly colored umbrellas of the vendors who
lined the entrance to the trust land. A column of armored cars raced past
them along the mountain highway, reducing its graded surface to scree
beneath their solid rubber tires and plated steel. The mission boys and servants would return to the glen in the coming years to fight each other in a
war of repression and liberation, and the soft ground tremors would be
replaced by a concussion of rockets and mortar shells that would shake
the sacred kopje apart, spilling out the crouching bones of the village
ancestors.

Once, midsermon, the Very Reverend had led his congregation of servants and troubled boys from the chapel out onto the bank of the lambent
current. "Look," he commanded us. "Fix this place in your hearts, so you
can return in the dark times to come."

The mountain shadows had retreated by the time I reached Madota's
house, leaving the valley bathed in sunlight. The rains had just ended.
Newly hatched locusts swarmed over the highlands to devour the tongues
of Moses-in-the-boat that filled the window box.

Mr. Takafakare stood over a sectioned cow that was dead of black leg
disease. I went over to help him clean the chain saw but he waved me
away. "Why do you always come sniffing about with all your talk! Leave us
alone, or I will take Madota far away from you."

I laughed at this. "You can't even leave the glen."

Madota's chimes shook, though there was no wind, and I realized the
ground was elastic with tremors. Mr. Takafakare tried to menace me with
the bloody chain saw but it would not start, and so he tore through his
own house in a fit of temper, kicking the cooking pot, overturning the

water bucket, upending the cardboard box, and strewing groceries across the room. He filled the box with Churchill's volumes and dropped them at my feet.

"Take them and go." He wanted to say more but a racking cough seized him. He stood before me, waiting for his lungs to quiet, wishing me away. Soon his chest would grow still altogether, as the earth would one day cease to shudder and sound Madota's bone-chimes.

Madota watched me from the threshold of the disordered house as I descended the kopje shouldering the burden of *The History of the English-Speaking Peoples*. There came to me the cracked, halting voices of the water drawers as they returned from the river, laden, and I set down my books and listened to the broken rhythm of their gait, the thud of their walking sticks, the telluric drone of shifting plates of granite. Always, they had bound the glen together with their lore. Without them to remark on the connection, the red locusts would no longer lay the eggs that brought the rains to the mountains, the river would run dry, and the glen would become a furnace where sacred places warped and rifted, the world unmade.

Susan Fromberg Schaeffer

Wolves

"WOLF," he said, without looking up from his paper.
Just one word: *wolf.*

A fly had been buzzing and thumping against the kitchen window, and without awareness her eyes had been following it, noting its tedious, almost suicidal attempts to penetrate the unaccountably stiff pane of shining air that held it back from the trees and the sun, wondering, without realizing she was wondering, how long it would take the fly to exhaust itself and fall to the sill. She looked at her husband to see if he expected an answer. No, he was absorbed in what he was reading. Probably, she thought, he was reading something about wolves—or one wolf. He had said "wolf," after all—not wolves. Not only did he not expect her to say anything in reply to his one word, "wolf"; he would have been startled if she had said something about wolves—or a wolf.

The fly buzzed and thudded.

But she could have said something. Once she would have. She would have said the word after him: wolf. Then they would have begun to play with the word, with the wolf. It would have run back and forth from his chair to her chair, changing the color of its fur as they changed their descriptions of the beast they had brought alive, a jagged scar suddenly appearing on one side of its nose as they invented its story, its near-disastrous encounter with an elk, its wheezing after it was caught in a rock slide and lay for two days in rain and snow, the time in the cave without food, the small animal that returned to its den only to find the hungry wolf there, the wolf sleeping with his head pillowed on the carcass of the dead animal, sleeping in the cave until his ribs healed.

And they would have gone on with the wolf, her husband sketching him on the backs of the envelopes she cut up into neat squares and kept on the shelf beneath the wall telephone, until the wolf walked out of the story and took up permanent residence in the vast photograph album that was their life together, and later they would open that album together, and he would say, "I remember I saw a wolf once," and she in her turn would remember the story about the boy who cried wolf and how it had always frightened her, as if you were destined to be pursued and eaten by the thing that frightened you, as if you somehow knew what was coming for you in the end, and yet you must be punished for crying out in fear, but who would not cry out when they could plainly see what was coming?

Then her husband would say the predictable thing, reassuring precisely because it was predictable, insisting that there was no such thing as fore-knowledge or premonition; it was all a question of statistics. There must have been hundreds of things she had feared that caused her to cry out, but because only one of those fears was realized, she believed it was the only fear she had ever had. Wasn't it true?

No, she didn't think it was true.

"When I think of all the illnesses you think you've had," her husband said, "all the fatal illnesses, and yet here you are."

Here she was. Silently repeating the word *wolf* again and again, *wolf, wolf, wolf,* a kind of a chant, as if she were calling to an animal, or as if she had heard an animal call to her and she was answering.

She put her cup on her plate, picked up her silverware, and went to the sink. Just as she turned on the water, the fly fell to the windowsill, the last of its strength spent. She contemplated the insect, still buzzing and whirring its wings, and decided against crushing it with a paper towel. It might yet rally. The inherent strength of things fascinated her. "Don't kill this fly on the windowsill," she said aloud. "I'm watching it."

"Why would I want to kill that fly?" her husband asked, just as she knew he would. He could not tolerate the least criticism. Like dust, he found it everywhere. Every request of hers had, according to him, a thorn of criticism buried in it. If she asked him, "Would you buy the paper?" he would say, "Don't I always buy the paper?"

No, he did not always buy the paper, but if she said so, her husband would accuse her of starting an argument. "Why are you always arguing?" he would ask her. She had read somewhere that old lovers spent their time quarreling their way to the grave. She was beginning to think it was true. After forty years, what was the point of answering, of defending herself? She had come to value peace and quiet. Suddenly, she thought, What if I kept the wolf for myself? It would be mine, not his. I'd take care of it myself. He wouldn't know anything about it. It would be my wolf. Eventually, I would give it a name and it would come when I called—if it was the right kind of wolf, a tamable wolf.

She took a piece of paper from the shelf, slid it beneath the fly, and transported the fly to a windowsill in the dining room. Her husband rarely went into the dining room. The fly would be safe there, as safe as it could be. If the insect tried again and failed, she would carry it outside.

So she had decided to keep the wolf, without giving more than an instant's thought to the nature of the beast she would be keeping. It might be a wild thing that could grow tame and loving, a strong, loyal animal that could protect her, or a wild animal that would never accept her but would circle her until her attention faltered and then it would tear her throat out.

"I should mow the lawn," her husband said. "It's getting long and raggedy."

"Yes," she said.

"On the other hand," he said, "we're due for a killing frost. I could leave it until next spring."

"You could," she said.

"Should I mow it or not?"

Some years ago—even two years ago—she would have lost her temper and raised her voice and said, "Do whatever you want to do!" because she knew, although he was asking her advice, he would in fact do precisely what he had decided upon. He was a curious mixture of passivity and defiance. "Either mow the lawn or don't mow it!" she would have said. "But don't discuss it forever!" She would have had a vivid image of the white house in which they lived surrounded and menaced by waving grass, grass taller and thicker than any grass ever before seen on earth. She would have heard him saying, inside the house, in their bedroom, the windows sealed by a dense curtain of impossibly tall grass, "Shall I get the sickle and clear the grass in front of the windows?" She would have seen herself lying on the bed and crying until she was so tired her breath sounded like the wind in the green blades beyond the windowpane.

"Why are you crying?" her husband asked her now.

Crying? Was she crying?

Lately, she had a bad habit of standing at the sink, looking out the window and crying, although she would have been hard-pressed to say about what. She was careful to stop crying when she heard her husband come in, and if she suspected her eyes were red, would rub them with the back of her hand as if she had gotten soap in her eyes.

"Oh," she said, "it's my brother. I always thought I would fall to pieces if anything happened to my parents, but I never thought about my brother."

"He was younger," her husband said. "You thought he'd always be around. Don't you think that's it?"

"Yes," she said, although she did not. They had always been scrambled somehow, she and her brother, as if their images had been placed one on top of the other, the paint not quite dry, and so the colors had bled through. It was too complicated to explain. "I miss him," she said tentatively.

"It's grief," he said. "That's all. Plain, old-fashioned grief."

Then they sat silently. She began to follow the long twisted black line that threaded its way through the map of their forty years together, and remembered their first drive together over the Brooklyn Bridge in his small green car. They had waited until after rush hour, so that when they came along the drive leading up to the bridge, all of Manhattan was a jagged landscape studded with chunks of illuminated amber and the tops of many buildings were jeweled. She already knew that New York City was not a place in which she wanted to stay. He drove silently, and in the silence, she frequently turned to watch him, and at unpredictable intervals, he would turn his head and smile at her. She was nervous in the quiet. Was he bored? Was he waiting for her to say something? Always it had seemed to be her responsibility to break a silence. Silence had been such a terrible thing in the house of her childhood, her father sitting in his undershorts and undershirt in the living room, scowling behind his paper. But now the stillness in the car seemed beneficent, seemed an entirely new thing, first frightening, and then soothing, lovely, precious. You could be silent, and in the stillness, you could be happy.

"Sometimes," she said aloud, "I think I fell in love with you because you taught me about silence."

"Not too well," he said, bent over the crossword puzzle in the paper.

"Don't you ever think about how we got from there to here?" she asked him.

"From where to where?" he asked, filling in a word.

"From what we were when we started to what we are now."

He looked up. "I'm surprised I'm still around. I always thought I'd die young."

"No," she said. "I mean, how much we've changed between now and then."

"I haven't," he said.

"Yes," she said. "Once you were more trusting."

"I was trusting?"

"Once," she said.

"And I'm not now?"

"No." Would he now accuse her of starting an argument?

"And you? Are you trusting?"

"Sometimes."

"Then tell me what you were thinking about before," he said.

"Before?" she said, startled, looking away. She had been thinking about the wolf: her wolf. "Nothing."

"You were thinking of something. You had that look."

She shook her head. "Nothing," she said. "Except that I shouldn't have teased Lizzie so much when she was a child. Remember that time at the river? I was in the water and she was stamping up and down about something, and I said, 'Go to your room!' and she screamed, 'It's not here!' She couldn't help it, how logical she was. Why did I have to ridicule her for it?"

"Not that again," he said, dismissing her, going back to his puzzle.

How do we get from here to there? she wondered. She stared at the wall until what she saw was a wide, clean road, a white road winding between white chalk cliffs, and along the road were various bodies, statues, really, lifeless, each one resembling the one before, but the latest one a little older, a little more wrinkled, its skin a little thinner, its hair a little shorter or dyed a different color, its hands slightly more swollen, its neck a bit thicker, its eyes hidden by glasses, but still, something in the eyes was the same, and down the road, near the vanishing point, which was where the road began, if you could see that far, was a tiny animal. It came up to the first body and crept inside. It had found its first home. Time passed. Then the creature was off again, down the road, until it came to the next body and crept inside. This time it entered with greater confidence, as if it knew it belonged. Each time, the body was different, but for a while, the face was almost the same face, although even the face was beginning to change—so hard to remember now what the little creature's face had looked like. But the look in the eyes: that was the same. All these bodies waiting for you.

She could have told him about her wolf. Couldn't she? She should have told him. But she had already decided to keep her wolf and it was to be her wolf, not their wolf. There were so many kinds of betrayal, so many things to be guilty about. She thought, I do not forgive myself my betrayals. I simply overlooked them. And then I grew monstrous, which was, she thought, the same as saying that I grew up. Wasn't it the same?

She knew the wolf was nearby and she knew the wolf was not tame, but was dangerous to her. She was aware of him in the woodshed, although she knew he was not in the shed itself. He was somewhere on the hill behind the house, in the thick stand of pines and yellowing ferns, watching her shadow as it moved back and forth across the window. The house was very old and the woodshed walls were made up of boards, now two hundred and fifty years old, nailed to beams. The window, made up of sixteen little panes, had long ago lost three of its panes to hurled snowballs. When she bent down to touch them, the boards of the woodshed were soft as felt in some places and crumbly as old pine needles. Every year they said they had to replace the missing panes, and every year they left the window exactly as it was. It made no difference after all. Beneath the window was stacked wood, already cut down and aged, and beneath the wood was the shed floor, already a cross between wood and wood dust. There was no warmth in the unheated shed with its thin, weathered wall-skins that offered no protection from weather or prowlers or thieves. One good blow from a fist and someone would be inside.

But now, she thought, the wolf could jump at this window and he would be inside. One jump, that would be all it took. And the stacked wood would muffle the noise. He was hungry. She tried to remember: did wolves attack people in order to eat them? She thought not.

I will feed you, she said.

In his hiding place, the wolf lay down to wait.

But what could she feed him? And was it safe to go outside with food? Might he not think he had to fight her for the food and attack her?

There are deer who come here, she told the wolf. Outside in the meadow, one of the apple trees is covered with frozen apples. The deer come for them at night. Wait for them.

At that, the wolf sneezed. She could hear him quite clearly. Now she began to see him. He was thin; his ribs protruded through his fur. He had not eaten in some time. There were yellow crusts at the corners of his eyes.

Just then, he picked up his left rear leg and began to scratch violently behind his left ear.

"What do wolves eat?" she said aloud. And he seemed to laugh at her, as if to say, A hungry wolf will eat anything, even oatmeal.

"Please do not eat me," she said to the wolf, although now she did not have to speak aloud. She knew he could hear her.

"I cannot promise," said the wolf. "You called me, but I have no idea who you are."

"I don't know what to say," she said.

"But you are not a wolf," said the wolf.

"No," she said uneasily.

"Once in a very cold winter, I shared my den with another wolf. We were starving. One night, the moon was bright and the light shone on one of the cubs. He was very fat. We fell on him. We tore him apart and ate him. You are not a wolf."

She considered. "I have torn apart and eaten my young," she said.

The wolf picked up his head and seemed interested.

"What did you tear off first? The arm? The leg? How long did the young one wriggle after you bit down? They are soft, the young ones," the wolf said. "And full of juice."

"Oh!" said the woman.

"You did not eat your young," said the wolf. "You are upsetting yourself over a figure of speech. You cannot eat figures of speech." The wolf stood and stretched himself in the snow. "But the old ones are not bad," he said. "Their bones make a satisfying snap, a loud noise. Their bones are like chicken bones. Wolves like to eat chickens."

"Wolves are loyal to one another," she said. "I read that somewhere."

"A starving animal is not loyal," said the wolf, "not even to the one who summoned him."

It seemed to her now that the wolf had come closer, that she could hear his breathing, a kind of panting, as if he had been running for some time. When he breathed in, she could hear a soft, grinding noise, as if metal plates were scraping together.

She had been standing with her back to the woodshed window, and the shed suddenly darkened and when she looked down, she found herself standing in the shadow of something cast from beyond the window, a shadow that seemed to move in and out. She was standing on the shadow of the wolf's rib cage.

She was afraid to turn around. Even if she had summoned up this wolf, she could not let it kill her. She turned and saw no wolf near the window. On the other side of the shed wall, the air was swirling with snow. If the wolf had been here, she thought, he would have left tracks. She went to the window and looked at the ground. It seemed to her that she did see tracks heading toward the apple tree beyond the pine outside the door, but the longer she looked, the less distinct the tracks grew because the snow was falling heavily now, and even deep tracks, even the tracks of her husband's snow boots, would have quickly been covered. It was cold in the shed and she shivered and turned to go back into the house. At that moment, something deep in the woods howled, a long, angry howl. But why assume it was a wolf? It might be a dog, caught in a snare left by an unscrupulous farmer who trapped deer throughout the winter.

When the animal howled again, a chill went through her, thousands of short, tiny needles drawing themselves over her skin.

She thought, I ought to tell my husband about the wolf, but she knew that she would do no such thing.

"I'm going to get some wood," she said. "It's going to get cold."

He looked up, shook his head, and went back to his paper. She knew he believed she could predict the weather. She knew that he thought she was uncanny in many ways. Animals followed her; he didn't understand it. Up on the hill, a man was raising buffalo for slaughter where they grazed, generally indifferent to human presence. She was the exception. Buffalo 246, Buffalo 793, and Sam, the bull of the herd, came running when she appeared at the electrified wire fence. When they ran, the earth shook. He didn't like it, the shaking of the earth. Suppose they forgot their fear of the fence and kept on coming?

But she was not afraid of them.

He began to stay in the car when she went to visit them. When she came back, she always felt as if she had learned something of enormous value. She could find animals when no one else could. She would be washing dishes and stop suddenly and say, "The cat's in the barn behind the old newspapers," and there the cat would be.

He did not like things for which there were no logical explanations.

Days passed. Wherever she went, whatever she did, she watched for the wolf, listened for him.

One night, she woke in the dark as if someone had been calling her name. As though she had no will of her own, she went downstairs, put her parka on over her nightgown, pulled on her boots, and went out through the woodshed into the snow. She walked straight into the woods like a sleepwalker. The wolf was on the path ahead of her. When he saw her, he lowered his ears, bared his teeth, and growled. Then he turned and walked into the woods and was gone.

She went back inside, took off her boots, hung up her parka, and went back to bed.

The next night, the same thing. This time the wolf tilted his head to one side when he saw her, as if he were puzzled. When she stretched out her hand, he bared his teeth and growled, but his tail began to wag slightly.

On the third night, the wolf was again waiting for her. This time, when she stretched out her hand to him, he lay down in the snow. "Can I touch your head?" she asked him. He growled and tossed his head. "Perhaps tomorrow," she said.

On the fourth night, she brought out slices of roast beef. She put the meat down in front of her and then moved back. The wolf looked at her, then at the meat, and back at her. He got up slowly and went over to the meat. It seemed to her that he swallowed it without chewing.

This went on, night after night, and would have, she thought, gone on forever, except that one night she decided that she did not care what happened; she was going to touch the wolf. She took a step toward him. He did not move. She took another step. Still, he remained where he was. Finally, she was close enough to bend forward and touch his head. She bent forward quickly and placed her hand between his ears. She was surprised by the bumpy feel of his skull and the wide space between his ears. The wolf growled but made no move to attack her.

Gradually, he became used to her, almost tame.

After dinner, her husband looked up from his paper. He loved corned beef and insisted she made it well, although as she repeatedly told him, all she did was cover the meat in garlic powder and pierce its fatty layer with cloves of garlic. Her father had been the same. Every Thanksgiving, he insisted that *this* turkey was the best turkey they had ever eaten. Somehow she had married her own father. And yet when she found her husband, she prized him expressly because he was, or so she thought at the time, a man who did not in the least resemble her father.

She picked up a section of the paper and pretended to read. After some minutes, she asked, "Are there wolves in the woods here, or wild dogs? They say there are more bears, and that wolves are coming down from Canada."

"Who does?"

"Who does what?"

"Who says there are wolves coming down from Canada?"

They say. He knew that *"They say"* meant no one in particular; it was a way of saying, "I heard someone somewhere who said this particular thing." And yet each time he would stop her and ask her, "Who says it?"

"The newspaper," she said.

"There are coyotes coming down from Canada," he said. "I don't know about wolves. There could be wolves. I wouldn't worry about it."

"But all those children taking their snowmobiles into the woods," she said.

"You can't worry about the whole world," he said.

"I heard something howling before," she said. "I could have sworn it was a wolf."

"I didn't hear anything."

"You wear those headphones," she said.

"All right," he said, "I'll call the Game Warden." He made the call. "Earl says there hasn't been a wolf sighting up here in eighty years. He wants to know where you got such an idea and he hopes you won't start talking about it in the general store when it's full of skiers. And that," he said, "is the end of that. Unless, of course, I open the door and find a wolf asleep on the doorstep, which I won't."

Perhaps, she thought, it might be possible to start their game again.

"If you could have whatever animal you wanted," she asked, "what would you have?"

"A giraffe."

"You would *not* have a giraffe!"

"A big black German shepherd," he said. "And you?"

"Oh, I don't want any more animals," she thought.

"Good," said the wolf, wherever he was.

"Do you ever miss the city?" she asked suddenly.

"Why should I miss it?" he asked. "You don't miss it. You never liked it."

"I couldn't like it."

"You refused to like it."

"All right, I refused to like it."

"That's what I said," he said, turning a page. "Anyway, all that's over and done with."

"Nothing is ever really done with," she said.

He looked at her as if considering, and his face softened. She saw that and held her breath. "All right," he said. "It only *looks* like the country. Outside there are really skyscrapers and paved streets and at night we can't see the stars."

"And that," she said, "is true."

He looked at her; again she felt something waver, and then it was gone. Instead, she thought, tomorrow when I go to the store, I'll buy a chicken and hide it out near the apple tree.

The next day, she brought the wolf a large roasting chicken. She unwrapped the chicken and washed it and carried it outside and scraped out a small indentation in the snowdrift in back of the big pine near the house. Her husband was in his study. His window faced the meadow on the opposite side of the house. Then she went inside and began unwrapping the other roasting chicken, the one she was to cook for their own dinner.

She thought about the chicken she had left for the wolf. Raw chicken. Salmonella. Perhaps she should have cooked it. But he was a wolf. Wolves hunted down their food, and when they brought down their kill, it was not cooked meat into which they sank their teeth.

She looked at her watch, a small, old-fashioned watch she had to wind daily, her grandmother's watch. She had worn it for years, its mainspring broken, the dial always announcing the same time: a quarter to four. Then one day her husband had said, "Give me that watch." He had taken it away, and when he brought it back, the watch was ticking. The second hand relentlessly swept away the minutes; the hour hand erased the hours as they passed. "I'm surprised it could be done," her husband said. "I thought there'd be too much rust. You kept wearing it into the shower."

"I never wore this watch into the shower," she said.

She was not happy to hear this watch ticking, as it did beneath her ear every night when she rested her head on her arm. Motionless and silent, it had been a perfect companion, an unchanging moon that traveled with you wherever you went. *Full moon, full moon, madness,* her grandmother used to sing, in those last days before she died, in the home for the aged, when she no longer knew who she was. She would look at the watch and sing, *Full moon, full moon, madness and love.*

"Will you stop that, Mother?" her own mother had said.

"Let her alone," she said. "Singing makes her happy."

"It makes *you* happy," her mother said. "It's a mad song."

"But she's happy."

"Happiness isn't everything," her mother said, sniffling into her tissue.

"What else is there?" her grandmother asked, looking up suddenly, lit sharply by a lightning flash of normalcy.

"Don't sing," said her mother to her grandmother, trying another tack. "She'll learn from you. She'll sing in a monotone, and no one will ever marry her."

"Are you seeing anyone?" her grandmother asked her.

"No," she said.

Her grandmother's eyes traveled over her, rested a moment on her eyes, and then narrowed. She resumed her singing. "Full moon, full moon, madness and love."

"Couldn't you have said you were?" her mother whispered to her.

"Were what?"

"Seeing someone!"

Outside, the day had been dimming. A quarter to four. In that place, it had always been a quarter to four.

It was a quarter to four now. At a quarter to six, the chicken would be finished.

She knew the instant the wolf found the chicken. She heard his deep, low growl; she heard the small snorts he made as he blew air out through his nose so that, when he next inhaled, he could smell the meat well. She knew when he decided the meat was safe and good and when he picked the carcass up in his mouth and carried it in his jaws, holding his head up high, carrying the chicken back into the woods behind the house. Some time passed before she heard the cold snap of bones. She knew when the wolf picked up the unfinished carcass and began digging out a hiding place in the snow. She could see him as he raced back and forth through pines, dragging boughs brought down by the last ice storm, covering the chicken, that treasure.

He doesn't have to do that, she thought. I can bring him another chicken. Or a corned beef. I wonder if he's ever eaten corned beef.

The wolf was sleepy and lay down in the snow, his head on his crossed paws. Then he got up, ran up the mountain to a little stream, drank, and returned to his place behind the house.

"That was a good chicken," said the wolf.

The woman told him that he did not have to hide the chicken, or save part of it. Every day she would leave something for him in the snow, or she would bring him something when she came at night.

"You say that now," said the wolf, "but what if something were to happen to you? What if you could not bring me any chicken? And what if I could catch nothing that day? In our language, carelessness and starvation are the same word."

"I wonder if you would like corned beef," she said.

"Does it have feathers?" asked the wolf.

"No."

"Then I would like it very much," the wolf said.

"I was going to buy one tomorrow anyway," the woman said.

She was tired; her eyes were closing. "Do wolves dream?" she asked.

"What is a dream?"

"Something that happens while your eyes are closed and you are sleeping."

"When we are sleeping, life goes on," the wolf said. "Is that part of life a dream?"

"We think so, yes," she said.

She closed her eyes.

Wolves put back their heads and began to howl.

"The chicken is good," her husband said.

"Mm," she said.

"It's always good."

"Mm," she said.

"You're not very talkative," he said, putting down his paper.

"Have you ever noticed the color of headlights at night?" she asked him. "They light everything up; they turn everything gold. But when the car passes, the headlights are pale yellow. Why is it?"

"I don't know," he said.

"The rear lights are red," she said. "We see those lights. Do you think our memory mixes the red and the yellow? The yellow is really almost white. The red and the yellow would make that gold color. I think so."

"Do you?" he asked her.

"Yes."

He put down his paper and was studying her. He started to say something, and then stopped. But he was still looking into her eyes. He said, "Sometimes I think the red lights of the cars are like the red eyes of animals that hunt in the dark."

"What kind of animals?"

"Wild animals."

"What kind of wild animals?" she asked. She felt him hesitate.

"Any kind of wild animal."

"A deer?"

"Not a deer. A hunting animal."

"What *kind* of hunting animal?" she asked him.

"Any kind of hunting animal!" he said, pushing his chair back violently.

She sat, looking down at her hands. He pretended to look at the table-top, but really, he was looking at her. *Tell me, tell me!* she thought, as if she could will him into speech.

"Wolves?" she asked. "Did you mean wolves?"

"Why are you whispering?" he asked loudly.

"Wolves?" she asked again.

"There are no wolves here! I told you!"

"They're in Canada, where they belong," she said. Her own voice sounded mechanical to her.

"There's no need to be sarcastic," he said.

She got up and began to carry the dishes to the sink. *What kind of animals was he thinking about?* He might still answer her. There was still a chance.

"Don't you want to watch that movie on TV?" he asked her.

"As soon as I finish washing the dishes," she said.

A trackless wood, she thought: or a wood with one track only. Which do I want? A trackless wood, she decided, turning on the hot water tap.

Often, when they sat in the living room watching television, she would barely see the screen at all; she would not hear the words the actors spoke. Instead, she began to open her own invisible photograph album, an album her husband had never seen. She thought of the album as so old that it had rough, black cardboard pages, the photographs in it were black and white and deckle-edged, and at each corner, a small black triangle held the photo in place. There were endless photographs of her first love, and every time she opened the album, the photos changed, as if someone else were keeping the album up.

Over fifty years later, and she still thought of him. She understood now why people had so much trouble forgetting their first loves—especially if that first love had grown old or died. Who else could remember him as he had been when they had both been so young together? Now, finally, she was the only one who could possess him as he had been then.

She turned the pages until she came to the pictures of her children. Who else could remember them as they were so long ago? The boiled red color her son's face turned in the sun, the mottled red of her daughter's face when she was crying? In the end, she had become like a tree heavy with pods, each pod full of memories. But the seeds in the pods were dead, she thought, as she closed the book. And then she would open it again and look for the picture of herself sitting on her first love's bicycle as he ped-dled along the gray stone streets of their university.

No one else can love you this way, she said to herself. Once she had said this to him, aloud. Finally, it was true.

And there were the pictures in the back of the book, visited less fre-quently. There she was, in the old house in the city, her black hair long and tangly with curls, her husband pulling a curl straight out, then letting it go. "I love to watch them jump back," he said. And later, children's friends, and still later, their own friends, asking, "How do you do it? How do you stay happily married so long?" Now that they had moved to a small town in the country, no one asked them how they had stayed married so long. Up here, couples married for over half a century were everywhere. Had the people here known from the beginning how to be happy? When it came to happiness, some people had the knack of it. Her daughter had that knack, that habit. She often asked herself: could complicated people think themselves into becoming simple people?

She closed her eyes so that her husband would think she had fallen asleep. Otherwise, he would ask her how she had liked the movie, and the corners of his mouth would turn down when he realized she had paid no attention to it. It occurred to her that if she loved her husband less, they would be happier together. As it was, she feared losing him, not to another woman—that was over—but to illness or accident or those disasters of the mind that overtook people their age. It was her fear that made her so spiky and critical. Her fear came between them. And he had the same fears. No wonder they had become so suspicious of each other, so touchy, each fear-ing desertion by the other, always on the alert, looking like maniacal de-tectives for signs of trouble, for the tiny clues, resentful before the event, asking, before any shadow fell, Why did you leave me? Why did you leave me here alone?

"Are you awake?" her husband asked.

"Mm," she said. And sat up slowly, as if she were just waking up.

"You never used to get so tired," he said.

"You never had gray hair," she said.

And surprisingly, they both laughed.

. . .

"Love?" said the wolf. The wind lifted the boughs of the pines and dropped them and when it did so a small snow was loosed from the branches and glittered through the moonlight around them. "We are bound together by smell. We are all one wolf. Until we begin to starve. Then we become one and one and one."

"And if one of you is sick?" she asked.

"We will stay with that one and bring him what food we can and at night we will sleep in a circle around him."

"And if he cannot go on?"

"We will stay. But often the sick one will chew through his own paw and bleed to death, and when he does, his smell changes, and we go on. My mother said, 'I will die now,' and closed her eyes and stopped breathing. We left her, but I think she breathed on."

"Then wolves are capable of sacrifice?"

"We are all one wolf," he said. "Unless we become one and one and one, and then we are unhappy."

"When I was a child, we lived in the city. I hated the city. When I grew older, I dreamed about the city. It was always night there and there were no people on the streets, only white statues, statues of my mother and father and my brothers and cousins and aunts and grandmothers and grandfathers. And there was a moon so their shadows were sharp. I was terrified of the statues. And during the day, when I was awake; the same statues were still there, just behind what everyone else saw.

"I hated rooms with drawn curtains. I thought there were people behind them. It was a haunted city. I could never grow to like it. Never."

The wolf was breathing deeply and slowly, in and out. She lay at right angles to his body, her head pillowed in the fur of his side. His smell was sharp, almost rancid. He smelled of leaf-mold and mud and cold snow and the blood of what he had recently eaten. When the temperature was above freezing, he groomed himself, but now it was so cold that he ignored the twigs caught in his fur, the dry leaf stuck to his back by tree sap. She turned on her side and pulled loose the leaf; she took a wide-toothed comb from her pocket and began to groom him. He snorted when she pulled too hard on his fur.

"Everyone must have a protector," the wolf said. "I will be your protector."

"What will you protect me from?" she asked. She was smiling.

"The statues and their shadows. You must not go to that city anymore."

She said she only went in dreams, but the wolf said that even in dreams she must not go there.

The wolf's breath was hot and rusty. In the beginning, she had turned her head away, disliking the smell, but she had come to like it. Now she would bury her head in the wolf's fur when his back was dry, although almost always he was damp.

"I should clean your ears," she said.

"No."

Playfully, she reached up toward his ear, but the wolf growled deep in his throat. "Do not make me stand up and pin you to the ground," he said. "You will struggle like a rabbit but you will not get free. And," he added, "I can hear for miles."

"Then tell me what my husband is doing," she asked him.

"He is snoring through one half of his nose, but he is sound asleep," said the wolf.

The wind picked up and lifted the snow into strange, drifting shapes as if there were hundreds of chimneys hidden in the floor of the woods, and this was the smoke that rose from them. "Today," said the wolf, "I came upon a deer more dead than alive. Dogs brought him down. His back legs were chewed. He whimpered in his throat. His neck had been gashed open but still he did not die. The dogs should have finished him. They left that for me."

"You killed him?"

"He was more than half-dead," said the wolf.

"Did you eat him?"

"I was not hungry," said the wolf.

"And if you found me in the woods, more than half-dead, would you kill me?"

"You are human," said the wolf.

"I would want you to kill me," she said.

"I am your protector," the wolf said.

Inside her parka, she shivered.

"You must go back," the wolf said. He began to stand up and she slid down his side until she was lying on her back in the snow, laughing and looking up at the stars.

The wolf waited for her to get up, and when she did, he began dashing from tree to tree, and then loped further up the hill, and ran down to her, running, faster and faster, to the stream up the mountain, down to where she waited.

"Now you have seen me run," the wolf said. "Now go back."

"Yes," she said. "I'm going."

She let herself in through the woodshed door, left the coat on the pile of wood near the inner door, and in her nightgown and boots walked into the house. She took off her boots and went up the steps and got into her bed. Her husband slept on his back, snoring through one nostril.

She did not smell of wolf. The twigs had vanished from her hair, and the snow, which had dampened her hair, had evaporated and her hair was perfectly dry. But what was that?—was it a scratch on her arm? She had put her hand in the wolf's mouth and he had gently closed his mouth, but perhaps he had not closed it gently enough? Probably the wolf had not scratched her at all. Probably she had scratched her inner arm above her wrist when she brought in wood from the woodpile. But perhaps the wolf *had* made the mark. She moved her arm to her lips and licked the scratch and then she was asleep.

Now, when she came back in from visiting the wolf, her husband would stir uneasily and begin to awaken. One night, he turned to her and said, "I don't like that smell."

"What smell?" she asked.

"Wet dog. Or something like wet dog."

"I don't smell anything," she said.

"Your nose is always stuffed up," he said.

"I hope another animal didn't die and fall in the well," he said. "Last time, all our towels smelled of that animal."

"There's nothing wrong with the well water," she said. "You must have been dreaming. About a wet animal."

"I smell it right now," he said.

After that, she was careful. When she came back in, she took off her clothing, put her nightgown and socks in the washing machine, and took a shower, washing her hair. Her hair was cut short and dried quickly. She sprayed perfume on her nightgown and then went up to bed. At times, her husband would awaken and although she could not see him, she knew he was regarding her with suspicion. This surprised her. For years, she had been waking in the middle of the night. She would spend two hours working—cleaning, writing letters, painting—and then go back to bed. He never seemed to mind.

She herself had noticed that her husband disappeared for longer and longer periods during the day. He had always gone for his midday walk, but she stopped accompanying him when her arthritic knee refused to bear her weight for more than twenty minutes. He always returned one half hour after the porch door slammed behind him. Now hours could pass. She thought she was imagining things, and so she looked at her little gold watch, timing him. One hour, two hours, two and a half hours. Where did he go? If he went deep into the mountains, he should take his rifle. Did he take it? She should remind him.

And if he met her wolf? What then?

He cannot meet my wolf, she told herself. My wolf makes himself known to no one else. He told me so. She settled herself in an armchair. The wood in the stove might burn down before he returned, she thought resentfully, but so far it had not. Before he left, he always filled the two woodstoves.

He is careful to fill it so I won't have cause for complaint, she thought.

And then one day he came back and when she picked up his coat—he always threw it over the back of a kitchen chair—she smelled something sharp and probably filthy. Wet dog, she thought.

"Some of those wild dogs are rabid," she said aloud, "vicious and mean, attacking people. The man down the road's been shooting at the ones who go after deer."

"What are you talking about?" her husband asked her.

"Don't go walking with a wild dog," she said.

"Why would I do that?" he asked her. But he did not look at her. He kept his back to her.

"This coat needs a washing," he said.

"It certainly does," she said

Now when she came back into bed, after her shower, after picking up the twigs that fell from her clothes when she came back to the house, it seemed to her that she could hear the wolf growl, a threatening sound, nasty, as if he were seeing something he did not like.

Of course. The wolf was jealous.

"Animals do not fall in love with all and sundry," the wolf had said.

"Neither do people."

One of her hands was cold. She took her hand from her pocket. The wolf began to lick her hand with his warm tongue.

"It is warm now," she said, withdrawing her hand, plunging it into her pocket.

"I have seen your husband in the woods," said the wolf.

"You mustn't harm him," she said.

"I won't harm him, but I won't help him, either," said the wolf.

She sat up and looked at him. The moonlight glittered in his eyes. In the center of each eye was a full moon.

"He has nothing to fear," the wolf began, "because . . ." And then he stopped himself.

"What were you going to say?" she asked him.

"He has nothing to fear," said the wolf. "He knows these woods as well as any animal."

"Do you think I'm an idiot?" she asked the wolf. "Even an animal can't know every inch of the woods. If something goes wrong, an animal can run, and in no time, he's miles away from the danger, but a man like my husband, how far could he get? What would he do? Climb a tree? Bears can climb trees too!"

"I am telling you," said the wolf. "He is in no danger at all." And he angrily turned his head on his powerful neck, so quickly that his long muzzle knocked her down. She lay on her back in the snow.

I will just lie here and let him see how he's knocked me down, she thought, not moving. Wolves, husbands—they were all alike.

The wolf clamped the collar of her parka in his teeth and hauled her to a sitting position. He stood over her.

"If you were a wolf, you could run through the snow. We could play."

"If I were a *young* wolf," she said.

"Even an old one could go fast enough," said the wolf. "And I am an old wolf. You could keep up with me."

By now she knew that the other wolves with whom he had hunted were gone—dead, although he believed they might come back. He told her that, sometimes, at night, he smelled them on the wind. "As you smell your dead," he said.

She shuddered. She said, "Human beings cannot do that."

"You can make them come back to you," said the wolf. "I have seen you do it."

She thought about her secret photograph album, that was not an album, but was, and said nothing.

"Sometimes I can do it," the wolf said.

"Where does my husband go during the day?" she asked him.

"Perhaps he has his own wolf," said the wolf.

"Does he?" she asked.

"No."

"But," she said, "he might have some other kind of animal."

The wolf didn't answer her. Her wolf would not lie, but neither would he volunteer the truth.

At night, she lay next to the wolf and spoke to him of the first man she had loved, of her father, who had beaten her with a belt and wooden hangers, of her children, who had disappointed her and then changed again and once more become lovely, and of her bones, which she could see, she said, when she held an arm up to the light. Her bones were thin and fragile and white and speckled, like shells she once saw on a beach, eaten away by salt and sun.

The wolf would lick her forehead, but not her hair, although at times he would close his teeth in her hair and shake her head this way and that.

"This is how a wolf stuns his kill," he told her.

And one night, the wolf said, "I could kill you."

"You won't," she said. "Unless I ask you."

"I could kill your husband," said the wolf. He put his head between his paws. "I think I could win," he said at last.

"Of course you could," she said. "You are stronger than my husband."

The wolf growled and was silent.

"You must not touch him," she said, sleepily. "Promise me."

"I won't. Unless you ask me to," said the wolf.

"I will not ask you," she said.

Lately, she and her husband were happier together. She knew why she was happy: she had her wolf, who perfectly understood her. Perhaps her husband was happy because she was happy. He always said his contentment came from giving her pleasure.

If he were younger, she thought, I would be sure he had found someone else. But here there *was* no one else. No other woman accompanied him on his trips into the woods.

And one day, she looked up from her book, and thought, I am perfectly happy, and she thought, Happiness is such a quiet thing.

The older you become, the quieter you grow.

Several weeks later, she thought, I am tired. And it was true. She was too tired to open the little, invisible black album she still hid from her husband, too tired to answer his questions, too tired to pull the blanket up beneath her chin when she lay on the couch watching television, so tired that her husband now pulled the blanket up for her—without being asked.

One day, she picked up her gold watch, warmed by the sun where it lay on the windowsill while she did the dishes, and saw it had stopped. She tried to wind it, but it was already tightly wound. She knocked it gently against the sink's edge. It would not start.

So it is over, she thought. Then she thought, I am ready for it to be over. And then she thought, my husband is also ready.

She turned around and saw her husband smiling at her with such perfect love that it frightened her.

That night, she went out. The wind blew the pine boughs. Spring was in the wind. It seemed to her that she could hear bulbs crackling beneath the snow and stirring like someone crumpling paper. The house was surrounded by their crackling as they split themselves open.

"I've had enough of spring," she told the wolf. "Look at the snow in this meadow, sinking and pocking, like decaying skin. Listen to that river. The water's so fast it can pick up the boulders and tumble them for miles."

"You could last for a while," said the wolf. "Two more winters, I think."

"Will you do me a favor?" she asked the wolf.

"If I stretch out my neck . . ." she began, but she didn't finish the sentence. The wolf buried his snout in the softening snow, and using his nose as a shovel, tossed some snow up into the air. It was wet, melting snow. It fell with little thuds.

"In the house," she said, "I have many bottles of yellow pills. I saved them up. I never wanted to die slowly. I never wanted people walking back and forth, with me planted like a bathtub in the middle of a kitchen, saying pitying things, washing me and holding their noses, asking themselves, 'Why won't she die?' But this, this would be better. It's a terrible thing to do to the ones who stay behind, ending your own life.

"They don't know about you. No one knows about you. They would say, 'She got like grandma; she went out walking in the middle of the night, and some animal got her.'"

"They will like that?" the wolf asked.

"It will be something to cry about," she said. "Something they think can't happen to them."

"Of course I can do it," said the wolf. "But not tonight. You must ask me again."

"Again?"

"I am your protector, not your slaughterer," the wolf said. "You must ask me again. The second time I will know you are sure."

That night, when she slipped into bed, her husband was awake. Moonlight glowed in the room.

"You smell of something wild," he said.

She took a deep breath. "So do you," she said.

He put his wrist to his nose. "It's true," he said.

She asked him, "How did we get so old?"

"The same hawk pulled out both our feathers," he said. Even in the dark, she knew he was smiling.

She nodded—in the dark. She was also smiling.

"You won't ever leave me?" he asked her.

"Not unless something happens."

"And I won't ever leave you," he said. "Unless something happens."

"When will something happen?" she asked.

"Oh, probably tomorrow night or the next day," he said, and they both laughed.

They fell asleep in the moonlight, their arms around each other. It seemed to them both that they had once more grown young.

The next night, she went out to the wolf. She unbuttoned her coat and stretched out her neck. "I am asking you again," she said.

"Are you sure? You won't change your mind?"

"I won't. But who will you have when I am gone? Will someone else call for you?"

"No one else will call me. But it is easy for me to die. I will go up in the hills and stop eating. I haven't eaten for days."

"But I've been feeding you!" she said. She sniffed the air. What was that smell? Was it a wolf-smell or a husband-smell? "Do you smell that?" she asked.

The wolf sniffed the air, but if he smelled anything out of the ordinary, he had nothing to say about it. Instead, he said, "I have not been eating."

"So you are going, too," she said.

"And your husband and his dog," the wolf said.

"Dog?" she asked, beginning to sit up.

"Change your mind," said the wolf. "Change your mind and I'll tell you."

"No," she said. She wished her throat were longer and whiter, a more worthy throat. "Here is my throat."

"Are you sure?"

"Yes."

"I am sorry to do it."

"Please."

With a strange and terrible growl, half a cry of joy, the wolf's jaws closed over her neck and broke it and tore open her throat so that the blood spurted far and high, so far that it drenched the pine nearest to them. Then the wolf got up, his mouth bloody, blood staining his fur, and looked down at the woman. He breathed in deeply and the smell of her blood filled his lungs. Then he loped away.

He left tracks in the snow.

Douglas Trevor

Girls I Know

GINGER AND I careened along Storrow Drive in her black Lexus, on our way to the Brighton Cryobank for Oncologic and Reproductive Donors. Ginger was a shitty driver in ways that I assume most spoiled rich girls are—blithe disregard for others' rights-of-way, refusal to slow down for pedestrians, etc.—but I can't be sure since Ginger is the only spoiled rich girl I've ever known. As she cut off a ConElectric truck I thought of Robert Lowell, the subject of my dissertation, and the time he had Jean Stafford in his father's car and ran into a wall, smashing her nose to bits. "There was about a 25 percent reduction in the aesthetic value of her face," Lowell's friend, Blair Clark, said. A short time later, Lowell asked Stafford to marry him. It was the honorable thing to do, marry the woman whose face he had ruined, and Lowell was nearing the height of his honorable phase, although I don't think he became a worse person necessarily as he grew older. The idea of virtue was always mesmerizing to him, only he could never live up to his ideals for very long. His life was filled with these bold gestures of magnanimity that were always, in the end, withdrawn—not out of insincerity as much as an insufficient attention span. The mania and mad delusions were symptoms, not causes, of his alternating embrace of piety and savageness, at least that's how I understood him back then. I don't think of Lowell that much now, at least not Lowell the person, although I still read his poems fairly regularly.

Shifting gears with her bare feet, her mouth filled with bubble gum, Ginger gave me a sidelong glance. "What you thinking over there, retard?" She dropped the second "r" out of the last word to imitate a Southie accent, which she did pretty well.

I told her about Lowell's car accident, how he lived—in part—off the royalties of Stafford's first book, *A Boston Adventure*, for several years before openly cheating on her with a visitor to their Maine home, prompting separation and then divorce. "If we got in a car wreck today and I fractured all my vertebrae," I cut to the point, "would you marry me?"

We had been hanging out a lot over the past month or so, ever since she had moved into my building at the end of May and mentioned casually—in response to the bewildering description I offered of my intellectual interests—that her grandfather had known Lowell at Harvard. They had played tennis together a few times, hung out some socially in the Yard, before Lowell decided to transfer to study with John Crowe Ransom and Allen Tate, first at Vanderbilt and then at Kenyon. That made Ginger, so knobby-kneed and awkward, suddenly shimmer in my eyes; she was two degrees separated from a major American poet, even if he had died right before she had been born. Growing up in Burlington, Vermont, the only people my childhood friends were two degrees separated from were French Canadian prostitutes. So my motives for getting to know her were compromised from the beginning, but I don't fault myself for that. I came to Boston to enter Lowell's world as best I could and now—years after basically giving up on that enterprise—Ginger had fallen into my lap.

"I don't think I'd marry you," she said slowly as we rounded a corner, "but my family would help you out financially—you know, redo your kitchen so you could reach all the cabinets from your wheelchair."

"Well, that's definitely something."

She adjusted the volume of one of her Radiohead bootlegs via an inconspicuous button on her steering wheel. "You should be writing on Bishop anyway," she said. "She's the one who grew up with her grandparents, not Lowell."

Early on I had let slip that I had never known my father and that my mother had died when I was eleven of ovarian cancer. Ginger never let go of the information and tried to read it into everything I did, so if I nursed a cup of coffee, or that hideous green tea she was continually brewing, and claimed it was because the beverage was too hot to drink, she'd shake her head knowingly, tap me on the arm and whisper, "detachment anxiety." I had wanted her to see me as transcending my background, even if I didn't believe such a thing was possible. That was the problem with Bishop: writing about someone who came from nowhere, or someplace even farther away than nowhere, Nova Scotia, would have just taken me back again and again to the clapboard house of my grandparents: the three of us playing Parcheesi while a PBS show on the National Park Service droned on in the background and Easter bread baked in the kitchen. So I tried to ignore her poems altogether, even though they spoke to me keenly.

"But I like the Brahmins," I replied that day, using the same hollow justification I always did. "I like their self-indulgence. Bishop, Stevens, Williams, they're all too sincere."

"You're a retard, Walt. Wallace Stevens kicks Lowell's ass, and he was an insurance lawyer. An insurance lawyer! No, Lowell knew he sucked; that's why, when he rewrote his poems, he tried to ruin them."

She baited me like this all of the time, which I secretly loved. My retorts were invariably pathetic, though. "His genius was self-consuming . . ." I mumbled.

Every other Wednesday was my drop day at the sperm bank. If I could persuade her, Ginger would give me a ride, and sometimes after I was done we'd spend the day together, either driving around Boston or trading Lowell lines back and forth over gin gimlets at her place. If she weren't around, I'd take the T out to Brighton by myself, do my drop, then come home and try to work on the dissertation. The premise of "Robert Lowell and the Poetics of Yankee Peerage" was, I had realized with some shame two years before, pathetically simple: Lowell's poetry was shaped by where he chose to live and who his parents were. Although I had been in graduate school in the English Department at B.U. for seven years, I had yet to complete a draft of my introduction, not to mention any of the other chapters. The project had long since lost the interest of my advisor, and the poetry world as well seemed to have lost interest in Lowell, although every thin volume of autobiographical lyrics published still owed its shape—I was convinced—to *Life Studies*, published in 1959. Outside of Boston, I learned secondhand from the few graduates of our program who had managed to secure assistant professorships, Lowell was thought to be unteachable. No one cared about the old South Boston Aquarium anymore, and Lowell's pedigree made him deeply suspect in curricula shaped by identity politics—even if he had stood as a conscientious objector to World War II, was in and out of mental wards his entire adult life, and traveled with Eugene McCarthy in his hopeless bid for the Democratic Party's presidential nomination. He had also broken Stafford's nose not just once, in their car accident, but another time with his bare hand, versified excerpts from the letters of his second wife without her permission, even drowned three kittens given to him by a friend, although this last damning bit of information was never fully substantiated. Ginger was right; Bishop had become the preeminent poet of her generation, if posthumously, which meant that even while I had picked the right city in which to study poetry, I had also managed to pick the wrong poet.

There were faster ways to Brighton than Storrow Drive but that was the route we'd always take. It gave Ginger the opportunity to identify her Harvard classmates to me as they jogged along the Charles, the ones who had opted to spend the summer in Boston, taking over spacious apartments like the one she had sublet on the top floor of the building where I was the super. I'd ask endless questions about her acquaintances and she'd answer as many as she could, knowing how much I hungered for telling details: "Her dad invented antidepressants," she'd say, or, "He's in line for the Dutch throne." Half the time she was probably lying but I gobbled up the morsels she threw my way regardless. It was harder to get Ginger to talk about her own life but the pace she kept revealed a lot. She was always having to rush to New York for a family obligation, or drive to Mattapoisett for some aunt's anniversary. When she wasn't on the move she'd complain to me about what a boring and dreary summer she was having and how much nicer it would be to have no such encumbrances. "To have nothing to do but masturbate for money and read poetry," she'd say, "that sounds awesome." She never figured out, or at least never acknowledged, how absolutely broke I was, but that was probably her just trying to go easy on me. I so wanted her to see me as viable in some way, even though I was eleven years her senior and half her intelligence.

We turned onto Commonwealth Avenue, drove past those beautiful homes that poke out behind arbors, brick walls, and elm trees, then merged onto North Beacon. I can't remember when I've been happier than right then: in that beautiful car, angst rock blaring on the speakers. Since taking a year off from school to write *Girls I Know*, the book for which she would receive a six-figure advance at the end of that summer,

Ginger hasn't phoned me once. That's my fault, though, not hers, which is the odd thing: my self-pity crested that summer but I was the one, at the end of the day, who was bent on hurting others. It serves me right that now I orbit around those images I have of Ginger's self-conscious, endearing beauty, or recall the clever phrases she'd coin without any effort, all while I labored to be witty and edgy in her presence. How odd to think that it was me standing on the precipice that summer even as I did nothing. How odd that the inaugural moment for *Girls I Know* would mark my own entry into that unappreciated demographic of single men who—rather than be invited to the Cape with the young families squirting up like daisies all around—are instead pent in glass and sent floating through Boston to gaze all too surreptitiously on the unknowable gaggles of the city's borrowed beauties.

"What's it like, collecting jizz all day?" Ginger had produced a small, leather-bound notebook I had never seen before from her oversized straw bag while I signed in at the cryobank. The heavyset black nurse shot Ginger a cold stare before affixing labels to a couple of sample jars and walking around the counter. They had started two-cupping me a few months before, when my sperm count began to drop. Now I had to separate the first shot, in which my sperm concentration was the greatest, from the second. It was not an easy maneuver, not that anyone ever asked.

The nurse led me down the hallway toward one of the small private rooms. "Think of me, darling," Ginger shouted as she began to thumb through a *McCall's* in the waiting room. The donor rooms were filled with porn, but the waiting room didn't push the envelope at all—just your typical pile of outdated magazines, a few condensed books, and some pamphlets on STDs and bulimia.

I never used any of the donor aids; the magazines smelled of unwashed men's hands; the videos were too long and involved and the VCRs were typically broken anyway. I would think of the girl who worked at the convenience store across the street from our building, her pierced eyebrow, the apron she wore smeared with nacho cheese drippings, or that Israeli student I taught at B.U. two or three years before with jet black hair and leather everything. I never thought of Ginger.

. . .

Just a few months ago, Irena, a woman I know who works at the Victor Hugo Bookshop on Newbury Street, asked about my sperm. I don't know how she had learned about me whoring my DNA, but I had seen her more than once in the back row at the Grolier poetry readings with a woman I assumed was her girlfriend and I figured my part-time job was gossip that had bubbled up at one point. I told her that I was flattered by her interest and she quickly corrected me. "I don't want your seed," she replied, "I just want to know your lot number." It turned out, she explained, that some of the banks had a reputation for lying about the characteristics and backgrounds of their donors. I was intrigued and gave her my information. A week later I saw her in the bookstore, perched back behind that enclosed counter they have, chopsticks sticking out of her hair. "They say you're a six-one Ivy Leaguer with blue eyes," she said. *Was there,* I thought, *nothing of me worth advertising?* "You should be thrilled," she went on, knowing— I inferred later—enough of my intellectual interests to see the irony of it all. "In twenty years, every adopted WASP in Boston will look like you."

After I finished my drop that day we got on the Turnpike and raced back into town. No more meandering along the Charles, Ginger was either in a hurry to catch the shuttle back to New York or just feeling antsy, I wasn't sure which.

"What's with the notebook?" Its corner had poked out of her straw purse, reminding me of its earlier appearance at the sperm bank.

"Idea I have," she shrugged, "for a book."

My eyebrows arched.

"It'll be called *Girls I Know* and will be comprised of interviews I'll do with women from all walks of life: secretaries, custodians, lawyers, strippers, women who collect ejaculates at sperm banks—"

"Is that a word, 'ejaculates'?"

"I think so."

I shifted in the leather seat. "Did she talk to you, that woman, after your line about jizz?"

"She warmed up to me when I told her about the book project. Women like it when other women write down what they say."

"Is that right." I was feeling crabby suddenly, I wasn't sure why.

"She says it's a good job. They have really great benefits. She said lots of times the men can't produce their first time in. Did you have any problems?"

"No." We drove by a group of daycare kids walking in twos, holding on to a rope. "When did we start treating our young like cattle?" I wondered aloud.

"We love our children too much," she said. "We gag them with the idea of childhood as idyllic. 'Hold on to this rope and you'll be just fine.' It's ridiculous."

I loved it when she generalized facilely from her Upper East side upbringing. She pulled behind the building, into her reserved parking place, and we got out.

It was Ginger's book concept that had changed my mood; *Girls I Know* had begun to work on me, at first I wasn't sure why.

"How'd you come up with the idea for your book?" I asked.

"I want to write something without my own voice," she said. "I want to get out of myself."

"Don't we all," I replied, but I was kidding myself, I realize now. At the time I assumed that I was just as self-loathing as the next guy, or girl, but what I took to be self-evisceration back then was really just an artistic form of narcissism that characterized all the poems to which I found myself drawn. I was reading the same thing over and over again, and when I didn't find what I was looking for I projected it. Every poem was about the need to register one's self-disgust. Every poem was written with me in mind.

We walked into the building and she pushed the button for the elevator.

"Do you want to take a nap or something, after expending yourself?"

"No, I'm not tired."

We waited for the doors to open, then stepped inside the car. In her own at once vulnerable and sassy way, Ginger had been trying to seduce me for weeks, but I had resisted, mainly because I couldn't understand her attraction to me and thought—admittedly in a paranoid way—that if our bodies ever coupled she would never have anything to do with me again and I would lose my glimpse into American aristocracy once and for all. After I had rejected her for the third time the week before, she had refrained from asking me up, but that day I didn't really ask for an invitation; I just tagged along.

Although the apartment she was subletting from a family friend was a fully furnished two-bedroom, Ginger had pitched her camp in the living room. Her white futon was on the floor, her trunk open next to it, with expensive clothes piled around it, partially covering an enormous boom box and a bunch of worn paperbacks—books by Hans Küng, Sylvia Plath, and Cormac McCarthy. There were also snake droppings on the floor, left by her pet python, Sid, and the lingering odor of green curry, which she put in everything she cooked.

We sat on the edge of the futon, our feet touching, and began to kiss. I placed my hand on her nub of a breast and she leaned back but I didn't follow her lead. She stared up at the ceiling for a moment, then asked if I wanted some warm tap water and walked into the kitchen. "When you left," I called to her as she walked out, "I thought of you each hour of the day." "Each minute of the hour, each second of the minute," she hollered back. It was remarkable; after a single measly poetry survey course, Ginger had somehow managed to commit a whole pile of Lowell lines to memory. She came back in with Sid wrapped around her neck, having forgotten about the water. I was actually relieved to see the snake, hoping he'd give us something to talk about so that we wouldn't have to address why I was leading Ginger on and then pulling back.

"Look," she whispered to her pet, her fingers tickling his skin a few inches below his mouth, "it's the superintendent of the building, here to enforce the 'No Pets' rule and take you away." She held him out toward me.

"I, uh . . . that's okay." I didn't like to touch Sid; he scared the hell out of me. What's more, I knew—at the end of the summer—that I'd be the one scraping python shit off the floor. Ginger sat down a good three feet away from me, depositing her pet between us. He curled around her and slithered back into the kitchen.

I looked over at her, at her torn and patched jean cutoffs, the Green Day tee shirt off of which she had ripped the neckband. In a moment I was lost in one of those reveries that constantly sucked me in that summer: the two of us living in one of her family's seven vacation homes, dividend checks piled on Louis XIV dressers, my dog-eared copies of Lowell replaced with first editions. Through a staggering manipulation of connections, a professorship at Brown University had been secured for me. On the weekends we boated off Martha's Vineyard.

"I want a Twinkie," she said. I nodded my head eagerly, she grabbed her purse and we left.

The first day of her residency in my building, just a few scant hours after she had revealed her connection to Lowell while supervising the professional movers she had hired to drive a barely filled van one and a half miles from Harvard Square to the corner of Beacon and Mass Ave, I visited Ginger in her sublet. It had been my intention to leave her alone for a full day but I couldn't stop myself. In addition to her trunk, she had two enormous duffel bags, neither of which she would ever fully unpack, their unzipped tops disgorging clothes as if alive. In one of the bags, under a pair of silk pajamas, I thought I made out the hull of a vibrator. In another were piles of letters, bound with string, written—I would discover much later—by her grandmother, who, before dying of liver cancer, suffered from insomnia and wrote Ginger every night for three and a half years, mostly to complain of the infidelities of her long-dead husband and rail against the inadequate disposal of our nation's spent nuclear reactor rods, apparently her one current-events obsession.

Ginger watched me look over her belongings without making small talk. I asked her about the classes she had taken the previous year. "I don't remember the course titles," she said, "just the stuff we read."

"Well," I tried again, "what did you read?"

"In one class we read Aquinas. I remember his ontological proof for the existence of God: 'But as soon as the signification of the name *God* is understood, it is at once seen that God exists. For by this name is signified that thing than which nothing greater can be conceived. But that which exists actually and mentally is greater than that which exists only mentally. Therefore, since as soon as the name *God* is understood it exists mentally, it also follows that it exists actually. Therefore the proposition *God exists* is self-evident.'"

"Do all of your friends have photographic memories?"

She wrinkled her mouth. "I don't know. I don't have friends. I have acquaintances, classmates, cousins." She sat down on the floor, having yet to unfurl her futon. "In another class we read Faulkner. All I remember is Cash's line about Darl at the very end of *As I Lay Dying*: 'This world is not his world; this life his life.'"

I just smiled. I had never read a word of Faulkner—still haven't.

"I read Roethke in the same class that had some Lowell in it. Do you know 'I Knew a Woman'? 'These old bones live to learn her wanton ways.'"

"'I measure time by how a body sways.'"

"I like his poems more than Lowell's."

"Roethke!"

She smiled with her head bent down so that her eyes had to roll up in their sockets to look at me.

"Did your grandfather," I figured it was fair game now, since she had mentioned him before, "did he by chance remain friends with Lowell after he left Harvard?" I was on the hunt for an unknown correspondence, perhaps a letter or two that hadn't been picked over by other scholars.

"Nope. Sorry." She noticed me looking down at her own collection of yellowing envelopes and added, "No one in my family ever wrote, or received a letter from, Lowell. I don't think Grandfather liked him very much—something about his temper."

"He didn't have his first manic attack," here I had the opportunity to defend the patrician poet against his patrician detractor and I took it up eagerly, "until he was about thirty-two. But he was violent, even as a child. He beat up kids all the time at St. Mark's, punched his father out. That's why everyone called him Cal, for Caliban, or Caligula."

She didn't try to reclaim the conversation; she just let me go on for a while. I peppered her with a sampling of my Lowell anecdotes: him climbing up on a statue naked while in Argentina during a breakdown, getting lost in Caroline Blackwood's mansion the night before he died, refusing President Lyndon Johnson's invitation to read at the White House. She seemed neither entirely interested in what I had to say nor altogether bored.

"Do you ever feel so cramped in your own skin," she asked when I had exhausted myself, "that you'd do anything to crawl out? Do you ever look in the mirror and just want to erase your face?"

I paused, not sure of how to respond.

"I think it's a girl thing," she added, "wanting to make yourself disappear. Boys think of shooting people; girls think of starvation."

· · ·

After eating Twinkies and drinking Mountain Dew at the convenience store across the street from our building, Ginger decided to begin her research for *Girls I Know* and I tagged along. We went to the Glass Slipper. It's nice, entering a strip club with a young girl. The enormous black bouncer gave me a knowing nod and we were quickly ushered to a choice booth right in front just as the next dancer came down the staircase and onto the stage. The DJ situated in a booth on our left began to spin some techno music but the speakers were blown and the sound came out muffled. As my eyes adjusted to the half-light I noticed that the place was basically deserted. The stripper had on a business suit that was about two sizes too small and was holding a briefcase that she set down in the middle of the stage while looking menacingly at Ginger, her tongue heavy on her lower lip.

"Her tits are busting out," Ginger said. "I wish my tits busted out." She took out her notebook, looked around the place a little bit, then began to scribble furiously.

"It's the people who don't have any reason to give a shit that do things with their lives," I said, watching her write. "Why is that?"

She held up an index finger, finished her thought, then shut her book. "I don't know," she said in response, waving at one of the waitresses. "Maybe it's just easier than doing nothing."

I had been trying, roughly since Ginger was in middle school, to do something other than nothing, to get my Ph.D., and I wasn't finding it easy at all. A thin waitress in fishnet stockings and a strapless tank top sauntered over. She had dirty black hair tied off in a ponytail, dark eye shadow and lipstick.

"What can I get you?" Like everyone else in the place she looked at Ginger, not me.

"I'm writing a book about women," Ginger said, sliding over toward me and nodding at the space next to her. "Tell me your story."

The woman looked over her shoulder, then over at me. "You want something to drink?"

"Bud."

She nodded and looked at Ginger, who ordered a gin gimlet.

When the waitress walked away I knocked Ginger with my elbow to tease her about being shut down but she ignored me. Onstage, the stripper had opened her briefcase and taken out an enormous dildo that she waved at us like a handgun. Ginger pointed up at the ceiling, where there were mirrors I hadn't noticed. The dancer walked up the stairs, then came back down minus the suit and dildo, in a black teddy. She put her arms around the pole in the middle of the stage and began to buck and twist, the lingerie slipping to the ground. Looking at the woman's back as it was reflected off the mirrors behind the stage, I noticed a purple stain on her skin.

"Birthmark?" I asked Ginger.

"I'm thinking more burn than birth." She nodded her head authoritatively. We both looked at it for a few seconds. "It's shaped like Rhode Island," she added.

The waitress came back with our drinks. She asked me for nine dollars. I pointed at Ginger, who gave her twenty.

"So you're writing a book?"

Ginger nodded. *"Girls I Know."*

"Sheila," the woman nodded at another waitress, "can you get a scotch and soda for the guy at eight?"

I couldn't see Sheila's reaction but I did watch as the waitress set her tray down on our table and squeezed in next to Ginger. After the stripper in front of us had crawled over to pick a twenty out of Ginger's hand with her mouth, she told us about her life.

"I ran away from home at thirteen," she began. "We were living with my mom's boyfriend in Rumford, Maine, a piece-of-shit town. I don't remember the guy's name. He had two kids. One of them was mental—really big and strong but would spit up his food and crap on himself. The other went to juvenile hall cuz he kept on trying to rape the girls in his homeroom. He was a year older than me.

"Mom was diabetic and didn't work. She got disability money because her left eye was no good. The guy she was with then was real fat. He didn't work neither. The two of them would sit around, drink, and watch TV. Whenever I was alone with him, he would smile at me in a fucked-up way. He never touched me, though. I heard them talking about it one night and my mom was like, 'If you want it so bad go give it a try, just don't hurt her,' so I left.

"It wasn't like I meant to run away for good. I was really just planning on walking around. I went into a grocery store and decided I was going to buy some cigarettes only I didn't have any money, so I swiped a pack and then out in the parking lot this guy came up to me and said he had seen what I had done with the Marlboro Lights and he was going to turn me in. I begged him not to, I actually thought he could get me in trouble, and he said he wouldn't but that I should get home and he'd give me a ride. So I got in his car with him.

"He took me to his house all the way up near Oquossoc, me screaming the whole way, pounding on the window. No one in any of the cars we passed looked over at us. When we got to his place he locked me in his basement. A couple times a day he'd give me food. There was a sink and shower down there. I'd go to the bathroom in the sink. A few days later he came downstairs with a mattress and another man. The man gave him money to rape me. I don't know how much. I found out later that the guy had taken out ads in porn magazines. 'Young Girl Who Likes Pain.' It took me a month of getting the shit raped out of me to figure out a way out of there. I ended up knocking the door down with a section of pipe when he was gone one day.

"I didn't feel like I could go home after that so I moved to Waterville, then Berlin, New Hampshire, then Manchester. I did tricks, worked in a convenience store for a while. I didn't look like I was thirteen no more. I got arrested for stuff, nothing serious, mostly just cuz I had nowhere to go. Then I started doing speed and LSD and other shit guys would give me to fuck them or suck them off. I'm eighteen now. I take Concord Trailways down from Manchester on Monday and waitress and dance here through Wednesday. I can't dance on the weekends because they say my tits aren't big enough and I can't afford no enlargements. So I work and buy my shit down here for the week. One of my girlfriends looks after my boy while I'm gone in exchange for speed. I had him two years ago, Jayce. I work down here so it won't ever get back to him, how I make money."

A guy sitting a few tables away gave her a wave and she stood up, picked up her tray, and went back to work. As she walked off, I couldn't bear to look at Ginger. She had started scribbling notes again and I didn't want her to read my face. I was thinking that she might end up with a pretty good book.

.   .   .

When we got outside, we found broken glass all over the sidewalk on the passenger side of the Lexus. Someone had taken a crowbar to her dashboard in an attempt to swipe her disc player but had only gotten it halfway out. "At least finish the job," she said, surveying the damage.

An older man walked out of an adult bookstore across the street. "Is that your car?" Ginger nodded. "The alarm's been howling for the last twenty minutes. It just stopped."

She looked at him. "That's what alarms do, they howl."

He walked away while I tried to use one of my Birkenstock clogs to brush the broken glass off the front seats. It didn't work too well. We got in and took off.

Ginger drove through the city streets just as she did on Storrow Drive, carelessly aggressive. It wasn't rush hour yet but there were lots of pedestrians walking around and I stared at them, wondering what they were thinking, how it must have felt to have to get dressed up every day for work—exhausting, but then again you've got money in the bank at the end of the month and that doesn't sound all bad. I glanced over and noticed she was smiling. Ginger had three kinds of smiles: there was one that wasn't really a smile but a smirk, which she used when needling me about Lowell, another one that was a smile on the outside only, eyes vacant, kind of a social mask she had probably developed just to simplify her family encounters. The third smile was a girlish grin; it was my favorite one—very rare, but also very sweet. That was the one I glimpsed for a moment right then.

"What?" I asked her.

She shook her head.

"No, what?"

She shrugged. "I can feel shards of glass in my ass."

"Me too." We laughed.

She turned onto Mass Ave. In a few minutes we'd be home. I'd be listening to the phone messages by tenants who needed their toilets fixed; I'd be wondering how to avoid my dissertation on my own.

"'We're knotted together in innocence and guile,'" she said. Remarkably, she had settled on my favorite of all of Lowell's sonnets.

"'Yet we are not equal,'" I replied. I didn't say the rest of the line, not right then. We sat at a light that didn't want to change. Finally she turned to me.

"You know, Walt, it's not my fault that I have the background I do."

I was barely listening. The ingenuously simple premise of *Girls I Know* had reasserted itself in my mind and, horrifically, I found myself comparing it to my hieroglyphic of a dissertation, with envisioned chapters on Lowell and Boston infrastructure, the discernible metrical cadence of lithium, and an allegorical reading of "Sailing Home from Rapallo" as an anticolonial critique of French Symbolic Poetry. I thought of Ginger on the shuttle to New York, headed back for a weekend filled with parties, or having lunch with one of her professors at the Harvard Faculty Club, or just applying to Harvard in the first place. Had she even bothered to write a personal statement, or did people with last names like hers skip that step? And I thought of my grandfather up in Burlington, probably at that moment attempting once more to make it through some of Lowell's verse so that he could talk to me about my work, ask pertinent questions—try to be my father.

Now, in hindsight, I see it differently; I see, in her clumsy self-defense, one last attempt to reach out across the distance that I insisted existed between us, a distance made up of privilege and want that I felt—like some key to all mythologies—could explain every person or poem I encountered. Now I see her trying to become my friend.

"Yes it is," I said.

After reading poems from *Life Studies* that he sent her as he put the collection together, Elizabeth Bishop wrote Lowell a letter about what it felt like for her to see him write about his illustrious family. "I am green with envy of your kind of assurance," she said. "I feel that I could write in as much detail about my Uncle Artie, say—but what would be the significance? Nothing at all." She had an uncle, like everyone, but Lowell had something different, his genealogy. "All you have to do," she went on, "is put down the names!"

It has to be the most exasperated she ever sounded, at least on paper, but Bishop got over it; she continued to write her own kind of poems, and kept up her friendship with Lowell until the day he died. When he moved to England, Bishop took his place at Harvard, teaching poetry to kids like Ginger. He had so much acclaim in his life, she had some but not as much. When Lowell was playing as a boy on Revere Street in Boston,

Bishop was up in Nova Scotia, watching her grandparents grow older still. Where is her bitterness? It must be somewhere in her work and yet I can't seem to find it. For a time she seemed to consider wrecking herself— becoming an alcoholic, writing nothing at all—but she didn't. She went on in her quiet, quizzical way. I don't see how she did it.

"I have lived without sense so long the loss no longer hurts." That's the next line in the sonnet Ginger started to speak in her car that day. Like I said, it's a great poem.

There were other days we spent together after that one but not many. Ginger began to avoid me. I, as a result, started to pine for her—copying poems and leaving them on her door, even assembling a pyramid of Twinkies on her welcome mat late one night. She didn't tell me about her advance until the day she moved out, when her parents sent up their driver to take her stuff not over the Harvard Bridge and back into Cambridge but rather down to New York. "I'm going to write my book, I thought it might be easier in the city," she said with a shrug. I had to pry the monetary amount out of her by guessing incrementally larger dollar figures. When she pulled away it occurred to me that I had never seen Ginger with anyone other than me since I had met her—that maybe those acquaintances of hers that jogged every afternoon along the Charles were just that, acquaintances, and that her summer had probably been a lonely one, even with all the engagements.

In the past year I haven't gone anywhere; I'm still the super at the same building, although my dissertation has been redesignated in my mind as no longer stalled but abandoned. Generational shifts occur in Boston every four years; you last through one cycle of college students and suddenly you're on the inside of the outside, as close as you'll ever get to being *from* here, even if you grew up in a New England outpost, rooting for the Red Sox like everyone else. It's been almost a decade for me but I finally feel settled into life here, if in a permanently qualified way.

On the T yesterday I thought of those of us who migrated here for ridiculous reasons, because of a few lines of poetry, those of us whom the city has permitted to burrow into its hide even though we have nothing to offer, and I imagined, years down the road, when my artificially insem-inated sons have grown into boys, stepping onto the Red Line and suddenly finding myself surrounded by my likenesses. They might be slightly different shades of me, maybe different features here and there, but I will recognize them as my own, all squeezed together for a chance stop or two, reading their library books or just gazing out the window, oblivious to the presence of their father, the man who provided them with their ghostly parentage: with the unknowable lines of a peculiar, faint family.

Louise Erdrich

The Plague of Doves

S OME YEARS BEFORE the turn of the last century, my great-uncle, one of
the first Catholic priests of aboriginal blood, put the call out to his
congregation, telling everyone to gather at St. Gabriel's, wearing scapulars
and holding missals. From that place, they would proceed to walk the
fields in a long, sweeping row, and with each step loudly pray away the
doves. My great-uncle's human flock had taken up the plow and farmed
among Norwegian settlers. Unlike the French, who mingled with my
ancestors, the Norwegians took little interest in the women native to the
land and did not intermarry. In fact, they disregarded everybody but
themselves and were quite clannish. But the doves ate their crops just the
same. They ate the wheat seedlings and the rye and started on the corn.
They ate the sprouts of new flowers and the buds of apples and the tough
leaves of oak trees and even last year's chaff. The doves were plump, and
delicious smoked, but one could wring the necks of hundreds or even
thousands and effect no visible diminishment of their number. The pole-
and-mud houses of the mixed-bloods and the skin tents of the blanket
Indians were crushed by the weight of the birds. When they descended,
both Indians and whites set up great bonfires and tried to drive them into
nets. The birds were burned, roasted, baked in pies, stewed, salted down
in barrels, or clubbed to death with sticks and left to rot. But the dead only

fed the living, and each morning when the people woke it was to the scraping and beating of wings, the murmurous susurration, the awful cooing babble, and the sight of the curious and gentle faces of those creatures.

My great-uncle had hastily constructed crisscrossed racks of sticks to protect the rare glass windows of what was grandly called the rectory. In a corner of that one-room cabin, his twelve-year-old brother, whom he had saved from a life of excessive freedom, slept on a pallet of cottonwood branches and a mattress stuffed with grass. This was the softest bed the boy had ever had, and he did not want to leave it, but my great-uncle thrust a choirboy surplice at him and ordered him to polish up the candelabra that he would carry in the procession.

This boy would be my grandfather's father, my Mooshum, and since he lived to be over a hundred I was able to hear him tell and retell the story of the most momentous day of his life—which began with this attempt to vanquish the plague of doves. Sitting on a hard chair, between our first television and the small alcove of bookshelves set into the wall of our government-owned house on the Bureau of Indian Affairs school campus, he told us how he'd heard the scratching of the doves' feet as they climbed all over the screens of sticks that his brother had made. He dreaded going to the outhouse, because some of the birds had got mired in the filth beneath the hole and set up a screeching clamor of despair that caused others of their kind to throw themselves against the hut in rescue attempts. But he did not dare relieve himself anywhere else. So through a flurry of wings, shuffling so as not to step on the birds, he made his way to the outhouse and completed the necessary actions with his eyes shut. Leaving, he tied the door closed so that no other doves would be trapped.

The outhouse drama, always the first scene in Mooshum's story of that momentous day, was filled with the sort of details that my brother and I found interesting; the outhouse—which was an exotic but not unfamiliar feature—and the horror of the birds' death by excrement gripped our attention. Mooshum was our second-favorite indoor entertainment. Television was the first. But our father had removed the television's knobs and hidden them. Despite constant efforts, we couldn't find the knobs, and we came to believe that he carried them on his person at all times. So instead we listened to our Mooshum. While he talked, we sat on kitchen chairs and twisted our hair. Our mother had given him a red Folgers coffee can for spitting snoose. He wore soft, worn green Sears work clothes, a pair of battered brown lace-up boots, and a twill cap, even in the house. His eyes shone from slits cut deep into his face. He was hunched and dried-out, with random wisps of white hair falling over his ears and neck. From time to time, as he spoke, we glimpsed the murky scraggle of his teeth. Still, such was his conviction in the telling of this story that it wasn't hard at all to imagine him at twelve.

My great-uncle put on his vestments, hand-me-downs from a Minneapolis parish. Since real incense was impossible to obtain, he stuffed the censer with dry sage rolled up in balls. Then he wet a comb at the cabin's iron hand pump and slicked back his hair and his little brother's hair. The church cabin was just across the yard, and wagons had been pulling up for the past hour or so, each with a dog or two tied in the box to keep the birds and their droppings off the piled hay where people would sit. The constant movement of the birds made some of the horses skittish. Many wore blinders and had bouquets of calming chamomile tied to their harnesses. As our Mooshum walked across the yard, he saw that the roof of the church was covered with birds that repeatedly—in play, it seemed—flew up and knocked one another off the holy cross that marked the cabin as a church. Great-Uncle was more than six feet tall, an imposing man, whose melodious voice carried over the confusion of sounds as he organized his parishioners into a line. The two brothers stood at the center, and with the faithful congregants spread out on either side they made their way slowly down the hill toward the first of the fields they hoped to clear.

The sun was dull that day, thickly clouded over, and the air was oppressively still, so that pungent clouds of sage smoke hung all around the metal basket on its chain as it swung in each direction. In the first field, the doves were packed so tightly on the ground that there was a sudden agitation among the women, who could not move forward without sweeping the birds into their skirts. In panic, the birds tangled themselves in the cloth. The line halted suddenly as the women erupted in a raging dance, each twirling, stamping, beating, and flapping her skirts. So vehement was the dance that the birds all around them popped into flight, frightening other birds, and within moments the entire field was a storm of birds that roared and blasted down upon the people, who nonetheless stood firm with splayed missals on their heads. To move forward, the women forsook their modesty. They knotted their skirts up around their thighs, held out their rosaries or scapulars, and chanted the Hail Mary into the wind of beating wings. Mooshum, who had rarely seen a woman's lower limbs, dropped behind, delighted. As he watched the women's naked round brown legs thrash through the field, he lowered the candelabra that his brother had given him to protect his face. Instantly, he was struck on the forehead by a bird that hurtled from the sky with such force that it seemed to have been flung directly by God, to smite and blind him before he carried his sin of appreciation any further.

At this point in the story, Mooshum often became so agitated that he acted out the smiting and, to our pleasure, mimed his collapse, throwing himself upon the floor. Then he opened his eyes and lifted his head and stared into space, clearly seeing, even now, the vision of the Holy Spirit, which appeared to him not in the form of a white bird among the brown doves but as the earthly body of a girl.

Our family has something of a historical reputation for romantic encounters. My aunt Philomena, struck by the smile of a man on a passenger train, raised her hand from the ditch where she stood picking berries, and was unable to see his hand wave in return. But something made her stay there until nightfall and then camp there overnight, and wait quietly for another whole day until the man came walking back to her from the next stop, sixty miles ahead. My oldest cousin, Curtis, dated the Haskell Indian Princess, who cut her braids off and gave them to him the night she died of tuberculosis. He remained a bachelor, in her memory, until his fifties. My aunt Agathe left the convent for a priest. My cousin Eugene reformed a small-town stripper. Even my sedate-looking father was swept through the Second World War by one promising glance from my mother. And so on.

These tales of extravagant encounter contrasted with the modesty of the subsequent marriages and occupations of my relatives. We are a tribe of office workers, bank tellers, booksellers, and bureaucrats. The wildest of us (Eugene) owns a restaurant, and the most heroic of us (my father) teaches seventh grade. Yet this current of drama holds together the generations, I think, and my brother and I listened to Mooshum not only to find out what had happened but also because we hoped for instructions on how to behave when our own moment of recognition, or romantic trial, should arrive.

In truth, I thought that mine had probably already come, for even as I sat there listening to Mooshum my fingers obsessively spelled out the name of my beloved on my arm or in my hand or on my knee. I believed that if I wrote his name on my body a million times he would kiss me. I knew that he loved me, and he was safe in the knowledge that I loved him, but we attended a Roman Catholic grade school in the early nineteen-sixties, when boys and girls who were known to be in love hardly talked to each other and certainly never touched. We played softball and kickball together, and acted and spoke through other children who were eager to deliver messages. I had copied a series of these secondhand love statements into my tiny leopard-print diary, which had a golden lock. The key was hidden in the hollow knob of my bedstead. Also, I had written the name of my beloved, in blood from a scratched mosquito bite, along the inner wall of my closet. His name held for me the sacred resonance of those Old Testament words written in fire by an invisible hand. *Mene, mene, tekel, upharsin.* I could not say his name aloud. I could only write it with my fingers on my skin, until my mother feared I'd got lice and coated my hair with mayonnaise, covered my head with a shower cap, and told me to sit in a bath that was as hot as I could stand until my condition should satisfy her.

I locked the bathroom door, controlled the hot water with my toe, and, since I had nothing else to do, decided to advance my name-writing total by several thousand. As I wrote, I found places on myself that changed and warmed in response to the repetition of those letters, and without an idea in the world what I was doing I gave myself successive alphabetical orgasms so shocking in their intensity and delicacy that the mayonnaise must have melted off my head. I then stopped writing on myself. I believed that I had reached the million mark, and didn't dare try the same thing again.

Ash Wednesday passed, and I was reminded that I was made of dust only and would return to dust as soon as life was done with me. My body, inscribed everywhere with the holy name Merlin Koppin (I can say it now), was only a temporary surface, soon to crumble like a leaf. As always, we entered the Lenten season aware that our hunger for sweets or salted pretzels or whatever we had given up was only a phantom craving. The hunger of the spirit alone was real. It was my good fortune not to understand that writing my boyfriend's name on myself had been an impure act, so I felt that I had nothing worse to atone for than my collaboration with my brother's discovery that pliers from the toolbox worked as well as knobs on the television. As soon as my parents were gone, we could watch *The Three Stooges*—our and Mooshum's favorite, and a show that my parents thought abominable. It was Palm Sunday before my father happened to come home from an errand and rest his hand on the hot surface of the television and then fix us with the foxlike suspicion that his students surely dreaded. He got the truth out of us quickly. The pliers were hidden, along with the knobs, and Mooshum's story resumed.

The girl who would become my great-grandmother had fallen behind the other women in the field, because she was too shy to knot up her skirts. Her name was Junesse, and she, too, was twelve years old. The trick, she found, was to walk very slowly so that the birds had time to move politely aside instead of starting upward. Junesse wore a long white Communion dress made of layers of filmy muslin. She had insisted on wearing this dress, and the aunt who cared for her had given in but had promised to beat her if she returned with a rip or a stain. This threat, too, had deterred Junesse from joining in the other women's wild dance. But now, finding herself alone with the felled candelabra-bearer, she perhaps forced their fate in the world by kneeling in a patch of bird slime to revive him, and then sealed it by using her sash to blot away the wash of blood from his forehead, where the bird had wounded him.

And there she was! Mooshum paused in his story. His hands opened and the hundreds of wrinkles in his face folded into a mask of unsurpassable happiness. Her black hair was tied with a white ribbon. Her white dress had a bodice embroidered with white flower petals and white leaves. And she had the pale, heavy skin and slanting black eyes of the Métis women in whose honor a bishop of that diocese had written a warning to his priests, advising them to pray hard and to remember that although women's forms could be inordinately fair, they were also savage and permeable. The Devil came and went in them at will. Of course, Junesse Malaterre was innocent, but she was also sharp of mind. Her last name, which came down to us from some French *voyageur*, refers to the cleft furrows of godless rock, the barren valleys, striped outcrops, and mazelike configurations of rose, gray, tan, and purple stone that characterize the Badlands of North Dakota. To this place Mooshum and Junesse eventually made their way.

"We seen into each udder's dept'," was how my Mooshum put it, in his gentle reservation accent. There was always a moment of silence among the three of us as the scene played out. Mooshum saw what he described. I don't know what my brother saw—perhaps another boy. (He eventually came out to everyone at my parents' silver-anniversary dinner party.) Or perhaps he saw that, after a whirl of experience and a minor car accident, he, too, would settle into the dull happiness of routine with his insurance-claims adjuster. As for me, I saw two beings—the boy shaken, frowning, the girl in white kneeling over him pressing the sash of her dress to the wound on his head, stanching the flow of blood. Most important, I saw their dark, mutual gaze. The Holy Spirit hovered between them. Her sash reddened. His blood defied gravity and flowed up her arm. Then her mouth opened. Did they kiss? I couldn't ask Mooshum. She hadn't had time to write his name on her body even once, and, besides, she didn't know his name. They had seen into each other's being, therefore names were irrelevant. They ran away together, Mooshum said, before either had thought to ask what the other was called. And then they decided not to have names for a while—all that mattered was that they had escaped, slipped their knots, cut the harnesses that their relatives had tightened. Junesse fled her aunt's beating and the endless drudgery of caring for six younger cousins, who would all die the following winter of a choking cough. Mooshum fled the sanctified future that his bother had picked out for him.

The two children in white clothes melted into the wall of birds. Their robes soon became as dark as the soil, and so they blended into the earth as they made their way along the edges of fields, through open country, to where the farmable land stopped and the ground split open and the beautifully abraded knobs and canyons of the Badlands began. Although it took them several years to physically consummate their feelings (Mooshum hinted at this but never came right out and said it), they were in love. And they were survivors. They knew how to make a fire from scratch, and for the first few days they were able to live on the roasted meat of doves. It was too early in the year for there to be much else to gather in the way of food, but they stole birds' eggs and dug up weeds. They snared rabbits, and begged what they could from isolated homesteads.

On the Monday that we braided our blessed palms in school, braces were put on my teeth. Unlike now, when every other child undergoes some sort of orthodonture, braces were rare then. It is really extraordinary that my parents, in such modest circumstances, decided to correct my teeth at all. Our dentist was old-fashioned, and believed that to protect the enamel of my front teeth from the wires he should cap them in gold. So one day I appeared in school with two long, resplendent front teeth and a mouth full of hardware. It hadn't occurred to me that I'd be teased, but then somebody whispered, "Easter Bunny!" By noon recess, boys swirled around me, poking, trying to get me to smile. Suddenly, as if a great wind had blown everyone else off the bare gravel yard, there was Merlin Koppin. He shoved me and laughed right in my face. Then the other boys swept him away. I took refuge in the only sheltered spot on the playground, an alcove in the brick on the southern side facing the littered hulks of cars behind a gas station. I stood in a silent bubble, rubbing my collarbone where his hands had pushed, wondering. What had happened to our love? It was in danger, maybe finished. Because of golden teeth. Even then, such a radical change in feeling seemed impossible to bear. Remembering our family history, though, I rallied myself to the challenge. Included in the romantic tales were episodes of reversals. I had justice on my side, and, besides, when my braces came off I would be beautiful. Of this I had been assured by my parents. So as we were entering the classroom in our usual parallel lines, me in the girls' line, he in the boys', I maneuvered myself across from Merlin, punched him in the arm, hard, and said, "Love me or leave me." Then I marched away. My knees were weak, my heart pounded. My act had been wild and unprecedented. Soon everyone had heard about it, and I was famous, even among the eighth-grade girls, one of whom, Tenny McElwayne, offered to beat Merlin up for me. Power was mine, and it was Holy Week.

The statues were shrouded in purple except for our church's exceptionally graphic Stations of the Cross. Nowadays, the Stations of the Cross are carved in tasteful wood or otherwise abstracted. But our church's version was molded of plaster and painted with bloody relish. Eyes rolled to the whites. Mouths contorted. Limbs flailed. It was all there. The side aisles of the church were wide, and there was plenty of room for schoolchildren to kneel on the aggregate stone floor and contemplate the hard truths of torture. The most sensitive of the girls, and one boy, destined not for the priesthood but for a spectacular musical career, wept openly and luxuriantly. The rest of us, soaked in guilt or secretly admiring the gore, tried to sit back unobtrusively on our bottoms and spare our kneecaps. At some point, we were allowed into the pews, where, during the three holiest hours of the afternoon on Good Friday, with Christ slowly dying underneath his purple cape, we were supposed to maintain silence. During that time, I decided to begin erasing Merlin's name from my body by writing it backward a million times: Nippok Nilrem. I began my task in the palm of my hand, then moved to my knee. I'd managed only a hundred when I was thrilled to realize that Merlin was trying frantically to catch my eye, a thing that had never happened before. As I've said, our love affair had been carried out by intermediaries. But my fierce punch seemed to have hot-wired his emotions. That he should be so impetuous, so desperate, as to seek me out directly! I was overcome with a wash of shyness and terror. I wanted to acknowledge Merlin, but I couldn't now. I stayed frozen in place until we were dismissed.

Easter Sunday. I am dressed in blue dotted nylon swiss. The seams prickle and the neck itches, but the overall effect, I think, is glorious. I own a hat that has fake lilies of the valley on it and a stretchy band that digs into my chin. At the last moment, I beg to wear my mother's lace mantilla instead, the one like Jackie Kennedy's, headgear that only the most fashionable older girls wear. Nevertheless, I am completely unprepared for what happens when I return from taking Holy Communion. I am kneeling at the end of the pew. We are instructed to remain silent and to allow Christ's presence to diffuse in us. I do my best. But then I see Merlin in the line for Communion on my side of the church, which means that on the way back to his seat he will pass only inches from me. I can keep my head demurely down, or I can look up. The choice dizzies me. And I do look up. He rounds the first pew. I hold my gaze steady. He sees that I am looking at him—freckles, dark slicked-back hair, narrow brown eyes—and he does not look away. With the Host of the Resurrection in his mouth, my first love gives me a glare of anguished passion that suddenly ignites the million invisible names.

For one whole summer, my great-grandparents lived off a bag of contraband pinto beans. They killed the rattlesnakes that came down to the streambed to hunt, roasted them, used salt from a little mineral wash to season the meat. They managed to find some berry bushes and to snare a few gophers and rabbits. But the taste of freedom was eclipsed now by their longing for a good, hot dinner. Though desolate, the Badlands were far from empty; they were peopled in Mooshum's time by unpurposed miscreants and outlaws as well as by honest ranchers. One day, Mooshum and Junesse heard an inhuman shrieking from some bushes deep in a draw where they'd set snares. Upon cautiously investigating, they found that they had snared a pig by its hind leg. While they were debating how to kill it, there appeared on a rise the silhouette of an immense person wearing a wide fedora and seated on a horse. They could have run, but as the rider approached them they were too amazed to move, or didn't want to, for the light now caught the features of a giant woman dressed in the clothing of a man. Her eyes were small and shrewd, her nose and cheeks pudgy, her lip a narrow curl of flesh. One long braid hung down beside a large and motherly breast. She wore twill trousers, boots, chaps, leather gauntlets, and a cowhide belt with silver conchas. Her wide-brimmed hat was banded with the skin of a snake. Her brown bloodstock horse stopped short, polite and obedient. The woman spat a stream of tobacco juice at a quiet lizard, laughed when it jumped and skittered, then ordered the two children to stand still while she roped her hog. With swift and expert motions, she dismounted and tied the pig to the pommel of her saddle, then released its hind leg.

"Climb on," she commanded, gesturing at the horse, and when the children did she grasped the halter and started walking. The roped pig trotted along behind. By the time they reached the woman's ranch, which was miles off, the two had fallen asleep. The woman had a ranch hand take them down, still sleeping, and lay them in a bedroom in her house, which was large and ramshackle, partly sod and partly framed. There were two little beds in the room, plus a trundle where she herself sometimes slept, snoring like an engine, when she was angry with her husband, the notorious Ott Black. In this place my Mooshum and his bride-to-be would live until they turned sixteen.

In Erling Nicolai Rolfsrud's compendium of memorable women and men from North Dakota, "Mustache" Maude Black is described as not unwomanly, though she smoked, drank, was a crack shot and a hard-assed camp boss. These things, my Mooshum said, were all true, as was the mention of both her kind ways and her habit of casual rustling. The last was just a sport to her, Mooshum said; she never meant any harm by it. Mustache Maude sometimes had a mustache, and sometimes, when she plucked it out, she didn't. She kept a neat henhouse and a tidy kitchen. She grew very fond of Mooshum and Junesse, taught them to rope, ride, shoot, and make an unbeatable chicken-and-dumpling stew. Divining their love, she quickly banished Mooshum to the men's bunkhouse, where he soon learned the many ways in which he could make children in the future with Junesse. He practiced in his mind, and could hardly wait. But Maude forbade their marriage until both were sixteen. When that day came, she threw a wedding supper that was talked about for years, featuring several delectably roasted animals that seemed to be the same size and type as those which had gone missing from the farms of the dinner guests. This caused a stir, but Maude kept the liquor flowing, and most of the ranchers shrugged it off.

What was not shrugged off, what was truly resented, was the fact that Maude had thrown an elaborate shindig for a couple of Indians. Or half-breeds. It didn't matter which. These were uncertain times in North Dakota. People's nerves were still shot over what had happened to Custer, and every few years there occurred a lynching. Just a few years before, the remains of five men had been found, still strung from trees, supposedly the victims of a vigilante party led by Flopping Bill Cantrell. Some time later, an entire family was murdered and three Indians were caught by a mob and hanged for maybe doing it, including a boy named Paul Holy Track, who was only thirteen.

The foul murder of a woman on a farm just to the west of Maude's place caused the neighbors to disregard, in their need for immediate revenge, the sudden absence of that woman's husband and to turn their thoughts to the nearest available Indian. There I was, Mooshum said. One night, the yard of pounded dirt between the bunkhouse and Maude's sleeping quarters filled with men hoisting torches of flaring pitch. Their howls rousted Maude from her bed. As a precaution, she had sent Mooshum down to her kitchen cellar to sleep the night. So he knew what happened only through the memory of his wife, for he heard nothing and dreamed his way through the danger.

"Send him out to us," they bawled, "or we will take him ourselves."

Maude stood in the doorway in her nightgown, her holster belted on, a cocked pistol in either hand. She never liked to be woken from sleep.

"I'll shoot the first two of youse that climbs down off his horse," she said, then gestured to the sleepy man beside her, "and Ott Black will plug the next!"

The men were very drunk and could hardly control their horses. One fell off, and Maude shot him in the leg. He started screaming worse than the snared pig.

"Which one of you boys is next?" Maude roared.

"Send out the goddam Indian!" they called. But the yell had less conviction, punctuated, as it was, by the shot man's hoarse shrieks.

"What Indian?"

"That boy!"

"He ain't no Indian," Maude said. "He's a Jew from the land of Galilee! One of the lost tribe of Israel!"

Ott Black nearly choked at his wife's wit.

The men laughed nervously, and called for the boy again.

"I was just having fun with you," Maude said. "Fact is, he's Ott Black's trueborn son."

This threw the men back in their saddles. Ott blinked, then caught on and bellowed, "You men never knowed a woman till you knowed Maude Black!"

The men fell back into the night and left their fallen would-be lyncher kicking in the dirt and pleading to God for mercy. Maybe Maude's bullet had hit a nerve or a bone, for the man seemed to be in an unusual amount of pain for just a gunshot wound to the leg. He began to rave and foam at the mouth, so Maude tied him to his saddle and set out for the doctor's. He died on the way from loss of blood. Before dawn, Maude came back, gave my great-grandparents her two best horses, and told them to ride hard back the way they had come. Which was how they ended up on their home reservation in time to receive their allotments, where they farmed using government-issue seed and plows and reared their six children, one of whom was my grandfather, and where my parents took us every summer just after the wood ticks had settled down.

The story may have been true, for, as I have said, there really was a Mustache Maude Black who had a husband named Ott. Only the story changed. Sometimes Maude was the one to claim Mooshum as her son in the story and sometimes she went on to claim that she'd had an affair with Chief Gall. And sometimes she plugged the man in the gut. But if there was embellishment it had to do only with facts. St. Gabriel's Church was named for God's messenger, the archangel who currently serves as the patron saint of telecommunications workers. Those doves were surely the passenger pigeons of legend and truth, whose numbers were such that nobody thought they could ever be wiped from the earth.

As Mooshum grew frailer and had trouble getting out of his chair, our parents relaxed their television boycott. More often now, our father fixed the magic circles of plastic onto their metal posts and twiddled them until the picture cleared. We sometimes all watched *The Three Stooges* together. The black-haired one looked a lot like the woman who had saved his life, Mooshum said, nodding and pointing at the set. I remember imagining his gnarled brown finger as the hand of a strong young man gripping the candelabra, which, by the way, my great-grandparents had lugged all the way down to the Badlands, where it had come in handy for killing snakes and gophers. They had given their only possession to Maude as a gesture of their gratitude. She had thrust it back at them the night they escaped.

That tall, seven-branched silver-plated instrument, with its finish worn down to tin in some spots, now stood in a place of honor in the center of our dining-room table. It held beeswax tapers, which had been lit during Easter dinner. A month later, in the little alcove on the school playground, I kissed Merlin Koppin. Our kiss was hard, passionate, strangely mature. Afterward, I walked home alone. I walked very slowly. Halfway there, I stopped and stared at a piece of the sidewalk that I'd crossed a thousand times and knew intimately. There was a crack in it—deep, long, jagged, and dark. It was the day when the huge old cottonwood trees shed cotton.

Their heart-shaped leaves ticked and hissed high above me. The air was filled with falling down, and the gutters were plump with a snow of light. I had expected to feel joy, but instead I felt a confusion of sorrow, or maybe fear, for it suddenly seemed that my life was a hungry story and I its source and with this kiss I had begun to deliver myself to the words.

Xu Xi

Famine

I ESCAPE. I board Northwest 18 to New York, via Tokyo. The engine starts, there is no going back. Yesterday, I taught the last English class and left my job of thirty-two years. Five weeks earlier, A-Ma died of heartbreak, within days of my father's sudden death. He was ninety-five, she ninety. Unlike A-Ba, who saw the world by crewing on tankers, neither my mother nor I ever left Hong Kong.

Their deaths rid me of responsibility at last, and I could forfeit my pension and that dreary existence. I am fifty-one and an only child, unmarried.

I never expected my parents to take so long to die.

This meal is *luxurious,* better than anything I imagined.

My colleagues who fly every summer complain of the indignities of travel. Cardboard food, cramped seats, long lines, and these days, too much security nonsense, they say. They fly Cathay, our "national" carrier. This makes me laugh. We have never been a nation; "national" isn't our adjective. *Semantics,* they say, dismissive, just as they dismiss what I say of debt, that it is not an inevitable state, or that children exist to be taught, not spoilt. My colleagues live in overpriced, new, mortgaged flats and indulge 1 to 2.5 children. Most of my students are uneducable.

Back, though, to this in-flight meal. Smoked salmon and cold shrimp, endive salad, strawberries and melon to clean the palate. Then, steak with mushrooms, potatoes *au gratin*, a choice between a shiraz or cabernet sauvignon. Three cheeses, white chocolate mousse, coffee, and port or a liqueur or brandy. Foods from the pages of a novel, perhaps.

My parents ate sparingly, long after we were no longer impoverished, and disdained "unhealthy" Western diets. A-Ba often said that the only thing he really discovered from travel was that the world was hungry, and that there would never be enough food for everyone. It was why, he said, he did not miss the travel when he retired.

I have no complaints of my travels so far.

My complaining colleagues do not fly business. This seat is an *island* of a bed, surrounded by air. I did not mean to fly in dignity, but having never traveled in summer, or at all, I didn't plan months ahead, long before flights filled up. I simply rang the airlines and booked Northwest, the first one that had a seat, only in business class.

Friends and former students, who do fly business when their companies foot the bill, were horrified. *You* paid *full fare? No one does!* I have money, I replied, why shouldn't I? *But you've given up your "rice bowl." Think of the future.*

I hate rice, always have, even though I never left a single grain, because under my father's watchful glare, A-Ma inspected my bowl. Every meal, even after her eyes dimmed.

The Plaza Suite is nine hundred square feet, over three times the size of home. I had wanted the Vanderbilt or Ambassador and would have settled for the Louis XV, but they were all booked, by those more important than I, no doubt. Anyway, this will have to do. "Nothing unimportant" happens here at the Plaza is what their website literature claims.

The porter arrives, and wheels my bags in on a trolley.

My father bought our tiny flat in a village in Shatin with his disability settlement. When he was forty-five and I one, a falling crane crushed his left leg and groin, thus ending his sailing and procreating career. Shatin isn't very rural anymore, but our home has denied progress its due. We didn't get a phone till I was in my thirties.

I tip the porter five dollars and begin unpacking the leather luggage set. There is too much space for my things.

Right about now, you're probably wondering, along with my colleagues, former students, and friends, *What on earth does she think she's doing?* It was what my parents shouted when I was twelve and went on my first hunger strike.

My parents were illiterate, both refugees from China's rural poverty. A-Ma fried tofu at Shatin market. Once A-Ba recovered from his accident, he worked there also as a cleaner, cursing his fate. They expected me to support them as soon as possible, which should have been after six years of primary school, the only compulsory education required by law in the sixties.

As you see, I clearly had no choice but to strike, since my exam results proved I was smart enough for secondary school. My father beat me, threatened to starve me. *How dare I,* when others were genuinely hungry, unlike me, the only child of a tofu seller who always ate. *Did I want him and A-Ma to die of hunger just to send me to school? How dare I risk their longevity and old age?*

But I was unpacking a Spanish leather suitcase when the past, that country bumpkin's territory, so rudely interrupted.

Veronica, whom I met years ago at university while taking a literature course, foisted this luggage on me. She runs her family's garment enterprise, and is married to a banker. Between them and their three children, they own four flats, three cars, and at least a dozen sets of luggage. Veronica invites me out to dinner (she always pays) whenever she wants to complain about her family. Lately, we've dined often.

"Kids," she groaned over our rice porridge, two days before my trip. "My daughter won't use her brand-new Loewe set because, she says, that's *passé*. All her friends at Stanford sling these canvas bags with one fat strap. Canvas, imagine. Not even leather."

"Ergonomics," I told her, annoyed at this bland and inexpensive meal. "It's all about weight and balance." And cost, I knew, because the young overspend to conform, just as Veronica eats rice porridge because she's overweight and no longer complains that I'm thin.

She continued. "You're welcome to take the set if you like."

"Don't worry yourself. I can use an old school bag."

"But that's barely a cabin bag! Surely not enough to travel with."

In the end, I let her nag me into taking this set, which is more bag than clothing.

Veronica sounded worried when I left her that evening. "Are you *sure* you'll be okay?"

And would she worry, I wonder, if she could see me now, here, in this suite, this enormous space where one night's bill would have taken my parents years, no, *decades*, to earn and even for me, four years' pay, at least when I first started teaching in my rural enclave (though you're thinking, of course, quite correctly, *Well, what about inflation,* the thing economists cite to dismiss these longings of an English teacher who has spent her life instructing those who care not a whit for our "official language," the one they never speak, at least not if they can choose, especially not now when there is, increasingly, a choice).

My unpacking is done; the past need not intrude. I draw a bath, as one does in English literature, to wash away the heat and grime of both cities in summer. *Why New York?* Veronica asked, at the end of our last evening together. Because, I told her, it will be like nothing I've ever known. For the first time since we've known each other, Veronica actually seemed to envy *me*, although perhaps it was my imagination.

The phone rings, and it's "Guest Relations" wishing to welcome me and offer hospitality. The hotel must wonder, since I grace no social register. I ask for a table at Lutèce tonight. Afterwards, I tip the concierge ten dollars for successfully making the reservation. As you can see, I am no longer an ignorant bumpkin, even though I never left the schools in the New Territories, our urban countryside now that no one farms anymore. Besides, Hong Kong magazines detail lives of the rich and richer so I've read of the famous restaurant and know about the greasy palms of New Yorkers.

I order tea and scones from Room Service. It will hold me till dinner at eight.

The first time I ever tasted tea and scones was at the home of my private student. To supplement income when I enrolled in Teacher Training, I tutored Form V students who needed to pass the School Certificate English exam. This was the compromise I agreed to with my parents before they would allow me to qualify as a teacher. Oh yes, there was a second hunger strike two years prior, before they would let me continue into Form IV. That time, I promised to keep working in the markets after school with A-Ma, which I did.

Actually, my learning English at all was a stroke of luck, since I was *hardly* at a "name school" of the elite. An American priest taught at my secondary school, so I heard a native speaker. He wasn't a very good teacher, but he paid attention to me because I was the only student who liked the subject. A little attention goes a long way.

Tea and scones! I am *supposed* to be eating, not dwelling on the ancient past. The opulence of the tray Room Service brings far surpasses what that pretentious woman served, mother of the hopeless boy, my first private student of many, who only passed his English exam because he cheated (he paid a friend to sit the exam for him), not that I'd ever tell since he's now a wealthy international businessman of some repute who can hire staff to communicate in English with the rest of the world, since he still cannot, at least not with any credibility. That scone ("from Cherikoff," she bragged) was cold and dry, hard as a rock.

Hot scones, oozing with butter. To ooze. I like the lasciviousness of that word, with its excess of vowels, the way an excess of wealth allows people to waste kindness on me, as my former student still does, every lunar new year, by sending me a *laisee* packet with a generous check which I deposit in my parents' bank account, the way I surrender all my earnings, as any filial and responsible unmarried child should, or so they said.

I eat two scones oozing with butter and savor tea enriched by cream and sugar, here at this "greatest hotel in the world," to vanquish, once and for all, my parents' fear of death and opulence.

Eight does not come soon enough. In the taxi on the way to Lutèce, I ponder the question of pork.

When we were poor but not impoverished, A-Ma once dared to make pork for dinner. It was meant to be a treat, to give me a taste of meat, because I complained that tofu was bland. A-Ba became a vegetarian after his accident and prohibited meat at home; eunuchs are angry people. She dared because he was not eating with us that night, a rare event in our family (I think some sailors he used to know invited him out).

I shat a tapeworm the next morning—almost ten inches long—and she never cooked pork again.

I have since tasted properly cooked pork, naturally, since it's unavoidable in Chinese cuisine. In my twenties, I dined out with friends, despite my parents' objections. But friends marry and scatter; the truth is that there is no one but family in the end, so over time, I submitted to their way of being and seldom took meals away from home, meals my mother cooked virtually till the day she died.

I am distracted. The real question, of course, is whether or not I should order pork tonight.

I did not expect this trip to be fraught with pork!

At Lutèce, I have the distinct impression that the two couples at the next table are talking about me. Perhaps they pity me. People often pitied me my life. *Starved of affection,* they whispered, although why they felt the need to whisper what everyone could hear I failed to understand. All I desired was greater gastronomic variety, but my parents couldn't bear the idea of my eating without them. I ate our plain diet and endured their perpetual skimping because they did eventually learn to leave me alone. That much filial propriety was reasonable payment. I just didn't expect them to *stop* complaining, to fear for what little fortune they had, because somewhere someone was less fortunate than they. That fear made them cling hard to life, forcing me to suffer their fortitude, their good health, and their longevity.

I should walk over to those overdressed people and tell them how things are, about famine, I mean, the way I tried to tell my students, the way my parents dinned it into me as long as they were alive.

Famine has no menu! The waiter waits as I take too long to study the menu. He does not seem patient, making him an oxymoron in his profession. My students would no more learn the oxymoron than they would learn about famine. *Daughter, did you lecture your charges today about famine?* A-Ba would ask every night before dinner. *Yes,* I learned to lie, giving him the answer he needed. This waiter could take a lesson in patience from me.

Finally, I look up at this man who twitches, and do not order pork. *Very good,* he says, as if I should be graded for my literacy in menus. He returns shortly with a bottle of the most expensive red available, and now I *know* the people at the next table are staring. The minute he leaves, the taller of the two men from that table comes over.

"Excuse me, but I believe we met in March? At the U.S. Consulate cocktail in Hong Kong? You're Kwai-sin Ho, aren't you?" He extends his hand. "Peter Martin."

Insulted, it's my turn to stare at this total stranger. I look *nothing* like that simpering socialite who designs wildly fashionable hats that are all the rage in Asia. Hats! We don't have the weather for hats, especially not those things, which are good for neither warmth nor shelter from the sun.

Besides, what use are hats for the hungry?

I do not accept his hand. "I'm her twin sister," I lie. "Kwai-sin and I are estranged."

He looks like he's about to protest, but retreats. After that, they don't stare, although I am sure they discuss me now that I've contributed new gossip for those who are nurtured by the crumbs of the rich and famous. But at least I can eat in peace.

It's my outfit, probably. Kwai-sin Ho is famous for her *cheongsams*, which is all she ever wears, the way I do. It was my idea. When we were girls together in school, I said the only thing I'd ever wear when I grew up was the *cheongsam*, the shapely dress with side slits and a neck-strangling collar. She grimaced and said they weren't fashionable, that only spinster schoolteachers and prostitutes wore them, which, back in the sixties, wasn't exactly true, but Kwai-sin was never too bright or imaginative.

That was long ago, before she became Kwai-sin in the *cheongsam* once these turned fashionable again, long before her father died and her mother became the mistress of a prominent businessman who whisked them into the stratosphere high above mine. For a little while, she remained my friend, but then we grew up, she married one of the shipping Hos, and became the socialite who refused, albeit politely, to recognize me the one time we bumped into each other at some function in Hong Kong.

So now, vengeance is mine. I will not entertain the people who fawn over her and possess no powers of recognition.

Food is getting sidelined by memory. This is unacceptable. I cannot allow all these intrusions. I must get back to the food, which is, after all, the point of famine.

This is due to a lack of diligence, as A-Ma would say, this lazy meandering from what's important, this succumbing to sloth. My mother was terrified of sloth, almost as much as she was terrified of my father.

She used to tell me an old legend about sloth.

There once was a man so lazy he wouldn't even lift food to his mouth. When he was young, his mother fed him, but as his mother aged, she couldn't. So he marries a woman who will feed him as his mother did. For a time, life is bliss.

Then one day, his wife must return to her village to visit her dying mother. "How will I eat?" he exclaims in fright. The wife conjures this plan. She bakes a gigantic cookie and hangs it on a string around his neck. All the lazy man must do is bend forward and eat. "Wonderful!" he says, and off she goes, promising to return.

On the first day, the man nibbles the edge of the cookie. Each day, he nibbles further. By the fourth day, he's eaten so far down there's no more cookie unless he turns it, which his wife expected he would since he could do this with his mouth.

However, the man's so lazy he lies down instead and waits for his wife's return. As the days pass, his stomach growls and begins to eat itself. Yet the man still won't turn the cookie. By the time his wife comes home, the lazy man has starved to death.

Memory causes such unaccountable digressions! There I was in Lutèce, noticing that people pitied me. Pity made my father livid, which he took out on A-Ma and me. Anger was his one escape from timidity. He wanted no sympathy for either his dead limb or useless genitals.

Perhaps people find me odd rather than pitiful. I will describe my appearance and let you judge. I am thin but not emaciated and have strong teeth. This latter feature is most unusual for a Hong Kong person of my generation. Many years ago, a dentist courted me. He taught me well about oral hygiene, trained as he had been at an American university. Unfortunately, he was slightly rotund, which offended A-Ba. I think A-Ma wouldn't have minded the marriage, but she always sided with my father, who believed it wise to marry one's own physical type (illiteracy did not prevent him from developing philosophies, as you've already witnessed). I was then in my mid-thirties. After the dentist, there were no other men and as a result, I never left home, which is our custom for unmarried women and men, a loathsome custom but difficult to overthrow. We all must pick our battles, and my acquiring English, which my parents naturally knew not a word, was a sufficiently drastic defiance to last a lifetime, or at least till they expired.

This dinner at Lutèce has come and gone, and you haven't tasted a thing. It's what happens when we converse overmuch and do not concentrate on the food. At home, we ate in the silence of A-Ba's rage.

What a shame, but never mind, I promise to share the bounty next time. This meal must have been good because the bill is in the thousands.

I pay by traveler's checks because, not believing in debt, I own no credit cards.

Last night's dinner weighs badly, despite my excellent digestion, so I take a long walk late in the afternoon and end up in Chelsea. New York streets are dirtier than I imagined. Although I did not really expect pavements of gold, in my deepest fantasies, there did reign a glitter and sheen.

No one talks to me here.

The air is fetid with the day's leftover heat and odors. Under a humid, darkening sky, I almost trip over a body on the corner of Twenty-fourth and Seventh. It cannot be a corpse! Surely cadavers aren't left to rot in the streets.

A-Ma used to tell of a childhood occurrence in her village. An itinerant had stolen food from the local pig trough. The villagers caught him, beat him senseless, cut off his tongue and arms, and left him to bleed to death behind the rubbish heap. In the morning, my mother was at play, and while running, tripped over the body. She fell into a blood pool beside him. The corpse's eyes were open.

He surely didn't mean to steal, she always said in the telling, her eyes burning from the memory. *Try to forget,* my father would say. My parents specialized in memory. They both remained lucid and clearheaded till they died.

But this body moves. It's a man awakening from sleep. He mumbles something. Startled, I move away. He is still speaking. I think he's saying he's hungry.

I escape. A taxi whisks me back to my hotel, where my table is reserved at the restaurant.

The ceiling at the Oak Room is roughly four times the height of an average basketball player. The ambience is not as seductive as promised by the Plaza's literature. The problem with reading the wrong kind of literature is that you are bound to be disappointed.

This is a man's restaurant, with a menu of many steaks. Hemingway and Fitzgerald used to eat here. Few of my students have heard of these two, and none of them will have read a single book by either author.

As an English teacher, especially one who was not employed at a "name school" of the elite, I became increasingly marginal. Colleagues and friends converse in Cantonese, the only official language out of our three that people live as well as speak. The last time any student read an entire novel was well over twenty years ago. English literature is not on anyone's exam roster anymore; to desire it in a Chinese colony is as irresponsible as it was of me to master it in our former British one.

Teaching English is little else than a linguistic requirement. Once, it was my passion and flight away from home. Now it is merely my entrée to this former men's club.

But I must order dinner and stop thinking about literature.

The entrées make my head spin, so I turn to the desserts. There is no gooseberry tart! Ever since *David Copperfield*, I have wanted to taste a gooseberry tart (or perhaps it was another book, I don't remember). I tell the boy with the water jug this.

He says. "The magician, madam?"

"The orphan," I reply.

He stands, openmouthed, without pouring water. What is this imbecility of the young? They neither serve nor wait.

The waiter appears. "Can I help with the menu?"

"Why?" I snap. "It isn't heavy."

But what upsets me is the memory of my mother's story, which I'd long forgotten until this afternoon, just as I hoped to forget about the teaching of English literature, about the uselessness of the life I prepared so hard for.

The waiter hovers. "Are you feeling okay?"

I look up at the sound of his voice and realize my hands are shaking. Calming myself, I say, "*Au jus.* The prime rib, please, and escargots to start," and on and on I go, ordering in the manner of a man who retreats to a segregated club, who indulges in oblivion because he can, who shuts out the stirrings of the groin and the heart.

I wake to a ringing phone. Housekeeping wants to know if they may clean. It's already past noon. This must be jet lag. I tell Housekeeping, Later.

It's so *comfortable* here that I believe it is possible to forget.

I order brunch from Room Service. Five-star hotels in Hong Kong serve brunch buffets on weekends. The first time I went to one, Veronica paid. We were both students at university. She wasn't wealthy, but her parents gave her spending money, whereas my entire salary (I was already a working teacher by then) belonged to my parents. The array of food made my mouth water. *Pace yourself,* Veronica said. *It's all you can eat.* I wanted to try everything, but gluttony frightened me.

Meanwhile, A-Ba's voice. *After four or more days without food, your stomach begins to eat itself,* and his laugh, dry and caustic.

But I was choosing brunch.

Mimosa. Smoked salmon. Omelet with Swiss cheese and chives. And salad, the expensive kind that's imported back home, crisp Romaine in a Caesar. Room Service asks what I'd like for dessert, so I say chocolate ice-cream sundae. Perhaps I'm more of a bumpkin than I care to admit. My colleagues, former students, and friends would consider my choices boring, unsophisticated, lacking in culinary imagination. They're right, I suppose, since everything I've eaten since coming to New York I could just as easily have obtained back home. They can't understand, though. It's not *what* but *how much.* How opulent. The opulence is what counts to stop the cannibalism of internal organs.

Will that be all?

I am tempted to say, Bring me an endless buffet, whatever your chef concocts, whatever your tongues desire.

How long till my money runs out, my finite account, ending this sweet exile?

Guest Relations knocks, insistent. I have not let anyone in for three days. I open the door wide to show the manager that everything is fine, that their room is not wrecked, that I am not crazy even if I'm not on the social register. If you read the news, as I do, you know it's necessary to allay fears. So I do, because I do not wish to give the wrong impression. I am not a diva or an excessively famous person who trashes hotel rooms because she can.

I say, politely, that I've been a little unwell, nothing serious, and to please have Housekeeping stop in now. The "please" is significant; it shows I am not odd, that I am, in fact, cognizant of civilized language in English. The manager withdraws, relieved.

For dinner tonight, I decide on two dozen oysters, lobster, and filet mignon. I select a champagne and the wines, one white and one red. Then, it occurs to me that since this is a suite, I can order enough food for a party, so I tell Room Service that there will be a dozen guests for dinner, possibly more. *Very good,* he says, and asks how many extra bottles of champagne and wine, to which I reply, As many as needed.

My students will be my guests. They more or less were visitors during those years I tried to teach. You mustn't think I was always disillusioned, though I seem so now. To prove it to you I'll invite all my colleagues, the few friends I have, like Veronica, the dentist who courted me and his wife and two children, even Kwai-sin and my parents. I bear no grudges; I am not bitter towards them. What I'm uncertain of is whether or not they will come to my supper.

This room, this endless meal, can save me. I feel it. I am vanquishing my fear of death and opulence.

There was a time we did not care about opulence and we dared to speak of death. You spoke of famine because everyone knew the stories from China were true. Now, even in this country, people more or less know. You could educate students about starvation in China or Africa or India because they knew it to be true, because they saw the hunger around them, among the beggars in our streets, and for some, even in their own homes. There was a time it was better *not* to have space, or things to put in that space, and to dream of having instead, because no one had much, except royalty and movie stars and they were *meant* to be fantasy—untouchable, unreal—somewhere in a dream of manna and celluloid.

But you can't speak of famine anymore. Anorexia's fashionable and desirably profitable on runways, so students simply *can't see the hunger.* My colleagues and friends also can't, and refuse to speak of it, changing the subject to what they prefer to see. Even our journalists can't seem to see, preferring the reality they fashion rather than the reality that is. I get angry, but then, when I'm calm, I am simply baffled. Perhaps my parents, and friends and colleagues and memory, are right, that I *am* too stubborn, perhaps even too slothful because instead of *seeing* reality, I've hidden in my parents' home, in my life as a teacher, even though the years were dreary and long, when what I truly wanted, what I desired, was to embrace the opulence, forsake the hunger, but was too lazy to turn the cookie instead.

I mustn't be angry at them, by which I mean all the "thems" I know and don't know, the big impersonal "they." Like a good English teacher I tell my students, you *must* define the "they." Students are students and continue to make the same mistakes, and all I can do is remind them that "they" are you and to please, please, try to remember because language is a root of life.

Most of the people can't be wrong all the time. Besides, whose fault is it if the dream came true? Postdream is like postmodern; no one understands it, but everyone condones its existence.

Furthermore, what you can't, or won't see, *doesn't* exist.

Comfort, like food, exists, *surrounds* me here.

Not wishing to let anger get the better of me, I eat. Like the Romans, I disgorge and continue. It takes hours to eat three lobsters and three steaks, plus consume five glasses of champagne and six of wine, yet still the food is not enough.

The guests arrive and more keep coming. Who would have thought all these people would show up, all these people I thought I left behind. Where do they come from? My students, colleagues, the dentist and his family, a horde of strangers. Even Kwai-sin and her silly hats, and do you know something, we *do* look a little alike, so Peter Martin wasn't completely wrong. I changed my language to change my life, but still the past throngs, bringing all these people and their Cantonese chatter. The food is not enough, the food is never enough.

Room Service obliges round the clock.

Veronica arrives and I feel a great relief, because the truth is, I no longer cared for her anymore when all we ate was rice porridge. It was mean-spirited, I was ungrateful, forgetting that once she fed me my first buffet, teasing my appetite. *Come out, travel,* she urged over the years. It's not her fault I stayed at home, afraid to abandon my responsibility, traveling only in my mind.

Finally, my parents arrive. My father sits down first to the feast. His leg is whole, and sperm gushes out from between his legs. *It's not so bad here,* he says, and gestures for my mother to join him. This is good. A-Ma will eat if A-Ba does, they're like that, those two. My friends don't understand, not even Veronica. She repeats now what she often has said, that my parents are "controlling." Perhaps, I say, but that's unimportant. I'm only interested in not being responsible anymore.

The noise in the room is deafening. We can barely hear each other above the din. Cantonese is a noisy language, unlike Mandarin or English, but it is alive. This suite that was too empty is stuffed with people, all needing to be fed.

I gaze at the platters of food, piled in this space with largesse. What does it matter if there *are* too many mouths to feed? A phone call is all it takes to get more food, and more. I am fifty-one and have waited too long to eat. They're right, they're all right. If I give in, if I let go, I will vanquish my fears. *This* is bliss, truly.

A-Ma smiles at the vast quantities of food. This pleases me because she so rarely smiles. She says, *Not like lazy cookie man, hah?*

Feeling benevolent, I smile at my parents. *No, not like him,* I say. *Now, eat.*

Lara Vapnyar

Puffed Rice and Meatballs

O NCE, IN A hazy, postcoital silence, Katya's lover came back from a
shower, dropped the towel to the floor, climbed into the bed, and
said, "Tell me about your childhood. Tell me about the horrors of Communism."

Katya sat hugging her knees so that her body resembled a triangle with
her head as an apex. She had put on her bra and panties—she hated
nakedness, how it turned into something sadly irrelevant after sex.

The request startled her. What exactly were the horrors of Communism? Katya's childhood coincided with the stagnation period. People
weren't killed or put in prisons as easily as before, there was plenty of space
in mental hospitals, and as for the freedoms of speech, residence, and
such—what did little Katya need them for? Was it horrible to have to wear
a red tie, or stand in a two-hour line to see Lenin's body in his tomb, or
stand in an even longer line to buy toilet paper? Katya didn't think so. It
was rather funny, even nostalgic now.

So then why would a man with whom she'd gone on only a few dates
and exchanged a few embraces be interested in something as intimate as
her childhood?

She stared at her lover suspiciously.

He had propped up his head with his elbow. His expression was of calm anticipation. He didn't want to know her better. The man was simply asking for some entertainment—for an easy, amusing, and preferably sexy story about the exotic world to which his lover belonged. Katya's shoulders relaxed.

After some mental probing she picked a story. She wasn't sure if it had anything to do with Communism, but she thought that with a few effective details she would be able to make the narrative exotic enough. She put her right cheek on her knee and turned to her lover.

"Do you want to hear about my first sexual encounter?"

"Gladly!"

"When I was little, I attended a daylong preschool, like most city kids. We were on a very strict schedule similar to a prison, or a labor camp. Every day, at 1 PM, we had a nap. Our teacher—I remember only that she had red ears and a long, lumpy nose—put us in two lines and led us to the bedroom, a gloomy semidark room, where blinds were drawn at all times, where the beds stood in tight rows, a girl's bed alternating with a boy's."

"I see," Katya's lover noted with enthusiasm. "So you were sandwiched between two boys."

"Not exactly. Between a boy and a wall, because my bed was the last in a row.

"We stripped to our underwear—boys and girl had identical white underpants and undershirts—climbed into the beds, pulled the blankets to our chins, and turned to the right side. We weren't allowed to sleep on our backs or left side. As soon we all were in bed the teacher said: 'I'm going now, but if I hear even a squeak from you, I'm coming back and I'm coming back with the thing!' Nobody knew what 'the thing' was, and nobody wanted to find out.

"'And if you go to the bathroom, it better be an emergency!' she added before leaving for the dining room.

"I couldn't sleep on my right side. I just lay there scared and bored, facing the back of the boy next to me, staring at his blanket's pattern through the rectangular slit in the blanket cover.

"Delicious sounds coming from the dining room distracted me even more. I listened to the plates' clatter and the persistent scraping of a serving spoon against a pot's bottom. I knew that in a few minutes the teacher would open the entrance door and let in her sons, twin boys, nine years of age. She would seat them at our tables and feed them the food left over from our lunch. I saw them once, when I pleaded an emergency and ran through the dining room to the bathroom. Their plates were piled up with shrunken meatballs and pale mounds of mashed potatoes. Their knees were bent awkwardly under our kid-size table. Their ears moved along with their jaws.

"I tossed in bed and thought about meatballs, which during the nap time always seemed awfully tempting, even though I'd repeatedly refused them during lunch. 'Want to be hungry—fine,' the teacher had said, hastily taking away my plate. 'This school is no place for picky eaters.'"

Katya's lover listened with a warm and amused expression, tinted with slight shadows of impatience. She didn't know why she mentioned the teacher's boys at all. She'd better hurry up and get to the sex part.

"'Hey, are you asleep?'" she continued. "A thin voice from the next bed interrupted my meatballs fantasies. The voice belonged to a chunky, blue-eyed boy named Vova. He had turned to me and lay blinking with his white eyelashes.

"'Can't you see that my eyes are open?' I asked.

"'Shh,' he pointed in the dining room's direction. The white eyelashes blinked some more. 'I'll show you my *peesya* if you show me yours.'

"I didn't have any problems with that.

"We moved our blankets aside and pulled down our underpants. We craned our necks. We stared.

"'Mine's better,' Vova said at last.

"I agreed. His was better. His looked like something you could play with.

"'It's so pretty and small,' I said."

That was the only time when I didn't lie about a man's size, Katya wanted to add, but then changed her mind.

"'What do you do with it?'

"'Not much really,' he shrugged, tucking his *peesya* into his underpants. 'I pee with it, I pull on it sometimes. Not much.'

"'Not much?' I frowned. Such a pretty, fun toy. I would have known what to do with it! For one thing I would've dressed it in all the clothes from my tiny dolls collection. I would've tried little hats, socks, and dresses on it. Then I would've tried to feed it and put it into bed."

"Classic case of penis envy," Katya's lover said, laughing. He was playing with her bra straps.

"Oh, no, not at all. I didn't feel envy. It was rather a feeling of waste that such a promising thing wasn't properly used.

"Anyway, I was excited, and I couldn't wait to go home and tell my mother. In fact, I didn't wait. I told her on the way from school. I stopped in the middle of the dry summer sidewalk, let go of my mother's hand, and said, 'Mom, you wouldn't believe what I saw today!'

"Several hours of yelling, sobbing, and hysterical phone confessions to her friends followed. Then there was a lecture. My mother led me into a room that we shared—my little bed stood perpendicular to her big one— sat me on a little chair in the corner, and walked to the middle of the room, her arms folded on her chest and her brows furrowed. I think I might have spurted a giggle, because I remember my mother suddenly yelling: 'It's not funny. It's a very serious matter.'

"The lecture wasn't long. I remember sitting patiently through the whole of it, and I couldn't have possibly done that if the lecture lasted more than twenty minutes. At one point, my mother broke into sobs at midsentence and ran to lock herself in the bathroom."

"Oh, my god. It could've left you scarred for life."

Katya stopped. Her lover looked mildly horrified. He'd even freed his fingers from under the straps of her bra.

It would've been a bad idea to mention that she then banged on the bathroom door, yelling, "Mommy, please, please forgive me!" It would've been even worse to add that she dropped to her knees and tried to calm her mother by whispering through the slit under the door. The last thing Katya needed was to show her scars.

She continued in a lighter tone.

"After my mother had gone, I decided to go on with the lecture. Probably wanted to try on the role of an authority figure. I gathered all my dolls—some I had to pull from under the beds and bookcases—and sat them on little chairs from my toy furniture set. It was a peculiar group with the dolls ranging from one inch to three feet high, a few with missing body parts. 'Listen to me,' I said, looming above them with my arms folded on my chest. 'Listen hard, you bunch of stupid, irresponsible dolls. And don't you giggle! Never ever show your little *peesya* to anyone. First of all, good dolls don't do that. Second of all, you can go to prison for that.'"

Katya paused before a punch line.

"And guess what? They never did."

The punch line worked. Katya's lover lifted his hands back to her bra straps, and he even laughed.

"But you did. You did! You weren't as obedient as your dolls."

"No, I wasn't," Katya agreed, and helped him to unhook her bra.

The story was a success. It was certainly better than watching the news broadcast, as they had the last time. "You were great," he had said, pulling on his socks afterward, but she hadn't been sure whether he referred to their lovemaking or her ability to patiently watch the news.

It wasn't until much later, when Katya returned to her Brooklyn apartment, that the story started to bother her. It felt like the onset of a toothache—a vague gnawing sensation that would grow into real pain at any moment. Katya brewed some bitter, dark tea right in the mug and opened a jar of walnut jam, which having cost her a ridiculous $5.99 still didn't taste like home. It was too sugary—wrong, just like her story. The very lightness of her carefully dispensed jokes made her shiver with disgust now. "It's not funny!" she wanted to scream like her mother, whom she'd just betrayed for a strange man's entertainment.

Katya became awash in shame, for herself, for her mother, but most of all for the teacher's hungry boys who had to eat leftovers at the kids' tables.

At the bottom of her mug sat a little pile of tea leaves. Years ago, Katya attempted to read the leaves with her best friend, Vera. They sat leaning over their mugs, the tip of Katya's yellow braid touching the table. "I don't see anything," Vera complained. "I see a shape," Katya said. "A shape of what? A man?" Katya shrugged. "A shape of something."

Katya peered into the pile and tried to determine whether she would ever meet a man who would understand her pity and her shame, to whom she could tell her real stories, the ones that mattered, the ones that haunted her, without dressing them up to his taste.

There were two things I craved as a child—imported clothes and imported junk food in crunchy bags, she would have started her real story. One day I came close to having the one and the other.

It happened soon after I turned thirteen. I remember the year exactly, because it was the year I developed breasts, and it was also the year my aunt Marusya returned from West Germany and brought me a bunch of hip German clothes. "Here. Ransack it!" she said, handing me a tightly packed plastic bag.

I ran to my room and shook the bag's contents right onto the floor. The clothes made an impressive pile. I wanted to dive in and swim in that colorful sea of fabric. Instead I sat in the middle of the pile and ran the material through my fingers—I felt like somebody who'd opened a treasure box. I stretched stockings, I stroked fuzzy sweaters, I played with shiny metallic belts. I even kissed one nylon blouse I particularly liked. Then I hurried to try them on, afraid that if I waited, they might disappear. I pulled the pieces on, one by one, admiring my reflection in the shiny glass doors of the bookcase. The clothes, even obscured by the reflected book covers, looked divine, even more than divine—they looked just like the ones in the dog-eared JCPenney catalogue I'd once seen at my best friend Vera's place.

The last piece in the pile was a modest beige sweater with funny shoulder straps. Why would somebody sew shoulder straps to a sweater, I'd thought when I saw it first. And why bother spending precious currency when you could buy a simple thing like that here. But I was wrong, I was very wrong. And I saw it as soon as I tried the sweater on. The pale, unimpressive piece of fabric could perform miracles. I didn't know whether it was because of the shoulder straps or some other tailor's trick, but it made me appear as if I had breasts! I couldn't believe my eyes. For several months I'd been staring into a bathroom mirror hoping to discover much-desired swellings on my chest. I kneaded and pinched myself, but no matter how hard I tried, it didn't work. My chest was as flat and as hard as my grandmother's washing board. Drink more milk, my happier, breasts-equipped girlfriends advised. I did. I drank about six to eight glasses a day, fighting the spasms of nausea. It didn't work.

And now here they were. Two soft little knobs pushing against the beige fabric. They were my very real breasts. They were beautiful. The girl who blinked at me from the bookcase's glass surface was beautiful. She was not just pretty or cute, as people mistakenly called her. She was strikingly, undeniably beautiful. Apparently, the beauty had always been there, but buried under the wrong clothes.

I had to show it to the world.

I dialed Vera's number and asked her to meet me by the playground.

I threw on a new miniskirt and new tights and ran to the door past my parents, who were getting drunk on foreign liquor and Aunt Marusya's stories of foreign life.

Clomping with my shoes on the steps of the littered staircase, I suddenly thought of my newfound beauty as a burden. Being beautiful couldn't be easy. It could be troublesome, and even embarrassing. People would stare at me now; I would produce some reaction in the outside world, make some change. And I would have to react back. But how? What exactly was a beautiful person supposed to do? What was I supposed to do when boys stared at me and at my breasts, which I was certain they would? I had a surge of titillating panic as I opened the entrance door and stopped, blinded by the orange rays of the setting sun.

I'd just keep my eyes down, I decided. I'd let them stare, but I'd keep my eyes down.

Vera presented a bigger problem. Would it be possible to stay friends? Vera, with her flat, square face and thick waist, wasn't even pretty, let alone beautiful, and about 80 percent of our conversations had consisted of berating the stupid and boy-crazy pretty girls. Yet, she'd been my best friend for years and I didn't want to lose her.

She loped toward me now, swinging a canvas bag in one hand and waving a wad of money with the other. Was she ungraceful! I slouched and messed up my hair, trying to make my beauty a little less obvious.

But when Vera drew near, I saw that my worries had been in vain. Her nose and forehead were covered with sweat, her eyes bulged with excitement—she clearly was oblivious to everything in the world, including the sudden beauty of her friend.

"The puffed . . . puffed, the puffed rice," she panted. "They are selling puffed rice in the little store." She clutched my sleeve and tried to catch a breath. "American puffed rice in crunchy bags! A friend of my mother's hairdresser told us. We have to run because the line is getting bigger every second."

"But I don't have any money!"

"I'll lend you some."

And we loped in the store's direction together.

We were two hundred fifty-sixth and two hundred fifty-seventh in the line. The reason we knew it was they had scribbled the numbers in blue ink right on our palms. I had to keep my marked hand outslung, so the number wouldn't rub off accidentally, as happened to a woman who stood ahead of us. She kept showing her sweaty palm to everybody and asking if they could still read her number, when there wasn't anything but a faded blue stain. I was sure they would turn her away at the counter. The subjects of clothes, boys, and beauty lost their importance somehow, or maybe it was just hard to think of such nonsense while guarding your marked hand.

The line moved slowly. Everybody shifted from one foot to the other waiting to take a step forward. They let in people in batches of ten or twelve—as many as could fit into the narrow strip of the store.

I bit on my ponytail. Vera rolled and unrolled the ruble bills in her hand. We were too tired to talk, as were other people. All eyes focused on the exit door, where the happy ones squeezed by with armfuls of crunchy, silver-and-yellow bags. The people looked shabby and crumpled, but the bags shone winningly in the orange rays.

"Let's buy two each," Vera suggested when the line advanced to the hundreds. I nodded. She smoothed the crumpled ruble bills in her hand. There were five of them, enough to buy ten bags of puffed rice or two bags and a round can of instant coffee in the big store next door, as Vera's mother had suggested. I thought what a good friend Vera was. Another person would've just taken all the money, without sharing it with me. I asked myself if I would've done the same thing for Vera. I wasn't sure.

"Let's buy six," Vera said, when we advanced to the store doors. I nodded.

She reached with her hand and touched a bag of puffed rice in somebody's arms. It crunched just as I'd expected.

"You know what, let's buy ten," Vera decided.

I nodded.

My feet hurt and my lips were parched. But instead of craving for a drink, I craved dry and salty puffed rice.

We stood just a few people away from the doors now. They'd let us in with the next batch! It would take just a little bit longer before I could feel the crunchy surface of a bag, before I could rip it open, before I could let the golden avalanche pour into my hands. I licked a trickle of saliva off the corner of my mouth.

Then a saleswoman appeared in the doorway.

"Seven o'clock. The store is closed," she said.

For a few moments nobody moved. Nobody made a sound. People just stood gazing at the woman intently, as if she spoke a foreign language and they were struggling to interpret her words. Then the crowd erupted. The feeble, polite pleas grew into demands, then into curses, then into angry, unintelligible murmur.

The woman listened with a tired and annoyed expression. She shook her head and pulled on the door. She wore a white apron and a white hat above thin dark hair gathered in a loose bun. She had a smooth round birthmark on the right side of her chin. I had never hated anybody as much as I hated her. My hands clenched into fists. I prepared to punch her in the face. Even though I had never done that before, I knew exactly what it would be like. I heard the swishing sound of my striking arm and her scream. I saw the thin skin of her cheeks breaking under my knuckles. I saw her blood. I saw her sink to the floor. Then I realized it was somebody else who punched her.

Almost immediately I felt a strong shove in the back and found myself swimming inside the store. I was squeezed between other bodies and I was going in. I was going in! In! We were storming the store. Just like the crowd that stormed the Tsar's palace in all the Revolution movies. Only now I was more than the audience—I was a part of the crowd.

There was a drunken determination on people's faces. We crashed through the entrance, and the last thing I saw on the outside was Vera, who had been pushed away.

"Vera!" I yelled halfheartedly, because in my toxic excitement I didn't really care whether she'd make it or not.

Soon I found myself pushed to the very back of the store, next to the cracked plywood door that led to the storage area. I was squeezed in among twenty or thirty people filling the tiny space between the entrance and the back door. There wasn't any puffed rice around, but I was sure they had more in the storage.

"Bring it out, you bitch! We won't leave," piercing voices screamed behind me. I wiggled to turn away from the door and see what was happening.

The saleswoman had scrambled onto her knees and stood by the entrance holding her cheek. Her face flinched with a cold hatred.

"Ivan, Vasyok!" she called to somebody in a tired voice. "Where the hell are you? Call the police!"

People kept pushing. An old man to my left shoved me between my ribs with his elbow, somebody hit me in the stomach, somebody stepped on my foot, the light hair of a woman in front of me stuck to my sweaty nose.

The excitement had faded. All I wanted was to get out. I looked for the slightest opening between people's bodies, where I could sneak through. There wasn't any.

Then a man appeared, either Vasyok or Ivan. He pushed through the plywood door and stopped right behind me. I managed to turn my head sideways to look at him. He wasn't tall but rather broad and heavy, like my grandmother's commode. He smiled.

"Why are you standing there like an idiot?" the saleswoman screamed. "Do something! Call the police!"

Vasyok or Ivan snorted.

"Why police? No need for police." He rolled up his sleeves and smiled again. His arms were red and perfectly round with pale hairs scattered among scars and tattoos.

He drew some air in and huffed into my neck. His breath was hot and garlicky-wet.

I screamed.

"No need for police," Vasyok repeated in the same calm and cheerful tone.

And then he lifted me off the ground. It was the first thing that I noticed, the sensation of being in the air, of losing control. His hands were on my chest, right where I'd felt the precious little knobs just a couple hours earlier. His index fingers crushed my nipples to the bone, while his thumbs pressed into my back ribs, an inch away from my shoulder blades. Half-crazy with fear and pain, I kicked with my knees, which was exactly what he needed. He used me as a battering ram, crashing me into the crowd to push people out of the store.

I don't remember how long it took him to clear the room. I don't remember at which point my feet met the ground, and whether I fell or not. It is strange, but I don't even remember if Vera was waiting for me at the store doors or if I had to walk home alone. I don't remember whether I walked or ran.

I do remember that after changing into my pajamas that night, I took the new sweater, folded it several times, and shoved it into the garbage pail between an empty sour cream container and long strings of potato peel. And I do remember thinking that I wasn't beautiful and never would be.

Later, when I lay in bed trying to fall asleep, I heard the rumble of a refuse chute—my mother was taking the garbage out. I pressed my face into the pillow and sobbed, suddenly regretting that I'd thrown the sweater out.

Katya peered into her mug again. The tea leaves looked like a bunch of dead flies. They didn't show the face of a man, nor did they give any hint of his name. If they knew something, they certainly kept it secret. Katya put the mug away and went to brush her teeth.

Melanie Rae Thon

Letters in the Snow—for kind strangers and unborn children— for the ones lost and most beloved

S*WEET LADY IN WHITE!*
I almost love you. I do love the way your red lipstick matched your little red purse so beautifully. I loved your white fur coat, soft and plush but not real. No creatures died for you. In this, as in all things, you are forever innocent.

We met by chance. Two days ago, I watched you choosing fruit and vegetables. Such bliss! One Fuji apple, green and rosy, one grapefruit blushing pink, one fat orange orange, one small bright banana. You held each piece of fruit as if to weigh it in your hand and heart, as if to see inside, beyond its perfect size and color.

You reminded me of my mother, once upon a time, not so long ago, when she remembered my name and knew me as her daughter, before her lips were cracked and her fingernails broken.

She said, *I remember the important things. I remember that I love you.* She couldn't pull my name from the air, but when I said, *Nicole,* she nodded.

Now I could be anybody: night nurse with her magic meds or cruel cousin Pearl Kane, long dead, long lost, and now returned to mock and tease, pearl divine, this ghost of childhood.

Mother never knows: have I come to ease her pain, or take pleasure in her torment?

Kind Stranger! You left your red purse open in the cart. You turned your back and walked away. The beauty of green beans held you in rapture. I imagined God through you did this on purpose.

You offered a small, good gift with perfect humility. Jesus flooded into your heart. Your mind didn't know what your body was doing.

Dear Lydia, I know your name now, your height and weight, your birthday, all this printed on your driver's license. Five-foot-two and eyes of blue, Lydia Kobell, seventy-six years old last January, hair still blond and full of light. Even in the harsh glare of the grocery store you looked radiant.

I know your children and your children's children. I was tempted to keep them, to stuff their little photographs and all their precious names into my pocket so that I might pretend they were my people. Five siblings, eight nieces, four nephews! Surely one strong brother would see my trouble and let me hide for a month or a year in a dark room in his damp basement.

I didn't keep them. I thought you might be afraid if they were gone too long, that you might imagine some thief with sinister intentions. I left your family in your wallet, in the glove box, all of them safe with your credit cards and license.

Lydia, before I knew your name or loved your grandchildren, I walked swiftly out of Albertson's with your wallet in one pocket of my coat and your car keys in the other. Terrified as I was, I did not scurry. Still, people stared. The throbbing bruise around my eye flared blue and green, a peacock's royal fan of feathers.

Even in the parking lot I did not run. I felt strangely calm: by you and God, silently protected. I punched the lock release on your keys till I saw taillights wink and the trunk of a silver sedan spring open.

I took it as a sign. I took it as a blessing.

Oh Lydia! How grateful I am for your love of vegetables. Your search for the beans most green and glossy gave me time to reach in your little purse, to feel, to find, to take only what I needed. You were in the checkout line and I was thirty-nine miles west before you realized what was missing.

Lydia, I confess. Once I lifted seven dollars from my mother's purse. I bought Kools and Coke. I smoked and drank in the woods by the river with Trina Flynn and Marlee Troyer. We blew smoke into one another's mouths. We coughed and laughed. We never called it kissing.

I entered my new life: ten-year-old thief, prepubescent addict. She knew, of course, my sly detective, my dark-eyed diminutive mother. Why couldn't I be sweet and good like my one and only little sister Lora? If I stole twenty dollars or Mother lost it, what did it matter? In my house, I was always to blame: bridal lace snipped in half, purple grape juice spilled on a pale carpet—china doll dropped on her head, china skull shattered to pieces.

When I was bad enough, Mother said, *You almost killed me once, and you haven't stopped trying.*

My weary father who died too soon said, *Why do you do this?*

It's true. I did borrow Mother's Carmen Miranda Red lipstick and dangling sapphire earrings. Nine years old, Nicole Odair—gloriously, fabulously beautiful. I lost one earring, of course: hanging upside down, skirt flying over my head, careless Nicole exposed on the monkey bars.

Mother charged me ninety-two dollars so that she could buy a new pair. But they were too dear, those sparkling jewels, a great-grandmother's last gift, *Here, my darling, be wonderful.* To punish us, Mother never replaced them.

Still, I paid. Ninety-two dollars. I was a child with no piggy bank full of coins, no secret savings, no allowance. *You can pay it off in work,* she said. *Thirty cents an hour.*

Nine, ten, eleven years old, she hoped I'd learned my lesson.

I did learn. I learned my soft-skinned mother who spoke Spanish with a rippling tongue could turn mean in my language, could cling to loss, could hurt as long as memory lasted.

Mother! I can't forgive you. To forgive, some place in the heart has to remain hard, has to hold a stone of blame to cast in silence. I am washed clean by grief and guttered out by the strange sound of merciful laughter.

Mother is a problem at the Sunny Arms Adult Care Center. The three drawers of her little nightstand are full of other people's treasures: a wedding band, a note of sympathy, pine-scented shaving cream, a tiny glass rocking horse, suffering Jesus on a silver cross, two photographs of a thin soldier boy, a box of chocolate cherries, a strand of pearls. If you accuse her of theft, she says, *They're mine,* or *I don't know how they got there.* She suspects Daisy Lee Valentin, the lady down the hall, the one who shuffles up and down all day, carrying her walker. That eighty-three-pound pixie would walk all night if the aides didn't strap her to the bed rails. Mother says, *She's a witch. She put those things in my drawers while I was sleeping.*

Why speak now?

The bitter child I once was might say she deserved this, to be scolded to tears by two exasperated attendants, to see her drawers emptied on the bed, to have all her wealth redistributed. *Justice divine,* I might say, *justice hilarious.* Now I know: we deserve nothing, neither the blessings nor misfortunes that befall us.

Lydia! I committed crimes worse than theft against my mother. Once, by accident, I saw her naked. Dripping wet, she stepped from the bathtub and I caught her reflection in the mirror, one breast gone and the other one withered. I was in her bedroom, in her closet, tying silky scarves around my throat and ankles. I saw the deep scar from me across her belly, tiny baby Nicole scooped out six weeks early.

My father said, *You were so small we dressed you in doll clothes and you lived in a little dollhouse and we took you for walks in a little doll carriage.* Nobody ever knew when Daddy was joking! All stories are true. I slept in a dollhouse. I woke in an incubator. My mother's blood pressure soared and the masked man sliced her open to save us.

Sweet Rose! Your body, not mine, was the first to betray you.

Lydia, bless you for your rosy-cheeked grandchildren. I carry them in my heart though I left them in your wallet. I name one Rose, after my mother. Forgive me for any grief I caused if you thought for a moment your darling ones had fallen into the hands of someone dangerous. The one named Soshana was a special comfort. She'd written a note on the back: *This is me. I'm five. I love you.* One thin blond boy in a group of seven stood apart, leaning toward the edge of the frame as if he wanted to step out of it. I could see from his knobby joints he'd already suffered. Heart murmur or brain tumor, Crohn's disease or juvenile arthritis. He was mine, and I loved him. *Isaac Jerome, far left,* it said on the back, and I thought he might be gone because his was the only name you'd written. I loved him, yes, but I left him in the glove box with Soshana and their cousins.

My mother was sixty-six, my father dead two years, and Doctor Julian said, *Probably Alzheimer's.*

Too young! Lora and I cried out together. But it can start anytime. You might be thirty-five. You might be ninety.

Four years since that day. She no longer knows my name. She does not remember I am her daughter. She no longer asks, *Where's Lora?* She no longer pleads, *Help me break out of here.*

In her fast fingers, in her bedazzled eye, in her search for shiny things that bring brief solace, she is mine, and I am hers, in love at last, beyond all shame, beyond all doubt, the good thieves, right hand, left hand, mother and daughter.

Oh my Rose of all roses, in your closet, I found a lady's red wig, a man's boot and prosthesis. I know I shouldn't be glad. I know I shouldn't find us amusing. But I am and I do when my heart isn't shattered.

Dear Cody,

You looked like a pirate from my high school play: pale scruff of beard and gold rings through pierced earlobes. *Shy Cody, my slender-hipped swashbuckling hero,* when you found me, I'd been shivering in the rain almost two hours. I'd smoked my last cigarette down to the nub and was looking for butts in the ash can. You took pity on me, this stringy-haired wet rag of a woman with a battered face: one eye swollen shut, one wild eye popped too far open.

I told you my husband and I had had a fight, that he'd torn off with the two kids while I was in the ladies' room. You believed me. It wasn't such a terrible lie. There was a kind of truth imbedded in it.

I'd ditched Lydia Kobell's car behind a burned-out bar in Big Timber, walked back to the highway and caught a ride with Wyatt Derosa, a trucker hauling ice augers and snowshoes to Missoula. He was nice enough at first. He said I looked hungry, and yes, I was, so Wyatt stopped in Livingston to buy two supersize coffees and six maple doughnuts.

When he got back in the truck, he touched my face, the edge of the bruise. *Cody!* He looked so tender I wanted to love him, to lay my head against his wide chest and hear the valves of his heart opening and closing. But Wyatt Derosa said, *It's almost beautiful.*

I flinched, then laughed. *Beautiful* is a cruel word for a person who's been pummeled. He said, *I mean, a woman so small, a bruise like that, I just want to protect you from everybody.*

Cody, I'm an idiot. I went back to Dixon Spark eleven times after he smacked me. I let him hold me naked in his lap; I listened to the rain; I let him weep; I let him lie, *Never again, baby.* But thick as I am, I've learned one thing in thirty-seven years: there's not much distance between a man who loves to touch a bruise and a man who needs to make one.

I got rid of Wyatt outside of Butte, high on the windy rim of the Continental Divide, bent spine of the earth, at the rest stop where you saved me.

I told him I had a brother down in Wisdom. I pretended to call. I said I'd be fine: Mick was on his way. If I did have a brother, one I could really call, would he be like you, or would he be like my sister and disown me?

Cody, it makes me sick to think I left you, that you might have been scared or cold. I know how that is. You were generous and too kind. We were friends before I betrayed you. You asked about my eye. You thought it was him, of course, the husband I'd invented. I didn't want to lie to you, but the lies had already started. I said, *No, not that, a swing in the park, playing with my kids and my nieces and nephews.* I imagined all the children in Lydia Kobell's photographs. I thought of my sister Lora's girls, Ingrid and Emily, not as they are now, but younger, when I was still allowed to visit.

I loved the story I spun, me in the park with sixteen kids, all of us yelping. *It didn't hurt that much, the swing, because I was happy.*

Later you told me you had a girlfriend named Joy, nineteen and pregnant, the baby not yours. You met her after. You said, *I'd marry her in a minute.* You said, *She laughs at me. My mother hates her.*

You were on your way to Eureka to help your mom clear out your grandfather's house. Last May, he fell off the roof, fractured his jaw and pelvis. He never walked again, never again chewed anything solid. It took him six months to die. With his jaw still wired shut, he scrawled a note to your mother. *Don't let them do this.* That was four months ago, when the doctor put a tube in his stomach.

Grandpa had a Christmas tree farm. He never retired. Once you got lost in the maze of miniature trees. You were four feet tall and they were four inches taller. *But I wasn't afraid. I heard voices like bees and the smell was delicious.*

I hope you weren't afraid after I left you, that the smell of pines was sharp and sweet, that you heard the voices of bees inside you. *Don't be afraid. If there's a way in, there's a way out. You'll find it.* I hope you could always see a light, a farmhouse in the distance. I dropped your bag of Oreos and thermos of hot chocolate at the side of the road. I pray they sustained you.

My thin gypsy, to say I love you is unfair, a burden you shouldn't have to carry. But it's true. I do love you. And it's true. You did save me. You gave me hope—not just for the days ahead, but for the hours and years behind me. Inside your little emerald green Ford Ranger, in the perfect Montana dark, on the cutoff between Avon and Helmville—there, sheltered from snow, sheltered from all things outside us, I was a girl again, fourteen and maybe a little buzzed, stomach empty and just enough wine to be giddy.

I saw you exactly as you are: Cody Weaver, sixteen years old, the faithful son, the benevolent boyfriend, the one not afraid. I saw another life I could have had, another world of possibility.

If it's true time is a circle and not a line, then there might be a way for us to meet on the other sides of our lives, not as thief and child, but as friends or lovers.

I'm sorry for myself, now that I've lost you. It was easy, like the grocery store in Billings, the red purse, Lydia's keys and wallet. You had to take a whiz. You were suddenly shy. You walked deep into the grove of tall pines. You left me alone in the truck with the keys and your trust. I saw my chance, and I took it.

Dear Kirk and Trudie Iyler,

I lived in your elegant cabin above Swan Lake for twenty-eight hours. You were courteous and wise to leave a spare key where I could find it. I busted no locks; I broke no windows. I swear I had a vision: a tall man tipping a clay flowerpot on the porch, a slender red-haired woman sliding a key on a yellow string under it.

I tipped the pot, and there it was, the key and all it promised.

You are clean people, you and your three grown children: Lance, Duncan, Amanda. I saw their names and numbers on the refrigerator and wanted to call them. I thought I'd say, *I'm your cousin Nicole. I'm at the cabin. Come get me.*

I found the breaker box in the bedroom closet and parted your clothes to flip the switches for your pump and hot water. It took two hours for the water to heat. I heard the hum and groan, the song of pipes expanding. *Trudie!* It was worth the wait, every minute. If it's true God is everywhere in everything, he was the warm water in your bathtub. God the womb. God the mother.

I meant to be considerate, to hang your towels and wash your dishes. I meant to turn your heaters off, and now, I know, your warmth is wasted. Forgive me. The tracks through your house are my confession: *The bad sister of Goldilocks was here. I rumpled your bed. I devoured your porridge.* I ate a whole can of pork and beans. I slurped three bowls of instant oatmeal. If I survive another night, know that your food has become my flesh. Know that you have saved me.

Your towels were rolled, not folded—swirls of green and gold—crimson, copper, burnt sienna—wind through tamarack and pine, the autumn forest. *Trudie,* I imagined you and Lance, your quiet son, peacefully rolling these towels together.

Every corner of your house breathed *hallelujah*, a song of joy in praise of beauty: the towels, a bowl of tiny translucent soaps, a jar of shells, the flagstone mosaic of the fireplace. You and Kirk and your beloved children must have gathered each sea star and slab of rock with gratitude and awe for its singular size and shape and color.

I entered your cabin, your family, your bed. I was one with you, embraced, *holy child*, the long-lost piece of your fabulous puzzle.

Kirk, thank you for the fireplace so carefully laid with logs and kindling. I crumpled paper under the grate, and with your patience in my heart, I torched it. The leather of your couch and the fur of your plush pillows smelled of the animals they once were, and I thought they had sacrificed their lives for me so that I might live one night in heaven.

Oh, merciful strangers! You gave me refuge in the darkest hour, on a night when I wanted to go, but could not go, to my mother, my father, my sister, my children. Your cabin is almost as glorious as my sister's house at the edge of the Rimrocks overlooking the river. My sister's house, from which I have been exiled forever.

Lora, I swear: anything I have could be yours in an instant. When I hammered out the glass of your basement window with a rock and dropped into your house that night three years ago, I didn't think of it as breaking and entering. I thought of it as seeking sanctuary. I was safe at last, *home*, in hiding.

When I drank Stephen's cognac, I didn't think of it as theft, I thought of it as necessary comfort. When I slipped into your bed, I thought, *Soon, so soon, my sister will come home and hold me.* I whispered, *When I wake, I won't be alone and I won't be afraid of anyone.*

I didn't know how badly I'd cut my hand on the glass. I didn't intend to streak your sheets and nightgown. I didn't plan to drink as much as I did. I didn't deliberately drop the goblet. But oh, what a sound as it splintered on tile: bell of joy, bright laughter!

I'm sorry I scared Ingrid and Emily, the children I love beyond all reason. I promise: I didn't come to cause an argument between you and Stephen. And though I see all the trouble I caused, it still seems unnecessary for you to have your own sister arrested, to let her nieces see her hauled away: Aunt Nicole, stumbling drunk, wrists clamped behind her back in handcuffs.

Anybody could have looked at my face—split lip, broken nose—and seen I'd had a bad night already. I could have offered more evidence: bruised wrists and ribs, three fingers fractured. Those fingers healed bent and now cannot be straightened.

I'll say this for what you did: two nights in jail kept me safe from Dixon, and when I got out, he was the one to come, to rock, to kiss, to hold, to love me, and he brought me home, and we took a shower, and the rain came, and I was cold, and we lay together, and I heard the rain on the roof and the leaves and the grass and the windows, the endless rain making everything whole, bringing everything together, and we didn't make love, we just lay there till his skin was cool and mine was warm and it rained all night and it never stopped raining, and the rain was his voice and I knew he was sorry and one of us began to cry or we both did or it was just the rain, and I learned if you go back once, you'll go back forever.

Lora, your good husband Stephen, your brilliant entrepreneurial wonder who was clever enough to invest in land twenty years ago before the movie stars made Montana famous—Stephen, who has earned himself and you a fortune five times over, this man who could so easily afford to be generous, forbids me now and for all time to see your children. And you, my sister, my only one, you have agreed to the terms of Stephen's love, a husband's bitter reconciliation.

Most precious sister, at eight I became a monarch butterfly; at five you emerged as a tiger swallowtail. That Halloween, we disguised our slender bodies in black tights and leotards. We grew lovely wings of colored silk and wire. Lora and Nicole, magically remade by our magical mother. We were luminous. Light glowed through our wings. Our sweet Rose had transformed us.

At nine, I borrowed the sapphire earrings; at ten, I smoked Kools and kissed my girlfriends by the river. Six years later I lost, I gave up, I abandoned my first child. I saw my squalling son whisked away; I never held him! *Too hard,* the Lutheran lady said. *Believe me, this is better.* Now he's twenty-one. I meet him everywhere. He waves to me as I drive through a construction zone. He walks past me in the park holding his wife's hand, carrying their first baby like a kangaroo, in a soft pouch against his chest and belly. Sometimes I find him alone in the merciful light of a roadside bar, and he thinks I'm younger than I am, and he flirts with me and I flirt back—our faces reflect, a natural attraction. Johnny Mathis sings just for us from the jukebox, his voice smoldering so close I think he's really there, in the dark, swaying in the corner of the room where nobody else can see him, and this child of mine, this man, asks me to dance and I do, cheek to cheek, *oh my love,* rib to rib, *my darling,* and I feel him, *I've hungered for your touch,* I swear, *a long, lonely time,* cradled inside me.

At twenty, I let a doctor scoop me out. *Better* this *way,* I thought. I let a nurse flush me. Gone, this fast, my second child. *You were so small and you slept in a little dollhouse forever and ever.* My children! One walks the earth and one I carry still: she's a fist in the heart, a pulse in the pelvis. She could be anywhere, any age, her spirit returned in any body. *Be kind,* she says, *you owe me.* And I am kind. When I see a child sobbing in a grocery cart, when his mother walks away and leaves him stranded, I mouth the words, *You're mine; I love you,* and the child sees it's true, and by some miracle stops howling. And God says, *I don't forgive because I never blamed you.* But oh, how he grieves for me and my children.

Lora, repentance is not a single act; repentance is an endless turning, and this is why it broke my heart to hurt Cody—Cody, my child—Cody, the boyfriend who would have married me when we were both children. Lora, you have wounded me a thousand times by forbidding me to see your daughters. You can't imagine how Ingrid and Emily heal me with love, theirs for me and mine for them, and oh my darling, the pain of love is sweet and the pain of love is tender.

I would have been a lousy mother at sixteen and even worse at twenty. Every choice was wrong, the ones I made, the ones I didn't.

You think your girls are safe in your house on the hill. Thirteen-year-old Ingrid plays the flute. Eleven-year-old Emily plays the cello. She runs the 400-meter dash faster than any girl or boy in her school. Ingrid does back handsprings in the yard. Ingrid does double somersaults from the high board at the pool. They don't have time to be bad; they don't have time to get in trouble.

But I know this secret. One day last summer I spied on little Emily in the park. She wore a tight white T-shirt and short pink shorts. She was rolling down a hill with a boy, and they kept rolling into each other and bouncing apart, and I heard them laugh, and then I saw them stop, and Emily lay in the grass, and the boy rolled on top of her, and they lay very still and were endlessly silent.

Oh, children! Perilous are your years.

One day a group of boys circled me in the hallway so each could take his turn sliding up close, unseen, to touch me. Fast hands flicked over all the sweet little-girl curves of me. Their twelve hands didn't hurt, but they spoke only Spanish, these white boys, and their quick tongues made it all happen in another country. Five boys scattered when the bell rang, but one lingered long enough to speak my language: *We learned every word from your mother.*

Later that one found me alone. Later: his car, the stars pouring in, the night, the river.

Lora, I'm not saying Emily will end up like me, fifteen and pregnant, sixteen and childless. I'm just saying you never know and nothing in the real world will save us. One false step leads to another. The wrong path may open onto a field of forget-me-nots and poppies.

We do forget in the end. Our mother forgets her mastectomy. It is a grief relived every morning. She forgets the word: *breast.* She forgets: *el cáncer del seno.* She lays her hand on the sunken place, *mi corazón.* She says, What happened here? She opens her robe to show me.

Oh, our beautiful shape-shifting mother! Sometimes I glimpsed her in the classroom of our high school. I'd hear a silvery sound, her voice a moonlight dance on water. She was a new Rose, a Rose reborn, not the mother I'd seen naked. Our Rose in Spanish rhyme, tempting all the boys with language. Long ago, this Rosa was the first and only child of Presbyterian missionaries—clever Rosa, three years old and already singing

Spanish in a Guatemalan village. She learned what her thin parents never learned: she learned to love her body.

Lora, is this punishment or mercy?

My Sister, because I could not come to you, or Rose, or Daddy, I fled, and these strangers—Lydia, Cody, Kirk, Trudie—have saved my life, and so I must believe I have a life worth saving.

Most gracious ones, it was my second night in your cabin. I'd slept eighteen hours the day before, and now, again, was sleeping. The jangling telephone jolted me into panic, three thirteen, exactly. I thought it must be Dixon. I thought somehow he'd found me. I imagined him a mile up the road, the Window Wizard in his white truck, calling from his cell phone: *Nicole, I'm here. I'm coming.*

Crazy, I know, to leave the safety and solace of this place, to bolt out into the winter night, into the snow, the moonlit woods, to clamor and climb up the ridges above Swan Lake when everything in your cabin said, *You're warm, you're safe, wrong number, don't worry.*

It seemed like another vision. This time, I saw the truck, the snow, his name painted on the side, *Dixon Spark—Window Wizard,* Dixon in red letters blazing.

Sweet strangers! I could almost hear your voices. *We are keeping you very safe. We love you.* If only I'd held on to faith! If only I'd believed you.

Father,

Forgive me for my extravagant kisses the day you died. I'd told you to let go when you got too weary. I promised: *Lora and I will take care of Mother.* Liar! I said, *We'll be okay. We'll miss you.*

I thought you would go in the night and make it easy.

But I found you awake another day, alive to see another morning. With your eyes wide but not focused, you saw only light, all your people as shadows. *Daddy.* I covered your face with tears and kisses. *Thank you,* I said. *Thank you, thank you.*

You knew me as a thief then, a betrayer worse than Judas. We were *not* ready! We would never be okay. Lora and I could not take care of your Rose, your love, our mother.

All this you understood, beyond words, beyond your clouded vision. You knew long before we knew, long before we could bear to face it. You were the one to find her lost words, to finish her sentences, to whisper names in her ear, to hold her hand at a party, to match her socks, to wipe the smudge of lipstick from her face when the lips she drew were crooked. *Here, darling, let me help you.* She needed you, only you, partner of thirty-three years, keeper of faith, keeper of memory.

And so you lived another day. And so you struggled to the final hour.

In your suffering, you lived in truth, the pure pain of perfect compassion.

Why, when you loved us like this, did I choose a man like Dixon?

Father, you survived three heart attacks and two strokes, open-heart surgery, one clogged carotid artery. You lived with a cleaved chest and five bypasses. In the end, everything failed you.

I remember your hands, clean and soft. I remember: you wanted me beautiful. If you could see me now, all your loving work destroyed, my thin face realigned by the quick fist of Dixon Spark, you'd weep.

Daddy, I almost hear you.

You and Valerie murmured, *yes,* like Cody's bees, as you mended my teeth, filling the ones gone bad, capping the two I'd chipped, riding fast down the dirt path, flying head over handlebars from my blue bicycle. Ten years old. *Daddy,* I was fearless.

Dear Valerie. My oldest and your youngest cousin, your assistant for twenty-three years. She made you laugh. She'd loved you forever.

Valerie whispered as you worked. It could have been anything: the rain in the night, the new moon after—Troy's accident last winter, his foul moods, the shattered bones that never healed—Miranda in the school play, *Wizard of Oz,* Miranda the star, Miranda the lion.

You said: *pick, drill, gauze, water.*

She said, *I made cheesecake brownies yesterday. I brought you half. They're scrumptious.*

When I let go of words, I heard only love, you and Valerie praying over me.

Father, why have I forsaken you, accepting violence when you showed me the face of love and endless mercy?

Sometimes when you see a man and his family, you know his whole life, not as stories he tells, but as memories, as dreams, as dirt and barking dogs, as light in a window far away, your own burned wrists, your own blood trembling.

Dixon's brothers laugh like twins, erupting for no reason anybody else can fathom. Bald and bearded, Malcolm and Lee, the Spark boys—they even look like twins, though there are eight years, Dixon and Flora and Irene between them.

Dixon's the skinny one, the child lost, the boy in the middle. Dixon, thirty-six years old, and his brothers still tease him about the swish in his hips, the stutter that comes back when he's scared or excited. They love to excite him. They call: *Pretty Girl, Pretty Girl,* their voices high, two twittery parrots. They pat his butt and yip with joy as soon as Dixon's words start tumbling.

They're not mean to be mean. *Boys will be boys,* they say. *We can't help it.* Malcolm's thirty-two, and Lee is pushing forty.

Harmless, their sisters say. *Mush melons.* Irene says, *It's the quiet ones who cause you trouble. Dixon was the one up the tree with his slingshot and pellets, killing little birds, wounding cats and squirrels.* Flora says, *Dixon was the one under my bed with a box of mice or snakes or lizards.*

They're big girls, Irene and Flora. They laugh big laughs. They say, *If he tries anything now, we'll sit on his lap and squish him.*

Daddy, I'm not saying this is why. I'm not offering up excuses.

The laughing Spark brothers go hunting and come back with tall tales of a fourteen-point whitetail buck and a grizzly that almost ate them. They see a field of grass shimmering before a hundred elk rise and run. *Out of range,* Lee says. *Too bad. I'd like an elk head for the office.*

They promise to take Dixon next time, but they forget, or he refuses. Not joking, Dixon says, *If they get me in the woods alone, they'll shoot me.*

Later, drunk on Dixon's Jack Daniel's, the three of them sit on the couch, arms looped over shoulders, with Dixon, the favorite tonight, cradled in the middle. Malcolm starts humming "Edelweiss," and Lee joins him. Dixon's the only one who knows the words, and so he leads, and the three of them get so sad and sweet they're practically weeping.

There are mysteries in every man's life, love and grief beyond all telling.

In a dream, I'm buried in the woods, damp earth packed tight around me. The Spark boys have left only my nose exposed. My eyes and mouth fill with dirt as I struggle. I kick and claw, twist my way free at last, and run toward home as night falls. I hear the brothers, each hard breath, each footfall. They could catch me anytime, but the chase is deeper pleasure. They carry BB guns and little knives, ropes to burn my wrists, a dirty rag to use as a blindfold. They toss firecrackers in the trees. Every burst becomes a spark, a laughing boy inside me.

I hear Odile's dogs and nobody's coyotes. When I see the lights of home at last, it's not ours: it's Dixon's double-wide trailer. His father never built a house. Jackson Spark was too busy building kennels. Through little lit windows I see Mother, Father, Irene, Flora. I won't cry. I won't confess. The ones inside will tease or scold if they see me scared and filthy.

I love Dixon like this. I dream his dreams for him.

Dixon's parents breed Rottweilers and travel four states to sell them. A Rottweiler will herd cattle or sheep, goats or children. People with kids need to be careful. Anything that runs is his. His stamina is endless. But when the dog dreams, a cat hissing in the yard is a mountain lion come down to eat him. He whimpers in his sleep, panting hard, legs twitching.

Odile Spark is a tiny woman: four feet, eleven inches—eighty-nine pounds and shrinking. A male Rottweiler weighs thirty pounds more than she does. The whole pack might be snapping and snarling, but when Mama steps into the yard, they shiver with delight and lick her.

My tough guys, Odile says, *my babies.* She sits on Malcolm's lap. He's huge, and she's scrubbed clean, a shiny doll or strange child. *He came from me,* she says. *Can you believe it?* He's her sweetheart, her youngest, *My big boy,* her biggest.

Odile doesn't understand fear. She doesn't believe in unnecessary comfort. She doesn't cook or sew. Jackson Spark, six-foot-three, a thin giant of a man who has to stoop to enter the trailer, mends his own shirts and washes their laundry. He fries the eggs and bakes the chicken. He makes the bed. He washes the dishes. Like all Odile's boys, he's absolutely devoted.

Five kids and seventeen Rottweilers. If one of them cried in the night, nobody whispered, *What's wrong?* Nobody ran to give solace.

I love Dixon like this, as if he is my lost-in-the-middle child, as if I alone can give back what he didn't know was stolen.

Daddy, how could I ever leave him?

But two nights ago, back in Billings, he shot me, and I knew at last, I believed: *Yes,* I said to myself, *this man will kill me.*

Only a toy, Trevor's revolver, metallic gray with a narrow black handle, a perfect grip for a woman or child—small, yes, but its weight felt true, and its silhouette looked convincing. I didn't steal it exactly.

The kid had wounded me all day, puny Trevor, that seven-year-old jack-in-the-box, weird wide grin and skinny neck, a vision of Dixon as a child. Trevor popped up from behind my chair. Trevor lay coiled under the bed. Trevor crouched behind the shower curtain. He squealed every time: *You're dead. Fall down. I shot you.* Dixon found the whole thing hopelessly amusing.

So I failed to mention the gun under the sofa when Vanessa picked him up, when lovely lush Vanessa said, *I hope he wasn't any trouble.* She thinks she's better than I am. She has Dixon's kid, but no Dixon. Once she said: *We should talk. Call me.*

I carried the heavy toy for three days. I liked the shape of it, the tug, the weight, the slender grip, the serious intention.

I didn't plan to show it to anybody. Next time Trevor came, I'd leave it somewhere obvious. But two nights ago I got home late from work, four hours late, 9:30. Vince had a hard case, Sean McVey, fifteen years old and up as an adult for murder. I write Vince Kassela's letters, interview witnesses, search the books for precedents. Vince says, *You should have been a lawyer.* Nights like this, we take turns arguing mitigating circumstances.

Sean McVey shot the man who found him sleeping in the back seat of his red Riviera. He was sorry now, just a terrified runaway boy seeking refuge, just a scared shooter with his father's gun, 9mm, stolen from the drawer of Christopher McVey's nightstand.

But the man he killed, Terry Simone, taught sign language to the parents of deaf children, so that they could talk to their kids, so that they could learn to laugh and clap, hands held high above their heads, all ten fingers fluttering. He had three deaf daughters of his own, a pregnant wife, another girl in March coming.

Sorry as he was, the boy was not sympathetic: he'd fired three times; this was a problem. Sean McVey is one of those kids who never looks clean, big for his age and pissed off at the world. His father spoke with his hands, too: with a paddle across the butt when Sean was small, with a swift box to the ears when Sean got too strong to bend over a knee and wallop.

That night, before he lay down in the car, I think Sean watched Terry Simone through his living room window. I think he saw the man's delicate hands and wanted to die, or wanted to kill him. Sean made the mistake of revealing Terry's last words: *What is it, son? Can I help you?* I think he hated the man. I think he found kindness unbearable.

But Sean McVey's grief was no consolation to Lily Simone, who had to explain it all with her own hands to little Kira and Iris and Natasha. Her fingers became birds. They flew out the window and disappeared. She clutched them in tight fists and held them hard against her chest. No matter how wide she spread her fingers, when she opened her hands again, they were always empty.

Who, besides God, could convince a jury this boy's life—any boy's life—was worth saving? Vince said, *He'll come out of prison in twenty years, and he won't be reformed, he'll be crippled.* Vince said, *I need your brain tonight. We must have missed something.*

So I called Dixon, and I left a message, three messages, and I know he heard, but he didn't believe me. He was always jealous of Vince. He thought he came up short by comparison: *Harvard lawyer, Window Wizard.* He had some wild idea that Vince Kassela might want to jump me. A fantasy, and I thought it was sweet, so I let him keep it.

Vince and his wife and three kids camp together, sleep in one tent, catch forty rainbow trout, then float the river. They're a team: they bike a hundred miles and earn three hundred dollars for kids with spina bifida. Gwen is a hospice nurse. Luke plays the organ for the Methodist choir. Last winter, Janaya and Dorrie built a snow family: five fat happy people who stood in the yard for a month melting. To risk a family like that for a woman like me, a man would have to be delirious.

Three years ago, Vince talked Stephen and Lora into dropping their charges, breaking and entering. Vince said, *I'll help you with Dixon, too, whenever you're ready.*

I said, *We're fine.* I touched my face. *Oh this,* I said, *I fell down the basement stairs with a basket of laundry.*

Vince said, *Any time, Nicole. Just tell me.*

Vince, I'm ready now. Help me.

I didn't go to him two days ago. I was too ashamed. Becoming a thief felt familiar. Safer, I thought, for everybody—me and Vince, Gwen and the children—safer, yes, mostly for Dixon.

Dixon Spark, Window Wizard. He repairs cracks and chips in glass doors and windshields. He'll come to your house to lift scars from your windows. He can heal a twenty-inch fracture. It's a wonder, a miracle. In the beginning, I called him Doctor Spark, and he laid his hands on me, and said, *Here, be well again, be healed.* And we laughed and made love, and this was the first time.

The Window Wizard was home when I got home, but I didn't know it. I called his name when I opened the door. He didn't answer. I must have walked right past him. My jack-in-the-box sat in the dark, coiled up tight as Trevor.

When I felt him, I was in the bathroom, panty hose around my knees, squatting on the toilet—a bit of an emergency, so I still wore my coat, and Trevor's gun was there, still in my pocket. I'd left the door half open, no time to spare, bladder bursting.

Then I knew. I smelled him, that dangerous Dixon energy. He sprang into the bathroom, and I reached for the revolver. A reflex, a joke, a stupid mistake. I saw from his face, I wouldn't get out of it.

He grabbed the gun before I could laugh, before I could say, *Trevor's.* He wrenched it from my hand, and with me shackled by my panty hose, trapped on the toilet, he pulled the trigger. *Daddy!* He shot me.

It was hilarious, really, the ridiculous pop of the toy gun, me squatting there, Dixon furious. But neither he nor I were laughing. He used the gun to hit me hard, my eye; I thought I heard the socket cracking. I can't repeat the words he said, not to you, my father.

He pulled me to the floor, kicked my ribs, my head, my belly. I curled up small and hoped he'd stop before he killed me. I don't know when or why he did. Maybe he got scared too. Maybe he thought he was finished.

Daddy! You came! You and Valerie, murmuring, praying as you fixed my teeth, *only chipped,* you said, *not too bad. Like that other time. You'll be good as new by morning.*

Valerie laid her small hands on my eye and pelvis. She mended the bones; she left the bruises. You told her to bring an ice pack for my face. When I woke, I thought I'd have this as proof: a wet rag, the ice melted. But you or Valerie took it back before you fled. She left a dry towel by the sink. She put the ice in the freezer. I had to take your visit on faith. I had to accept the ice in the freezer as evidence of love and comfort.

I feel you now as I stumble in deep snow. You give me strength. You whisper, *I'm here, baby, right beside you.*

Father, I confess, I tried to take care of your Rose, but I couldn't. Before she lost so many words, she kept her Spanish. Three times I found her with Ana Arredondo, the plump little nurse's aide, a refugee from El Salvador. They giggled like lovers. They spoke as birds sing, their whole hearts spilling out of them.

I tried not to hate the woman, not to wish her back the way she'd come fifteen years before, walking with goats across the Sonoran Desert.

I thought Mother remembered everything from her life in another country: little Rosa playing in the dirt, little Rosa swimming in the river. Rosa speaking Spanish rhyme faster than the village children. *Daddy,* I saw her come alive in a language we never spoke, in a tongue that doesn't include us.

But you saved pretty Rosa's teeth. Twenty-nine years old and she'd never seen a dentist. You were her first, and then you were her husband. Four root canals and two extractions, three white caps and six gold fillings. You'd seen worse, you said. But later confessed: *Not many.*

Rose said you saved her life. Rosa said you saved her Spanish.

Last October, Mother stole Dwight Wilken's yellow sweater. She wouldn't give it up to me or Dwight or Caitlin, the attendant. I felt stupidly joyful. The sweater looked like one of yours, a gift from me, soft cotton. I thought she might remember us, our lives together, some tiny fragment.

Limp with rage and tears, Rose finally surrendered. I helped her then. I found her red sweatshirt, her blue fleece slippers. I expected her to be sad, but when the sweater was gone, it was gone—like you and me, perfectly forgotten.

I took her to the sun porch, and we sat there, warm behind windows. It was cold outside, bright blue, and the last yellow leaves quivered.

To my rescuers in the snow,

I feel you climbing toward me. I give you names—Sam LaRue, Loy Kemmerick, Neville Gaye—men who have been kind to me. Terry Simone appears in camouflage: winter white with tangled branches. He carries his own broken bones. He wears an elk's antlers. His breath hangs in the air. When he opens his mouth, white birds fly out of it.

Last night the phone rattled me from bliss and I ran and I climbed till I fell down, exhausted. As I lay me down to sleep, my father came and said, *Have I told you lately that I love you?*

I finally heard him with my heart. I finally, truly, could believe him. I woke in a bed of snow, the sky clear, the earth glittering. I saw every color spark in white: violet, green, rose, amber. The whole world trembled. I could see each particle of air. I could hear it vibrate. I thought I was dead. I thought, *This is the Kingdom.* I was free of pain and cold and loss and hunger.

I laughed out loud. Nothing hurt me.

Then an angel appeared, a small mule deer. She stepped into the clearing and stood close, barely the length of a body between us. Face in shadow, she seemed dark and her wide eyes even darker, but the fine hairs of her outline caught the sun and burned, a radiant halo.

I wanted to hold her in my arms. I wanted her to step out of her body, so that we might meet in the space between, as light on snow, as blue day breaking. It almost happened. I shivered with the pure joy of it. Then my body began to shake, violent spasms, and this was the end, my jolting return to life in the world. I coughed and my ribs pierced my lungs, and the deer leaped and was gone, and I spat blood in the snow, and the cold was so cold it scorched me.

Later, I crawled, blinded by sun on snow.

I prayed for clouds, and God answered with the wind. Needles of ice cut my face, sharp and invisible.

Now the dark light comes, now the night is falling.

Sweet Saviors, build your fire high and hold on to hope till daybreak. Your faith has made you climb. Your love has pulled you up this mountain.

I have made a bed of boughs. In soft fir, I am cradled.

I might live another night, and wake again tomorrow.

I lie down in my father's arms.

Hush now, precious one.

I hear my father's voice.

Be not afraid, my darling.

Deborah Eisenberg

Window

NOAH IS SETTLED down on his little blanket, and Alma has given him some spoons to play with. High up, a few feet away, Alma and Kristina drink coffee at the shabby kitchen table. Noah, thank heavens, has been subdued since Alma opened the door to them, no trouble at all.

In this new place he seems peculiarly vivid—not entirely familiar—as if the way Alma sees him were trickling into Kristina's vision. Kristina contemplates his look of gentle inquiry, his delicate eyebrows, gold against his darker skin, his springy little ringlets. He looks distantly monumental in his beauty, like an idol at the center of a pond, sending out quiet ripples.

"You better do something about that cold of his," Alma says. "He looks like he's got a little fever." She exhales smoke carefully away from him. "Or is that asthma?"

Kristina's gaze transfers to Alma's face.

"Does he have asthma?" Alma says.

"He'll be better now we're out of the car," Kristina says.

Yesterday afternoon and last night, and most of today, too, nothing but driving in rain, pulling over for patchy sleep, Noah waking over and over, crying, as he does these days coming out of naps, bad dreams sticking to him. Or maybe he's torn from good ones.

Or maybe dreams are new to him in general and it's frightening—one life sinking into the shadows, the forgotten one rising up. How would she know? He's talking pretty well now—he's got new words every day—but he doesn't quite have the idea yet of conversation and its uses.

Driving up, Kristina saw water just out back of the house, and tangled brush still bare of leaves, but Alma has taped plastic over her kitchen window to keep out the cold, and the plastic is blurry, and denting in the wind. The water can't be seen. All that's visible are vague, dark blotches, spreading, twisting, and disappearing. Anyone could be walking along the shore now in the gathering dark, looking in, and you wouldn't know.

Alma's saying that her friend Gerry is going to come by and then they're going out to grab a bite. "I won't be back too late, I guess." She glances at Kristina as impersonally as if she were checking something on a chart. "I'll pick up something at work tomorrow for the baby's cough." A psychiatric facility is what she called the place she works, but it sounds like a hospital.

A clattering over by the fridge makes Kristina's heart bounce, and there's a large man—stopping short in the doorway.

"Gerry, my sister Kristina," Alma says. "Kristina, Gerry."

"Your sister?" is what the man finds to say.

Alma reddens fast to an unpleasant color and looks down at her coffee cup. "Close enough. Same dear old dad, or so they told us."

"Hey," Gerry says, and gives Alma a little pat. But it's too late. Kristina was always the pretty one.

Gerry has a full, frowzy beard and a sheepish, tentative manner, as if it's his lot to knock over liquids or splinter chairs when he sits. Kristina picks up Noah to get him out from underfoot. "Can you say hi?" she asks him.

He observes Gerry soberly while Gerry waves, then burrows his head against her shoulder.

"Cute," Gerry says to Kristina. "Yours?"

Alma sighs. "No, ours." And then it's Gerry's turn to become red.

"Is there a store near here where I can get some milk and things for him?" Kristina asks. "We kind of ran out on the way."

Alma grinds her cigarette out on her saucer, staring at it levelly. "I would have stocked up if I'd known you were coming," she says.

"I tried to call from the road," Kristina says.

"McClure's will still be open," Gerry says.

Alma looks at him without altering her expression, and turns back to Kristina. "Gas-station type place a few miles down. Not the answer to your dreams, maybe, but you'll find the essentials."

"Which way do I go?" Kristina asks.

Alma looks at her for a long moment. "If the car goes glub glub? Try turning around."

By the time Kristina returns from McClure's, Alma and Gerry are gone. Entering the house for a second time, this time with a key, juggling Noah and a bag of supplies, Kristina could practically be coming home. The mailbox says she is; that's her name there—a durable memento from the man who slid out of Alma's life soon after Alma was born and about a decade later, when Kristina was born, slid out of hers.

When Kristina first had seen the house this afternoon, she had felt the sort of shame that accompanies making an error. She hadn't realized she'd been expecting anything specific, but clearly there'd been a place in her mind that was larger or brighter—more cheerful. Still, it's what a person needs, four walls and a roof, shelter.

She supplements the graham crackers from McClure's with a festive-looking package of microwave lasagna that was sitting in the freezer. "Isn't this fun?" she says to Noah. "All we have to do is push the button."

Noah stares intently. Behind the window in the glossy white box, plastic wrap and Styrofoam revolve turbulently as intense, artificial smells pour out into the room. Shadows move in Noah's dark eyes, and he turns away.

"What?" she says.

He leans against her leg and says something. She has to bend down to hear.

"Not today. Thumb, Noah," she says as he puts his into his mouth. "No doggies today."

Alma might have thought of canceling her date with Gerry, Kristina thinks. It's been years since the two of them have seen one another, and it would be awfully nice to have some company. But there's Noah to concentrate on, anyhow. She urges him to eat, but he doesn't seem to be hungry. For that matter, neither is she. She spreads a sheet out on the futon that she and Alma dragged from the couch frame earlier onto the floor, and there—she and Noah have their bed.

Outside, the wind is still hurtling clumsily by, thrashing through the branches and low, twiggy growth, groaning and pleading in the language of another world. But she and Noah are hidden under the blankets. She'll turn out the light, the night will be a deep blue swatch, Noah's cold will die down, and in the morning the wind will be gone and sunlight will stream through the window. She reaches up to the switch.

The whoosh of darkness brings Eli—surging around her from the four corners of the earth, bursting Alma's tinny little house apart.

She gasps for breath and flings aside the churning covers; she stumbles into the kitchen where she stands naked at the window. A dull splotch of moonlight on the plastic expands and contracts in the wind.

"Kissy?" a tiny, hoarse voice says behind her.

The small form hovers in the shifting darkness. It holds out its arms to be picked up. The blank dark pools of its eye sockets face her.

"Go back to bed," she says as calmly as she can. Fatigue is making her heart race and churning up worries. Little discomforts and pains are piping up here and there in her body. "Now, please." She turns resolutely away and sits down at the kitchen table. After a few seconds she hears him pad away.

Fortunately, there's an open pack of Alma's cigarettes out on the table. Her hands shake slightly but manage to activate a match. Flame from sulfur, matter into clouds . . .

Everything that happens is out there waiting for you to come to it. One little turn, then another, then another—and by the time you think to wonder where you are and how you got there, it's dark.

She can't see back. It's like looking into a well. She sees her long hair ripple forward. There's nothing in front of her. But then rising up behind her, the moving shadows of trees, of the muddy road, of cars, of faces—Nonie, Roger, Liz, the girls from the distant farms, Eli . . . At the dark center of the water her own face is indistinct.

And then there she is, standing indecisively at the bus station, over a year and a half ago, in the grimy little city where she grew up. She was a whole year out of high school, and there had been nothing but dead-end clubs and drugs, and dead-end jobs. Years before, Alma had told her, go to college, go to college, but when the time came she couldn't see it—the loans and the drudgery and then what, anyhow. There was talk of modeling—someone she met—but she was too lanky and maybe a little strange for catalog work, it turned out, and too something else for serious fashion. Narrow shoulders, and the wrong attitude, they said; no attitude, apparently. So for a while, instead of putting clothes on for the photos it had been taking them off, and after that it was working in a store that sold shoes and purses.

When she was little there had been moments like promises, disclosures—glimpses of radiant things to come that were so clear and sharp they seemed like erupting memories. A sudden scent, a sudden slant of light, and a blur of pictures would stream past. It was as if she'd been born out of a bright, fragrant life into the soiled, boarded-up room of her present one. She chose the town from the list of destinations at the bus station for its name.

Soft hills flowed in distant rings around the little country town, and a chick-colored sun shone over it. Out in front of the pretty white houses were the bright, round-petaled flowers. Sheep drifted in the meadows like clouds.

Every day she awoke to the white houses and the gentle hills, and it was like looking down at a tender, miniature world. The sky was as clear as glass; the planet spun in it brightly, like a marble.

Tourists came on the weekends for the brilliance of the sky, the charged air, and the old-fashioned inns. With so many people coming to play, it had been easy to get work.

The White Rabbit . . . with that poor animal, its petrified red glass eyes staring down at her and Nonie from over the bar. It wasn't enough they shot it and stuffed it, Nonie had said; they had to plunk it down right here to listen to Frank's sickening jokes.

A pouty Angora mewed up at them from its cushion near Kristina's ankle. Good thing they didn't call this place the White Cat, huh, you, she'd said, and just then Frank craned into the dining room. Girls—ladies. A lull is not a holiday. A lull is when we wipe down tables, make salads, roll silver . . .

Or the White Guy, Nonie said.

Nonie—all that crazy, crimpy hair—energy crackling right out from it!

Her new friend. Nonie had a laugh like little colored blocks of wood toppling.

It wasn't long before she moved into a room in the pretty white house Nonie and Munsen were renting. Nonie was still waiting tables on weekends then, saving up; Nonie was planning to buy a bakery. She and Munsen were hoping to have a baby.

How nice it had been when Munsen came home on his lunch breaks to hang out in the kitchen, and they were all three together. Munsen, looking for all world like a stoopy plant, draped in the aroma of butter, smiling, blinking behind his gold-rimmed specs, drinking his coffee, sometimes a beer.

And Nonie—that was a sight to see! Little Nonie, slapping the dough around, waking the dormant yeast as if she were officiating at the beginning of the world.

How had Nonie figured out to do that, Kristina had wanted to know.

No figuring involved, Nonie told her; when she was a kid she was always just sort of rolling around in the flour.

She'd given Kristina a little hug. Never mind, she said. You'll find something to roll around in.

Anyhow, Munsen said, it's overrated.

Sure, Nonie said, but it what?

Munsen had sighed. It all, he said.

One star and then another detached from its place and flamed across the dark. The skies were dense with constellations. Whole galaxies streamed toward the porch where she sat with Nonie and Munsen on her nights off, watching the coded messages from her future, light-years away.

She helped, but maybe she slowed things down a bit. Well, she did, though Nonie never would have said. So while Nonie carried on, she would take Nonie's beat-up old car and deliver orders of bread and pastries to various inns and restaurants. And Nonie and Munsen let her have her room for free.

Save those pennies! Nonie said.

For what? she had thought; uh-oh.

. . .

Every day there were new effects, modulations of colors and light, as if something were being perfected at the core. Going from day to day was like unwrapping the real day from other days made out of splendid, fragile, colored tissue.

The tourists started swarming in for the drama of the changing leaves. Every weekend the town bulged with tourists. Someone named Roger took her to dinner on one of her nights off, to the Mill Wheel, where she subbed sometimes.

Roger had waxy, poreless skin, as if he'd spent years packed in a box, and his blue eyes shone with joyous, childlike gluttony, lighting now on booty, now on tribute.

It had come to him, he told her, that it was time to make some changes. He was living in the city—toiling, as he put it, in the engine rooms of finance, but one day not long ago his company had vanished, along with so many others, in a little puff of dirty smoke. What was he to do? His portfolio had been laid waste. So, the point was, he could scrounge for something else, but it had occurred to him, why not just pull up stakes and live in some reasonably gratifying way? There wasn't any money to speak of out there these days, anyhow.

Money to speak of. A different kind of money from the kind her mother had counted out for groceries.

So why not look at this period of being broke as an opportunity, he was saying, that might not come again? Because this was, he'd informed her, one's life.

The waiter poured a little wine into Roger's glass. How is that, sir? the waiter said.

Fine, Roger said, very good. He beamed as the waiter poured out a full glass for Kristina.

Thanks, Artie, she said, and Artie had bowed.

You know everyone! Roger observed.

Yeah, well, she knew Artie, unfortunately. A tiny chapter her history would have been better off without.

What is it? Roger asked. He'd smiled quizzically and taken her hand. What are you thinking?

She'd looked at him, smiled back, and withdrawn her hand.

Roger's marriage, for better or worse, had come to its natural end, he was saying. And while he looked for the occasion to make that clear, in a sensitive manner, to his wife, he was scouting out arenas in which to mine his stifled and neglected capacities.

As he talked, he gazed at her raptly, as though she were a mirror. When he reached for his wallet, to show her pictures of his children, she withdrew her hand from his again, and concentrated on drinking the very good wine. By the time they had polished off neatly two bottles and Roger was willing to throw in the towel, the Mill Wheel had almost emptied out, and Artie was lounging at the bar, staring at her evilly.

After that evening, she turned down dinner invitations, and eventually she started wearing a ring. At some point it came to her attention that Roger had indeed moved to town. In fact, he was increasingly to be seen in the afternoons hanging out at one of the bars or another, brainstorming his next move in life with the help of the bartenders.

The brilliant autumn days graded into a dazzling, glassy winter with skies like prisms, and then spring drifted down, as soft as pale linen. She painted her room a deep, mysterious blue.

Where on earth was she going to go if Nonie and Munsen had this baby they kept talking about?

She kept seeing women around her age, or anyway not much older, coming into town in their beat-up old cars or pickups, to stock up. They looked sunburned and hardy and ready for the next thing, as if they were climbing out of water after a swim. Big, friendly dogs frisked around them.

Where could they be coming from? From out in the country, of course—way out, from the wild, ramshackle farms, where the weeds shot up and burst into sizzling flowers.

The kitchen is freezing. She goes into the bedroom and selects a worn chenille robe from Alma's closet. Alma's clock, with the big, reproving green numbers, says ten thirty.

So, where is Alma? Way back, when they were growing up almost next door to each other in the projects, and their mothers let Alma exercise her fierce affections on the little girl she knew to be her half sister, Alma took care of her while their mothers worked.

And young as Kristina was, Alma confided in her. Back then, Kristina felt Alma's suffering over boys like the imprint of a slap on her own skin. Evidently things haven't changed much for Alma, and it's saddening now to picture Alma's history with Gerry: the big guy on the next bar stool, a few annihilating hours of alcohol, a messy, urgent interval at his place or hers, the sequence recapitulated now and again—an uneasy companionability hemmed about with recriminations and contingencies . . .

In her peripheral vision, Eli appears.

It was busy, and she didn't get a good look at him right away, but even at the other end of the room, sitting and talking to Frank, he was conspicuous, as if he were surrounded by his own splendid night.

It must have been several weeks later that he was there again with Frank. She'd felt the active density right away, before she even saw him. And when Frank got up to strut, and sniff around for mistakes, Eli looked right at her and smiled—not the usual sort of stranger's smile, like a fence marking a divide. Not a stranger's smile at all.

It was a Friday night; the tourists started to pour in, and when she had a chance to peek back at him he was gone.

He didn't reappear.

Then one night she glanced up from the table where she was taking an order and he was sitting at the bar. A little shock rippled through her. Evidently she'd been waiting.

He was looking for Frank again of course, but, as she explained, it was Frank's night off. Too bad you didn't call first, she said.

No phone, he told her, lightly.

No phone. Okay, but how did he find people when he wanted to?

Finding people is easy, he'd said; it's not getting found that's hard.

It was a slow evening, and early. They stood side by side at the bar. She could feel his gaze; she let herself float on it. How long had he and Frank been friends, she'd asked.

He'd seemed amused. Strictly business, he'd said. And what about her? Who was she? Where was she from?

As she spoke, he looked at her consideringly, and sorrow rose up, closing over her. How little she had to show for her eighteen years on the planet! And there were long years ahead of her; in an hour or so the room would be filled with frenetic diners, killing time until it killed them. They might as well be shot and stuffed themselves.

I don't know about this town, though, she'd said. I'm starting to feel like I'm asleep.

So, maybe you need your sleep, he said. This isn't a bad place for a nap. Why not nap? Soon you'll be refreshed and ready to move on out.

She took to sitting at her window. Haze covered the hills in the distance; the sky had become opaque, and close. Where had that real day gone?

Sometimes after she finished delivering the orders in Nonie's old car she'd just drive around, down the small highways, to the shady dirt roads. Sometimes she thought she'd caught a glimpse of Eli in town, rounding a corner, disappearing through a doorway; she wasn't well, she thought—maybe she never had been.

It was time to locate a basis, she thought. If she wasn't careful, she could end up like her mother and Alma's—always behind, sliding around, helpless. Alma had gone to school; she wasn't planning to just toss her life away, she'd told Kristina once.

Maybe I'll try to find myself a place out in the country, she said to Nonie, and get my own car.

That would be great, Nonie said. I'll help you look, if you want.

Wouldn't you even miss me? she'd said.

Of course, Nonie said. But you wouldn't be far. You'd come see us all the time.

And I'd keep helping you, she'd said.

And you'd keep helping me, Nonie said.

She can still see in perfect detail Zoe's face as she saw it, in The White Rabbit, for the first and only time. Truly she could only have glimpsed it—in profile as Zoe and Eli left, or in the mirror over the bar—but she might as well have scrutinized it for hours. It's almost as if she had been inside Zoe, looking into that mirror over the bar herself, seeing herself in the perfect dark skin, the perfect head, her hair almost shorn. She can feel Zoe's delicate body working as if it were her own, and she can feel the weight of the sleeping baby strapped to Zoe's back.

The lovely face with its long, wide-set eyes floats in Alma's plastic-covered window now, unsmiling, distant.

Eli had waved to her as he and Zoe left, but it was as if she was watching him from behind dark glass; she didn't wave back, or smile.

And Zoe appeared not to have seen her. The fact is, Zoe appeared not to see anything at all; Zoe had looked unearthly and singular, as if she were a blind woman.

Nonie was five months pregnant by the time she and Munsen told Kristina. She was superstitious, she said, and she'd had trouble before. But this is getting pretty obvious, she said. She chuckled, and patted her stomach. I figured you were just being polite.

For months Munsen and Nonie had been aware there was a baby in the house.

Oh, her blue room! It was pretty poor comfort that day.

Of course, it hadn't really been her room for the five previous months.

And the lady at the real estate office! Irritably raking back the streaky hair, the rectangular glasses in their thin frames, the expectant expression that went blank when Kristina spoke, or changed to a hurried smile . . .

A little less than fifteen hundred dollars! Every penny she'd saved. Not quite enough, was it, even for some crumbling hut out there, all made out of candy.

While Nonie baked rolls and Munsen sanded down to satin the cradle he'd built for the invisible baby, she'd flipped through Munsen's atlas. Chicago, Maine, Seattle, Atlanta—or why not go to one of those places really far away, where people spoke languages she couldn't understand at all? Because that was the point—this direction or that—apparently it didn't matter where she went.

The end of summer was already sweeping through town, hectic with color and heat, as if it were making a desperate stand against the darkness and cold ahead. Nearly a year had passed.

He was watching her as she walked right by him at the bar. Hey, he said, and held his hand out. No handshakes? No greetings, no how are yous, none of the customary effusions?

She had blushed deeply; she shook her hair back. All right, she said, greetings.

She remembers standing there, waiting for the blush to calm while he stretched lazily.

Well, since you ask, he'd said, here's the data. A lot of travel, recently, a lot of work. And my girlfriend is gone.

She glanced quickly at him and away. It was as if there were other words inside those, in the way there are with jokes. That's too bad, she said.

Why, exactly? he said, and the mortifying blush flared again.

To tell you the truth, he was saying, it was obvious almost from the beginning that there were going to be problems.

That woman had looked like someone with problems, she remembers having thought; that woman in the mirror looked like she was drifting there between the land of the living and the land of the dead.

And what was she up to herself, these days, he'd wanted to know.

She took a deep breath to establish some poise in her thoughts. Since you ask, she said, I think naptime is just about up for me.

That very night, when she got back after work, he was there in the kitchen. He and Munsen were drinking beer, and he must have just finished saying something that made Nonie and Munsen laugh. She'd stood in the doorway, silenced.

There she is, Nonie said. How come you never brought this guy around? He's okay.

Guess I don't need to introduce anyone, she'd said.

Nonie and Munsen were sitting at the table, but he was lounging against the wall, looking at her, not quite smiling. It seemed I might not have a whole lot of time, he said. So I thought I'd drop on by to ask for your hand.

He waited for her to approach. She couldn't feel herself moving. She laughed a little, breathlessly, as he removed her ring, looking at her. Dollar store, she said, and he dropped it into the ashtray on the kitchen table.

Wow! Munsen said. Okay!

There's some stuff I have to deal with tonight, Eli said. Sit tight. I'll be back in for you at noon.

·   ·   ·

Roger was already at the bar of The White Rabbit when she went in to leave a note for Frank the next morning. His arm was around one of the new waitresses. His wife and kids were where by then, she wondered. Probably living in his abandoned SUV on just the same street where she and Alma grew up, all those years ago. Hey, she'd said. Hey, he said cheerfully. Actually, he hadn't seemed to quite remember who she was.

Wear something pretty, Eli had said the night before as he left, and so she was wearing her favorite dress, with its little straps and bare back. Her hair was pinned up. He swung her suitcase into the back of the truck, and then they climbed in.

Beyond the windshield, the hills had an unfamiliar, detailed look. Red and gold were beginning to edge into the leaves. The hills were like inverted bowls or gentle cones, covered with trees. She had the impression that she could see each and every tree. The trees, like the hills, were shaped like gentle cones or inverted bowls. Would you look at that, she said.

Huh, he said. A nice little volumetric exercise.

He reached over and unpinned her hair.

This is a very crazy thing to do, she said.

Which is crazier? he said. This, or not this?

She must have been smiling, because he'd laughed. What a skeptic, he'd said. It's a risk, okay, but a risk of what? Look, here's the alternative: we meet, we like each other, we say hello, we say goodbye. Now there's an *actual* risk. That's pure recklessness. So, maybe you're scared, maybe I am too—is that so bad? Because when you're scared, you can be pretty sure you're on to something.

She remembers a sudden, panicked sensation that something was wrong, and then all her relief because it was only the ring—she wasn't wearing her dime-store ring.

It's pretty clear, he was saying, the things people know about each other in an instant are the important things. But all right, let's say the important things aren't everything. Let's say the unimportant things count too—even a lot. The point is, though, we can spend as long as we like learning those unimportant things about each other. We can spend years, if we want, or we can spend a few hours. If you want, I can bring you back here tomorrow. We can say goodbye now, if you want.

They watched each other, smiling faintly. The silence raced through her over and over.

Say the word, he'd told her, and you're back where you were.

Past the gorge, where she went to swim sometimes with Nonie and Munsen, past the old foundry, past the quarry, the hills flowing around them, mile after mile, so little traffic on the highway, the sweet air pouring by and the sun ringing through the sky like trumpets. Then they were in the woods, among the weaving streamers of sunlight and shadow. The dirt road was studded with rocks, and grooved, tossing her around as if she were on the high seas.

None of her drives in Nonie's car had taken her in that direction, or nearly that far. There were no other people to be seen. Every leaf and twig signified, like a sound, or a letter of the alphabet.

By the way, she said, how did you know where to look for me last night?

Hey, he said. In a town that size?

Light brimmed and quivered through the leaves in trembling drops. All around was a faint, high, glittering sound. The cabin was a maze of light and shadow—all logs with polished plank floors, and porches. And with the attic and lofts and little ladders and stairs, you hardly knew whether you were inside or up in a tree house.

There was running water, and there was even electricity, which he used mainly for the washing machine and the big freezer at the back. He brought her out past a group of sheds to the vegetable garden he'd been clearing and tending, and to the shiny little creek. If you walked into the woods, within just a couple of minutes, you couldn't even see the cabin. When the sun began to set they came back, and he showed her how to light the kerosene lanterns and the temperamental little fire-breathing stove.

There was a lot of game in the freezer, Eli said; hunters often gave him things. But he'd kept it simple tonight—for all he knew, she might be the fainthearted sort.

He opened a bottle of rich red wine and they ate wonderful noodles, with mushrooms from the woods and herbs, and a salad from the garden. He watched, with evident satisfaction, her astonishment at the bright, living flavors.

You have to live like this to taste anything like this, he said. Streamline yourself. Clear away the junk. Prepare for an encounter.

But anyhow, she said, and in the stillness she'd felt like a dancer, balancing—I'm not fainthearted.

How on earth was she accounting in those first hours, she wonders now, for the baby she had seen at the bar with Eli?

Well, if she'd thought of too many questions out front, she'd probably still be rotting away in that little town, living in somebody's spare room. She'd been in no position at that moment to be thinking of the sort of questions whose answers are, Go back to sleep.

They were finishing off the bottle of wine when he explained that his partner Hollis and Hollis's girlfriend, Liz, were taking care of Noah right now, as they did from time to time. It was all kind of improvisational, not ideal, but Zoe had been erratic and moody, so anyhow it was an improvement over that situation.

He rested his hand on her neck, and stars shot from it. If it had been up to her, the dishes would have stayed in the sink till morning—till winter. But Eli just held her against him for a blinding moment. Here's some of that new stuff to learn about me, he said. I am very, very disciplined.

And what had she been dreaming about that first morning? She was hidden behind something. Something was about to happen to someone very far away, who was her. There were showers of burning debris. The noise that woke her came into the dream as an alarm, she thinks, but it all dissolved like a screen over the morning light, and there was Eli lying next to her, his eyes still closed, shadows of leaves moving across him like a rich, patterned cloak.

A mechanical growl was pushing through the racket of birds and leaves. She peered out and a mottled green truck came into view. The sun must have been up for some time—it was so bright! The door of the truck slammed, and Eli groaned. Hollis, he said, and opened his eyes.

She wrapped herself around him, but he kissed her, untangled himself, and drew his jeans on. There were dogs barking. Powder! T-bone! someone yelled—Down!

Well, they're here, Eli said, and tossed her dress to her.

She watched from the top of the stairs as Liz transferred the baby over to him. The baby whimpered, and Eli put him on his shoulders.

A cigarette dangled from Hollis's mouth, and a line of smoke swayed up past his gray eyes. Would you mind kindly keeping that shit out of the house, please? Eli said. And away from my kid in general?

Hollis pinched the cigarette out with his fingers and flicked it through the door. So how about some coffee? he said.

The dogs were milling and bumping at things. Don't rush me, don't rush me, Eli said. He stretched, and reached over to tousle Hollis's floppy brown hair. I just got up.

Hollis inclined his head. Impressive, he said. Outstanding.

They looked like a tribe, Hollis and Liz and Eli, tall and slouchy and elastic. Kristina sat on the stairs, rags of her dream still clinging to her, until he called for her.

It was Hollis who tracked down the guns, and kept on top of the orders and sales. Because this guy's too pure in heart to have a computer in his place, Hollis had said, tilting back to appraise her.

No phone line, Eli said, unruffled.

My point, Hollis said to her. So I'm stuck with it. He shook his head. Too fucking poetic, this guy.

You are so jealous, Liz told Hollis, sliding her hand inside the back of his jeans.

The good weather continued, and there was the garden and clearing away the persistent brush. There was plenty else, too, of course—cleaning and dealing with the wood for the stove, and endless laundry.

Mostly, of course, there was Noah. Eli was doing a lot of things to the cabin, and the wood chips and splinters and chemicals were flying around everywhere. And there were always tools, and work on the guns going on in the sheds.

You've really got to watch him every second. Eli said. And I mean every second.

It was true; if she turned around for a *second* he'd have gotten himself over to the stove or the door or a pail of something. So she watched and she watched. But at night, when Noah was asleep, she had Eli to herself, and that was well worth all the trouble of the day, and more.

. . .

Mostly, it was he who cooked. Sometimes just vegetables, but sometimes rabbit or venison or little birds. Often, as evening came, the sky turned greenish—a dissipating, regretful color.

She remembers his voice coming through that color from outside, asking her to get the stove going. But when he came in almost half an hour later, she hadn't managed. I'm sorry, she said. How tired she used to get, back at the beginning! And she'd actually started to cry.

He looked at her and sighed. Here, he said. I'll show you again.

Sometimes the woods shook and flared with thunder and lightning. The deer came crashing through the trees. Way down in the valley the little foxes jumped straight up from the grass. Sometimes, walking near the creek with Eli, Noah on his shoulders or back, she would hear just a little whisper or rustle somewhere, or there would be a streak in the corner of her eye. Are there snakes? she asked.

He folded his arms around her and explored her ear with his tongue. Not to worry. They won't bother you unless you do something to stir them up.

At first Noah would go rigid when she tried to hold him. He'd swat at her if she bent down for him, and he'd scream when it seemed he thought Eli was in earshot.

And then Eli had to come in from outside and hold him or swing him around while she looked on. There we go, Eli would say when Noah calmed down. And sometimes he'd go back out hardly looking at her.

Noah was still only a baby then, but every day he was looking more like a little boy; every day he figured out new ways to resist and defeat her.

Just pick him up like a big ham, Eli said. Look. Like this, right, Noah?

He smiled at her as he went out, but later he'd taken her by the shoulders, and looked at her very seriously. I know it's hard, he said. But you've got to start taking some more responsibility around here. She averted her face as he leaned over to kiss her; she'd just sneaked a cigarette.

It was early on that they talked about Zoe. She wasn't ready, Eli said; it wasn't her fault. In fact, there was a lot that was his fault, really a lot, he hated to think about it. But anyhow, it was just the way she was constituted—she lacked courage. She was always dissatisfied. And she always would be, because she didn't have the courage to face the fact that what happens to you is largely of your own choosing.

He turned back, then, to whatever it was he'd been doing. But she was still listening, she remembers; something was still flickering in what he'd said.

Does she want to see Noah? she asked after a moment.

That's not a possibility, he said.

She couldn't see his face; his back was to her.

She was willing to leave her kid, Eli said. And that one's on her.

Noah isn't sounding so good. She can hear him snuffling from the kitchen. She goes to check. He's a bit sweaty—maybe Alma's right, that he's got a little fever. But little kids get sick all the time. Anyhow, what makes Alma the authority? The hospital she works at is for crazy people, not for little kids.

Tomorrow she'll get him some kind of treat—a fuzzy doggie toy, maybe, or something. Not that there's money to burn.

She remembers one day trying honey in his milk, trying a story, promising maybe a trip into town later with Eli, but Noah still whining and crying hour after hour. All right, that's it, you behave now, she'd said. Or you're going right in your crib and you're not going to be seeing that bottle of yours anytime soon.

He let out a little yelp of fury.

Fine, then, scream, she said. Go ahead and scream. Just cry until you melt yourself away for all I care. You know he's not going to hear you out there over all that noise. They stared at each other. He is not going to hear you.

She turned away from him and opened one of Eli's books. When she glanced back Noah was still standing there, looking at her. What? she said.

He wobbled for a moment on his feet, and then plopped down on his rear end, crying again.

Eli went into town to get supplies and took Noah with him. To give her a break, he said.

She'd listened to the truck heaving itself out on the rutted road. It was the first time she'd been truly alone in the cabin for more than a few minutes. Sunlight and silence shimmered down through the leaves all around it. In the sparkling dimness the floor shone like a lake. All around her there was a tingling quiet. She shivered, then sat very still, to enter it.

It was like a garden, or park, that opened out forever. Peaceful, clever animals, invisible in the abundance, paused to take note of her. She had found her way through patience and good fortune.

How's it been going? Eli said, when he returned, looking around at the cabin. She'd finished the dishes and tidied up. Any lions or tigers?

Hollis's green truck pulled up, waking her. The sheets still noted Eli's body, but they were cold. She watched from a window upstairs. The dogs were huffing and circling in back, and Hollis and Liz got out. Eli was carrying Noah. He handed Noah over to Liz. He called something up to Kristina, and then he and Hollis got into Eli's truck and pulled back out onto the dirt road.

She heard Liz downstairs with Noah. After a while she came down herself. Hi, Liz said. Eli told me you might want some help with Noah today. She yawned, and twisted her quantities of straw-colored hair into a rope. She opened a cupboard absently, and shut it again.

Oh, thanks, Kristina had said. But we'll be fine.

That's okay, Liz said, flopping herself down on the couch. Just toss me out when you get sick of me.

Sorry not to have given you a heads-up, Eli said later. But we had an unexpected opportunity. To do an errand for your old pal, Frank.

Frank, she said. What did Frank want?

He's into Mausers these days, I'm sorry to tell you. He had his tender heart set on a 1944 Kreigsmodell, and we just happened to come across one at a reasonable price. Oh, give me the sweet old American revolver guys any day. Or the Derringer guys, or the Winchester guys. Anyone at all—the Finnish military model guys. I've got to admit it's not necessarily a super high IQ clientele, but Frank is special. It's amazing he hasn't already blown his brains out by mistake.

Frank! To think of the way that freak had gotten her to scurry around. Like a rabbit! She let out a little whoop.

What, Eli said. Oh, right—like how would anyone know if he had.

. . .

I don't really need Liz to come help, she said the next time he had to go off for the day.

He looked at her. It doesn't hurt to have reinforcements, he said. And I'll have her bring any supplies you might need from town.

The leaves were truly turning when she first went back into town with Eli. The cycle of the year had locked tight, but she'd slipped out in time.

Past the quarry and the foundry and the gorge, into the painted, prissy town. She'd lived there only months ago, and yet it didn't look like a real place any longer—it just looked like a picture of a place.

She cast her mind back, and saw Zoe—the way Zoe had looked carrying Noah, gliding and regal.

Want me to carry you? she said. Noah protested, but Eli slung him onto her back.

He was heavy, and she had to cede him to Eli pretty soon, but for a while as they went about their errands, buying food and batteries and seeds, she felt, in the weight of him, her elevated station. And when they went to the diner for lunch, people she had barely spoken to in the old days came over to admire him.

They went to one of the fancy tourist stores, and Eli picked out two dresses for her. Back in the truck, with Noah settled on her lap, she felt in the bag at the slippy, lovely fabric.

Anything you particularly want to do before we head home? Eli said.

Home. The way she had lived at Nonie and Munsen's—like a little animal! I bet Nonie and Munsen would enjoy seeing Noah, she said.

Are you saying you'd like to stop by there now? he said.

She glanced at him, then shrugged. We're here.

He was looking at her steadily. Do you want to see them?

It's been a while, she said.

All you have to say, he said. All you have to say is that you'd like to see them.

But neither Munsen's car nor Nonie's was out in front.

Well, too bad, Eli said.

Eli had so many books. How nice it had been to take them down from the shelves and look at them. In the one about the ocean, the prettiest fish imaginable hovered so weightlessly you could almost see them moving—

rising, lingering, darting down with the flick of a tail. And the gorgeous plants and flowers around them were really other animals.

How did he get out? Eli was saying. He was in front of her, holding his machete in one hand and Noah by the other, and rage was flashing off him in sheets, like lightning. *It was just luck I didn't kill him with this.*

She was still shaking when Eli returned outside. She could hardly stand. Her hand was clamped around Noah's shoulder. If you want something you come to me, do you hear? she told him, her voice tight and shaking. You come to me. You do not go outside to bother your father. Try some stunt like that again and I'll—I don't know what I'll do—

On rainy days when Eli wasn't working, she curled up against him while he read out loud. Noah curled up at his other side, or played quietly nearby. Eli read from books about history or animals or the earth and other planets. The world was living and breathing, each bit in its place. When the weather was good the three of them played together in the woods.

Whenever Eli went away for the day, Liz came in her pickup, and stayed on and on. Noah would go rigid with joy when the big, patient dogs, with their amazing tails and fur and tongues, came huffling toward him through the door, but Kristina set herself to endure some bad hours.

Sometimes for days afterward, Kristina felt like a swan that had gotten caught in an oil slick—sticky and polluted, not fit to be near Eli. How could he deal with Liz? Her loudness, her opinions about every pointless thing, her gossipy chattering, the way she made everything ordinary . . . Eli had shrugged: she was an old, old friend, there was a lot of history, she was as loyal as a person could be.

Noah was making his way toward them, holding his empty bottle. Hey, Noah, Liz said. You're really getting that locomotion thing down! Wow, I can't believe how fast he's growing, look at him. Noah! She grabbed him up and tickled him, blowing hard into his hair.

Kristina remembers watching as Noah exploded into giggles.

Does he still cry for Zoe? Liz said, when Noah had run back to the dogs.

For Zoe? she'd said.

Wow, it used to be Mama, Mama, Mama just the whole fucking time, Liz said. Poor little sweetie. It used to drive Eli nuts.

I guess he's forgotten about her, she'd said.

That's great, good for you, she was a major pain, if you ask me, Liz said, Miss Too Gorgeous for This World. I always felt like smacking her myself, to tell you the truth. She didn't appreciate what she had in Eli. Eli's intense, so what? He's got his own way of looking at things. He's more evolved than other people. Plus, he gave her everything. He was fucking great to her, and he put up with her shit a long, long time before he even *began* to lose patience. Liz was holding one of the dish towels, creasing it absently and fiercely.

They've been gone so long, Kristina remembers saying. Did they say when they were planning to get back?

Oh, you never know with those two, Liz said. She tossed the towel onto the table. They take their time with the custom work. Of course that's why they've got such a great reputation, obviously. Hollis can find just about anything, and Eli can convert just about anything. He's got great hands. She pushed her hair back and eased a pack of cigarettes from her pocket. Great, great hands . . . She lit a cigarette and inhaled, closing her eyes.

Kristina watched her for a while. Liz, she said, but her voice came out fuzzy. Can I take one of those?

Help yourself. Liz opened her eyes; she'd sounded almost angry. I won't tell.

The next time Eli and Hollis went off, Noah played happily with the dogs while Liz talked on, but then suddenly Liz had exclaimed, and put her hands to her forehead.

Are you okay? Kristina asked.

Sorry, Liz said. I've been getting these crucifying migraines these days.

Do you want to lie down? she asked. Then her breath caught for a moment. Do you want to leave?

Would you mind? Liz said. You don't have to mention to Eli it was so early, though. But if I don't get out of here fast, basically, I'm not going to be able to drive till probably tomorrow.

That afternoon, with Liz and the dogs gone, no matter how often Kristina explained that Eli was coming back soon, Noah cried and fussed, swatting at her with his little hands.

You'd be less cranky if you ate something, she said. What about some applesauce?

No, Noah said.

Well, then, a graham cracker. Don't you like your graham crackers anymore?

No, he said.

Such a tiny word. Such a tiny voice.

Do you know how furious your father's going to be if I have to tell him you refused to eat one single thing all day? Do you know how angry he's going to be with you? Are you going to make me tell him?

He looked at her, swaying a bit on his feet. Bad Kissy, he said.

Not bad me, bad you! Bad you! Do you want me to smack you? Because I'm just about ready to.

Bad Kissy, he said. Bad Kissy.

Don't you talk to me like that! Don't you look at me like that! Do you think I like picking up after you all day long? And getting you your food when you do deign to eat? And cleaning up all your mess? I know you don't like having me around. And do you know what? I think I've just about had it with you! One more sassy word and I'm going to walk right out that door, and you'll just have to take care of yourself. Now you eat your graham cracker this minute, or I'm out of here.

But then he was screaming and kicking and banging his head against the wall.

It was the moment; it was their chance, and thank God she'd recognized that. But just remembering the struggle, she starts to sweat—scooping him up and trying to hold him still, and all the time he was kicking at her and screaming. And clinging to her so fiercely she could hardly get him over to the sofa to sit down with him.

It must have been over an hour that she was holding on to him before he was calm enough for her to speak. All right then, Noah, she said.

He had gone limp. She held him steadily on her lap and broke the graham cracker in half. She wouldn't let him avoid her eyes.

I'm not going to leave you alone, she said. Listen to me. This is a promise. I am not going to leave you alone.

Tears were still rolling down his cheeks, and he hiccuped.

They watched each other as she ate her half of the cracker. She nodded, and held the other half of the cracker out to him. Slowly, gulping back the last of his sobs, still watching her, he chewed it laboriously down.

When Eli returned, Noah was still in her lap, asleep. Where's Liz? he said.

You just missed her, she said.

Huh, Eli said. And this one—trouble?

She rested her cheek against Noah's springy hair and tightened her hold on him for a moment before handing him over. No, she said. No trouble.

The cold came, and kept them frequently inside. Eli was working in the shed a lot, and from time to time he'd have to take a trip or go to a show with Hollis. When they were away, Liz showed up for the daylight hours. When her truck finally pulled away, darkness folded in over the cabin.

When Eli was home, he was quiet. He read to Noah, and when he grew tired of it he went to his own reading. He was looking a little pale, she'd thought. Eli? she said.

What's that? he said, pausing on his way up to the loft.

She shook her head: Nothing.

Noah pined and clamored for his friends the dogs. Shh, she told him, and took him where he could play without disturbing Eli.

Once in a while a car would pull up, and some man or other would get out and Eli would take him around back to the sheds. She stayed upstairs then with Noah.

While Noah played with the blocks Eli had made him, she watched out the window as the men returned to their trucks or cars, and headed off to the hills, or the hills beyond them, or the hills and cities beyond those—glinting pins springing up on the map.

And she watched Noah as he concerned himself with the blocks or with his crayons and paper. Playing, it was called—the deep, sweet concentration, the massive effort to familiarize himself with the things of the world. Can she remember that, being so little herself, being so lost? Not at all. Probably Alma had already been around, looking out for her, but she can't find a trace of that time in her mind. It had happened, it had made her, and then it had sunk away out of sight.

Want me to carry you? she'd ask, and he'd raise up his little arms to her.

She held him as he woke from his naps, and felt the damp heat coming off his gold skin and little ringlets. He snuggled against her, and in an attic-dark area of her sleeping thoughts, things clarified for a moment, and aligned.

He never fussed anymore. He had made his choice; he had forgotten.

Sometimes Kristina felt Zoe hovering nearby, drawn by her need, watching along with her as Noah played. But Noah never even looked up.

Yes, he had surely forgotten. Poor little thing—he was a prisoner.

Are you not talking to me? Eli said one day.

Not talking to you? she said. She looked up. He was sitting across the room, looking at her. The book he'd been reading was closed, resting on his lap.

You don't seem to be talking to me.

You were reading, she said.

Now I'm not reading, he said.

She looked at him for a clue. Is there something you want me to talk about?

He sighed and opened his book again, but a moment later he looked up at her again. You're happy, he said.

Yes, she said—he seemed to be gazing back at her sadly from some time in the future—I'm happy.

Well, good, then. He walked over to her and stroked the back of her neck, looking at her thoughtfully. He kissed her temple and then he returned to his book.

He picked up some yeast for her in town. She baked bread the way Nonie had showed her to, and the companionable aroma brought Nonie to visit.

She remembers the way she imagined showing Nonie around the cabin. It was as if she were unfolding it and spreading it out flat, like a map, so she could see all of it at once, herself.

How's Eli these days? Liz said.

Fine, she said.

Well, I'm glad one of them is keeping it together, Liz said. Hollis is fried. But everything always happens all at once, doesn't it.

I guess, Kristina said.

Well, but I mean what kind of dickhead doesn't back up the files? Liz said. I guess that genius they found, I hate to think where, is still saying he can resurrect the hard drive, but who believes that's going to happen? Anyhow, who cares. It's the thing with that Cunningham lunatic, obviously, that's really putting him around the bend.

Yes? Kristina said. The room darkened for a moment, and she'd sat down.

Well, it's sure getting enough attention. Eli must have told you. You literally can't turn on the TV for one second without seeing the pictures. God, those kids must have been cute! With that red hair?

Kristina had let out a little sound.

But anyhow they don't usually go after the source, Liz said. Unless like it's a kid putting holes in his parents or at school, something like that. And anyhow, according to Hollis for whatever that's worth, he did check the guy out, and there was no history.

Sleet coated the trees and power lines, and froze. For a day or two the woods were bright glass, and the branches snapped and fell under the weight of the ice. Nights were mostly bundled up in silence; you could hear the world breathing in its sleep. When she closed her eyes, she'd see the animals outside in the stark, brilliant moonlight, huddled, or wandering for food—the foxes and the deer, the badgers and the possums and the pretty black bear. The stars overhead contracted in the cold. From bed she could watch them oscillating with intensified light, as if they were about to burst into sharp, glittering fragments.

Is everything all right? she asked him.

Fine, he said.

Can I help with anything?

Can you help? he said. Can you do a conversion on a 1911 automatic with a broken drill press while some drooling trog breathes down your neck?

She went into town with him, and when they passed the old house, both cars were out front. Would you like to drop by? he asked.

I don't really care, she said.

It might be nice for you, he said. You probably miss your friends.

She reached over and stroked his beautiful hair. He could drop her and Noah off, she suggested, while he did errands.

We're in no rush, he said. I'll go in with you.

Nonie was practically a sphere. She greeted Kristina with a little shriek of joy, and cried a bit.

How fussy the kitchen looked to Kristina now, with its shiny appliances and painted walls.

Nonie cut up pieces of her bread with homemade jam for everyone, and Munsen took a couple of beers from the fridge. Eli? he said.

No, thanks, Eli said.

Kristina?

Not for me either, Munsen—thanks.

He put one bottle back, and opened the other for himself. Well, better a full bottle in front of me than a prefrontal lobotomy, he said, ruefully. Then he set Noah on his lap, and while Nonie recounted goings-on at The White Rabbit, which were exactly the same old thing, it seemed, Munsen told Noah the true-life adventures of a lonely bottle of beer.

What a fuss Nonie made over Noah! He's going to have a friend soon, she said.

Kristina glanced at Eli. He was standing, leaning against the door with his head bowed.

Nonie gave Noah one of the soft little rag dolls she'd made for her own baby, with a little plastic ring in its navel. Noah looked at it with great seriousness, and then rubbed it against his cheek. He looked up at Nonie, who laughed happily and knelt down to give him a squeeze.

So little real time had passed, but she might as well have spent it living at the bottom of the sea with its creaturely landscape, or on the white polar tundras. And all the while Nonie and Munsen had been confined to the little painted town. Goodbye, she thought. Goodbye.

They had almost reached the cabin when Eli finally spoke. That is one inane guy, he said. I wonder how your friend can stand having him around.

The next morning, Kristina couldn't find Noah's new rag doll anywhere.

She was searching through a heap of laundry for it when she realized Eli was in the doorway, watching her. Everything okay? he said.

She turned and they looked at one another. Fine, she said.

. . .

Look, I've got to go away tomorrow for a few days, Eli said. But Liz will come over during the days and help.

Eli, she said.

What?

Eli, she said again.

What? he said. Speak to me.

Do you have to go?

Yes, he said. Obviously. Yes, I have to go.

Eli, can't I come with you?

And do what with him?

Bring him along. Can't we come?

No, you cannot come.

Why not?

Why not? It goes without saying why not.

She was twisting one of Noah's little T-shirts in her hands, she realized. But maybe I could be helpful.

Maybe you could, he said. Maybe you could bring a little sunshine into the lives of some lonely gun collectors.

She looked at him, but he was sealed up tight. But please, please, don't send Liz at least.

Fine, he said. No Liz. And you'll do what for food? You'll do what if you need something? You don't have a phone. You don't have a car.

If you're worried about us, we could go stay with Nonie and Munsen.

With Nonie and Munsen, he said. Would you be happier there?

It's just—she was saying, and then all she really remembers is her surprise, as if his fists were a brand-new part of his body.

A little blood was coming from somewhere; she felt something on her face, then checked her hand. Her tooth felt wobbly, she noted; the thought sat as a salty little pool around the tooth.

She heard the bare branches clacking together outside in a slight breeze. Then he picked her up from where she'd fallen back.

She registered Noah's eyes, enormous and blurry-looking. What will he remember? He was sucking at his blanket as Eli carried her upstairs.

. . .

He postponed his trip for a few days, and stayed with her, curled up next to her in the loft, holding her hands, looking through his books with her. He taught her the names of all the little birds that lived in the leaves around them. He brought her meals on a tray. Noah played quietly downstairs, and sometimes Eli brought him up to be with her. He'd wake her urgently in the night, and after they made love, he kissed her ankles, her toes, her temples. The air was sweet with the delicate freshness of approaching spring. They lay next to each other, their fingers laced together. Whatever barrier had been between them was gone now, completely.

She stroked his thick, coarse hair. She can feel it under her hand now—almost feel it. Sometimes as he slept she ran her hands over his beautiful face. Poor Eli. He lived with danger all the time.

It wasn't long before the swellings went way down, and she could get around pretty comfortably, as well. The day he left, she found a tube of makeup out on the bureau. Evidently he'd picked it up in town, for the bruises.

She's sure there were marks but nothing too conspicuous by the time she'd finished applying it. She watched carefully for Liz's expression when she opened the door in her sunglasses.

She's reviewed it so often she's worn away the original, but she knows perfectly well what it was.

She saw Liz register the sunglasses, the masked bruises. She saw Liz politely covering her surprise. And then she saw the thing that she had hoped so fervently that she would not see: she saw that Liz was not very surprised at all.

What did they talk about that morning? Not Eli, that's for sure. Or Hollis, or themselves. They did not, of course, allude to Zoe. Kristina felt Zoe's volatile essence as a slight trembling in the air. Eventually, she remembers, Liz began leafing through some trashy magazine she'd brought in with her and paused to study the picture of two pretty faces, empty of anything except a pitiful falseness. They broke up! she exclaimed, looking up at Kristina. Can you believe it? How sad is that!

. . .

It was the next day—the second of the three he was to be gone—that Zoe's sorrowing angel spirit passed her hand across Liz's brow, and Liz winced, pressing her hand to her eyes.

And there it was. The opportunity that was as clear as a command. For a moment Kristina just stood there.

Migraine? she had asked then quietly. Want to go home and lie down?

It was a hard trip into town, and of course you always had to worry about who it was who would stop. But thank heavens it wasn't raining, at least. Feel better, she'd called to Liz, waving from the door as the pickup pulled out, and then as fast as humanly possible, she'd thrown a few necessities for Noah and a change of clothing for herself into a satchel. It wasn't heavy, but progress down the muddy road out to the highway was arduous; something in her side still hurt a lot when she tried to carry Noah.

Hey, it's you, Nonie said when she opened the door. And then her smile was gone. Wuh! Take off those sunglasses for a moment, girl.

Noah let himself be transferred over, and clung to Nonie as she put juice into a bottle for him. Come see the baby, she said.

The baby was red and gummy. Could Noah ever have looked like that? That's incredible, Kristina said.

So, could Nonie and Munsen manage with one car, she'd asked? She could give them over a thousand dollars for Nonie's. She hadn't spent so much as a dime the whole time she'd been with Eli, she realized; he'd taken care of her completely.

Well, you could pay me down the line somewhere, Nonie said. But I'm not really sure I want to know you've got it, if you see what I mean.

That was a good point.

I guess you could report it stolen, Kristina had said. But maybe not for a while? And I guess I'll have to figure out about changing the plates . . .

They'd looked at each other, frowning. Damn, Nonie said. You'd think a person would know how to steal her own car.

And for just a moment, Kristina remembered the way she'd felt sitting around that kitchen in the old days.

. . .

Dull moonlight sloshes around like rainwater in the plastic over the window. Alma still hasn't come in. But Kristina's just as glad to have had this time with Eli.

This afternoon, when Alma answered the door she looked silently for a moment at Kristina, with her bruises and the beautiful, dark child. Then she stood aside to let them in. Heaven knows what she thinks—she didn't ask questions.

When Kristina was young she idolized Alma. It was Alma who looked out for her, and she never doubted for a moment that Alma would gladly take her in if the time came. It hardly matters now that it seems not to be the case. She looks around at Alma's cheap, carelessly ugly place—home for nobody, really. Oh, those shining floors, that quiet, the breathing shadows! Will she ever see it again?

Noah coughs raspily in his sleep. She puts her hand to his hot forehead, and he opens his eyes, just for a moment.

Stolen car! Kidnapped child! How can those words mean her? The deer come crashing through the woods, Zoe holds her breath, Eli's rage is all around them, the red net casting wide. What's right outside? Keys hanging from the warden's belt? The men with the guns? Just guns, or guns and badges . . .

No one looks at anyone—really completely looks—the way he looked at her. She never imagined, or even dared hope, that she would meet such a man or have such a time in her life. Better keep moving. New names, new histories, a nondescript room in a busy city where she'll be able to lose herself and Noah. Watching, hiding, running—that way at least she'll be with Eli for good.

Reading *The O. Henry Prize Stories 2006*

The Jurors on Their Favorites

Each juror read all twenty stories without knowing who wrote them or where they were published.

Kevin Brockmeier on "Old Boys, Old Girls" by Edward P. Jones

Five notions regarding "Old Boys, Old Girls" by Edward P. Jones:

1) I did not realize that I loved "Old Boys, Old Girls" until I was midway through the story. The key moment came for me when Cathedral, Caesar's friend and protector, whose mind has been broken by visions of the young bachelor he has killed, tells him, "What we need is a new God." Up to this point I had certainly appreciated the story for its pugnacity and its momentum and the steel suggestiveness of its imagery, but I did not yet love it. Then I read Cathedral's monologue about the senselessness of the world, and it was as if a wave ran through the rest of the pages. Everything that had come before "and everything that would come after" suddenly rose into place. It seems appropriate that a narrative about how even the most barren lives can be unexpectedly transfigured would be transformed in this way by a sentence about the need for a new God.

2) One of the things I like best about "Old Boys, Old Girls" is the ease with which Edward P. Jones manipulates time. Fully eight years pass between the opening paragraph and the final sentence of the story, and yet the events Jones presents are so rich, you never get the sense that any phase

of Caesar's life has been neglected or trimmed away. In addition, the story regularly sends out feelers into both the past and the future, quick little one- or two-sentence glimpses of other times and places, which seem to hint that the actions of the characters are shaped not only by what has already happened to them but by what has yet to occur. The narrative establishes a world governed as much by expectation as by memory, in which the future as well as the past sheds its light over the present.

3) After I finished reading the manuscript for this anthology "minus the author names or sources of publication" and decided to write about "Old Boys, Old Girls," I conducted an Internet search to find out who the author was, which was how I discovered that the story revisits the lives of several of the characters from Edward P. Jones's 1992 collection *Lost in the City.* If I had not stumbled across this piece of information, I would never have guessed that the story arose out of an earlier piece of fiction, since the approach it takes to its characters and the settings they inhabit feels so bountiful, so comprehensive.

4) There is a John Updike statement about how the ending of a piece of fiction is where you discover whether the story you have been reading is the same story the writer thought he was writing. "Old Boys, Old Girls" ends with a moment of hopeful suspension involving both Caesar and a little girl who is watching him as she tinkers with her bicycle (and I'll stop to mention here how much I like the fact that although "Old Boys, Old Girls" is mainly about Caesar, it is continually ready to share its space with other characters, even characters who brush up against the action for only a moment before they take their leave). I must have read the story half a dozen times now, including this final scene between Caesar and the little girl, and it is a testimony to its power that when their hearts pause, my own heart continues to pause along with them.

5) Of course, a reader could finish "Old Boys, Old Girls" without taking note of any of the things I have mentioned and still appreciate it thanks to an entirely different set of considerations. There is a largeness to the story, a vitality and a freedom of meaning, that makes it possible to follow any number of pathways from the beginning to the end. It is the kind of story I like best, one that gives its readers plenty of wandering room.

Kevin Brockmeier is the author of the novel *The Truth About Celia*, the story collection *Things That Fall from the Sky*, and two children's novels,

City of Names and *Groove: A Kind of Mystery.* His most recent novel is *The Brief History of the Dead.* His stories have appeared in many magazines and anthologies, including *The New Yorker, The Best American Short Stories, The Year's Best Fantasy and Horror,* and in *The O. Henry Prize Stories* three times. Brockmeier lives in Little Rock, Arkansas.

Francine Prose on "Window" by Deborah Eisenberg

Were I to attempt to summarize "Window"—which I wouldn't, for fear of spoiling the reader's pleasure in its delicate plot shifts and in the elegant pace at which it reveals essential information—it would probably not sound anything like the marvelous story Deborah Eisenberg has written. Because to summarize is to separate the bones of plot from the flesh of language, and what makes this story so incandescent is the language in which it is written: the way each precisely chosen and resonant word demonstrates the most profound respect for the reader, and for the story's characters. It's assumed that we will be able to understand a fiction that so fully inhabits its protagonist's consciousness that there is no need—no place—for conventional exposition. Just as it is assumed that Kristina—jobless, homeless, down on her luck—has a complex sensibility and an inner life rich enough to afford the most inspired use of metaphor, the most original and penetrating responses to her situation and to the world around her. In just a few words, we are made to understand exactly why Kristina (why anyone) would be attracted to someone like Eli, and, just as she does, we see and ignore the warning signs, the low thrum of menace that sounds beneath the buzz of attraction. Even the title is beautifully chosen, because to read the story is to feel as if one window after another were opening, allowing us a series of fleeting and privileged glimpses into the human heart and soul.

Francine Prose is the author of eleven novels, including *Blue Angel,* which was nominated for a 2000 National Book Award. Her most recent books are *A Changed Man,* a novel; *After,* a novel for young adults; *Sicilian Odyssey,* a travel book; *The Lives of the Muses: Nine Women & the Artists They Inspired; Gluttony,* a meditation on a deadly sin; and a biography, *Caravaggio, Painter of Miracles.* Prose lives in New York City.

Colm Tóibín on "Passion" by Alice Munro

The story is framed; what happens is told in the light of many years later. We are allowed to guess what sort of person Grace became in the years that followed. We know, and we believe, that she has come back to this place because something defining occurred here. The story then is not simply something she remembers, or something strange or poetic, a tale worth telling, but it is a crucial moment in Grace's young life, a line she crossed that made all the difference.

A novel is a thousand, maybe two thousand details. A story too is all details, but each of them has to do more work, tell us more, like a telling detail in a play that will lead to something. The job of the writer is not to use these details too tactlessly, not to offer them a burden they cannot hold. They must be telling and also seem natural. In a story they also have to have a sort of magic about them.

The names of the places in "Passion" are remarkably ordinary; there is a constant use of tentative description, in which Grace "has located Sabot Lake, or thinks she has" and in which the village may not really be a village "because she does not see a post office or even the most unpromising convenience store." This sense of things studied carefully and reported accurately runs right through the story. "Mr. Travers had built the house," we are told. And then: "that is, he'd had it built."

Everything said about Mr. and Mrs. Travers at the beginning of the story makes clear that they are neither good nor bad, and installs the illusion that they may be ordinary. Her telling stories and imitating people; his friendly taciturn nature. They can be read either way, as signs of uneasiness or signs of ease.

Grace is both the central consciousness of the story and an aspect of the reader. The reader, too, is more interested in Mrs. Travers and her household than in her son Maury. Thus Grace's interest in seeing the family rather than dating the son is made to seem natural, almost ordinary too. Even the bitterness of her response to "Father of the Bride" seems part of her general intelligence, although it is also the first real clue offered that she is trouble, or troubled, or both.

The story is a set of unfoldings. First the framing sequence, then the Travers couple, then the story of how Grace met them; then, when we have seen Grace respond to a number of things and feel we know her slightly, Grace's background is offered.

The story now can go many ways. It is open for Maury and Grace to marry; it is open for Maury and Grace to break up; it is open for Grace to fall in love with Mrs. Travers; it is open for Grace to remember this summer simply as the beginning of her education. Instead, much stranger, more bizarre, and more engaging things are about to happen. The extraordinary thing is that we think we know Grace as a character before they happen, as she thinks she knows herself. She seems quiet, watchful, a conformist. Opinionated and ambitious, but polite.

The first sign comes with Mavis, the wife of Neil, a doctor, who is the son from Mrs. Travers's first marriage. She is an outsider in the family, ready to disrupt the harmony, the very opposite, it seems, of Grace. Neil, her husband, does not appear until almost halfway through the story and then only as described by his mother: "Neil is very bright. I don't mean that Maury isn't—you certainly don't get to be an engineer without a brain or two in your head—but Neil is . . . He's deep."

Soon afterward it emerges that Mrs. Travers is not merely funny and wise and intriguing; she also suffers. Such ease as hers has its dark side, and this discovery is also part of Grace's education.

The events that make all the difference happen on Thanksgiving Day. The great family occasion is punctured first by Grace's breaking her sandal and then cutting her foot. This is a cue for Neil to arrive, and the story now needs a most skillful teller so that it can be turned and refocused, like someone working with glass, where one wrong turn of the wrist will destroy a most ambitious project.

The moment where the real genius of the story shows is when Grace is in the emergency ward and she has one second to decide to stay with Neil, who she knows is drunk, or to go with Maury, who she knows is dull. The reader will at least expect her to consider the matter, but, strangely and subtly, all the reader's expectations have been undermined. We notice in the exchange on which everything depends that Grace remains silent. But she is not absent. We can almost hear her breathing. And finally when she is asked if she wants to go home now, she replies: "No." She says it "as if she'd seen the word written in front of her, on the wall. As if she were having her eyes tested."

She is not the character she thought she was, or we imagined she was. She emerges, like the story itself, as surprising and complex. The story offers no character who is easy to explain, or whose motives or actions follow simply from their clearly delineated personality. And this goes against the grain of pure simplicity and controlled clarity in the prose and becomes, for that, all the more surprising and, at times, almost alarming. This way of hiding the sheer complex nature of Grace by making her appear simple and natural is part of the pure genius of the story.

Colm Tóibín was born in Enniscorthy, County Wexford, in the southeast of Ireland in 1955, and educated at University College, Dublin. His novels include *The South, The Heather Blazing, The Story of the Night, The Blackwater Lightship*, and, most recently, *The Master*. His works of nonfiction include *The Trial of the Generals, The Sign of the Cross: Travels in Catholic Europe*, and *Love in a Dark Time*. Tóibín lives in Dublin.

Writing *The O. Henry Prize Stories 2006*
The Authors on Their Work

Karen Brown, "Unction"

I begin most stories with place, and this one is no exception. As a teenager, I worked a summer job in a small bookbinding machine shop. The heat-filled boredom, the smell of the oiled parts, all of this came back to me. Just as often when I begin a story, I read—books pulled almost at random from my shelves. In my notes I had copied Updike's epigraph to *Rabbit, Run,* and lines from poet Robert Pawlowski's *Seven Sacraments.* The characters emerged in phrases of description, a mix of memory and invention. I discovered Lily's fearless sexuality, and the sensuous nature of a sacrament that involves anointing the body. I wanted to play with the idea of Grace. I thought of us all in our clumsy, human forms, bestowed with the capacity to administer aid. These pieces converged in the writing, on a rainy weekend in Florida, and of this there are no notes—as always, the story is its only record.

Karen Brown grew up in Connecticut. Her stories have appeared in *Epoch*, *StoryQuarterly*, *The Georgia Review*, and the *Graywolf Annual*. She lives in Tampa, Florida.

George Makana Clark, "The Center of the World"

I grew up in the eastern highlands of Rhodesia (now Zimbabwe), shouting distance from Mozambique. I've since forgotten more than I remember about the place. Several years ago, it occurred to me that my most resonant memories of the highlands are embedded in its stories and lore. In "The Center of the World," I tried to pull together the threads of all the place-stories I collected long ago when I was a troubled mission boy looking for my own place in the world.

George Makana Clark's stories have appeared in *The Georgia Review*, *Glimmer Train*, *The Massachusetts Review*, *The Southern Review*, *Transition*, *Zoetrope*, and elsewhere. His collection of stories is *The Small Bees' Honey*. He has been the recipient of a National Endowment for the Arts Fellowship and a finalist for the Caine Prize for African Writing. He teaches at the University of Wisconsin—Milwaukee. Clark lives in Milwaukee, Wisconsin.

Deborah Eisenberg, "Window"

This is a story that I failed to write over a period of years. That is to say, I failed to know what it was, though certain of the elements were clear to me. I knew about the two little houses, the house in the woods and the house on the water (though it was some time before they moved into the same story), and I knew about the baby. I suppose I was very interested in exploring the growth of violence where there is no enmity. And I was also interested in the inscrutable—as distinct from unpredictable—shape of certain lives, that there are lives which appear to be moving in a fairly orderly way in one direction, but are then revealed to have been moving in a fairly orderly way in quite another direction.

Deborah Eisenberg's fourth collection of short fiction is *Twilight of the Superheroes*. She teaches part of every year at the University of Virginia in Charlottesville. Eisenberg lives in New York City.

Louise Erdrich, "The Plague of Doves"

More than any story I've ever written, "The Plague of Doves" came to me with an urgency and insistence so strong that I felt at times I was taking dictation. I had all the parts of it for years and years—the doves, the

Mooshum, Mustache Maude—but I sat for a long time under the nearest cottonwood to know the ending.

Louise Erdrich was born in 1954, in Little Falls, Minnesota, and is a member of the Turtle Mountain Band of Chippewa. Her latest novel is *The Painted Drum*. "The Plague of Doves" will be included in her next collection. Erdrich lives in Minnesota.

Paula Fox, "The Broad Estates of Death"

"The Broad Estates of Death" grew out of several known elements in my own life, and a good many unknown! I spent three months in Taos, New Mexico; I met a district nurse, and Ben is based on the father of someone I lived with in Taos.

Paula Fox was born in 1923 and has been writing since she was in her early twenties. Since her first novel, *Poor George*, and first book for children, *Maurice's Room*, she's published books for young people, as well as novels and short stories. *The Coldest Winter: A Stringer in Liberated Europe*, a memoir, is her most recent book. Fox lives in Brooklyn, New York.

Edward P. Jones, "Old Boys, Old Girls"

"Old Boys, Old Girls" began with "Young Lions," a story in *Lost in the City*. At the end of that first story, Caesar Matthews is a young thief and estranged from the world. I never planned to go back to the people in *Lost*, but one by one, they returned to my imagination. And when it was Caesar's turn, he had murdered two men.

Edward P. Jones is the author of *The Known World*, a novel that won the Pulitzer Prize and the National Book Critics Circle Award for fiction, and *Lost in the City*, winner of the PEN/Hemingway Award in 1992. He was the recipient of a fellowship and award from the Lannan Foundation. Jones lives in Washington, D.C.

Jackie Kay, "You Go When You Can No Longer Stay"

Some stories take weeks and weeks; and others you write in the one sitting. This story I wrote in a single evening. I had had the idea for some time. I was interested in trying to write about how long-term couples often merge identities, and in seeing whether or not it'd be possible to find any humor in a breakup. I'd noticed going through various breakups with different friends, how when people are splitting up, they emphasize their differences; but when they are together they look for similarities. They want to say things like "I thought of that at exactly the same time as you." But when they are breaking up they want to push all that away. I also wanted to write about the safety of the mainstream.

Jackie Kay grew up in Scotland. Her first book of poems, *The Adoption Papers*, tells the story, her story, of a black girl adopted into a Scottish family. Her novel *Trumpet* won the Guardian Fiction Award. Her short-story collection is *Why Don't You Stop Talking*, and her most recent book of poems is *Life Mask*. Kay lives in Manchester.

David Means, "Sault Ste. Marie"

When I was writing "Sault Ste. Marie" I tapped into several images I had floating around from my youth, waiting to be used when the time was right. One of them was Sault Ste. Marie, Michigan, and the visitors station where you could watch the rise and fall of ships in the Soo locks and examine a model of the St. Lawrence Seaway. I remember being impressed by the huge boats, their weight, being moved up and down. I began the story with that image—and the sense that the town at that time, like so many in Michigan, seemed sucked dry, a relic of the Industrial Age, a place of transport and constant transition. Although there seems to be a lot of death in the story, it's not clear, even to me, if anyone dies.

David Means was born and raised in Michigan. He is the author of three books of fiction, most recently *The Secret Goldfish: Stories*. His second collection, *Assorted Fire Events*, won the Los Angeles Times Book Prize for Fiction and was a finalist for the National Book Critics Circle Award. He teaches at Vassar College. Means lives in Nyack, New York.

David Lawrence Morse, "Conceived"

Once in a museum in Russia—it might have been a folk art museum— I came across a wooden sculpture of a village living on top of a fish. I supposed at the time that the sculpture was meant to represent the dependence of the sculptor's village on fish for its sustenance. But when I remembered the fish many years later, this explanation seemed too simple—and failed to explain why or how that sculpture had remained in my memory all that time. I had a look at some wonderful myths of big fish—Jonah and the whale, also the story of Saint Brendan, a Celtic monk whose boat landed on what he assumed was a small island but was in fact a whale named Jasconius. In my first drafts of this story, I tried to concoct a kind of philosophical satire that spent overmuch time explaining how a group of people came to be living on a fish—sailors, ahoy!, shipwreck, etc. But here again I was resorting to simple explanations, and it's no wonder these drafts fizzled out. It was only when I took life on the fish as a given that the story held my interest. I spent the next couple of weeks doing almost nothing but writing the story, staring at an illustration mounted on the wall of a smiling blue whale.

David Lawrence Morse grew up in south Georgia and has since lived in North Carolina, Washington, D.C., and Iwakuni, Japan. "Conceived" is his first published story. He teaches at the University of Michigan. Morse lives in Ann Arbor.

Alice Munro, "Passion"

When I was driving around the Ottawa Valley with a friend, I heard his story about cutting his foot on a shell, and how the family entertaining him insisted he be treated by a family member who happened to be a doctor and a drunk. His impression was that they were all hoping against hope for the rehabilitation of this man—who seemed, to my friend, to be proud, sad, irretrievable. From that, and some notion of the way young and not-so-young women are sexually drawn to such men, I made my story.

Alice Munro was born in 1931 in Wingham, Ontario. Her most recent short-story collection is *Runaway*. She is a three-time winner of the Governor General's Literary Award; the Lannan Literary Award; and the W. H. Smith Award. Her stories have appeared in *The New Yorker*, *The Atlantic Monthly*, *The Paris Review*, and other publications, and her collections have been translated into thirteen languages. She divides her time between Clinton, Ontario, and Comox, British Columbia.

Lydia Peelle, "Mule Killers"

In 1919, there were 26.5 million mules and horses in this country. By 1945, less than a tenth of that number remained. They simply disappeared from the landscape. I was reading about this one hot summer in Tennessee, and thinking about the echoes of loss. At the time I was living in a small town just north of Nashville and didn't see many people from day to day. Walking along the roads and through the old fields, I often had a sense of these animals—not their ghosts, exactly, but some vestige of their recent presence. Their reverberations. It was the same feeling that you can have when, upon entering a room, you somehow know for certain that someone has recently left it. I was living in an old house that baked in the afternoon sun, writing most days at a desk that was steps from my bed. It was so hot and muggy that I could only write for brief spurts of time before exhaustion took over. When it did I would creep over to my bed, lie down, and close my eyes. This story started out as I lay curled there, with an old man saying, *Mercy, mercy, mercy,* and the rest of it came slowly, not at the desk, but in those moments when I was very still and quiet. This is what convinces me that this story, or one very much like it, was there already, deep in the land's memory. I just happened to be in the right place at the right time to set it all down on paper.

Lydia Peelle was born in Boston in 1978. "Mule Killers" is her first published story. She is a Poe-Faulkner fellow in creative writing at the University of Virginia. Peelle lives in Charlottesville, Virginia.

Stephanie Reents, "Disquisition on Tears"

When I began writing "Disquisition on Tears" I was interested in how individuals react to horror. This was after 9/11, and the newspapers were full of people's stories, some of them about the lucky string of events that made them late for work that morning, others about the terrifying process of getting out of the buildings. (Of course, there were still more stories about the lives of people who remained there and died.) In the account that stayed with me, a man described holding the hand of another person and running for safety. When the building fell, the man looked down and saw that he was only holding an arm. The body had vanished.

As I considered how I would react if faced with a similar situation, the following line came to me: "A woman stood at my door with her head in her hands." Because I wasn't sure that I was committed to looking at a headless woman, I liked the ambiguity of the sentence. I wrote for several weeks about the physical presence of the woman with the detachable head and my narrator's reaction to her. Then, I began to consider to whom a headless woman might appear, and this made me realize that the headless woman wasn't as scary as the situation that led to her.

Stephanie Reents is a native of Idaho. Her stories have appeared in *Epoch*, *Gulf Coast*, and *Pleiades*. She was a Wallace Stegner Fellow at Stanford University.

Susan Fromberg Schaeffer, "Wolves"

One snowy night, my husband and I were in Vermont, reading. The house was very quiet and I realized that this silence was emblematic of how drastically our lives had changed since the children left the house. At the same time, I thought about the neighbors who had recently told me that bears, foxes, and perhaps a wolf had been seen nearby. The silence began to interest me and I found myself wondering if silence is, perhaps, for many people, a kind of emptiness. I also asked myself how time takes many things from us, and then it was a short step to wondering how many losses a person can withstand and still want to survive. This was how the story of "Wolves" began, a couple in a silent house, one of whom is unable to accept how her life has changed. The wolf soon comes to visit the woman. Whether or not there is a real wolf is irrelevant; to her, the wolf is real. Psychological reality is as true as, or truer and more definitive than, the reality we normally acknowledge. In "Wolves," that reality has become very despairing. Hence the ending of the story.

Susan Fromberg Schaeffer was born in Brooklyn, New York. The most recent of her twelve novels is *The Snow Fox*, and she's published five books of poetry, a collection of stories, and two books for children. Her awards include two previous O. Henry prizes and a John Simon Guggenheim Fellowship. Since 1999, she has taught at the University of Chicago. Schaeffer lives in Chicago.

Terese Svoboda, " '80's Lilies"

In 1983, the USSR shot down a Boeing 747, killing all 269 passengers flying from the United States to Seoul via Anchorage. The flight, numbered 007, was suspected of espionage because it had veered off course over secret Russian installations. At the time, the Cold War felt very hot. My husband and I had been too young to do anything other than duck and cover during the Cuban Missile Crisis and now we had a new baby to protect. Perhaps we overreacted, but we maxed our gold card and fled to New Zealand. This was just months before Carl Sagan announced the realities of nuclear winter, which knocked out any idea of real escape.

For fifteen years after our return to the United States, I puzzled over my fevered impressions of New Zealand, trying to articulate why we didn't stay. Slowly I realized it wasn't just that immigration wanted only plumbers and nurses or that world politics had quieted down. It took another five years to convince myself that the story had indeed found its shape.

Terese Svoboda's writing has appeared in *Bomb*, *Conjunctions*, *The Yale Review*, *Tin House*, *The Atlantic Monthly*, *The Paris Review*, *The New Yorker*, and *Grand Street*. She's won awards and grants in essay, translation, playwriting, fiction, poetry, and video. Her opera *Wet* premiered in Los Angeles at Disney Hall. Her most recent novel is *Tin God*. Svoboda lives in New York City.

Melanie Rae Thon, "Letters in the Snow—for kind strangers and unborn children—for the ones lost and most beloved"

Two images converged and sparked this story. In the winter of 2000–2001, somebody broke into my parents' cabin on Bitterroot Lake in northwestern Montana. Whoever it was didn't take much—just some food and warm clothing—but s/he lived there several days, as if taking refuge. I started to wonder who this person was, and what dangers or difficulties s/he might be fleeing. Then in June of 2001, I had one of my weird accidents and battered my right eye rather spectacularly. Yes, a peacock bruise like Nicole's, brilliant rings of violet, blue, and green. It was so extreme some people thought I'd painted it on, and others (strangers in grocery stores, for instance) winced in pain when they saw me. I noticed an odd pattern: suddenly men of all ages were flirting with me. I had my own theories about this, and finally a man twenty years younger than I confessed: "There's something irresistible about a battered woman." Nicole came alive in my mind and body. I felt her. I began to know her. She was wonderfully mysterious to me and also frighteningly familiar.

Melanie Rae Thon's latest novel is *Sweet Hearts*, and her story collections are *First, Body* and *Girls in the Grass*. She teaches at the University of Utah. Thon divides her time between the Pacific Northwest and Salt Lake City.

Douglas Trevor, "Girls I Know"

I wrote the story because I was interested in the class differences I noticed while I was a graduate student in the nineties. I'm sure there are plenty of middle-class undergraduates at Harvard; I just never met any. The ones I knew were affluent and savvy—smart too, but in a different world from my friends in the graduate college, most of whom subsisted on all-carb diets and worried endlessly about ever being employable as "intellectuals." I liked the idea of modeling the friendship of Ginger and Walt on that of the poets Robert Lowell and Elizabeth Bishop, since relative social class was an issue in their relationship, and I was also intrigued by how a self-loathing character like Walt would gravitate toward Lowell.

One of my closest friends had supported himself in graduate school as a sperm donor. He told me about how he discovered that the people at his sperm bank were lying about his physical appearance, and I knew I wanted to use that in the story, since it seemed to encapsulate a similar kind of erasure that can occur in graduate school: one in which you feel forgotten while at the same time you're anonymously productive—reading voraciously or working as a teaching assistant.

I was determined to have another voice speak in the story; I was worried that the reader would otherwise be asked to sympathize too much with someone who doesn't have it that bad. So I put in the waitress who tells a truly horrific tale, unmediated by any conscious appreciation of narrative techniques. She can just talk, whereas everything Walt tries to write has to be filtered through what he has read. Ginger's desire to record the waitress's plain speech is supposed to complement Walt's belief in the power of "higher" art forms; I wanted the two of them to attest to the importance of listening for stories in unlikely places, and caring about art even if you can't explain why exactly you do.

• • •

Douglas Trevor's stories have appeared in *The Paris Review, Glimmer Train, Epoch, New England Review*, and other journals. His first collection, *The Thin Tear in the Fabric of Space*, won the Iowa Short Fiction Award, and he is the author of *The Poetics of Melancholy in Early Modern England*, a study of self-described depressives in sixteenth- and seventeenth-century England. Trevor lives in Iowa City, Iowa.

William Trevor, "The Dressmaker's Child"

[No author statement from William Trevor—*LF*]

William Trevor was born in 1928 at Mitchelstown, County Cork, and spent his childhood in provincial Ireland. He has written many novels, including *Fools of Fortune, Felicia's Journey*, and most recently *The Story of Lucy Gault*. He is a renowned short-story writer and has published thirteen collections, from *The Day We Got Drunk on Cake* to *A Bit on the Side*. Trevor lives in Devon, England.

Lara Vapnyar, "Puffed Rice and Meatballs"

I have always felt compelled by the theme of sexual awakening in a country as bizarre as Soviet Russia. The comical was often blended with the tragic, and we never knew if a certain episode would with time turn into an amusing memory or a long-lasting trauma.

"Puffed Rice and Meatballs" is based on two real episodes. Both made a deep impression on me, yet for some reason I kept telling the first episode to many different people under different circumstances and in very different forms, while the second episode stayed buried in my memory. I often wondered why people choose to share certain episodes, and try to suppress the others. I think this wondering made me write "Puffed Rice and Meatballs."

Lara Vapnyar emigrated from Russia to New York in 1994 when she was twenty-three. Her stories have appeared in *The New Yorker, Zoetrope*, and *Open City*, and are collected in *There Are Jews in My House*. Her first novel is *Memoirs of a Muse*. Vapnyar lives in New York City.

Neela Vaswani, "The Pelvis Series"

The story came from my reading, in a dentist's office, a magazine article about the dwindling chimpanzee population in Africa. Chimpanzees were losing their natural habitat and being hunted for food (in some cases because people were starving, in others for "bushmeat trade") and "exotic markets" (chimpanzee hands sold as ashtrays). The article ended by mentioning an American Sign Language chimpanzee. I thought about the cut hands of chimps in Africa, and the chimps in the States who had been trained by scientists to converse, with hands, in a human, American language; I thought about power, brutality, the responsibilities that come with being on top of the food chain, and I cried my eyes out in the dentist's office (the sound of the drill did not help). So the story is my emotional response to the grotesque inequality that allows a market for chimp hands as ashtrays. I also wanted to explore the idea that no connection is impossible. A woman and a chimpanzee can communicate, can be family to each other. And in that way, any communication, any understanding, any family, is possible.

Neela Vaswani's stories have appeared in *Shenandoah*, *Prairie Schooner*, and *American Literary Review*, among other publications. Her first collection of stories is *Where the Long Grass Bends*. She lives in New York City.

Xu Xi, "Famine"

I began writing "Famine" because I wanted to revisit a youthful obsession—"above life" versus "under life"—first articulated in my journals when I was a teenager. Through much of my early twenties in Hong Kong, I was convinced that functioning in my world depended on keeping these two lives in balance: the "real" above life of family, friends, work, and society, against my "unreal" under life of desires, lusts, dreams, solitary retreats, and an intense longing for identity—political, cultural, and linguistic. Despite the lip service paid to the importance of learning the language, Hong Kong remains linguistically Cantonese, and for the vast majority its English voice is reluctant or, at best, pragmatic; since our return to China, Mandarin has become the voice to acquire. Arguably, my city has no real "mother tongue."

As I drafted my way through the story, I realized I was writing about those who may consume as much as they wish but remain hungry, because what they ingest does not nourish. I also had in mind the famine in China under Mao during which over a hundred million people starved even as the chairman remained convinced that his farming collectives were a success.

I've only been in the Plaza Hotel once, for a Christmas party of a Wall Street law firm I used to work for, which is what suggested the use of that hotel. Having spent time in international five-star hotels for business travel, I wanted to re-create the peculiarly impoverished sensation I experienced, as well as the opulence of life in that world.

Xu Xi is a Chinese-Indonesian native of Hong Kong. She has written three novels, three collections of stories and essays, *Overleaf Hong Kong, History's Fiction*, and *Daughters of Hui*, and coedited two anthologies of Hong Kong literature in English. Her fiction and essays have appeared in *Ploughshares, Manoa, The Literary Review*, and elsewhere, and have been anthologized worldwide. Xu Xi lives in New York, Hong Kong, and New Zealand.

Recommended Stories

Publications Submitted

Because of production deadlines for the collection, it is essential that stories reach the series editor by May 1 of the year in which they are published. If a finished magazine is unavailable before the deadline, magazine editors may submit scheduled stories in proof or in manuscript. Stories may not be submitted or nominated by agents or writers. Please see our Web site, http://www.ohenryprizestories.com, for more information about submission to *The O. Henry Prize Stories.*

The address for submission is:

> Professor Laura Furman
> The O. Henry Prize Stories
> English Department
> University of Texas at Austin
> One University Station, B5000
> Austin, TX 78712

The information listed below was up-to-date as *The O. Henry Prize Stories 2006* went to press. Inclusion in the listings does not constitute endorsement or recommendation.

580 Split
Mills College
P.O. Box 9982
Oakland, CA 94613-0982
Michelle Simotas,
Managing Editor
editor@580split.com
www.580Split.com
Annual

96 Inc
P.O. Box 15559
Boston, MA 02215
www.96inc.com
Annual

African American Review
Saint Louis University
Humanities 317
3800 Lindell Boulevard
St. Louis, MO 63108
Jocelyn Moody, Editor
keenanam@slu.edu
http://aar.slu.edu/
Quarterly

Agni Magazine
Boston University
236 Bay Street Road
Boston, MA 02215
Sven Birkerts, Editor
agni@bu.edu
www.bu.edu/agni/
Biannual

Alaska Quarterly Review
University of Alaska Anchorage
3211 Providence Drive
Anchorage, AK 99508
Ronald Spatz, Editor
www.uaa.alaska.edu/aqr
Quarterly

Alligator Juniper
Prescott College
220 Grove Avenue
Prescott, AZ 86301
aj@prescott.edu
www.prescott.edu
Annual

American Literary Review
University of North Texas
P.O. Box 13827
Denton, TX 76203-1307
Lee Martin, Editor
americanliteraryreview
@yahoo.com
www.engl.unt.edu/alr/main.html
Biannual

Another Chicago Magazine
3709 North Kenmore
Chicago, IL 60613
Barry Silesky, Editor and
Publisher
editors@anotherchicagomag.com
anotherchicagomag.com
Biannual

Antietam Review
41 South Potomac Street
Hagerstown, MD 21740
Philip Bufithis, Editor
antietamreview
@washingtoncountyarts.com
http://www.washingtoncounty
arts.com/antietam_review.htm
Annual

The Antioch Review
P.O. Box 148
Yellow Springs, OH 45387
Robert S. Fogarty, Editor
review@antioch.edu
http://review.antioch.edu
Quarterly

Apalachee Review
P.O. Box 10469
Tallahassee, Florida 32302
Laura Newton, Mary Jane Ryals,
Michael Trammel, Editors
http://apalacheereview.org
Biannual

Arkansas Review
Department of English and
Philosophy
Box 1890
Arkansas State University
State University, AR 72467
Tom Williams, Editor
tswillia@astate.edu
www.clt.astate.edu/arkreview
Triannual

Ascent
Department of English,
Concordia College
901 South 8th Street
Moorhead, Minnesota 56562
W. Scott Olsen, Editor
ascent@cord.edu
www.cord.edu/dept/english/
ascent
Triannual

At Length
P.O. Box 594
New York, NY 10185
Jonathan Farmer, Editor
info@atlengthmag.com
www.atlengthmag.com
Quarterly

Atlanta Review
P.O. Box 8248
Atlanta, GA 31106
Daniel Veach, Editor and
Publisher
Dan@atlantareview.com
www.atlantareview.com
Biannual

The Atlantic Monthly
77 North Washington Street
Boston, MA 02114
Benjamin Schwarz, Literary
Editor, and C. Michael Curtis,
Senior Editor (Fiction)
Letters@theatlantic.com
www.theatlantic.com
Monthly

The Baltimore Review

P.O. Box 36418
Towson, MD 21286
Susan Muaddi Darraj,
Managing Editor
www.baltimorereview.org
Biannual

Bellevue Literary Review

Department of Medicine, Room
OBV-612
NYU School of Medicine
550 First Avenue
New York, NY 10016
Ronna Wineberg, JD,
Fiction Editor
www.blreview.org
Biannual

Beloit Fiction Journal

Box 11
Beloit College
700 College Street
Beloit, WI 53511
Shawn Gillen, Editor in Chief
http://www.beloit.edu/~english/
bfjournal.htm
Annual

BIGnews

302 East 45th Street
4th Floor
New York, NY 10017
Ron Grumberg, Editor
MainchanceNY@aol.com
www.Mainchance.org/BIGnews
Monthly

Black Warrior Review

Box 862936
Tuscaloosa, Alabama 35486-0027
Laura Hendrix, Editor
bwr@ua.edu
webdelsol.com/bwr
Biannual

Blue Mesa Review

1 University of New Mexico
MSC03 2170
Albuquerque, New Mexico
87131-0001
Daniel Mueller, Editor
bluemesa@unm.edu
http://www.unm.edu/~bluemesa/
Annual

Bomb

594 Broadway, 9th Floor
New York, NY 10012
Betsy Sussler, Editor in Chief
bomb@echonyc.com
www.bombsite.com/
firstproof.html
Quarterly

Book

252 West 37th Street
5th Floor
New York, NY 10018
Jerome V. Kramer, Editor in Chief
bookmagazine.com
Bimonthly

Border Crossings
500-70 Arthur Street
Winnipeg, Manitoba R3B 1G7
Canada
Meeka Walsh, Editor
bordercr@escape.ca
www.bordercrossingsmag.com
Quarterly

The Boston Book Review
331 Harvard Street, Suite 17
Cambridge, MA 02139
Kiril Stefan Alexandrov, Editor
www.bookwire.com/bookwire/
bbr/bbr-home.html
Monthly

Boston Review, A Political and Literary Forum
E53-407 MIT
Cambridge, MA 02139
Deborah Chasman, Joshua
Cohen, Editors
www.bostonreview.net
Published six times per year

Boulevard Magazine
6614 Clayton Road, Box 325
Richmond Heights, MO 63117
Richard Burgin, Editor
www.richardburgin.net/boulevard/
Triannual

The Briar Cliff Review
3303 Rebecca Street
P.O. Box 2100
Sioux City, IA 51104-2100
Tricia Currans-Sheehen, Editor
currans@briarcliff.edu
www.briar-cliff.edu/bcreview
Annual

Callaloo
English Department
4227 TAMU
Texas A&M University
College Station, TX 77843-4227
Charles Henry Rowell, Editor
callaloo@tamu.edu
http://xroads.virginia.edu/
~public/callaloo/home/
callaloohome.htm
Quarterly

Calyx, A Journal of Art and Literature by Women
P.O. Box B
Corvalis, OR 97339-0539
Beverly McFarland, Senior Editor
calyx@proaxis.com
www.proaxis.com/~caylx
Biannual

Canadian Fiction
P.O. Box 1061
Kingston, Ontario K7L 4Y5
Canada
Geoff Hancock, Rob Payne,
Editors
Biannual

The Carolina Quarterly
Greenlaw Hall CB# 3520
University of North Carolina
Chapel Hill, NC 27599-3520
Tessa Joseph, Editor
cquarter@unc.edu
www.unc.edu/depts/cqonline
Triannual

The Chariton Review
Truman State University
Kirksville, MO 63501
Jim Barnes, Editor
Biannual

The Chattahoochee Review
Georgia Perimeter College
2101 Womack Road
Dunwoody, GA 30338-4497
Marc Fitten, Editor
gpccr@gpc.edu
www.chattahoochee-review.org
Quarterly

Chelsea
P.O. Box 773
Cooper Station
New York, NY 10276-0773
Alfredo de Palchi, Editor
Biannual

Chicago Review
5801 South Kenwood Avenue
Chicago, IL 60637-1794
Joshua Kotin, Editor
humanities.uchicago.edu/review
Triannual

Cimarron Review
205 Morrill Hall
English Department
Oklahoma State University
Stillwater, OK 74078
E. P. Walkiewicz, Editor
cimarronreview@yahoo.com
cimarronreview.okstate.edu
Quarterly

Colorado Review
Department of English
Colorado State University
Fort Collins, CO 80523
Stephanie G'Schwind, Editor
creview@colostate.edu
http://www.coloradoreview.com
Triannual

Commentary
165 East 56th Street
New York, NY 10022
Neal Kozodoy, Editor
editorial@commentarymagazine.com
www.commentarymagazine.com
Monthly

Concho River Review
P.O. Box 10894, ASU Station
Angelo State University
San Angelo, TX 76909
Mary Ellen Hartje, Editor
www.angelo.edu/dept/english/
Biannual

Confrontation
English Department
C. W. Post Campus, Long Island
University
720 Northern Boulevard
Brookville, NY 11548-1300
confrontation@liu.edu
www.liu.edu/confrontation
Biannual

Conjunctions
21 East 10th Street
New York, NY 10003
Bradford Morrow, Editor
conjunctions@bard.edu
www.conjunctions.com
Biannual

Crab Orchard Review
Department of English
Southern Illinois University
Carbondale
1000 Fauer Drive
Carbondale, IL 62901-4503
Allison Joseph, Editor
www.siu.edu/~crborchd
Biannual

Crazyhorse
English Department
College of Charleston
66 George Street
Charleston, SC 29424
crazyhorse@cofc.edu
http://crazyhorse.cofc.edu
Biannual

The Cream City Review
University of Wisconsin—
Milwaukee
P.O. Box 413
Milwaukee, WI 53201
Phong Nguyen, Editor
www.uwm.edu/dept/english/ccr/
Biannual

Cut Bank
English Department
University of Montana
Missoula, MT 59812
cutbank@selway.umt.edu
www.umt.edu/cutbank
Biannual

**Daedalus, Journal of the
American Academy of Arts
& Sciences**
Norton's Woods
136 Irving Street
Cambridge, MA 02138
James Miller, Editor
daedalus@amacad.org
Quarterly

Denver Quarterly
University of Denver
Department of English
2000 E. Asbury
Denver, CO 80208
Bin Ramke, Editor
www.denverquarterly.com/
index.cfm
Quarterly

Epoch
251 Goldwin Smith Hall
Cornell University
Ithaca, NY 14853-3201
Michael Koch, Editor
www.arts.cornell.edu/english/
epoch.html
Triannual

Esquire
823 Eleventh Avenue
New York, NY 10019
Adrienne Miller, Literary Editor
www.esquiremag.com
Monthly

Faultline
English and Comparative
Literature Department
University of California—Irvine
Irvine, CA 92697-2650
faultline@uci.edu
www.humanities.uci.edu/faultline
Annual

Fence
303 East Eighth Street, #B1
New York, NY 10009
Lynne Tillman, Fiction Editor
fence@angel.net
www.fencemag.com
Biannual

Fiction
English Department
City College of New York
Convent Avenue at 138th Street
New York, NY 10031
Mark Jay Mirsky, Editor
www.fictioninc.com
Biannual

The Fiddlehead
Campus House, 11 Garland
Court
University of New Brunswick
P.O. Box 4400
Fredericton, New Brunswick
E3B 5A3 Canada
Ross Leckie, Editor
fiddlehd@unb.ca
www.lib.unb.ca/Texts/Fiddlehead
Quarterly

First Intensity
P.O. Box 665
Lawrence, KS 66044
Lee Chapman
leechapman@aol.com
members.aol.com/leechapman
Biannual

The First Line
P.O. Box 250382
Plano, TX 75025-0382
David LaBounty, Jeff Adams,
Editors
info@thefirstline.com
www.thefirstline.com
Quarterly

Five Points
P.O. Box 3999
Atlanta, GA 30302-3999
David Bottoms and Maggie
Sexton, Editors
http://www.webdelsol.com/
Five_Points/
Triquarterly

The Florida Review
Department of English
P.O. Box 161346
University of Central Florida
Orlando, FL 32816
Jeanne M. Leiby, Editor
flreview@mail.ucf.edu
www.flreview.com
Biannual

Fourteen Hills:
The SFSU Review
Department of Creative Writing
San Francisco State University
1600 Holloway Avenue
San Francisco, CA 94132-1722
Kristine Leja, Editor in Chief
hills@sfsu.edu
http://14hills.net
Biannual

Fugue
Department of English
Brink Hall 200
University of Idaho
Moscow, Idaho 83844-1102
http://www.uidaho.edu/fugue
Biannual

Gargoyle
P.O. Box 6216
Arlington, VA 22206-0216
Lucinda Ebersole, Richard
Peabody, Editors
atticus@atticusbooks.com
http://www.atticusbooks.com
Annual

The Georgia Review
University of Georgia
Athens, GA 30602-9009
T. R. Hummer, Editor
garev@uga.edu
www.uga.edu/garev
Quarterly

The Gettysburg Review
Gettysburg College
Gettysburg, PA 17325
Peter Stitt, Editor
pstitt@gettysburg.edu
www.gettysburg.edu/academics/
gettysburg_review
Quarterly

Glimmer Train
1211 NW Glisan Street
Suite 207
Portland, Oregon 97209-3054
Susan Burmeister-Brown,
Linda B. Swanson-Davies, Editors
eds@glimmertrain.com
www.glimmertrain.com
Quarterly

Good Housekeeping
959 Eighth Avenue
New York, NY 10019
Ellen Levine, Editor in Chief, and
Laura Mathews, Literary Editor
www.goodhousekeeping.com
Monthly

Grain Magazine
Box 67
Saskatoon, Saskatchewan
S7K 3KI Canada
Kent Bruyneel, Editor
grainmag@sasktel.net
www.grainmagazine.ca
Quarterly

Granta
1755 Broadway
5th Floor
New York, NY 10019-3780
Ian Jack, Editor
www.granta.com
Quarterly

**The Green Hills Literary
Lantern**
P.O. Box 375
Trenton, MO 64683
Joe Benevento and Jack Smith,
Editors
http://ll.truman.edu
/ghllweb
Annual

The Greensboro Review
MFA Writing Program
English Department
134 McIver Building, UNCG
P.O. Box 26170
Greensboro, NC 27402-6170
Jim Clark, Editor
jlclark@uncg.edu
www.uncg.edu/eng/mfa/gr
Biannual

Gulf Coast
Department of English
University of Houston
Houston, Texas 77204-3013
Claudia Rankine,
Executive Editor
editors@gulfcoastmag.org
www.gulfcoastmag.org
Biannual

Gulf Stream
English Department
FIU Biscayne Bay Campus
3000 NE 151 Street
North Miami, FL 33181-3000
Lynn Barrett, Editor
http://w3.fiu.edu/gulfstrm
Biannual

Hampton Shorts
P.O. Box 1229
Water Mill, NY 11976
Barbara Stone, Editor
hamptonshorts@hamptons.com
Annual

Happy
240 East 35th Street
Suite 11A
New York, NY 10016
Quarterly

Harper's Magazine
666 Broadway
New York, NY 10012
www.harpers.org
Monthly

Harpur Palate
English Department
Binghamton University
P.O. Box 6000
Binghamton, NY 13902-6000
Catherine Dent, Editor
http://harpurpalate.binghamton.
edu/
Biannual

**Harrington Gay Men's Fiction
Quarterly**
English Department
Thomas Nelson Community
College
P.O. Box 9407
Hampton, VA 23670
Thomas L. Long, Editor in Chief
www.tncc.vccs.edu/faculty/longt/
HGMFQ/
Quarterly

Harvard Review
Lamont Library
Harvard University
Cambridge, MA 02138
Christina Thompson, Editor
harvrev@fas.harvard.edu
www.hcl.harvard.edu/houghton/
departments/harvardreview/
HRhome.html
Biannual

Hawaii Pacific Review
Hawaii Pacific University
1060 Bishop Street
Honolulu, HI 96813
hpreview@hpu.edu
Annual

Hayden's Ferry Review
Box 875002
Arizona State University
Tempe, AZ 85287-5002
Salima Keegan, Managing Editor
hfr@asu.edu
haydensferryreview.org
Biannual

Hemispheres
1301 Carolina Street
Greensboro, NC 27401
letters@hemispheresmagazine.
com
www.hemispheresmagazine.com
Monthly

High Plains Literary Review
180 Adams Street
Suite 250
Denver, CO 80206
Robert O. Greer, Jr., Editor in
Chief
Triannual

The Hudson Review
684 Park Avenue
New York, NY 10021
Paula Deitz, Editor
www.hudsonreview.com
Quarterly

The Idaho Review
Boise State University
English Department
1910 University Drive
Boise, ID 83725
Mitch Wieland, Editor in Chief
english.boisestate.edu/
idahoreview/
Annual

**Image, A Journal of the Arts
& Religion**
3307 Third Avenue West
Seattle, WA 98119
Gregory Wolfe, Editor
image@imagejournal.org
www.imagejournal.org
Quarterly

Indiana Review
Indiana University
Ballantine Hall 465
1020 East Kirkwood Avenue
Bloomington, IN 47405-7103
Grady Jaynes, Editor
http://www.indiana.edu/
~inreview/index.html
Biannual

Inkwell
Manhattanville College
2900 Purchase Street
Purchase, NY 10577
Jeremy Church, Editor
inkwell@mville.edu
http://www.inkwelljournal.org
Annual

The Iowa Review
308 English/Philosophy Building
University of Iowa
Iowa City, IA 52242-1492
David Hamilton, Editor
www.uiowa.edu/~iareview
Triannual

Italian Americana
University of Rhode Island
Feinstein College of Continuing
Education
80 Washington Street
Providence, RI 02903-1803
Carol Bonomo Albright, Editor
http://www.uri.edu/prov/italian/
italian_pub.html
Biannual

The Journal
Department of English
Ohio State University
164 West 17th Avenue
Columbus, OH 43210
Michelle Herman, Fiction Editor
http://english.osu.edu/journals/
the_journal/
Biannual

**Kalliope, A Journal of Women's
Literature & Art**
Florida Community College
at Jacksonville
Kent Campus
3939 Roosevelt Boulevard
Jacksonville, FL 32205
www.fccj.org/kalliope/index.html
Biannual

Karamu
English Department
Eastern Illinois University
Charleston, IL 61920
Olga Abella, Editor
http://www.eiu.edu/~karamu/
Annual

The Kenyon Review
Kenyon College
Walton House
Gambier, OH 43022-9623
David H. Lynn, Editor
kenyonreview@kenyon.edu
www.kenyonreview.org
Triannual

Kiosk
State University of New York at
Buffalo
English Department
306 Clemens Hall
Buffalo, NY 14260
eng-kiosk@acsu.buffalo.edu
www.cuneiformpress.com/
2005.html
Annual

Knight Literary Journal
P.O. Box 449
Spout Spring, VA 24593
Charles Cutter, Editor
Annual

The Land-Grant College Review
P.O. Box 1164
New York, NY 10159
Dave Koch, Josh Melrod, Editors
editors@land-grantcollegereview.
com
www.lgcr.org
Biannual

The Laurel Review
Department of English
Northwest Missouri State
University
Maryville, MO 64468
William Trowbridge, David Slater,
Beth Richards, Editors
m500025@mail.nwmissouri.edu
Biannual

Literal Latté
Suite 240
200 East 10th Street, Suite 240
New York, NY 10003
Jenine Gordon Bockman,
Publisher and Editor
Litlatte@aol.com
http://www.literal-latte.com
Bimonthly

The Literary Review
285 Madison Avenue
Madison, NJ 07940
René Steinke, Editor in Chief
tlr@fdu.edu
www.theliteraryreview.org
Quarterly

The Long Story
18 Eaton Street
Lawrence, MA 01843
R. P. Burnham, Editor
rpburnham@mac.com
http://homepage.mac.com/
rpburnham/longstory.html
Annual

Louisiana Literature
Box 10792
Southeastern Louisiana University
Hammond, LA 70402
Jack Bedell, Editor
lalit@selu.edu
www.louisianaliterature.org/press/
Biannual

The Malahat Review
University of Victoria
P.O. Box 1700, STN CSC
Victoria, British Columbia
V8W 2Y2 Canada
John Barton, Editor
malahat@uvic.ca
http://malahatreview.ca
Quarterly

Manoa
English Department
University of Hawai'i
Honolulu, HI 96822
Frank Stewart, Editor
www.hawaii.edu/mjournal
Biannual

The Massachusetts Review
South College
University of Massachusetts
Amherst, MA 01003-7140
David Lenson, Editor
massrev@external.umass.edu
www.massreview.org
Quarterly

McSweeney's
826 Valencia Street
San Francisco, CA 94110
Dave Eggers, Editor
printsubmissions
@mcsweeneys.net
www.mcsweeneys.net
Quarterly

Michigan Quarterly Review
University of Michigan
3574 Rackham Building
915 East Washington Street
Ann Arbor, MI 48109-1070
Laurence Goldstein, Editor
MQR@umich.edu
www.umich.edu/~mqr
Quarterly

Mid-American Review
Department of English, Box W
Bowling Green State University
Bowling Green, OH 43403
Karen Craigo and Michael
Czyzniejewski, Editors
http://www.bgsu.edu/
studentlife/organizations/
midamericanreview/
Biannual

Midstream
633 Third Avenue, 21st Floor
New York, NY 10017-6706
Joel Carmichael, Editor
midstreamthf@aol.com
www.midstreamthf.com
Nine issues yearly

The Minnesota Review
Department of English
Carnegie Mellon University
Pittsburgh, PA 15213
Jeff Williams, Editor
editors@theminnesotareview.org
www.theminnesotareview.org
Biannual

Mississippi Review
Center for Writers
The University of Southern
Mississippi
Box 5144
Hattiesburg, MS 39406-5144
Frederick Barthelme, Editor
www.mississippireview.com
Biannual

The Missouri Review
1507 Hillcrest Hall
University of Missouri—
Columbia
Columbia, Missouri 65211
Speer Morgan, Editor
tmr@missourireview.com
www.missourireview.com
Triannual

Ms. Magazine
443 South Beverly Drive
Beverly Hills, CA 90212
Michele Kort, Fiction Editor
info@msmagazine.com
www.msmagazine.com
Quarterly

Nassau Review
English Department
Nassau Community College
1 Education Drive
Garden City, NY 11530-6793
Paul A. Doyle, Editor
Annual

**Natural Bridge, A Journal
of Contemporary Literature**
Department of English
University of Missouri—St. Louis
One University Boulevard
St. Louis, MO 63121
natural@umsl.edu
www.umsl.edu/~natural
Biannual

The Nebraska Review
University of Nebraska at Omaha
WFAB 212
Omaha, NE 68182-0324
http://www.zoopress.org/
nebraskareview/
Biannual

Neotrope
P.O. Box 172
Lawrence, KS 66044
Adam Powell and Paul Silvia,
Editors
apowell10@hotmail.com
www.brokenboulder.com/
neotrope.htm
Annual

Nerve
520 Broadway, 6th Floor
New York, NY 10012
Michael Mastin, Editor in Chief
Six issues yearly

New Delta Review
English Department
214 Allen Hall
Louisiana State University
Baton Rouge, LA 70803-5001
new-delta@lsu.edu
english.lsu.edu/journals/ndr
Biannual

New England Review
Middlebury College
Middlebury, VT 05753
Stephen Donadio, Editor
NEReview@middlebury.edu
www.middlebury.edu/~nereview
Quarterly

New Letters
UMKC/University House
5101 Rockhill Road
Kansas City, MO 64110-2499
Robert Stewart, Editor in Chief
newletters@umkc.edu
http://www.newletters.org/
Quarterly

New Millennium Writings
P.O. Box 2463
Knoxville, TN 37901
Don Williams, Editor
www.mach2.com
Annual

New Orleans Review
Box 195
Loyola University
New Orleans, LA 70118
Christopher Chambers, Editor
chambers@loyno.edu
www.loyno.edu/~noreview
Biannual

New York Stories
English Department, E-103
La Guardia Community
College/CUNY
31-10 Thomson Avenue
Long Island City, NY 11101
Daniel Caplice Lynch,
Editor in Chief
nystories@lagcc.cuny.edu
www.newyorkstories.org
Triannual

The New Yorker
4 Times Square
New York, NY 10036
fiction@newyorker.com
Deborah Treisman, Fiction Editor
www.newyorker.com
Weekly

**News from the Republic
of Letters**
120 Cushing Avenue
Boston, MA 02125
Keith Botsford, Editor
rangoni@bu.edu
www.bu.edu/trl
Biannual

Night Rally
P.O. Box 1707
Philadelphia, PA 19105
Amber Dorko Stopper,
Editor in Chief
NightRallyMag@aol.com
Triquarterly

Night Train Magazine
212 Bellingham Avenue, #2
Revere, MA 02151-4106
Rusty Barnes, Editor
submission@nighttrainmagazine.
com
www.nighttrainmagazine.com
Biannual

Nimrod
The University of Tulsa
600 South College Avenue
Tulsa, OK 74104-3189
Francine Ringold, Editor in Chief
nimrod@utulsa.edu
www.utulsa.edu/nimrod
Biannual

Noon
1369 Madison Avenue
PMB 298
New York, NY 10128
Diane Williams, Editor
noonannual@yahoo.com
http://www.noonannual.com/
Annual

The North American Review
University of Northern Iowa
1222 West 27th Street
Cedar Falls, Iowa 50614-0516
Vince Gotera, Grant Tracey,
Editors
nar@uni.edu
www.webdelsol.com/
NorthAmReview/NAR/
Published five times per year

North Carolina Literary Review
Department of English
2201 Bate Building
East Carolina University
Greenville, NC 27858-4353
Margaret Bauer, Editor
bauerm@mail.ecu.edu
www.ecu.edu/nclr
Annual

North Dakota Quarterly
University of North Dakota
Grand Forks, ND 58202-7209
Robert W. Lewis, Editor
ndq@und.nodak.edu
www.und.nodak.edu/org/ndq
Quarterly

Northwest Review
369 PLC
University of Oregon
Eugene, Oregon 97403
John Witte, Editor
Triannual

Notre Dame Review
840 Flanner Hall
Department of English
University of Notre Dame
Notre Dame, IN 46556
www.nd.edu/~ndr/review.htm
Semiannual

Now & Then
Center for Appalachian Studies
and Services
Box 70556
East Tennessee State University
Johnson City, TN 37614-1707
Nancy Fischman,
Managing Editor
cass@etsu.edu
cass.etsu.edu/n&t
Triquarterly

Nylon
394 West Broadway, 2nd Floor
New York, NY 10012
Gloria M. Wong, Senior Editor
nylonmag@aol.com
www.nylonmag.com
Monthly

Oasis
P.O. Box 626
Largo, FL 34649-0626
Neal Storrs, Editor
oasislit@aol.com
Quarterly

The Ohio Review
344 Scott Quad
Ohio University
Athens, OH 45701-2979
Wayne Dodd, Editor
The.Ohio.Review@ohiou.edu
www.ohio.edu/TheOhioReview
Biannual

One Story
P.O. Box 1326
New York, NY 10156
Hannah Tinti, Editor
questions@one-story.com
www.one-story.com
About every three weeks

Ontario Review
9 Honey Brook Drive
Princeton, NJ 08540
Raymond J. Smith, Editor
www.ontarioreviewpress.com
Biannual

Open City
270 Lafayette Street
Suite 1412
New York, NY 10012
Thomas Beller, Joanna Yas,
Editors
editors@opencity.org
www.opencity.org
Triannual

Orchid
P.O. Box 131457
Ann Arbor, MI 48133-1457
Keith Hood, Amy Sumerton,
Editors
editors@orchidlit.org
www.orchidlit.org
Semiannual

Other Voices
English Department (MC 162)
University of Illinois at Chicago
601 South Morgan Street
Chicago, IL 60607
Gina Frangello, Editor
othervoices@listserv.uic.edu
www.webdelsol.com/Other_
Voices
Biannual

Owen Wister Review
University of Wyoming
Student Publications
Box 3625
Laramie, WY 82071
Annual

The Oxford American
201 Donaghey Avenue
Conway, AR 72035
Marc Smirnoff, Editor
oamag@oxfordamericanmag.com
www.oxfordamericanmag.com
Quarterly

Oxford Magazine
English Department
356 Bachelor Hall
Miami University
Oxford, OH 45056
http://www.units.muohio.edu/
cwe/Publish.html

Oyster Boy Review
P.O. Box 77842
San Francisco, CA 94107-0842
Damon Sauve, Publisher
email@oysterboyreview.com
www.oysterboyreview.com
Quarterly

The Paris Review
62 White Street
New York, NY 10013
Philip Gourevitch, Editor
www.parisreview.com
Quarterly

Parting Gifts
3413 Wilshire Drive
Greensboro, NC 27408
Robert Bixby, Editor
rbixby@aol.com
www.marchstreetpress.com
Biannual

Partisan Review
236 Bay State Road
Boston, MA 02215
partisan@bu.edu
www.partisanreview.org
Quarterly

Phoebe, A Journal of Literature and Art
MSN 2D6
George Mason University
4400 University Drive
Fairfax, VA 22030-4444
Ryan Effgen, Editor
phoebe@gmu.edu
www.gmu.edu/pubs/phoebe
Biannual

Playboy Magazine
680 North Lake Shore Drive
Chicago, IL 60611
Jonathan Black, Managing Editor
articles@playboy.com
www.playboy.com
Monthly

Pleiades
Department of English
Central Missouri State University
Warrensburg, MO 64093
Kevin Prufer, Editor
www.cmsu.edu/englphil/pleiades/
Biannual

Ploughshares
Emerson College
120 Boylston Street
Boston, MA 02116-4624
Don Lee, Editor
www.pshares.org
Triannual

Post Road
203 Bedford Avenue
Brooklyn, NY 11211
Mary Cotton, Managing Editor
fiction@postroadmag.com
www.postroadmag.com
Biannual

Potomac Review
Montgomery College
51 Mannakee Street
Rockville, MD 20850
Julia Wakeman-Linn, Editor
http://www.montgomerycollege.
edu/potomacreview
Biannual

Pottersfield Portfolio
P.O. Box 40, Station A
Sydney, Nova Scotia B1P 6G9
Canada
Douglas Arthur Brown,
Managing Editor
pportfolio@seascape.ns.ca
www.pportfolio.com
Triannual

Prairie Fire
Artspace
423-100 Arthur Street
Winnipeg, Manitoba R3B 1H3
Canada
Andris Taskans, Editor
prfire@mts.net
www.prairiefire.mb.ca
Quarterly

Prairie Schooner
201 Andrews Hall
University of Nebraska
Lincoln, NE 68588-0334
Hilda Raz, Editor in Chief
www.unl.edu/schooner/
psmain.htm
Quarterly

Prism International
Creative Writing Program
University of British Columbia
Buchanan E-462
1866 Main Mall
Vancouver, BC V6T 1Z1 Canada
Benjamin Wood, Fiction Editor
prism@interchange.ubc.ca
www.prism.arts.ubc.ca
Quarterly

Provincetown Arts
P.O. Box 35
650 Commercial Street
Provincetown, MA 02657
Christopher Busa, Editor
www.provincetownarts.org
Annual

Puerto del Sol
Department of English
New Mexico State University
P.O. Box 30001, Dept. 3E
Las Cruces, NM 88003
Kevin McIlvoy, Fiction Editor
puerto@nmsu.edu
www.nmsu.edu/~puerto/
welcome.html
Semiannual

Quarry Magazine
P.O. Box 74
Kingston, Ontario K7L 4V6
Canada
Andrew Griffin, Editor in Chief
quarrymagazine@hotmail.com
Quarterly

Quarterly West
255 South Central Campus Drive
Room 3500
University of Utah
Salt Lake City, UT 84112-0494
quarterlywest@yahoo.com
www.utah.edu/quarterlywest
Biannual

Raritan
Rutgers University
31 Mine Street
New Brunswick, NJ 08903
Jackson Lears, Editor in Chief
rgr@rci.rutgers.edu
Quarterly

Rattapallax
532 LaGuardia Place, Suite 353
New York, NY 10012
Martin Mitchell, Editor in Chief
info@rattapallax.com
www.rattapallax.com
Biannual

Red Rock Review
English Department, J2A
Community College Southern
Nevada
3200 East Cheyenne Avenue
North Las Vegas, NV 89030
Richard Logsdon, Editor in Chief
Biannual

River City
English Department
University of Memphis
Memphis, TN 38152-6176
Kristen Iversen, Editor
rivercity@memphis.edu
www.people.memphis.edu/
~rivercity/
Biannual

River Styx
634 North Grand Avenue
12th Floor
St. Louis, MO 63103
Richard Newman, Editor
www.riverstyx.org
Triannual

Rosebud
N3310 Asje Road
Cambridge, WI 53523
Roderick Clark, Editor
jrodclark@rsbd.net
www.rsbd.net
Quarterly

The Saint Ann's Review
129 Pierrepont Street
Brooklyn, New York 11201
Beth Bosworth, Editor
sareview@saintanns.k12.ny.us
Biannual

Salamander
English Department
Suffolk University
41 Temple Street
Boston, MA 02114
Jennifer Barber, Editor
http://members.bellatlantic.net/
~vzefh4r/index.html
Biannual

Salmagundi
Skidmore College
Saratoga Springs, NY 12866
Robert Boyers, Editor in Chief
rboyers@skidmore.edu
http://www.skidmore.edu/
salmagundi/
Quarterly

Salt Hill
English Department
Syracuse University
Syracuse, NY 13244
Ellen Litman, Editor
salthill@cas.syr.edu
Biannual

Santa Monica Review
Santa Monica College
1900 Pico Boulevard
Santa Monica, CA 90405
Andrew Tonkovich
atonkovi@uci.edu
www.smc.edu/sm_review
Biannual

The Seattle Review
Padelford Hall
Box 354330
University of Washington
Seattle, WA 98195
Colleen J. McElroy, Editor
seaview@u.washington.edu
http://depts.washington.edu/
seaview.html
Biannual

Seven Days
P.O. Box 1164
255 South Champlain Street
Burlington, VT 05042-1164
Pamela Polston, Paula Routly,
Coeditors
sevenday@together.net
www.sevendaysvt.com
Weekly

The Sewanee Review
University of the South
735 University Avenue
Sewanee, TN 37383-1000
George Core, Editor
www.sewanee.edu/sreview/
home.html
Quarterly

Shenandoah
Mattingly House
2 Lee Avenue
Washington and Lee University
Lexington, VA 24450-2116
R. T. Smith, Editor
shenandoah@wlu.edu
http://shenandoah.wlu.edu
Quarterly

Sonora Review
English Department
University of Arizona
Tucson, AZ 85721
sonora@u.arizona.edu
www.coh.arizona.edu/sonora
Biannual

The South Carolina Review
Center for Electronic and Digital
Publishing
Clemson University
Strode Tower, Room 611, Box
340522
Clemson, SC 29634-0522
www.clemson.edu/caah/cedp/
scrintro.htm
Biannual

South Dakota Review
Box 111
University Exchange
Vermillion, SD 57069
Brian Bedard, Editor
sdreview@usd.edu
sunbird.usd.edu/engl/SDR/
index.html
Quarterly

The Southeast Review
Department of English
Florida State University
Tallahassee, FL 32306
http://southeastreview.org
Biannual

Southern Humanities Review
9088 Haley Center
Auburn University
Auburn, AL 36849
Dan R. Latimer, Virginia M.
Kouidis, Editors
shrengl@auburn.edu
www.auburn.edu/english/shr/
home.htm
Quarterly

The Southern Review
Louisiana State University
Old President's House
Baton Rouge, LA 70803-0001
Bret Lott, Editor
southernreview@lsu.edu
http://www.lsu.edu/
thesouthernreview/
Quarterly

Southwest Review
Southern Methodist University
P.O. Box 750374
Dallas, TX 75275-0374
Willard Spiegelman,
Editor in Chief
swr@mail.smu.edu
www.southwestreview.org
Quarterly

St. Anthony Messenger
28 West Liberty Street
Cincinnati, OH 45202-6498
Pat McCloskey, O.F.M., Editor
StAnthony@AmericanCatholic.
org
www.americancatholic.org
Monthly

StoryQuarterly
431 Sheridan Rd.
Kenilworth, IL 60043
M. M. M. Hayes, Editor
info@storyquarterly.org
www.storyquarterly.org
Annual

StringTown
P.O. Box 1406
Medical Lake, WA 99022-1406
Polly Buckingham, Editor
Stringtown@earthlink.net
http://home.earthlink.net/
~stringtown/
Annual

The Sun
107 North Roberson Street
Chapel Hill, NC 27516
Sy Safransky, Editor
www.thesunmagazine.org
Monthly

Sycamore Review
English Department
1356 Heavilon Hall
Purdue University
West Lafayette, IN 47907
sycamore@expert.cc.purdue.edu
www.sla.purdue.edu/academic/
engl/sycamore/
Biannual

Talking River Review
Division of Literature and
Languages
Lewis-Clark State College
500 8th Avenue
Lewiston, ID 83501
Biannual

Tameme
199 First Street
Los Altos, CA 94022
C. M. Mayo, Editor
editor@tameme.org
www.tameme.org
Annual

Tampa Review
The University of Tampa
401 West Kennedy Boulevard
Tampa, Florida 33606-1490
Richard Mathews, Editor
utpress@ut.edu
http://tampareview.ut.edu
Biannual

The Texas Review
English Department
Sam Houston State University
Huntsville, TX 77341
Paul Ruffin, Editor
eng.pdr@shsu.edu
Biannual

Third Coast
English Department
Western Michigan University
Kalamazoo, MI 49008-5092
Shanda Hansma Blue, Editor
Shanda_Blue@hotmail.com
www.wmich.edu/thirdcoast
Biannual

The Threepenny Review
P.O. Box 9131
Berkeley, CA 94709
Wendy Lesser, Editor
www.threepennyreview.com
Quarterly

Tikkun
60 West 87th Street
New York, NY 10024
Thane Rosenbaum,
Literary Editor
magazine@tikkun.org
www.tikkun.org
Bimonthly

Timber Creek Review
8969 UNCG Station
Greensboro, NC 27413
John M. Freiermuth, Editor
Quarterly

Tin House
PMB #280
32 Seventh Avenue
Brooklyn, NY 11215
Rob Spillman, Editor, and
Win McCormack, Editor in Chief
tinhouse@pcspublink.com
www.tinhouse.com
Quarterly

Toronto Life
59 Front Street, East
Toronto, Ontario M5E 1B3
Canada
John Macfarlane, Editor
www.torontolife.com
Monthly

Transition Magazine
W.E.B. DuBois Institute
Harvard University
69 Dunster Street
Cambridge, MA 02138
Henry Louis Gates, Jr., and
Kwame Anthony Appiah, Editors
transition@fas.harvard.edu
www.transitionmagazine.com
Quarterly

Triquarterly
Northwestern University
2020 Ridge Avenue
Evanston, IL 60208
Susan Firestone Hahn, Editor
www.triquarterly.com
Triannual

Two Rivers Review
P.O. Box 158
Clinton, NY 13323
Phil Memmer, Editor
tworiversreview@juno.com
Biannual

The Virginia Quarterly Review
1 West Range
P.O. Box 400223
Charlottesville, VA 22903-4223
Ted Genoways, Editor
vqreview@virginia.edu
www.vqonline.org
Quarterly

War, Literature & the Arts
2354 Fairchild Drive,
Suite 6D45
United States Air Force Academy
Colorado Springs, CO
80840-6242
Donald Anderson, Editor
editor@wlajournal.com
http://www.wlajournal.com
Biannual

Wascana Review
English Department
University of Regina
Regina, Saskatchewan S4S 0A2
Canada
Michael Tussler, Editor
Michael.tussler@uregina.ca
www.uregina.ca/english/
wrhome.htm
Biannual

Washington Review
P.O. Box 50132
Washington, D.C. 20091-0132
Clarissa K. Wittenberg, Editor
www.washingtonreview.org
Bimonthly

Washington Square Review
Creative Writing Program
New York University
19 University Place, Room 219
New York, NY 10003-4556
washington.square.journal
@nyu.edu
http://cwp.fas.nyu.edu/page/wsr
Biannual

Watchword
P.O. Box 5755
Berkeley, CA 94705
liz@watchwordpress.org
www.watchwordpress.org
Biannual

Weber Studies
Weber State University
1214 University Circle
Ogden, UT 84408-1214
Brad L. Roghaar, Editor
weberstudies@weber.edu
weberstudies.weber.edu
Triquarterly

West Branch
Bucknell Hall
Bucknell University
Lewisburg, PA 17837
Paula Closson Buck, Editor
www.bucknell.edu/westbranch
Biannual

West Coast Line
2027 East Academic Annex
Simon Fraser University
Burnaby, British Columbia V5A
1S6 Canada
Roy Miki, Editor
wcl@sfu.ca
www.sfu.ca/west-coast-line
Triannual

Western Humanities Review
University of Utah
English Department
255 South Central Campus
Drive, Room 3500
Salt Lake City, UT 84112-0494
Barry Weller, Editor
whr@mail.hum.utah.edu
www.hum.utah.edu/whr
Biannual

**Whistling Shade, The Twin
Cities Literary Journal**
P.O. Box 7084
Saint Paul, MN 55107
Anthony Telschow, Rhoda Niola,
Editors
editor@whistlingshade.com
www.whistlingshade.com
Quarterly

Wind
P.O. Box 24548
Lexington, KY 40524
Charlie Hughes, Leatha Kendrick,
Editors
books@windpub.com
Biannual

Windsor Review
English Department
University of Windsor
Windsor, Ontario N9B 3P4
Canada
Katherine Quinsey,
General Editor
uwrevu@uwindsor.ca
Biannual

Witness
Oakland Community College
Orchard Ridge Campus
27055 Orchard Lake Road
Farmington Hills, MI 48334
Peter Stine, Editor
stinepj@umich.edu
www.oaklandcc.edu/witness
Biannual

Worcester Review
1 Ekman Street
Worcester, MA 01607
Rodger Martin, Managing Editor
www.geocities.com/Paris/
LeftBank/6433/
Annual

Wordplay
P.O. Box 2248
South Portland, ME 04116-2248
Helen Peppe, Editor in Chief
wordplay@maine.rr.com
Quarterly

Writers' Forum
University of Colorado
P.O. Box 7150
Colorado Springs, CO 80933
C. Kenneth Pellow,
Editor in Chief
kpellow@mail.uccs.edu
Annual

Xavier Review
Xavier University
Box 110C
New Orleans, LA 70125
Thomas Bonner, Jr., and
Richard Collins, Editors
rcollins@xula.edu
Biannual

**Xconnect: Writers of the
Information Age**
P.O. Box 2317
Philadelphia, PA 19103
D. Edward Deifer, Editor in Chief
xconnect@ccat.sas.upenn.edu
ccat.sas.upenn.edu/xconnect
Annual

The Yale Review
Yale University
P.O. Box 208243
New Haven, CT 06250-8243
J. D. McClatchy, Editor
yalerev@yale.edu
www.yale.edu/yalereview
Quarterly

The Yalobusha Review
Department of English
University of Mississippi
P.O. Box 1848
University, MS 38677-1848
yalobush@olemiss.edu
www.olemiss.edu/yalobusha
Annual

Zoetrope: All-Story
916 Kearny Street
San Francisco, CA 94133
Michael Ray, Editor
www.all-story.com
Quarterly

ZYZZYVA
P.O. Box 590069
San Francisco, CA 94159-0069
Howard Junker, Editor
editor@zyzzyva.org
www.zyzzyva.org
Triannual

Permissions

The series editor wishes to thank the editors of the participating periodicals, the agents of the authors, and the authors themselves for cooperation in assembling *The O. Henry Prize Stories 2006*.

Grateful acknowledgment is made to the following for permission to reprint previously published material: